FREDERICKSBURG LAW

FREDERICKSBURG LAW

THE STORIES OF PIKE HARDY

PATRICK LINDSAY

WOLFPACK
PUBLISHING
EST 2013

Fredericksburg Law: The Stories of Pike Hardy
Paperback Edition
Copyright © 2025 (As Revised) by Patrick Lindsay

Wolfpack Publishing
1707 E. Diana Street
Tampa, FL 33610

www.wolfpackpublishing.com

Paperback ISBN 979-8-89567-767-4
Ebook ISBN 979-8-89567-733-9

FREDERICKSBURG LAW

PART ONE

PIKE HARDY

CHAPTER 1

A FINE WELCOME

PEDERNALES RIVER, TEXAS, 1876

Something was wrong, and I couldn't quite figure out what it was. I don't mean the part about folks taking potshots at me for the last twenty minutes. I had all six foot one, one hundred eighty-five pounds of me scrunched down behind some scrub oaks and brush, and I didn't dare raise my fool head enough to get a better look at things.

No, that wasn't the part that had me confused. I'd spent many years in the army, and I knew when I was under fire. No doubt about that, I was under fire. Every once in a while they touched off another round to remind me, not that I was likely to forget.

I looked at my new hat, lying over there just a few feet away. I had just ditched my old cavalry hat and bought myself a new, wide-brimmed, felt cowboy-style hat in honor of my new job as sheriff of Gillespie County, Texas. Now it had a fresh bullet hole in it. That had me a little riled up, of course, but the funny thing is, I had a feelin' that's what the guy was shooting at. I had a feeling he could've put that bullet right through my noggin if he'd wanted to.

The sun started to climb, and I knew I would have a powerful thirst before much longer. I glanced over to my right. My canteen was on my horse, Hank, and Hank was grazing in a circle of post oak trees, maybe thirty yards away. Being an army horse before I'd brought him with me, he didn't run that far when he heard gunfire.

Like they had read my mind, those yahoos who'd been firing at me from the woods opened up with several rounds just over Hank's head. He snorted and ran another thirty yards before he stopped and went back to grazing. So, I thought, they didn't want to shoot my horse and strand me. They just wanted to drive me and my horse away. Not that I was interested in standing up and walking out of there.

I hated to admit it, but waiting was the best thing I could do right now. Waiting is hard for me because I am a man of action. I squirmed just a bit, trying to find a better position, and got rewarded with a rifle shot that came too close for comfort. I muttered under my breath and thought about how I'd come to be in this jam in the first place.

My name is Pike Hardy and I'm twenty-five years old. I can't say if I look like either one of my parents because I hadn't really known either of them. A man named Jed Hardy had taken me in when I was little and I had taken his name. The army became my home when I was eighteen, and I'd only recently come to Fredericksburg, Texas. It had actually started to feel like home here, too. At least until those buzzards over there in the woods had started shooting at me.

Sometimes I wondered if I looked like my pa. I don't guess I'll ever know the answer to that question. I have thick, wavy, dark hair and I get a tanned face faster'n most folks. Once in a while a girl has told me I'm handsome, but I noticed they had to squint at me a little before they said it.

A few more shots sounded, but they weren't close. I looked over and saw they were driving Hank a little farther away. He trotted out of the grove of trees where he'd been, dipped down into a gully of some kind, and emerged on the other side, then stopped to crop the grass.

Watching Hank had given me an idea. Hank stood behind me and off to my right, and the gully ran from where he stood. I guessed I would have to cross about fifteen or twenty yards to get to the gully. I laid there and weighed the possibilities. They would have already hit me if they really wanted to. That only made me feel a little better, though. My fingers curled around my Winchester, lying on the ground beside me. Luckily, I had the instincts of an old army campaigner and I had grabbed the Winchester before bailing off Hank and hitting the ground.

If I could reach the ditch, I figured I could find enough cover to return fire and make it hot for them over there. It might be enough to make them pull back. I turned my head and surveyed the ground behind me. There wasn't much in the way of cover—just a few scraggly mesquite trees and some brush. No point in trying to crawl. I would just have to break for the gully and run myself a little zig-zag route.

Being that I'm not a patient man, like I said, I decided to make a break for the gully. I didn't really have enough cover to hold out much longer where I was lying right now. My left hand closed around a small rock and I gathered myself slowly to my hands and knees.

I threw the rock, hoping to distract 'em just a little. Then I took off, covering those fifteen yards just about as fast as I've ever moved. Shots kicked up dirt around me, and if they were missing on purpose, it wasn't by much. When I reached the edge of the gully, I tossed the Winchester and dove after it. A few more shots rang out, then it got quiet.

I crawled down the gully for several yards, then eased up for a quick look. More shots sounded, but they were having some target practice with my new hat. They shot several more times until the hat skittered over the edge and landed in the gully behind me. One look told me I could never get that hat patched up. Not that I'd had much hope for it before.

Things got quiet for a while and I decided to keep it that way. Firing back at them from the gully was what I wanted to do, but I didn't want to give away my position. They knew I'd gone into the ditch, but they couldn't see my movements now, and they might feel a little jumpy about the possibility of return fire.

I crawled farther along the gully toward Hank, hoping he would follow me without drawing any more fire. That's the way it worked out, which was about the first good thing that had happened to me all day.

I made a clucking noise as I moved past him, which was how I called him. Hank picked up his ears and started following. I stopped once in a while and let him go back to grazing, hoping it would make it less obvious that my horse was following me.

Finally, there was nothing to do but make my move. I came out of the gully, moving at a slow trot, circled around Hank, shoved the Winchester into the scabbard, and swung aboard. I leaned low and over Hank's shoulder. We wasted no time getting out of there. There were no more shots fired as I left.

I went back the way I had come, riding next to the Pedernales River, following it east until I took the trail north to go home to Fredericksburg, Texas. I had time to think about what had just happened, so that's what I did. I just didn't have much luck making sense of it.

I had been sheriff in this county for just a few months. I'd spent most of that time settling into the job in Fredericksburg, the county seat and biggest town. The man who had brought me to Texas and helped me get the sheriff's job after he retired was a man named Jake McCabe.

Jake is a good friend and a wise man, and he suggested I take a little time to travel around the county, stopping off at some villages and meeting the ranchers and farmers in the county. That's what I had been doing when a shopkeeper in a little town called Crabapple came out of his store and hollered to get my attention. This guy looked like he'd lived in Crabapple since maybe George Washington became president. He came up to me and said he was scared.

"Scared of what?" I asked.

The old-timer pulled at his beard, scratched himself, and leaned over to spit in the dirt. "Folks that moved here a couple years back," he announced. "Hill folks, I expect. Not from around here. They carry some old Henry rifles to town with 'em. I suppose they can hit what they shoot at. Try to steal stuff when I'm not lookin', they do."

I stared at him, trying to decide whether I should look into it. "Where do they live?" I asked finally.

He pointed west. "Out there, along the river, I expect." He spat into the dirt again, then went back into his general store and pulled the door shut behind him.

That was the conversation that had started me down the Pedernales River, looking for settlers along the way. I hadn't really seen much of anything except a big horse ranch with some rich folks livin' there until the rifles had opened up on me, coming from a thick stand of trees set back from the river. No wonder the old-timer feared them.

It looked to me like I would have to sneak up on these boys if I came back to pay them a visit. That part would come naturally for me. Even *hill folks*, as the old-timer described them, would have trouble outdoing me if I decided to sneak up on them.

I had been just five years old, living up north of here near Hico, Texas, with my family, when a raiding party of Comanches had swooped in out of nowhere. They had killed both my parents and taken my older sister and me captive. They had taken her away, and I never saw her again.

The Comanches raised me like one of theirs, teaching me how to use a bow and arrow, ride a horse with the best of 'em, and how to live off the countryside, moving around without being seen or heard.

I was about eleven, I reckon, when I got smallpox. The Comanches were terrified of it. They left me with a Mexican girl they had taken captive named Isobel and moved on. Isobel took care of me and nursed me back to health. She wanted to go back to her family in Mexico, so she left. That's when I met a man named Jed Hardy.

Jed was a mountain man from way back. He'd spent thirty years, he said, in the mountains of Colorado, trapping, living in a cabin he'd built himself, and eating whatever he could shoot for food. One day he decided he'd had enough of that, moved to Texas, bought a little land, and became a farmer and small-time rancher.

Jed had caught me breaking into his smokehouse to steal some beef. He'd gone easy on me. He let me have the beef and gave me some beans and cornbread to go with it. When I was done eating, he asked me if I would like to do a little work to earn some more meals. I said yes.

Seven years later, Jed had become sort of a dad to me. I think he hung around Texas because of me, even though he thought about going back to Colorado. He made me get some schooling and taught me a little about ranching. He gave me his name. When I decided I would join the army, he said he planned to sell the place and go back to the mountains. Said he might come back to Texas someday. I wondered if I would see him again.

I got to town in Fredericksburg without having decided exactly what I wanted to do about those folks back there on the Pedernales River. I knew they owed me a hat, though.

My deputy, Hostler, wasn't at the sheriff's office, and I had a pretty good idea he had parked his feet under the dinner table at Jake and Julia McCabe's house. After puttering around the office for a while, I decided Hostler had the right idea. I had a standing invitation over there, so I locked up the office and stepped out to unhitch Hank. I always enjoyed dinner at the McCabe's house.

Maybe Jake would have an idea of what to do about those people back there on the river.

———

A voice from down the street stopped me as I made ready to swing aboard Hank. I knew that voice. My stomach tightened up a little and I forced a smile onto my face as I turned around.

"Pike!" the voice said again.

Clara Morgan, owner of a dress shop down the street, was hurrying toward me as I looked up. I took a fast look to see if she was bringing another picnic basket. I was relieved to see that she wasn't. She had brought one earlier this week and left it when I was out of the office. My deputy, Hostler, had belted that one down. That was okay with me.

"Clara..." My voice trailed off as I tried to figure out what to say. She pushed past me and looked at the office door.

I stayed where I was and fiddled with the office key, which was still in my hands. There was a gleam in her eye that had me kinda nervous, I have to admit. I took a step in the other direction, toward my horse.

"I have to go," I explained, hoping it sounded official. "Some things I have to look into, you know."

Her smile faded, but she stepped back and nodded. "Sure," she said, "another time."

I waited for a moment as she walked back down the street, then swung aboard Hank. Hostler, my deputy, was gonna give me a hard time about it if he got word. Clara was ten years older than me, maybe twelve or fifteen. I sighed and turned Hank toward the McCabe spread.

Maybe, I thought, Julia McCabe could give me a tip on what to do about this.

_____

The road out to the McCabe place was getting pretty familiar. I suspect Hank knew the way without my help now. Jake and Julia shared the place with Julia's parents, Ike and Jeanne Hawkins. Julia's little brother, Isaac, had moved out to the bunkhouse with my deputy, Hostler. There was another brother who had moved into town.

Myself, I stayed at a boarding house in town, close to the jail and office. Hostler had worked for Ike Hawkins until the deputy's job opened up. He decided to stay out at the McCabe's place even after he quit working for them. I suspect it was the meals that he stayed for.

I pulled off the trail and wound down a path until I could see the big stone house in front of me. I dismounted and saw Hostler coming out of the bunkhouse while I unsaddled Hank and turned him into the corral.

I waited for Hostler—it looked like he had something on his mind. He leaned on the rails of the corral and told me we'd had a visitor at the office that day.

"George Lynch," he said, launching right into things. "George came by today, and he was some upset, I'd say."

My eyebrows climbed up a little. George Lynch had a big spread west of town. I'd actually ridden past it today. Thousands of acres, I'd heard. I had only ridden by the place a time or two before today, but it was a big ranch. He had some cattle, but mainly he loved horses. I waited for Hostler to explain a little more.

"Lynch was pretty worked up," Hostler said. "Told me

he'd had several horses rustled. One of his best stallions was taken, that's what he said. I promised him we'd look into it right away."

"Yeah, we will. For sure." I stepped out of the corral and thought about what I had going on tomorrow. "You and me," I said. "Let's ride out there tomorrow and talk to Lynch."

Hostler nodded and trailed after me up to the house. Julia threw the door open and gave me a kiss on the cheek. "Just in time," she told me. "I'm dishing up supper right now."

I followed Julia into the kitchen, sniffing the air as I went. It was enough to make a man drool. Julia handed me a dish to carry out to the table. "How's it going?" she asked.

I knew exactly what she meant. She was mighty curious if I'd found a lady in town, and she had been there when Clara Morgan had brought me the picnic basket.

"You didn't get another picnic basket, did you?" she asked, grinning just a little and trying not to.

"Basket?" That came from Hostler, who had come through the door behind me. He'd eaten most of the last one. "That was some mighty good fried chicken and apple pie in the last one." His Adam's apple bobbed up and down while he thought about it.

"No basket," I told him as I pushed him out the door. "You'll be the first to know if I get one."

Julia dished up some stew, looking thoughtful. "Maybe," she said, "she needs to meet somebody else and set her cap for another man. I'll see what I can do."

I told her I would be entirely grateful for the help and helped her carry the meal out to the table. I tried not to watch Hostler during dinner. It reminded me of a pack of coyotes on a fresh carcass.

———

After dinner, I went out to the porch with Jake, Ike, and Hostler. Everybody settled down with a satisfied sigh and leaned back. Boone, Jake's old deputy, showed up and joined us. Boone came from somewhere up in the hills of Tennessee, not too far from where Jake was born. He'd been living in these parts for longer than any of us. Now he and his wife lived in a line cabin somewhere on this property.

Boone lit up a foul-smelling cigar and put his feet up on the porch rail. "What've you been doin'?" he asked, directing that question at me.

"Well," I said, "I spent today gettin' shot at. Not sure who did the shootin' or why."

CHAPTER 2

MOONSHINE AND HORSE RUSTLING

Well, I had everybody's attention now. All the eyes were on me. Jake leaned forward. His sheriffing days weren't that far behind him, and this was his old county.

"Shot at where?" was his first question.

"Out west of here," I told him. "Near that little town of Crabapple. Old-timer that runs a grocery store in town told me there's some rough folks settled in those hills near town. Thought they were stealin' stuff from his store. I went out to take a look."

Boone left off puffing that nasty cigar and put his feet down. "So, you just rode up, and they started whangin' away at you?" he asked.

"That was just about it." I nodded. "I rode west out of town, following the Pedernales River, looking for a house or a shack or something. I got close to some pretty heavy woods, set back there in some nice rolling hills, and they opened up on me."

"So," Jake said, looking thoughtful, "they were back

in the trees, set up on a rolling hill or two, and they just opened fire. Nobody said anything?"

"Nope," I said. "I didn't get close enough to do any talking, what with all the lead in the air." I stopped and shook my head. "Funny thing is," I said, "I don't think they were trying to kill me. They shot my new hat off my head and filled it full of holes, but they didn't hit me."

Jake glanced over at Boone, who had stopped to light up that cigar again. He looked like he had a little smile on his face.

"Water?" Boone asked. "Was there a stream or a little crick comin' off that river or anything like that?"

I stopped to think that one over. "Maybe," I said. "Could have been a little creek or something flowing down from those hills. Like I said, I didn't get too close."

"Yup," said Boone. He looked over at Jake. "Sounds like a prime spot to me," he said. That grin was back on his face. "Somebody's makin' shine back there."

Jake nodded. "You're not from the hills back east like Boone and Ike and me," he explained. "If you were, you'd know you just described a place set up for a still to make some moonshine. When you said they were just shootin' to scare you away, that clinched the deal."

"They don't want me to find the still," I mumbled.

"Revenuer!" Ike boomed. "They see a badge, they see a revenuer!"

I leaned back in my chair and started talking it through in my head. "They're hidden pretty good back there, I guess. If we get too close, they might start shootin' for real."

"You're gonna try to close down the still??" Boone looked injured. The cigar was taking a beating.

"It's against the law, right?" I said.

"Yankee law!" Boone growled.

"You're right," Jake told me. "It's against the law. I've wondered a few times if we had some moonshine outfits around here. I guess it doesn't surprise me." He stopped and drummed his fingers on the arm of his chair.

"Maybe we can talk about it some more later," he told me. "I might have a few ideas about it. In the meantime, you're right—if you get too close, they'll figure you've had your warning and might just open up for real. Take Hostler with you and be careful."

"I will," I said. This one would take some planning.

The rest of the evening was some talk about the ranch and cattle and such. I got up to leave after an hour.

"See you at the office in the mornin'," I told Hostler. "Don't forget we're going to ride out and see George Lynch."

———

I was in the sheriff's office bright and early the next morning when Hostler rode up, followed by Julia McCabe, driving her buggy. I stepped out the door to say hello when the door to the dress shop opened down the street and Clara Morgan came out.

"I've got it," Julia told me with a wink.

She hopped down from the buggy and started down the street. "Clara," I heard her say, "there's somebody I think you would like to meet who just started work down at the bank."

Clara turned and went with her, glancing back over her shoulder from time to time. I heaved a sigh of relief and went back into the office with Hostler.

"You can quit grinning any time," I told him.

We turned a couple of people out of the jail who had been getting a little rowdy in the saloon last night, picked up a little breakfast from the bakery on the next block, then moved out for the ride to George Lynch's ranch.

Hostler passed over a map Lynch had given to him when they had talked yesterday. I laid it across the saddle horn and looked at it.

"Huh," I said finally, passing the map back over to Hostler.

He stuffed the map in his pocket and waited.

"That's close to where I was yesterday," I told him. "If I had turned north a mile or so before I did, I would have been in George Lynch's ranch. Passed by it." We rode a few miles in silence. "What's this George Lynch like?" I asked.

Hostler shook his head. "He ain't trying to make any friends," he finally answered. "Sounds like he's from up north somewhere. Pretty much came in and ordered me to bring you out there and arrest whoever's been stealing his horses. Wouldn't tell me much else about how it happened."

———

When we turned in through the gates at the Circle L Ranch, the first thought that went through my head was that George Lynch was a lucky man. Maybe that was the second thought, too.

There were rolling hills in front of me, with some burr oaks growing near a stream flowing down to the Pedernales River. The stream looked like it pretty much cut the property down the middle. The pastures were lush with spring grass. Some bluebonnet and Indian paintbrush wildflowers were scattered around.

Hostler walked our horses toward the big house at the end of the trail. We passed a paddock where some horses were being exercised. We pulled up for a look. I'm not an expert on horses, but I spent some time in the cavalry, and these looked like some fine horses to me.

Hostler pulled up alongside and let out a low whistle. "Those horses look better'n the ones we hitched up to pull old Napoleon," he said.

I chuckled. Napoleon was the name we gave to an old Civil War cannon our unit had used at the fort in New Mexico. Hostler could hit just about any target he aimed at with that cannon.

"Yeah, they look just a tad better," I agreed.

"You know, I found an old cannon like Napoleon," Hostler said.

I stared at him. "A cannon? You've been looking for a cannon? What would we do with it?"

Hostler shrugged and started to answer when we heard a shout from behind us.

"Hey! What are you doing here? Get off the property!"

I turned around to see a man on a palomino horse galloping toward us. He was leaning forward, like he couldn't wait to shoot us or beat us with a whip, which- ever came first. His hand moved to the pistol in his gun belt as he closed in on us.

I reached up slowly and pulled my vest aside to show him my badge. He slowed down just a tad, but his hand stayed on the gun. Hostler moved his horse to the side to flank him, and he didn't like it.

"Nick! Back off! I told 'em to come out here." The voice came from the house down below. A tall, stocky man was riding toward us. The guy who'd been ready to shoot us stared at me for a minute, then wheeled around and rode off.

I turned back to watch the guy riding in from the house. I figured this must be George Lynch. He didn't look any friendlier than the first one, but at least he didn't have his hand on his gun. He looked at Hostler, then at me.

"You Hardy?" he barked.

"Yeah, that's me. Pike Hardy." I held out my hand.

He ignored the hand and wheeled the horse around. "Come on, then," he growled. "Time's wasting. Follow me and I'll show you where they stole the horses." He spurred his horse and rode off without looking back.

"Told ya," Hostler muttered under his breath.

Lynch galloped across a pasture on our west side, slowing down only to splash across the stream I'd seen cutting across the property. He picked up speed again on the other side, and Hank was hard-put to keep up. Lynch was well-mounted, no doubt. Hostler trailed a little behind me. We caught up again when we reached a fence.

Lynch rode down the fence line until he came to a gate. He swung down, opened the gate, and waved us through. We followed him again until he came to another stream, bordered on both sides by a thick stand of trees. I could see about fifteen horses, maybe yearlings, by the look of them. They were grazing or drinking from the stream.

I dismounted and looked around. I noticed Lynch stayed on his horse, watching me.

"They took the horses here?" I asked.

Lynch nodded.

"How many? And can you describe them?"

Lynch was lookin' around like he was bored and ready to leave. "Three," he snapped. "Black stallion, about sixteen hands. Two chestnut geldings, both about fifteen hands. It's the stallion I really want back. Paid a lot for him. Get that one back." He wheeled his horse around, then looked back. "Stop at the house before you leave. Tell me what you've found." He spurred the horse and galloped away.

Hostler was staring at the split-rail fences on the sides of the pasture. They ran down to the edge of this stream and seemed to end at the edge of the stream, bordering it north and south. "What keeps 'em on this side of the water?" he asked.

I dismounted and strolled through the trees down to the water's edge, then leaned for a closer look. "Huh," I said. "Whaddya know?"

I waded into the water. Halfway across the stream, I found several strands of wire stretched lengthwise down the stream. I touched the sharp tips of wire sticking up from the strands every few inches.

Hostler splashed in to join me, then waded up and down along the wire fence for several feet.

"What is it?" he asked.

"Called barbed wire," I told him. "I've heard of it but never saw it before. Anyway, that's what keeps 'em in this pasture." I began to trace the wire fence down the stream. "Unless," I said over my shoulder, "somebody's cut the wire."

I followed the wire down the stream for another twenty yards until I found the spot I was looking for. They had cut the top two strands of wire through, leaving just the bottom strand uncut, just above the water level. I could see a few tracks leading out on the other side. I stepped over the bottom wire and followed the tracks up the mud on the bank on the far side.

Climbing up the bank, I could follow the tracks for only a few yards to the west. Hostler came up behind me, leaning down to look at the tracks.

"Too much rain lately," he observed.

"Yep." I looked at the land in front of me. The pasture rose slightly and gave way to more trees and thick brush. I moved down to the edge of the Pedernales River and looked up the slope again.

"I was here yesterday," I told Hostler.

He stopped trying to follow the tracks and straightened up. "Yesterday, when you got shot at, this is where you were?"

"Yeah, this is it." I took a minute to get a better look. There were more hills back there, probably another stream or two feeding into the river, maybe even a natural cave or two where the hills rose. I could see a few rocky faces and jagged drop-offs.

"No way I'm just riding in over there," I told Hostler. "Let's get back across the stream and follow the stream up a little farther from Lynch's side."

We crossed back over and I took a minute to get my bearings so I could tell Lynch where they had cut his fence. I wondered if he really didn't know about this. That seemed like the first thing to look for.

We mounted up and followed upstream for several hundred yards. Lynch's property seemed to run all the way to hills on the north side. The pasture land extended to another rail fence. That looked like the border of his land on this north side. The stream seemed to be fed by a runoff from the hills. The barbed wire fence hooked into the split-rail fence where the ground began to rise.

I got down where the fences met and stared up the hill. There was an old house there—more like a shack, really. There were no windows, just a chimney running up the back wall and a broken-down porch out front. The runoff from the hills above fed the stream just below it. There was something familiar about it, but I couldn't quite place it. After a while, I noticed Hostler was standing beside me.

"Know this place?" he asked.

I shook my head. "I don't think so," I told him. "It just...seems like I do, somehow." I shrugged and walked over to Hank. "Let's go back and tell Lynch what we know," I said. "I'm bettin' he won't be happy if we don't ride up to his house with prisoners."

———

We approached the big house slow and easy. I was watching for that gun-happy foreman we'd seen before. He wasn't around, but I saw a lot of men hanging around a bunkhouse, and all of them seemed to be heavily armed and not doing much.

The house was impressive—a big brick house with a wide veranda. It was big and expensive, for sure, but nothing about it made me feel comfortable. I didn't feel welcome, I knew that.

We started up the steps to the front porch, then I stopped and looked around. I glanced over at Hostler.

"How many cows have you seen on this place?" I asked him.

Hostler scratched his head and thought about it.

"Mebbe only a few dozen," he said. He looked around. "There might be some more in other pastures we didn't see," he offered.

"Yeah," I muttered under my breath. "Just seems like a lot of cowboys for no more cattle than what we've seen around here. Kinda strange, if you ask me. They don't have to herd the horses—just exercise 'em and stuff. What do they need all these men for?"

The front door opened, and a woman stepped out onto the porch. "Sheriff," she said, "I'm Maribel Lynch, George's wife. Please come in. George wants to hear what you've found out about the rustling."

"Ma'am." I took off my hat as we walked in and I nudged at Hostler to do the same. I could see and smell a cloud of cigar smoke coming from a room off to the left.

"Come in!" Lynch bellowed.

We walked in and took a seat opposite a massive oak desk. It was pretty clear this was Lynch's study. I parked my hat on my knee. Lynch fixed me with a glare.

"Well?" he barked.

"They cut through your barbed wire across the stream," I said. "Did you know about that?"

Lynch shrugged. "I figured as much. Did you trail 'em? Where'd they go with my horses?"

"They crossed the creek and went up the bank on the other side, for sure," I said. "The tracks fade out after that. Too much rain lately. Do you know who owns the land to the west of your place?" I asked.

Lynch waved his cigar in the air. I was wondering how he managed to stay in here without opening a window. "Some no-accounts from way up in the hills somewhere, I think," he snapped. "Got them some big beards and ancient rifles they carry into town. Don't know anything else about 'em. Did they take my horses?"

"That's the first place I'm going to look," I assured him. "They headed west from the stream, and there's no place where they have doubled back. They could have taken the horses south across the Pedernales River, but I'm betting west."

"Why aren't you out there doing that, arresting these guys?" Lynch leaned across the desk and glared at me. "Why'd you come back here?"

"I was over there once, just yesterday," I told him. "They opened fire on me. I'll go back when they can't see me coming."

"Yeah, okay." Lynch stubbed out his cigar and picked up some papers. I figured that meant he was done talking to us, so we got up to go.

"Did you fix my fence?" He stopped me in the doorway with that question.

I couldn't believe he'd asked me that. "No," I told him, "I'll get your horses back, but I don't fix fences."

Lynch's jaw dropped and his face went several shades redder. I guess he wasn't used to being talked to like that. He started up out of his chair, then his wife darted through the door. I had a feeling she'd been listening outside.

"George," she reminded him. "You have to get into town and pick up Norah at the train station."

Lynch's jaw twitched while he kept staring at me. Finally, he shrugged and brushed past me. "Okay," he said to his wife, "I'll go pick her up."

Maribel Lynch showed us to the door. "Please forgive my husband," she said. "He's used to just giving orders to the people who work for him. He's upset about losing some of his excellent horses. Thank you for looking into this."

That calmed me down a bit. Hostler and I walked outside and mounted up. Then Hostler started chuckling. "I've been wantin' to talk to him like that since the minute I met him," he said. "Brightened up my day a bunch when you said that."

————

We were two miles down the road toward Fredericksburg when I remembered something Hostler had said to me before we got to the horse ranch.

"You said something about finding an old cannon like Napoleon," I reminded him. "What in the world would you want a cannon for?"

Hostler grinned. "Well, for starters," he said. "You told me there's a still out there in those hills somewhere. I'll bet I could get their attention if I flatten the still."

CHAPTER 3

THE OLD SHACK

Malachi Hall was a hot-tempered man, and that was just on an average day. Today wasn't average. His sons, Zeb and Caleb, were having a hard time remembering when they had seen him this mad. This wasn't how they had pictured things going down. What with all the land they were living on here in Texas, they didn't figure their pa would ever notice those stolen horses. They'd gone to some trouble to hide the horses in some trees and brush.

"Do you wanna bring the whole county down on us?" Malachi thundered. "We had a revenuer out here yestiddy. Why not just bring the army out here too?"

Zeb tried to interrupt and calm his father down. It was a mistake. "Pa," he pleaded, "do you know how many hosses they got over there? It could mebbe be a month afore they even miss these three! We could, uh, we could take them back before anybody knows they're gone."

Malachi's face turned an even deeper shade of red, which his boys hadn't really thought was possible. "Won't miss 'em? Won't miss 'em? Just one of those hosses would sell for more than the two of you would sell for, both of you put together! Which you would know, if you knew hosses from...from..." Malachi couldn't find the word he wanted and punched the wall instead.

Zeb and Caleb kept their mouths shut this time and watched while Malachi resumed pacing in the little shack they called home. "Your Ma, God rest her soul, spoilt you two. I tole her time and agin to quit makin' excuses for yore tomfoolery." He stopped pacing long enough to glare at them. "I expect she dropped both of you on yer noggins a time or two. Neither one of you has a lick of sense."

Malachi stopped in mid-stride, whirled around, and pointed a finger at them. "You been in the 'shine?" he bellowed. "Is that what put such a fool idea in yore heads?" A vein throbbed in his forehead while he waited for an answer.

"No, Pa," they said in unison. They glanced at each other sideways. They both had a gallon-sized bottle of moonshine tucked away in a cave behind the still. They snuck out to tie one on every night after Malachi fell asleep. It was easy to hear his snoring clear out in the cave, so they always knew when it was time to sneak back into the shack. Just as soon as the snoring stopped, they let themselves in the back door.

Malachi, his chest heaving, was just about done with his tirade. These things really took it out of him. He waved a hand in the air. "Just take the hosses back where you got 'em!"

Caleb spoke for the first time and was immediately sorry he had. "Now, Pa?" he asked, genuinely puzzled.

"No, not now!!" Malachi came off the ratty old armchair where he'd collapsed. Caleb shrank back, afraid he had set off another round of bellowing. "Are ye tetched, boy? After dark, take the hosses back!"

Caleb raised a hand in the air and backed off a full two paces. "Yes, Pa," he mumbled. "After dark, we'll take 'em back." He glanced at his brother, and they both fled out the back door before Malachi could get up another head of steam.

Malachi collapsed back into the armchair and let his breathing slow down to normal. He tried to ignore the fluttering in his chest. After a while, he walked outside and sat on the porch of the shack. He reached under his chair and brought out a jug. He knew about the jugs the boys had hidden in the cave. He really couldn't get that mad at the boys for sampling the product. Malachi did a lot of that himself. Now, for instance, he popped the cork and tilted the jug back.

Malachi wiped his sleeve across his mouth and put the jug back under the chair. "If only," he grumbled to himself, "if only either one of 'em had a lick of sense in their skulls." He growled to himself and leaned back in the chair.

He'd moved the boys from Tennessee after their mother died. Too much feudin' and too many folks making 'shine back there in those hills. They had a chance here to do better for themselves. Not too much 'shine being made when they'd got here, and they were starting to get some customers.

He looked around him. He didn't know who owned this land, but it really didn't matter. He'd heard somebody back east had bought the land a few years ago, but whoever it was stayed back east and didn't visit much. Perfect. He and the boys stayed hidden away out in the brush and he wanted to keep it that way. They visited town once in a while to get some supplies and watched their back trail when they came home.

Yesterday had worried him some. That feller with the badge, he thought to himself, what was he doin' out here? The boys had opened up with their Henry rifles and scared him off, but he might come back. For sure, he thought, that badge would be back if the boys did any more horse stealing. Fastest way he knew for a man to get hisself hanged in Texas.

He'd ordered the boys not to shoot at the revenuer if that guy showed up around here again. They could hide out in the hills and the caves, he was sure of that. *Nobody knowed more about hidin' in the hills*, he told himself, *than an old boy from the backwoods of Tennessee*. They could leave the still behind and set up somewhere else if they had to, he told himself.

That's if those fool boys of his took the horses back. He growled to himself and reached for the jug again. How didn't they know better? Zeb was twenty-one and Caleb nineteen. He would, he vowed to himself, knock some sense into their heads with a two-by-four if he had to.

———————

Out in the cave, Zeb and Caleb had both lowered the level of their jugs by a couple of inches. They admitted to each other they hadn't seen their pa that angry. Not ever. They were well on their way to forgetting about this whole thing with some help from the moonshine. They still had to do some thinking about their plan to rob the bank in the town of Cain City. That's what they needed the horses for. The old nags they rode into town every week couldn't outrun a mule, let alone a posse.

Warned by some shouts and stomping around in the shack, they stowed the jugs back in their hiding places and braced themselves for Malachi to storm into the cave. When he didn't show, they both heaved a sigh of relief.

Caleb tiptoed to the mouth of the cave and risked a glance outside. Malachi wasn't there.

"What are we gonna do with those hosses, Zeb?" he asked.

Zeb, still feeling the moonshine, belched and yawned. "I really want that black stallion," he muttered. "We could give back the other two and keep the stallion, mebbe." He looked at Caleb hopefully.

His brother shook his head back and forth vigorously. "They probly want the black stallion the most of those three theirselves," he pointed out. "We gotta at least take the stallion back."

Zeb glanced over at the hiding place for his moonshine, then decided against it. He settled down to think about things. Caleb watched hopefully. When his brother's forehead got all scrunched up like that and he talked to himself, that meant Zeb was thinking. Caleb walked over, sat down, and waited.

"Got it!" Zeb slapped his leg so hard it made Caleb jump. "Here's what we do," Zeb said importantly. "We can hide the hosses for a night or two somewhere else. We'll tell Pa we taken 'em back. Then we use the geldings to rob the bank in Cain City, like we planned. Then we take the hosses back."

Caleb opened his mouth to say something, but Zeb held up a hand to stop him. Zeb was under a full head of steam now. "We use the money from the robbery to buy us a couple of decent hosses. Mares we kin breed. Maybe," he continued, "we can sneak into Lynch's pasture at night and breed 'em to the black stallion." Zeb was so excited now that he had staggered to his feet and started pacing.

Caleb rubbed a hand across his forehead and thought the plan over. "Where are we gonna tell Pa we got the new hosses from?" he asked. "He knows we don't got enuf money to buy hosses. Not good hosses anyway."

Zeb's pacing slowed down and stopped. His jaw sagged a little while he considered this new problem. "Well," he drawled, "we could just hide 'em in the new spot for a while. We can tell Pa we're saving all our money from sellin' shine to get us some new hosses. Then one day we just bring 'em back here with us and tell Pa we had enuf money saved up."

Caleb stared at the back wall of the cave while he thought it over. Finally, he nodded slowly. "Might work," he agreed.

Zeb puffed out his chest and went back to pacing. "We got to move these hosses tonight," he said. "We've got to hide 'em good, someplace Pa never goes." He jerked a thumb toward the west. "There oughtta be a good draw or some woods over there. We wait until Pa is good and likkered up tonight before we move 'em. Then we wait till he goes to town in Crabapple. He's been plannin' on going in tomorrow or the next day. That's when we rob the bank in town over at Cain City."

Caleb's eyes shone with admiration. "You was always the smart one, Zeb," he declared. "Ma always said you was the smart one."

————

That little cabin on the edge of Lynch's property was still in my mind, kinda buzzing around in the back of my brain all the way back to Fredericksburg. I had been there before, I was pretty sure of that now. But it must have been a long time ago, maybe while I was still with the Comanches or a little while after I came to Jed Hardy.

I turned that one over in my head while we rode. Hostler looked over at me from time to time, but he knew me well enough to leave me to my thinking when I had to study something through.

The Comanches had taken me up north of here. A considerable way north of here, I was sure of that. Up around Hico, Texas. We had drifted mostly south, though. Isobel, the girl who nursed me back to health, was from Mexico. They had kidnapped her on a raid down near the Mexico border, then drifted back north. I had met up with Jed Hardy when Isobel left me to go home. That was near San Antonio. His spread was west of there, and that's mostly where we had been until I left to join the army.

That first summer, though, he had taken me to a place where he said he had a little cabin. A place, he said, where a man could just let the wind blow through his ears and clear his head. I grinned at the thought. Old Jed had a way of saying things.

Hostler glanced over again but decided not to ask me why I was smiling. I clucked at Hank to speed him up a little and went back to thinking about that place where Jed had taken me that first summer. I had only been about ten years old, and I wasn't used to marking signposts on the trail and studying where I was going. It could have been north though. It surely could have been.

That cabin had looked deserted. Looked like they had

deserted it a while ago. Of course, it had been fifteen years since I had been there with Jed, if that was the place. I searched my brain for more memories about the cabin, about the fishing, about anything. I couldn't come up with much. It just had a feel about it that seemed familiar.

We reached town in Fredericksburg and dismounted in front of the sheriff's office. I tethered Hank to the rail and decided I would step inside for a minute before I took him down to the livery. The door opened to Clara's dress shop, and I jumped over toward the office door. I shot a glance down the street and relaxed when I saw it was just a customer coming out. I was getting gun-shy, no doubt about it.

I kept hightailing it for the door, anyway. Behind me, I heard Hostler snort a couple times.

"Oh, shut up," I told him.

I found Boone in the office, which didn't really surprise me. He didn't work as a deputy anymore, but he liked to ride along with us or maybe just come down to the office, make some coffee, and talk. I suspected his wife, Alice, would have put him to work if he'd stayed around their place. The coffee was terrible, as usual, but I helped myself to some anyway.

I sprawled in my chair and looked over at Boone. "You ever been out to the Lynch place?" I asked him.

Boone rolled his eyes. "That there is quite a spread," he nodded. "Didn't care to visit more'n once, on account that Lynch feller having a burr under his saddle all the time. How'd he treat you?"

"Like I'm the hired help," I said. "An' that's if he don't much like his hired help. I would hate to work for that guy. Can't say I'm much excited about going back to find his horses."

"You didn't find 'em, then?" he asked.

"No, didn't find them, but I'm thinking the moonshiners took them." I went on to explain how I had found the tracks leading across the stream and pointing me toward the area where I had been shot at yesterday.

Boone took his feet off the desk and let out a low whistle. "Moonshine is one thing, but stealing horses is somethin' else altogether," he allowed. "What are you boys planning to do about it?"

I gulped some of the coffee and set it down. I could only handle a couple of swallows at a time. "We'll go back, Hostler and me, probably in the morning," I said. "We'll come in when there's enough light they won't shoot us. Well, at least they won't shoot because they're thinkin' we're varmints. Early enough they might still be sleeping it off. We'll circle around and come in from the other side."

"Good plan," Boone said. "Stay under cover a little better this time though. They'll know it weren't no accident, comin' up on them this time. They might mean business now, and those mountain boys tend to hit what they're aimin' at."

"Yup. We'll do that."

It came to me that Boone had been in these parts for just about as long as anybody else I knew here. I wondered if he knew anything about that cabin just past the edge of the Lynch horse ranch. I described it to him and asked what he knew about it.

"It was off to the west of the big house," I told him. "Across a couple of wide pastures, you come to a creek flowing down from some hills and into the Pedernales

River. It was just off the Lynch property. An old cabin, hasn't been used in a while, I would say. Just off Lynch's ranch."

Boone leaned back and put his boots up on my desk. "Yeah, maybe," he said after a while. "Back before Lynch moved out there and decided he was King George or something. There was nothing much more than a shack there, had it a porch out front. Looked like you could fish in the crick off the porch."

I sat up and stared at him. "I think I did that," I said excitedly. "I think I can remember fishing off a porch somewhere."

Boone leaned forward and put his elbows on the desk. "Cain't remember much more," he said. "Never met the guy. Heard he pretty much kept to himself and wasn't there at the shack very often. Came from somewhere else, don't know where. Out west, maybe."

Boone knew most of my story. He got up and paced around a little. "You said you lived with this guy, he was kinda a pa to you. Had a spread down around San Antone, right, west of San Antone?"

"Right," I said.

"Uh-huh." Boone paced around a little more. "Well," he said, "it ain't much to go on, but you sure seemed to remember the fishing. The guy's name was Hardy. What was his first name?"

"Jed," I told him. "Jed Hardy."

"Okay." Boone reached down, picked up his hat, and pulled it down firmly on his head. "Not much to go on," he repeated, "but there's a few old-timers out that way I could ask about it. I'll see if anybody remembers the name and knows what might have become of him."

I sat at my desk for a couple of minutes after Boone

left. I hadn't expected this. Jed Hardy would be about seventy by now if he was still alive, but he was a tough old codger. He could be around here somewhere. If he was alive, I wanted to see him again.

I got up and put my hat on. We still had to do something about those stolen horses and the moonshiners out there, if they were really making moonshine out in the hills. I picked up my half-cold cup of Boone's coffee, took a sip, then leaned over and spat it in a bucket. There was coffee down at the café that was a whole lot better than this stuff.

I took Hank down to the livery, unsaddled him, gave him a rub, and told the stable boy to give Hank an extra bag of oats tonight. If we had to chase a couple of moonshiners riding George Lynch's horses, Hank was going to have his work cut out for him tomorrow.

CHAPTER 4

TRAINING WITH MCCABE

G eorge Lynch pulled out his buggy and hitched up a pair of young geldings, watching over his shoulder as the sheriff and deputy left his house. He'd thought he could put a little fear in the new sheriff and get his way. He was used to doing that. He hadn't gotten the result he'd expected.

Lynch climbed up in the buggy and set off for Austin. He would have to be a little careful with this guy Hardy. He didn't need to give the sheriff a reason to keep an eye on his horse ranch. Even more, he didn't need the guy getting wind of his operation in South Texas. The horse ranch was his passion, but the money was in the cows from Mexico. They were free.

The drive to Austin to pick up his niece gave him a little time to clear his head. Ordinarily, he would have been making a trip to his ranch near Laredo, down in South Texas. He would have to postpone that in order to get his niece, Norah, and bring her back to his home.

Funny thing about this niece, he reflected. She had lived her whole life in New York, losing her mother at an early age. George's brother had also passed away just recently, and the girl decided she wanted to come to Texas. It was the horse ranch—that's why she was coming. Lynch knew that much. The girl had been crazy about horses from the time she was little. Coming to Texas, though—that was going to be a whole different thing. Plus, it made one more person—along with his wife, Maribel, who lived with him—who couldn't know how he really made his money.

Taking Mexican cattle up the trail to Kansas was the perfect way to make money. Especially when a man wasn't too particular how he got those cattle. Lynch grinned to himself as he whipped the horses to pick up the pace. There were some bodies buried down there in Mexico. Who was going to miss a vaquero or two anyway?

His man down at the South Texas ranch, King Simms, took care of things. Lynch liked it that way, and he shared the money from the cattle business pretty freely with Simms. Simms did his job well, and Lynch didn't ask too many questions. Still, he planned to go along on one of the trips to Mexico soon, just to get a feel of how things were getting done. The Texas Rangers had sent a special company to South Texas to keep the peace. Sometimes a man had to lay low a little bit to stay out of trouble. It might be time to lay low, but he would judge that for himself.

Then there was Forster, his foreman at the horse ranch. Forster was another hothead, but he got things done. He would go after a man with his fists or his pistol, but he preferred using his fists.

Come to think of it, Lynch would have a word with Forster when he got home. If this new sheriff, Hardy, hadn't recovered his horse and dealt with the moon-shiners by the time he got home, he would send Forster in with a couple guys. There were plenty of places to bury a moonshiner or two. Nobody would miss them, either.

The ride to Austin seemed short. Lynch rolled into town and looked for a hotel on Guadalupe Street, not too far from the train station. For some reason, the girl had booked a train coming in at seven thirty in the morning —not an hour Lynch was used to. Lynch found his hotel and drove another two blocks to a livery stable, where he left the buggy and horses. He grabbed his overnight bag, slung it over his shoulder, and walked back to the hotel.

He wondered what his niece was like now that she was grown. He and Maribel had last seen her when she was twelve, coming to visit the horse-breeding farm he'd owned in New York. She had been a pretty girl, but head-strong and a little sassy. She would have to mind her manners if she lived under his roof, Lynch promised himself.

He checked into his room in the hotel and went looking for a drink and some dinner, in that order. Lynch decided he would give Norah a horse or two, maybe let her train a horse. Maribel could look after her. That would keep his niece out of his hair and not nosing into his business. Maybe this could work out all right after all.

———————

"Hold those hands a little higher," Jake McCabe told me. "You gotta protect your face with that right hand." He circled me a couple more times, throwing fake punches at me, aiming the punches at my face and my ribs.

After a while, he stopped circling and started talking

about how I move my feet. I'd never guessed there was this much involved in a good knuckle-and-skull fight. I figured I needed to learn everything I could. Jake had been in a unit, back in the war, that had a sure-enough prizefighter teaching him how to box.

"Okay," Jake said after a while. "Now you throw some punches at me. I waded in a little closer, taking one swing at his face and another at his belly. He blocked them both like he wasn't even working at it.

"Come a little straighter at me with that overhand," he said. "Don't try to loop that one. Come straight at my face." I did that a time or two, and it must have been better because he switched to something else.

"Now," he said, "try hooking up at me from below. Use your left hand too. You gotta have him worried about both hands. That'll keep him backed off a little." After I did that for a while, I was starting to suck some air.

I was hoping we were done, but he had a little more to go. "You're a tall man," he said. "That means you'll have longer arms most times. We gotta use that some more. You got to come in short and straight, hit him right in the eyes sometimes. That'll make him swell up, make it hard to see the other punches coming."

We practiced that for a while until Jake called a stop to it. "Just one more thing to keep in your mind," he said. "Most of these guys that want to mix it up are big guys who got used to knocking a feller cold with one big punch. Don't let 'em do that. They want to take a big swing, that's okay. They generally start that punch from down around their waist and you can see it comin'—just step inside it and come back with that straight overhand. If that doesn't stop 'em in their tracks, they'll get tuckered out, swingin' away like that. That's when you can take them down."

I thought we were done for sure, but he switched me over to practicing with my Colt. He set up some bottles on a log, like we always did, then watched while I drew and fired at the bottles. I shattered five out of six on the first try. I knew better than to puff out my chest about that. Jake just wasn't gonna be that impressed.

"Pretty good," he said, looking at the bottles. "You're definitely getting better shots off." He watched me draw and fire a couple more times. "Be sure you're clearing leather on the first try," he advised. "Don't get into such a hurry you get hung up at the top of the holster. You ain't gonna get a chance to draw twice. Make sure you get it clear at the top and aim, just one smooth motion."

I tried a few more times until he was satisfied. "Good, you're doing good," he said. "Remember, make the first shot count. There's lots of guys up in Boot Hill that were faster. Somebody else just shot straighter."

I knew Jake had put one or two of those guys in Boot Hill himself, so I paid attention. All the same, when he called it off for the day and asked if I wanted to go get a beer, I was all for it. We saddled up and headed for the Main Street Saloon and sat down by the window. Jake kept one eye out the window all the time. I guess the old sheriffin' habits die hard.

Jake turned away from the window. "I guess you and Hostler didn't get back out there to check on the stolen horses and moonshiners and whatever you got going on out there," he observed.

I shook my head. "Tomorrow," I told him. I filled him in on the tracks leading across the creek and fading out on the other side. "We couldn't get away soon enough today," I told him, "but Hostler and I will be out there first light in the morning. Lynch has him a foreman that'll probably shoot the horse thieves himself if we don't get there first."

I went on and told him about the little shack at the corner of Lynch's property and how I thought I'd remembered fishing off that porch the first summer I spent with Jed Hardy. I asked if he knew anything about it.

Jake considered it for a minute, then shook his head no. "That would have been a few years before I got here," he said. "I think I remember the shack out there, but there was never anybody livin' in it during my days as sheriff. Is Boone gonna look into it?" he asked.

"Yeah, he said he would," I said.

Jake finished off his beer, tossed a coin on the table, and stood up. "Good," he said. "If anybody can find an old coot out there who remembers something, Boone will find him. In a saloon, most likely." He stopped and grinned.

"No wonder Boone volunteered," Jake said. "He's gonna like this."

I stayed for a while after Jake left, just watching out the window. That seemed like a pretty good habit to get into. My mind went back to the horses stolen from Lynch. One thing kept nagging at the back of my mind. Why would moonshiners who almost never even get into town want to steal such valuable horses? It would be pretty likely that folks in town would recognize the horses if they rode them to the store or whatever. Why would they risk it? And what else would they do with the horses if they didn't take them to town? It didn't make sense to me.

I stood up and tossed another coin on the table to go

with Jake's. Then the thought hit me: fast horses. Maybe they needed horses faster than the old nags they were probably riding. Why would they need fast horses? The answer was obvious when I thought about it that way.

I headed out the door to talk to Hostler. We had shown ourselves in Crabapple just a few days ago. The only other town close to that area was Cain City. Maybe we needed to check things out over there tomorrow, then head over to look for moonshiners and stolen horses. Lynch could wait that long.

———

"Zeb! Caleb!" Malachi stood in the door of the shack and bellowed the names. He seemed to be pretty cross-grained today, but that wasn't anything they weren't used to. Especially when he'd had a pretty good nip at the shine the night before.

They scrambled out of the sorry-looking little garden Malachi made them tend out at the side of the shack and screeched to a halt in front of him. Malachi looked them up and down, then surprised them both.

"I need you boys to go to town today," he informed them. "Not Crabapple, go to Cain City."

Zeb and Caleb looked at each other sideways. This fit right in with their plan. Did Malachi suspect something? This had to be a trap of some kind. Old Malachi was cagey like that.

Zeb found his voice first. "Why Cain City, Pa? We allus go over to Crabapple. It's five miles closer. That's what you tell us all the time."

Malachi's eyes flared open and he gathered a lungful of air to bark at his oldest boy, then he thought better of it. He'd always told them to use their heads. At least Zeb had asked a good question.

"'Cause we need supplies," he told them. "Corn and sugar, and I want to buy a lot this time. I think we got some good orders for moonshine comin'. I don't want to buy them all in one place. Somebody's gonna get their nose outta joint and ask what does an old man and two boys want with all that corn and sugar? I'll git half of it in Crabapple tomorrow. You boys git half in Cain City today."

"Yessir." The boys said it together, turned on their heels, and saddled up two of the old nags in what passed for the corral out back. They came back and stood in front of Malachi again. "How much should we buy, Pa?" Caleb asked. "How much money we gonna need?"

Malachi did the arithmetic in his head and told them how much to buy. He reached into the pockets of his coveralls and came out with ten dollars, which he handed over to Zeb. The money went into Zeb's pocket, but both boys stayed where they were.

"What?" Malachi barked.

Zeb was the older one, but Caleb was always a little braver. "That's how we'll pay for the supplies, Pa," Caleb mumbled. "But, uh, there's a saloon there in Cain City, and Zeb and I don't never get into town..."

Malachi grumbled under his breath but fished around in his pockets again and came out with another two dollars. He fought to keep a little smile off his face as he handed it over. Both boys turned and sprinted for the horses. They left for town, trailing an old pack mule behind them.

Malachi watched them go, thinking he needed to do more of this. These boys were in their twenties, well

Caleb was close and Zeb was twenty-one. Malachi wouldn't be around forever. They needed to know how to do for themselves after he was gone.

He felt the flutter in his chest again and flopped down into the ratty old armchair on the porch. The flutters were coming more often now. He knew he needed to take things a little easier. The boys needed to do more for him.

Zeb and Caleb had just left the hills behind them and found the dim trail toward Cain City when Zeb reined his horse to the left and splashed into the creek flowing down alongside the trail.

Caleb followed suit, but he stopped Zeb when he reached the water. "What are we doing this for?" he demanded. "Much easier on the nags and on us to ride the trail."

"Tracks," Zeb said smugly. "We don't want to leave no tracks." He urged his horse forward along the creek bed.

"Who cares about tracks?" Caleb flared. "We're just goin' into town on our own horses. Who's gonna be tracking us?"

"What about tomorrow?" Zeb called out over his shoulder. "We can rob the bank tomorrow when Pa goes into Crabapple to buy them other supplies. We don't want to have any tracks on that there trail, either from today or tomorrow. That's how we git away with it."

Caleb's eyes shone with admiration. "You're the smart one, Zeb," he said. "Ma allus said you was the smart one."

————

Four hours later, with the corn and sugar divided between the pack mule and the two horses, they steered out of the saloon and mounted up. Moonshine was faster, they agreed, but a couple shots of whiskey and several beers could do the same thing for 'em. And, they agreed, it was a lot more fun to hang out in the saloon and watch the serving girl.

The bank in Cain City looked easy. Really easy. Nobody watching the place, no marshal or law of any kind. Just an old manager in the bank and an old clerk. Easy stuff. They would come back and do the job tomorrow.

———

Boone dismounted and walked into what passed for the only saloon in Crabapple. The old guy who ran the general store had a room in the back where he served beer and something he called whiskey. Boone knew he would stick to the beer in this place. The whiskey, well, he'd tried that once, a long time ago. He knew exactly how that whiskey was made.

You started with pure alcohol, then threw in some red pepper to give a bite, a plug of tobacco to give it some color, and a bar of soap to give it a bead. Add in some water so it won't be strong enough to kill anybody. No matter how you looked at it, beer was a better choice.

Boone pushed into the back room and let his eyes adjust to the darkness. He saw the guy he was looking for, way back in the corner, slumped over a table but still awake so far. No telling how much of his life the old guy had spent in this place.

"Herbie, that you?" Boone asked as he walked over to the table.

Herbie looked up and worked on bringing Boone into

focus. A smile slowly split his face. "Boone? You old sodbuster, you!" He shoved a chair in Boone's direction.

Boone took a seat and waved for a beer. He turned back around to look at Herbie. He was gonna have to get his question in fast. Herbie looked like he was about to have a long nap, anytime now.

"I wanted to ask you if you remember an old-timer, used to live in a shack out by the Lynch ranch."

"HUH?" asked Herbie. He cupped a hand up to one ear. "Whatdja say?"

Boone raised his voice to a low roar and repeated the question at full volume. Herbie picked up his empty whiskey glass and stared sorrowfully into the bottom of it. "Let's see now, old shack..." He thumped the empty glass down on the table.

Boone stared at the empty glass in disbelief. "You're kiddin'," he said. "You want more of that stuff?"

Herbie blinked slowly. His bleary eyes swam for a second, then focused. "Yup," he stated. "Mother's milk, that is."

Boone waved for a whiskey refill and waited for Herbie to slurp it down. "Old shack, Lynch's place," he repeated.

Herbie nodded slowly. "Yup, old boy used to visit jest once in a while, then he come back several years ago to live there all the time." He wiped his mouth with his sleeve and peered into the bottom of the glass again. He was a gen-u-wine old mountain man, folks said."

Boone sat up straight and stared. "Old mountain man?"

Herbie nodded again. One elbow started to slide toward the edge of the table. Herbie grabbed hold of the table to look up at Boone again. "Too bad, there at the end," he slurred. "Some folks think he was shot or somethin'. Jest disappeared one day and nobody ever saw him again."

Herbie's face planted into the table and he stopped moving. Boone jumped up and looked around. The old guy who owned the place came into the back and hauled Herbie's limp form out of the chair. "He can sleep it off in the corner, just like always," he said. "He sleeps here most nights, anyway."

Boone watched while the guy dragged Herbie over to an old mattress in the corner. He put some money on the table, went outside, and mounted up. He paused before taking the trail home. Was this something, he wondered, that he should really tell Pike about? Sometimes it was best just to let sleeping dogs lie.

CHAPTER 5

BEST LAID PLANS

Nick Forster considered himself to be a lot more than just George Lynch's foreman at the Circle L Ranch. He knew his horses, all right, and he had hired the guys that knew how to breed horses, how to train them, exercise them, all that stuff. Forster didn't have to know how to do it all himself. He just had to make sure it got done. He did that, with his fists and his guns if he had to.

No, that wasn't the most important part of what he was. Forster liked to think he was a businessman. Lynch had put him in charge of the cattle coming in from somewhere down south. Forster didn't know much about those details, but the cattle were unbranded and there were several dozen head just dribbling in all the time. It didn't take a genius to figure they were probably stolen in Mexico.

That's where the businessman came in, as Forster liked to think of it. Lynch couldn't get too close to the operation. Forster was pretty sure Lynch's wife didn't know about it. So, Forster was totally in charge of meeting up with the cowboys bringing the cattle up the trail, paying them off, and moving the cattle to pastures in the Circle L. They kept moving, so nobody noticed much about the cattle coming and going.

Forster would bring the cows in, then split off two or three of them and send those cows to a pasture on the far north side of the ranch. Those were his cows. When he took some of Lynch's cows to join a cattle drive to Kansas, he took *his cows* with them. Lynch paid pretty well, but Forster's side business paid better. If any of his hands asked about the cows in the north pasture, he told them to keep an eye on them but otherwise mind their own business.

Now, Forster was wondering about the horse thieves. Not who the horse thieves were, he was pretty sure about that. He'd been down into that stream bed and he'd seen where the tracks were leading on the other side, and he was pretty sure Lynch had looked at that too.

No, the question was more about what he should do about the moonshiner horse thieves. He would hang a horse thief, of course, or dry-gulch them if he had to. Forster just didn't know what Lynch wanted to do about them, and he didn't want to miss out on his pay packets around here.

Before he'd left for Austin, though, Lynch had growled something about horse thieves and how he would take care of them himself if that *yellow-dog sheriff* didn't do it. That sounded like the boss might appreciate Forster doing something about it.

His mind made up, Forster had slipped out of the bunkhouse in the early morning hours to do a little more scouting on those stolen horses. Finding the moonshiner shack hadn't taken that long at all. Forster stayed back in the trees, watching the place as the dawn light started to make things a little clearer. Nothing was stirring.

Forster reined his horse around and continued to the west. It wasn't likely at all that they would hide stolen horses this close to the Circle L. There were woods, hills, and gullies off to the west. That's where the horses would be.

He put about two hundred yards between the shack and himself, moving to the west with the rising sun behind him. Then he slowed down as he reached more cover from oak trees and little draws and gullies in the land. He cut back and forth, looking for horse tracks. After ten minutes, he found the first set of tracks. He dismounted for a closer look, a small smile spreading across his face. These guys were just about the worst horse thieves he'd ever run across. He figured that was about to cost 'em their lives.

Another ten minutes of following tracks was all it took. All three missing horses were there, staked out on some good grass with a small pond to give 'em water. Forster stayed just long enough to check them over. They were fine.

He climbed back into the saddle for a ride back to the Circle L. First, he would get the firepower he needed to take care of the horse thieves. Then he would bring the stolen horses back. If Lynch asked what he did with the thieves, maybe Forster would tell him the truth, maybe not. Maybe Lynch wouldn't bother to ask.

Riding up to the bunkhouse a half hour later, Forster knew who he needed for this job. Jackson was the man he needed. Jackson was the best shot with a Winchester. Forster preferred things a little more up close with his pistols and fists. Jackson, though—

Jackson could make that Winchester 73 stand up and sing.

Just as he'd suspected, Jackson was still snoring in his bunk. Forster walked over and kicked the bunk. Jackson came up spluttering and pawing at his eyes. He settled down when he saw Forster.

"Git yer clothes on and meet me outside," Forster growled. "You'll need yer Winchester."

Five minutes later, clutching a coffee mug in one hand and the Winchester in the other, Jackson came out and walked over to Forster. He had a pretty good idea what he was going to do with the Winchester, he didn't really need to ask. He'd done this kind of thing before, and the money was pretty good.

———

Malachi had been awake for half an hour—he could hear Zeb and Caleb outside, trying to stay quiet out there. Malachi didn't want them to know he was awake because he didn't know what he wanted to do yet. He couldn't believe his boys had been stupid enough to steal hosses belonging to George Lynch in the first place. Malachi had to figure out how to keep them all from getting hung for horse thieves.

He'd waited until they had left for Cain City yesterday before he went out to see if they had returned the hosses last night like they had promised to. They hadn't. They had 'em staked out in a little valley west of here. He was going to have to take them back himself, and he had to do it fast.

Malachi decided what to do. He made sure he made a lot of noise getting up and banged around inside while he made some coffee and fried some bacon for breakfast. Finally, dressed for town, he pushed the door to the shack open, nodded at the boys, mumbled something about going to Crabapple, and went out to saddle up his ancient horse.

He put a lead rope on the old mule, stepped into the saddle, and started down the trail toward Crabapple. When he reached a bend in the road, Malachi pulled off into the trees, tethered the animals, and crept back toward the shack to see what Zeb and Caleb were doing.

The boys made a good show of hauling the corn and sugar they'd bought yesterday down to the still, then came back and trudged off to the garden like they were actually going to do some work. After a while though, they laid down their tools, saddled up their horses, and rode off to the west. Malachi cursed under his breath, remounted, and followed them from a distance.

It turned out he'd followed at too much of a distance. Malachi cursed out loud this time when he reached the place where he'd found the horses. The black stallion was still there, but the chestnut geldings were gone. The boys' old nags were there instead. Malachi looked at the tracks leading out and sat down heavily on a log. They were headed toward Cain City with the two stolen horses. Nothing good could happen over there. The flutter in his chest came back. Malachi sat for a while and waited it out.

When the flutter settled down a little, he got up, took a lead rope from his horse, and went over to calm down the stallion long enough to slip the rope over his neck. The stallion followed along quietly enough. Malachi had to hope he could get close to the Circle L without being seen, slap the stallion on the rump, and send him back across the crick. He would have to deal with the geldings and his sons later.

————

Hostler and I got an early start on our way to Cain City. I had a hand-drawn map Boone had given me last night at the sheriff's office. He hadn't stayed long, just dropped the map I'd asked him for on my desk and said he had to get home. Normally he stayed and talked my leg off, but last night, he said the missus was waiting and rolled right out the door.

We found Cain City with no problems. The few shops along the street were opening up. A gray-haired man with spectacles, slightly stooped over, was opening up what passed for a bank. Hostler and I hitched our horses to the rail and waited for him to get the door open.

He finished opening the door, turned around, and looked at the badges. He walked over to us.

"Albert Webster," he said, holding out his hand. "You must be the new sheriff for the county."

"Right," I told him. I introduced myself and Hostler. He invited us into the bank, waved us into a couple of chairs, and walked around to sit behind a big desk. He looked a little worried, glancing back and forth at us.

"Is there trouble?" he asked. His voice wavered just a little. I wondered how old he was.

"No trouble," I said. No need getting him more worried than he already was. "I'm just making the rounds in the county," I said, "getting to know folks and see if everything is okay with you."

He looked relieved. I was afraid he was about to break out sweating. He offered us some coffee, which we accepted, and just talked about the town and such for a while. After Webster looked like he wanted to get some work done, Hostler and I let ourselves out the door.

We stood on the porch and looked around. "Looks peaceful," I observed, "but let's just show ourselves around town for a little while. If those shiner boys show up with some robbery in mind, they might just get discouraged and go home first." I looked across the street, where there was an old wooden building. I could just make out the word *café* on the door.

"How's your stomach?" I asked Hostler.

He looked across the street and grinned. "I lived on that food at the fort 'most as long as you did," he boasted. "I'm up to it if you are."

I led the way. "Ya never know," I told him. "It might be good."

The food turned out to be a lot better than what I expected. I had some eggs and biscuits, then waited while Hostler waded through the same thing, plus a steak. I thought the coffee was better over at the bank, but I wasn't gonna complain.

Hostler finished up and looked across the table at me. "You remember," he said, "when I talked about getting an old cannon like Napoleon an' we could maybe use it for things like busting up the still? Assumin' there is a still, I mean."

I stared across the table at him. "I remember," I nodded.

Hostler gulped the last of his coffee. "Thing is, I found one," he said. "On my day off, place down the trail over toward Austin, got them some old army stuff. Found me another Napoleon. Fifty bucks."

I was still staring. "You bought it already?" I asked.

"I did." Hostler set the coffee cup down. "Jake said I could haul it out to their ranch and fix it up. Fire a couple test shots even."

I sat back in my chair and started to laugh after a while. "Well," I said, "I guess if Jake don't mind, it'll give you something to do on your days off. Tell you what," I said, "if we wind up needing it to take out the still, I'll split the fifty with you."

I stood up, left some money on the table, and motioned at the door. "Let's just check around a little more before we go," I told him.

We walked down to an old general store. The sign outside said it was a general store and saloon. I shook my head. That was a first. An old guy about the age of Webster, over at the bank, came out. I was starting to wonder how old you had to be to live in this town.

"Gleason," he said. "Good thing you boys are here today," he said, pointing at my badge.

"Why?" I asked. "What's wrong?"

"Two boys, look like straight from the hills back east, been in town two days now, lookin' like they're up to no good, that's what." His arms were waving around in the air while he talked.

I shot a glance over at Hostler. "Two days, and they're here this morning?" I shot back. "Where are they?"

"Don't know," said Gleason. He folded his arms across his chest and stared at me.

"Well," I sputtered. "It's not a big town. Where are their horses? What about the horses?"

"They don't got no horses today," Gleason said. "They had a couple old nags they rode in on yesterday, they did, but they was just walkin' today. Left mebbe thirty minutes ago. Walked outta town, goin' that way." He pointed.

Hostler and I turned and trotted back to our horses, mounted up, and rode out of town the way Gleason had pointed. I wasn't going to waste my time looking for footprints, we just followed a faint trail until we saw hoofprints coming out of the woods. Two sets of 'em.

We picked up the pace and followed the tracks until they came to a narrow creek. The tracks disappeared into the creek. I pulled up and sighed in frustration.

"Whadda we do now?" asked Hostler.

I pulled Boone's map out of my pocket and studied it for a while. "Looks to me," I said, "like we can follow this creek and come out just west of Lynch's ranch. That's where they were takin' shots at me the other day. Let's follow the creek and pay 'em a little visit."

———

Today just wasn't going the way Zeb and Caleb had planned it out. It started out pretty good. The old man had taken his horse and the mule and ridden out to Crabapple, so they'd had a nice early start for Cain City, this time riding the stolen geldings and packing their pistols. They had ridden along the creek bed to cover tracks, just like they'd planned on.

Right at the edge of town, they had both gotten jumpy, riding on those stolen horses. Plus, if they got recognized, that was some serious trouble too.

Zeb pulled up right at the edge of town. Caleb reined in next to him. Both of them stared into the town. It seemed as sleepy a place as ever, but neither of them seemed to want to ride on in.

Zeb cleared his throat and held on to the saddle horn to steady himself down a little bit. "Why don't we pull back down the trail a little, tie the hosses in the trees and jest walk into town, you an' me?" he said. "Then we can check things out one more time afore we go in and take that bank."

Caleb nodded his head vigorously. Bank robbery was losing its appeal the closer they got to it.

Ten minutes later, they walked slowly down the street, hats pulled down low. Their beards were long and they couldn't wear the bandanas to cover them yet. That would be like wearing a sign that said *bank robbers*. They kept their heads down and walked past the bank, glancing in. Just the old man and the teller, like yesterday. Only three horses tied up at the rails.

Approaching the general store, they saw a guy staring out the window at them. Zeb and Caleb looked away, then Zeb looked back at the store window. The guy was still staring at them. Zeb turned slowly.

"Turn around, Caleb," he murmured. "That old boy in the store is givin' us the eye. I don't like it."

Caleb turned and took a step back in the other direction, then froze. "Zeb," he quavered, "I seen a badge. That guy in the black shirt, the big one. I seen a flash of light off it. He's got a badge."

Zeb's eyes followed the two men walking across the street. "You sure you seen a badge?" he demanded. Caleb only nodded.

The two men entered the café. "Okay," Zeb told his brother. "We jest walk back on out of town, real slow. We mount up and ride back to the shack. Today ain't a good day for robbin' a bank."

They retraced their steps, forcing themselves to take it

slow until they reached the edge of town. From there, they sprinted to their horses and galloped to the edge of the creek. Zeb slowed the pace only a little as they splashed down the creek, emerged, and rode hard for familiar ground.

They were feeling relief as they neared their hiding places for the horses. Stopping in his tracks, Zeb pointed. The black stallion was gone! Jumping down from the geldings, they swapped saddles for their own horses and were mounting on the old nags when they heard the gunshot.

CHAPTER 6

DRY GULCHED

Forster had Jackson stay behind him, weaving in and out of cover from the oak trees where they could find it. He was a little leery of getting within rifle range of the moonshiner's shack. He'd heard those boys had some skills with their old Henry rifles and he liked himself just fine without any bullet holes.

When they reached the edge of the clearing in front of the shack, he called a halt, then moved back into some trees. There was a pasture on his right and the clearing in front of him. He could see trees and better cover to his left, but that wasn't the direction he needed to take if he were going to recover those stolen horses.

Forster wasn't a patient man by nature, but he'd stayed above ground a couple times instead of going to Boot Hill when he'd waited something out instead of plowing ahead. His gut told him this was one of those times. He dismounted and told Jackson to do the same. They stayed in the cover of the trees and watched the shack.

Forster moved to his right until he could see into the

pile of posts and rope that the shiners used for a corral. His eyebrows rose a little when he saw no horses in the corral. Not even the scrawny old mule he'd seen in there before.

Feeling reassured, he retreated to Jackson's position and began telling Jackson in a muffled voice that they needed to mount up, move past the shack, and find the little valley where the horses were hidden.

No sooner had Forster stopped speaking than he heard what sounded like somebody talking to himself. Forster swung his head slowly in the direction of the noise. The old man was riding up out of a draw directly in front of them. As they watched, the black stallion, being led on a rope, came up out of the draw behind the old man.

Jackson reached slowly to pull the Winchester out of the scabbard and watched Forster. Forster was watching the old man.

"We done caught him red-handed with the stallion," Forster whispered. "I reckon Lynch won't mind if we skip the part where we take him to the sheriff." Forster moved toward his horse, ready to mount and go after the stallion. "Take him down," he told Jackson.

Jackson took a quick step forward to brace his Winchester against the trunk of a post oak tree and sighted down the barrel. He took a deep breath and released his breath slowly as he tightened his finger on the trigger.

———————

Malachi came up out of the draw, still talking to himself, just like he'd been doing ever since he'd found the black stallion. Just as bad, the two chestnut geldings weren't there, meaning his boys were riding stolen horses. "In Texas, of all places," he muttered to himself. That meant there were some ropes waiting to be stretched if he couldn't fix this.

It wasn't just about returning the horses. Lynch would know who took them. Malachi was sure of that, and he knew Lynch was a hard man. Malachi and the boys were going to have to close up the still, take what money they had, and clear out of there. That meant finding the boys and the other two stolen horses just as soon as he could get this one home.

Malachi's heart fluttered again, and he scowled as he felt a pain in his chest. It seemed like his entire chest was tightening up. He pulled back on the reins to slow down and forced himself to sit up straight. He reached out to hold the saddle horn.

Malachi never heard the shot that blasted him out of the saddle. He felt the punch in his chest and felt himself sliding off his horse. A brief glimpse of the blue sky was the last thing he remembered.

———

Forster kept his eyes on Malachi's old mare as he and Jackson burst out from the trees. The black stallion was rearing and plunging, but the mare moved only a few steps, then refused to be moved anymore. Forster swooped in, untied the lead rope for the stallion, and retied it to his own horse. He waited for the stallion to stop rearing and plunging, speaking as soothingly as he could while keeping an eye out for anybody else approaching the shack.

Finally, the stallion followed him back to the Circle L. Forster knew they were leaving tracks. Right now, he couldn't do anything about that. He barked at Jackson to fall in behind them and keep an eye on their back trail. He stayed on higher, drier ground where he could.

When they reached the creek bordering the horse ranch, Forster rode in to cut the remaining strand of barbed wire on the fence, then drove the black horse across. Jackson followed. He stopped when Forster barked at him.

"Hey! Hide that Winchester for a few days. Don't let nobody else see you with it."

Jackson nodded and drove the stallion a little farther across the pasture. When the stallion settled in and began grazing with some other horses, Jackson rode back to the ranch and stuffed the Winchester in the back of the woodshed.

Forster rode back out of the stream, staring at the tracks they had left. It was too hard, he decided, for anybody to know how many horses had come this way. If the sheriff showed up, Forster could tell him the black horse had come home on his own. As for the other tracks besides what the stallion would have left, well, of course, he and his men had ridden out a couple times, looking for the horse. No reason to think there wouldn't be some other tracks out there besides the stallion's.

———

Zeb was still looking around for the stallion when the shot rang out. When he looked at his brother, he saw the panic in Caleb's eyes. They froze for an instant, then

Caleb turned to switch saddles from the gelding to his own horse. Zeb stopped him.

"We might need the fast hosses," he told his brother. "Best leave the saddle on that one." He led the way toward the shack, but he stayed well into the trees and crept forward. Both feared what they were going to see.

When they saw the body lying on the trail, it was Zeb who reached out to hold his brother back. "We probly cain't help him," he mumbled. "He ain't moving. We don't need to git ourselves shot, too."

They waited in the trees for another ten minutes, watching and listening. There was nothing to see, and the only sound was Malachi's horse cropping grass. Finally, they moved out for a look.

Caleb turned toward the shack. "I'll git a shovel," he said. Zeb stopped him again.

"No time for us, Caleb," he said. "Somebody will give Pa a good burial. Whoever shot him is lookin' for us too, count on it." He shook his head. "He wasn't even wearing a gun."

They stopped at the shack just long enough to pick up an extra rifle, all the ammunition they could find, and food they could carry on the trail. They stepped out of the shack and looked at each other. Zeb checked his pockets. They had spent the twelve dollars Malachi had given them. He stepped back inside and pulled an old can from the back of a cupboard. He pocketed the twenty dollars inside.

"Where we gonna go, Zeb?" his brother asked.

Zeb stared at the ground. "Californy," he said. "How 'bout Californy? They won't foller us clear out there."

Caleb stared, his mouth working open and closed

with no sounds. "Sure," he finally said. "How we gonna git there?"

Zeb ran a hand through his hair. "We ride these hosses to Austin," he announced. "Then we sell 'em to somebody who ain't too worried about brands. We take a train as far north as it'll take us. We git far enough north, there's a train can take us clear to Californy. Pa told me about that one time."

Caleb's eyes showed hope for the first time that morning. "Do we know how to git to Austin?"

Zeb nodded. "Same way we came here in the first place. We foller the Pedernales River east, past Lynch's ranch. We got to do that part at night. We keep goin' along the Pedernales until we come to the big river." He knitted his eyebrows and concentrated. "Colorado. Foller the Colorado River to Austin."

Caleb nodded. "Whadda we do right now?" was his only question.

"We hide out in the woods till dark," Zeb answered. "We don't leave no tracks from here. Rake 'em over if we have to. We start down the Pedernales tonight." He ran his hand through his hair again. "We shave afore we git to Austin. We git a haircut when we git there and buy new clothes. Zeb and Caleb don't exist no more."

————

The buzzards were already circling the body on the ground when we rode up. I was careful, but not as careful as I'd been before. I had a feeling the fight had been knocked out of these folks. The only question was: who had done this to them?

I kneeled down next to the corpse. He was on his

back, facing up. His eyes were closed. I had a feeling somebody else had been here and closed the eyes. I looked around—there were at least three sets of tracks.

This was an old man, looking pretty worn and ragged. He was wearing a torn shirt and a pair of coveralls. His gray beard came down to his chest. He didn't look like somebody who'd been expecting visitors. I checked his pockets. They were empty.

"He wasn't lookin' for trouble, I don't think," I said to Hostler. "I'm thinking the trouble came to him."

Hostler nodded and knelt beside the body. He sniffed and backed off a little. "He smells like corn likker," Hostler observed. "This must be one of the moonshiners."

"Yeah, I think so," I agreed. "Looks like the daddy—the old bull of the woods. These guys work in families. That's what McCabe said. There might be a few others around." I saw two sets of tracks leading off into the woods. I followed them just that far and came back.

Hostler stood and looked off into the woods. "Do you think there might be more out there?" he asked.

I nodded. "We'd be fools to go in there right now though," I told him. "If there's more of 'em in there, they are forted-up and scared. We don't want to walk into that." I looked around and stared through the trees behind me. "There's some kind of shack down there," I said. "Let's go have a look."

We led the horses down a winding path toward an old shack, where the path stopped. I stayed behind a tree and hailed the house twice. Nobody answered, so we moved forward. I had my Winchester up and ready. Hostler did the same.

I glanced off to the side when we reached the door.

There was something that could have been a corral over there, but it wasn't enough to keep a horse in unless he was just old or used to standing there. I saw nothing but a sway-backed mule standing in the corner.

"No horses left here," I observed. I pulled my Colt and pushed through the door of the shack. It was empty. There was an old coffee can on the counter with the lid off, and stuff was strewn around the place like somebody had packed up in a hurry. Next to a mattress in one room, I found an old picture of a man and wife with two boys.

I passed the picture to Hostler. "I think the man in the picture was the guy out there on the trail," I told Hostler. "This place don't look like there's still a woman around. Those two boys would be bigger now, but they might be out in the woods somewhere."

I stepped outside and pulled the door shut behind us. "Let's see if we can find the still," I told Hostler.

—————

It didn't turn out to be hard at all, finding that still. There was a path worn from the back door of the shack, across a shallow creek, and into a thick stand of trees. We could smell the alcohol before we got there. We stepped into a cleared-out area screened off by a lot of thick brush and big oak trees. There were a couple of old barrels, some pipes, boards they probably used to stir things, and some jugs. I stepped across, picked up one jug, uncorked it, and took a sniff.

"It's moonshine, I'd say," I told Hostler.

I passed the jug across and he took a sniff. "How strong do you think it is?" he asked me.

I shrugged. "I wouldn't take a sip on an empty stomach," I told him. I took another sniff and put the cork back in. "I don't think I want a sip at all," I decided.

Hostler had stepped out of the clearing. I heard him call me and followed him into a little cave area. It looked like somebody had done some digging to hollow out a natural opening farther into the hillside. I stepped in and found Hostler kneeling down in the corner. He stood up and pointed.

"Supplies," he said.

I walked over and found bags of corn and sugar. There were a couple more jugs of moonshine next to two bedrolls. "Looks like two guys," I told Hostler. "Don't know if they lived out here or maybe lived in the shack and hid out here."

We stepped out of the cave and walked back to the clearing where we had found the still. "Whoever killed that old man out there on the trail," I told Hostler, "might just come back and look for somebody else he wants to kill around here. Considerin' the stolen horses and all."

I kicked around a little in the empty sacks and looked into the barrels. "We need to find the horse thieves, but I don't want somebody walkin' into an ambush and getting themselves murdered out here. We got to demolish this place."

Hostler had a little grin spreading across his face. "Sounds like a job for old Napoleon 2," he said.

"Napoleon 2." I started to chuckle. "That's gotta be what you named that old cannon you bought." I didn't even have to look at him to know I was right about that. "I think mebbe I can round up a little dynamite," I said. "That'll get the job done and won't be half as hard to haul out here."

I heard hoofbeats coming and waved at Hostler to

stay quiet. We crept out of the clearing and moved up toward the trail. Coming out of the trees, I could see somebody with his back to us, dismounted and pulling a rifle out of the scabbard. I took a closer look. It was George Lynch's foreman, Forster.

"Forster!" I called. He froze. I moved my hand up to my gun belt. He looked around at me, then slowly pushed the rifle back into the scabbard.

"Did ya catch those horse thieves?" he barked.

I ignored him, just looking him over, then I looked at the rifle. "You use that rifle lately?" I asked.

It was a shot in the dark, but it caught him off guard and it hit a sore spot. His head jerked up, and he stared at me. His eyes dropped and his look didn't miss my hand on my Colt. He walked over and got right in my face, tilting his head back.

"I asked if you caught them horse thieves?" he barked.

"I'm askin' the questions around here," I told him. "I might just have to take that rifle of yours and see if it's been fired lately. On account," I told him, "of the old man Hostler and I are gonna have to bury pretty soon."

Those eyes were getting a little crazy on me, but I had a feeling I was right about the dead man on the trail up there. "Did you bushwhack him?" I asked. "A man walks around talking big like you do, might just have a little yellow in him."

Jake was right about how guys like this one start a punch from the waist and you can see it coming. He was also right about stepping inside it and coming with the straight overhand punch. My fist smashed into his mouth and he fell over onto his back. He came up spitting blood and clawing for his gun. Mine was already out.

"You clear that leather by even one inch and I'll blow you into tomorrow," I snarled. "You just drop that gun back into the holster, walk over to your horse, and ride home. If I don't see both your hands the whole way, I'll bury you right next to that old man out there."

He went over to his horse, walking real stiff-legged all the way, but he kept his hands away from his guns. I kept my Colt handy.

He started to ride away, then turned his horse ever so slow, fished around in his mouth, took out a busted tooth, and threw it down in the trail. "Black stallion done come home," he said. "Geldings ain't back yet. I expect you to find 'em." He held my eyes a long time, then reined the horse around and rode toward the Circle L.

"I don't think he likes you, boss," Hostler observed.

"I think you're right," I agreed. I looked around. "Let's find us a shovel or two and bury the old man," I said. "Then we'll scout around for horse tracks. He's right about one thing—it's still our job to find the stolen horses."

CHAPTER 7

NORAH

The livery stable looked old and beaten down, but Zeb and Caleb were used to that. It reminded them a little of the kind of place they saw all the time back home in the Tennessee hills. Better than that, the old, sharp-eyed guy running the place didn't blink when he looked at the Circle L brand on the gelding and nodded. He knew that brand, but it didn't seem to bother him.

The old guy turned and looked at Zeb and Caleb. "Got yerselves a fresh shave, I'd say," he observed. He turned back to the horses. "I'd say I've seen that brand before." He shoved a toothpick in his mouth and scratched his ear.

"I'll give you a hunnerd forty for both hosses," he announced.

Zeb howled. "Those hosses are worth twice that much an' you know it," he protested.

The old guy shrugged. "Yeah, but these hosses need a little work on their brands. I think you know what I mean. That'll cost me some money."

Zeb and Caleb retreated and started talking to each other at a distance where the old guy couldn't hear. Zeb looked over his shoulder from time to time and tried to calm Caleb down. "He's plumb got us over a barrel," he kept saying.

"We kin sell 'em somewheres else," Caleb protested.

"An' mebbe git ourselves arrested," Zeb pointed out. "Them hosses is stolen and all three of us here know it."

Zeb turned back to the livery stable owner. "One hunnerd sixty an' we'll throw in the saddles," he offered.

The old guy walked over and looked at the saddles, mumbling to himself. He took out the toothpick and waved it in the air. "Done," he announced.

———

By the next morning, Zeb and Caleb both had a fresh haircut and some new duds. They boarded a train for Dallas and settled into their seats.

"Figger out a new name for yourself," Zeb told Caleb. "We got some money to git to Californy and start agin." He held out his hand. "No more hoss stealing and no more moonshine," he said. "Fresh start."

Caleb shook his hand. "Best idea you've had yet, Zeb," he told his brother.

———

Norah Lynch had already decided she liked Texas. Too many rules at her family's place in New York. They had told her it would be hot down here. She could get used to heat. Not much opera and ballet, they said. Lots of cows, horses, and cowboys. That sounded more like it to

Norah. Her mother had been disappointed in Norah's love of horses and the outdoors. Her dad shook his head about it, but she'd always noticed he grinned when he did.

She stared out the window of the train. It had taken a few weeks to get things wrapped up after her father's death. Her mother had passed away several years ago. The horse farm and house had been sold. Her lawyer had put her money in the bank and advised her not to talk about her money. That sounded like good advice to her.

The train ride had been a long one, lasting several days. She had stayed over for a night or two along the way just to break things up, but she was getting excited now that they were coming into Austin. She could see a lot of open country and some rolling hills in the distance. Her aunt and uncle didn't know it, but she had brought her favorite horse with her. She had high hopes for that mare as breeding stock.

She had talked with her father at the very end about moving to Texas to stay with her Uncle George. He had always encouraged her to pursue her interests, but she felt like he was holding back a little when he talked about his brother. She could see a little concern in his eyes. She had decided to make the trip anyway.

The train pulled into the station and screeched to a stop. Looking out the window, she could see her uncle already. They hadn't crossed paths in many years, but the resemblance to her father was obvious.

Norah stepped down from the train car and waved. Her uncle stared for a moment, then returned the wave and stepped forward to give her a hug. He stepped back, looking for her bag.

"Didn't know you for a minute there," he said. He

picked up her bag and moved toward a buggy he had waiting.

They waited to get her horse unloaded from the train. Norah noticed her uncle pulling a watch from his pocket to check it more than once. She pushed her luck by asking to tour Austin for a bit. Lynch forced a smile and agreed.

Norah insisted on taking a mule-drawn streetcar down Congress Avenue. She went into a few shops after the streetcar ride was over and mixed with the other shoppers. Her uncle finally got into the spirit of things a little by telling her how funding had been passed for a new capitol building. He pointed out the spot where he thought it would be built.

He spent most of the ride to the horse ranch talking about how she could "see the town with her Aunt Maribel." He clearly hadn't wanted to take the time with her himself, but expected Norah to go back with her aunt and maybe find a place to live in Austin. He dropped a question here and there about how much she might be able to afford and made a few other comments/questions about how much money her father had left her.

Norah said nothing at all about how much money she had, and talked about breeding and raising horses when George talked about moving to Austin. He seemed to grow more and more irritated with her and a strained silence grew between them for the last two hours of the ride.

When they reached the horse ranch, Norah's spirits lifted again. It was bigger than the farm her family had owned back east, fronting on a river with some rolling hills in the background. Norah was enough of a horse lover to see there was some good stock in the pastures on either side when they pulled up.

Her Aunt Maribel came from the house to give her a hug and promised to give her a tour of the place. Maribel urged her toward the house, but Norah hung back for a moment to make sure her horse was taken care of.

As she turned back toward the house, a man rode up and swung down to talk to her uncle. Norah was startled at his appearance, his face was swollen and turning an ugly yellow color where bruises were setting in. His lips were split in a couple places, and when he talked, it sounded like a tooth was missing. Norah leaned in to pick up the conversation.

"What happened to you, Forster?" Lynch demanded.

The man scowled and spat into the dirt. "That high-and-mighty new sheriff," he growled. He fingered his swollen mouth carefully and pointed off to the west.

"I was out with Jackson, uh, lookin' for the missing horses," he continued. "Found the black stallion and brought him back. Ain't found the geldings yet. Found an old codger layin' dead in the trail out yonder. Anyways, that new sheriff come ridin' up and accused me of killing the old codger."

Lynch stared at him, watching Forster's face. "What happened to the old codger? Was he a moonshiner? Did he steal the horses?"

"Probly," came the answer. "I dunno, but I found the stallion close to where he was layin' there in the trail. The old codger probly stole him, and then somebody shot him."

Lynch shrugged. It didn't matter whether or not Forster had shot the moonshiner, as long as it didn't point back to him.

"Then the sheriff rode up?" Lynch prompted impatiently.

"Yeah, the sheriff rode up, with that same deputy with him. Accused me of shootin' the old man. Asked if I had fired my rifle lately."

"What'd you say?" Lynch was starting to get a good idea of who had worked over Forster's face.

"I said I didn't...and told him it weren't none of his business." He pointed at his face. "He swung when I weren't lookin' and got in a lucky punch," he finished.

Lynch studied his face and barked out a short, ugly laugh. "Lucky or not, looks like he tore down your meathouse," Lynch said.

The man her uncle called Forster made another growling noise and spat in the dirt. Lynch glanced back over his shoulder at Norah, then put out his arm and steered Forster away. They kept talking, but Norah couldn't hear them anymore. Her aunt moved her toward the house, talking about taking her up to Norah's new room so she could freshen up after the long trip.

Norah followed her aunt, but her mind wasn't on the things Maribel was saying. Norah was shocked. The man, Forster, had been in a fight and was bruised and beaten. They had talked about stolen horses. Her uncle didn't seem surprised at having his horse stolen, and he didn't seem to care much about his man being beaten by a sheriff.

None of this fit in with the world she had known in New York. She wondered what kind of people these were. Norah decided she didn't much like or trust any of them. Forster was crude and had a bad temper. The sheriff sounded like a brute. She didn't much like or trust her uncle either. This didn't seem like a very good start for her new life in Texas.

————

I stopped off at the livery stable in Fredericksburg when I got back to town and looked for those stolen chestnut geldings, but I didn't have much hope of finding them there. Horse thieves have to be smarter than that if they don't want to get hanged. Sure enough, the geldings weren't there.

I went back to the office and was pretty happy when Jake McCabe and Boone showed up a little later. They usually stopped off if either one of them was in town. I told them about developments with the moonshiners, stolen horses, and my run-in with Lynch's foreman out on the trail.

Jake glanced over at my skinned knuckles. "Looks like you got in a pretty good shot," he observed.

"Yup, I got in a lick or two," I told him. "Thanks for the tip about the straight right hand over the top." I stirred a spoon around in my coffee.

"How can I find those stolen geldings?" I asked. "They could have gone anywhere on those horses."

Jake glanced over at Boone, who just shrugged. I think Boone was still upset that I planned on blowing up the still.

Jake leaned back and stared at the ceiling for a minute. "They're just going to get away from here as fast as they can," Jake advised. "Probably not much chance you'll see them around here."

He thought a little more. "You could send a wire to the Rangers over in Austin and give them a description of the horses. They could keep an eye out. They could maybe keep an eye on the horses being loaded at the train stations. Houston, Dallas, Ft. Worth, Austin. Horse thieves like to get those things out of the state. They'll have somebody who can do some tricky work with a branding iron and change those brands a little. The Rangers can look for that."

Jake got up and headed for the door. "I promised to do a little shopping for Julia," he told me. "See you later."

Boone hadn't moved. He was just stirring his coffee, then finally looked up at me. "Been decidin' whether I should tell you about this," he said abruptly. "But seein' as how this guy Hardy was like a pa to you, I decided to tell you."

I stopped fiddling with my coffee cup to give him my attention. He sounded serious.

"There's an old fossil that spends most of his time in the saloon in the back of the general store in Crabapple," Boone said.

I had been there, but not to the saloon in the back. I nodded.

"Anyways, that old boy told me he remembered Jed Hardy livin' in that old shack near the Lynch ranch. Said Hardy just came once in a while for a long time, but came back and was there all the time afore he died."

Boone glanced across the desk at me. "I guess mebbe he come back there after you left for the army," he said.

This was news to me. I thought Jed had gone back to Colorado, but what Boone said made sense. I just nodded again and waited.

Boone was staring at the desk now, but he looked up to tell me the last part. "That old boy at the Crabapple saloon thinks mebbe somebody killed old Jed Hardy. He didn't say much else—maybe he don't know much else. Sounds possible, though, that somebody murdered him."

———

It turns out there wasn't any dynamite in Fredericksburg. Mostly, folks used it in mining, with the coal mining in Texas being mainly south and east of us. I asked around and found out I could get some over in Austin. That was a two-day ride for me, but I wanted to meet up with an old friend in the Texas Rangers over there and ask him some questions.

I packed up some stuff, saddled Hank, and borrowed a mule over at the livery stable, then stopped off at the sheriff's office to give Hostler a few instructions before I left. Mainly, I wanted him to keep an eye out for the stolen horses and to let me know if Lynch or Forster showed up in town while I was gone.

Hostler was nodding while I talked, then he straightened up and stared past me down the street. "Well, I'll be..." he said.

I turned around to see what he was looking at. The new clerk from the bank was standing outside Clara Morgan's dress shop, holding some flowers. She wasn't open for business yet, but he knocked on the door, still holding the flowers. She opened the door, gave him a big hug, and pushed him inside.

I grinned. "Julia McCabe did me a big favor," I explained.

Hostler was still staring down the street. "Mebbe she can find a girl for me," he mumbled.

"Me first," I told him. Then I swung into the saddle and headed for Austin.

Leander McNelly was in his office when I showed up in Austin, and he waved me right in. I had been with the army when I met McNelly. We had been in a couple scrapes together—up in the Nation, and again at the Palo Duro Canyon last year.

McNelly pumped my hand, slapped me on the back, and offered me some really bitter coffee. I was used to what Boone makes, so it didn't bother me much.

McNelly pointed me at a chair. "What can I do fer ya?" he asked.

I started out talking about the stolen geldings, explaining what had happened at the moonshiner shack, and asked if he could help me with those chestnut geldings.

He tilted back in his chair and clasped his hands behind his head, staring at the ceiling. "How long ago did they steal those horses?" he asked.

"'Bout three days ago," I told him. "We looked around the place where we saw 'em last, but I suspect the old moonshiner maybe had a couple sons or cousins that took those horses and lit a shuck out of there."

"Mmmph," said McNelly. "Most likely rode 'em out of Texas, or maybe sold 'em to somebody who's gonna ship 'em out of Texas on a train. We can take a look down at the Austin station before you go."

"Mostly," McNelly went on, "we've been seein' horses stolen in Mexico and brought across the border. No brands on 'em—we call 'em *wet horses* because they got swum across the Rio Grande. Chestnut gelding with real good breeding ought to stand out."

I talked to him about Jed Hardy and asked if McNelly had heard of him.

McNelly shook his head. "Gonna be hard to find out anything about him if he's been gone several years," he observed. "You looked around that shack and didn't find anything?"

I shook my head. "I don't really know what to look for," I said. "There aren't any personal belongings or anything left there."

"Mmmph," he said again. "Did Jed Hardy know how to read or write?" he asked suddenly.

"Yep, he could," I answered. "He was downright proud of that."

McNelly nodded. "Sometimes, a lonely old man like that in his last years, he might take to keepin' him a journal, writin' things down," McNelly said. "It's kinda like talking to somebody when you've got nobody. There might be an old journal, under some boards or something. You could look for that."

Well, that was something to go on that I didn't have before. We left McNelly's office and went down to the train station. McNelly cornered a guy near the corral where they kept stock before loading them on the train.

"You been keeping an eye out for horses with no brands, like I told you?" McNelly demanded.

"Yup." The guy nodded his head up and down, but didn't look at McNelly, I noticed.

"How 'bout brands that look like they might've been reworked lately? Any of those? Pair of chestnut geldings, I'm thinkin' about." He looked over at me. "What was that brand?"

"Circle L," I answered.

The train station guy squirmed a little and looked away.

"Out with it," McNelly barked.

"Well," he drawled, "there was a couple of chestnut geldings, all right, left a couple days ago for Dallas.

"Brands?" McNelly boomed.

"Rocking K, they was. Kinda, uh..."

"Fresh brands, messy lookin'?" I put in.

The guy shoved his hands in his pockets and nodded. McNelly shook his finger under the guy's nose. "I'm watchin' you, buster," he warned. "You get any more like that and don't tell us and I find out, you're gonna answer to me."

We walked away. McNelly told me he would send a telegram to Dallas and pick up the horses there. He would be in touch, he said.

I picked up my dynamite and got a little extra in case I needed some again. I loaded it on the mule and went home to Fredericksburg, thinking about what McNelly said about maybe old Jed Hardy had kept a journal.

CHAPTER 8

KABOOM!

"**Y**ou sure you wanna touch this stuff off without knocking on the door and letting the folks at the Circle L know what we're doing?"

I stopped and looked over at Hostler, who had just finished dropping a stick of dynamite in each of the barrels at the still. I had bought some long fuses, and I was tying them together to let us get some distance away from the explosion. We had to be sure we were out of range when this thing went up.

I looked over at the fuse running out of the cave. I'd put a few sticks in there, too. It made a good hideout and storage place for the operation, so I was going to take that out of production along with this still.

Besides that, I wanted to shake them up over there at the Circle L. I wanted Lynch and Forster to worry about what I was doing. Before I left Austin, McNelly had told me there were a lot of raids across the Mexican border going on, and not just for horses. Cattle were being stolen and driven north to meet up with the trail drives to

Kansas. There was a lot of bad blood and there might be an ugly border war shaping up down there.

I knew that a lot of cattle were staged over near Austin to join the drives. It made sense, McNelly told me, that a lot of the stolen Mexican cattle might be driven up there to join the herds. Fredericksburg was a little out of the way to bring cattle through, but it wouldn't hurt for me to look around.

The funny thing about the Circle L Ranch was that I didn't see many cows at all. There were a lot of horses, of course, but it seemed like Forster had more hands than he needed for just a few dozen cows and breeding horses. A few dozen cows were all I'd seen, anyway.

I had scouted the trails going east from the Circle L toward Austin, and I found a lot of cattle tracks. Lynch didn't really have enough cattle to account for those tracks. That puzzled me. All in all, I figured I would just keep Lynch and Forster aggravated and nervous. Maybe they would do something stupid.

We spent another twenty minutes running fuses from the still and the cave, down into a gully far enough away and behind some trees. We knew we were safe from flying rocks and wood chunks down in the gully. We moved our horses well away and tethered them so they couldn't run off, then laid down in the gully next to the fuses.

Hostler pulled out a match and looked at me. "Ready?" he asked.

I looked at the sun overhead. "What is it, about eight o'clock?" I asked. "Ranch folks are up and getting' stuff done by now, I would think."

I pulled my hat down low and clapped my hands over my ears. "Touch 'em off," I told Hostler.

Norah prided herself on being an early riser, so it shocked her when she rolled over in the morning to see sunlight streaming through her window. Getting oriented took a minute longer. She was in Texas, at the end of a very long train ride. Maybe that was another reason she had slept this late. She hadn't gotten a lot of sleep on the train.

A loud *thump* interrupted Norah's thoughts. She jumped out of the bed and ran to the window. There was a cloud of dust to the west. She turned around and started to get dressed, then heard another explosion like the first one.

Looking out the window, Norah saw her uncle thundering down the porch steps, yelling at the hands in the bunkhouse, who had apparently been eating breakfast. Tin plates and coffee mugs flew as they scrambled to their feet. They swarmed toward the corral, trying to get their horses saddled while staring off at the dust cloud to the west.

Norah ran down the stairs and collided with Maribel, who was running up the stairs to find her.

"Stay here!" Maribel said. "George and the hands are going to see what this is about."

Norah hesitated only for a moment, then rushed around her aunt and out to the porch. Her uncle was riding out of the corral, followed by four or five hands, including the foreman, Forster. Norah rushed out to the corral and began saddling her mare.

"Norah!" She could hear her aunt calling, but she only waved her hand at the house.

"I'll be careful," she shouted, then she followed the

hands as they galloped across the pasture and toward the dust cloud.

Two minutes later, her mare stretched out flat and pulling at the bit, Norah saw the hands wading their horses across a creek. She followed, keeping just a little distance between them. Nobody was looking back.

They crossed another pasture, then she saw the men in front pulling up and dismounting just short of a stand of oak trees. A few hills rose in the background, and smoke and dust were heavy in the air. Norah smelled something she thought might be gunpowder.

She reined in and swung down outside the circle of men. Her uncle was in the front, shouting at a tall man wearing a badge. Another man with a badge stood beside him. Norah's eyes returned to the first man. This, she thought, must be the sheriff.

Her Uncle George was under a full head of steam. "What are you doing??" he shouted at full volume. "Was that dynamite?"

The sheriff leaned back and tucked his thumbs into his gun belt. "Yep, that's sure enough what it was," he said lazily. Norah noticed his eyes were anything but lazy, taking in everybody there. His eyes lingered on her.

"What are you doing, setting off dynamite and scaring my family before they're even up?" Lynch's eyes were popping out and a vein started throbbing in his forehead.

The sheriff rolled his eyes overhead and thought for a minute. "Well now, Lynch," he said quietly. "I figgered a hard-working ranch family such as yours woulda been up and at 'em for a few hours now."

Lynch snorted and stomped his foot. "You can't set off

dynamite on my property and scare my cows and horses!" he shouted.

The sheriff's eyes returned to Lynch. Norah noticed for the first time that though his complexion was dark, his hair was a dark-blonde color, and his eyes were an intense blue. Those eyes were locked in now on George Lynch.

"First of all, Lynch," he said, "this isn't your land. It's my county though, and if I decide to make it so the moonshiners don't come back, that's what I'll do." He rubbed his jaw thoughtfully, his eyes never leaving Lynch. "And by the way," he said, "speaking of cows, where are they? I don't see any, and you've got a lot of hands and a lot of land here."

Norah had circled to the side a little to get a look at her uncle. He stiffened the instant he heard the sheriff's comment about cows. His jaw worked open and shut without making a noise. That comment, she thought, had really struck a nerve with her uncle.

Lynch turned away, saying nothing, then saw Norah for the first time. His jaw dropped open. "What are YOU doing here?" he shouted.

Norah took a step back, shocked at his anger. "I saw the smoke, and I saw the hands riding in this direction," she said, watching as Lynch's face turned two shades deeper red. "I thought I would see if I could help."

"Help! Help?" Lynch took a step in her direction. "You stay out of things like this, or I'll..."

The sheriff took three quick steps to plant himself in front of George Lynch. "You'll do what, Lynch?" he asked. The mild, lazy tone he'd had earlier was gone.

"I'll do what I want with my family on my land!" Lynch spluttered.

"Let me remind you again, Lynch, this isn't your land," the sheriff said, some heat creeping into his voice for the first time. "And as far as doing what you want, if you lay one hand on this lady, you'll be my guest at the jail for a long time."

Norah saw, from the corner of her eye, that Forster, the foreman, was drifting to the side. It flashed through her mind that he had a clear shot at the sheriff from there. It wasn't lost on the deputy, either. He drifted to the side and slowly lifted his Winchester rifle. Forster stopped moving.

Lynch pulled back a step and seemed to force himself to calm down. He turned away from the sheriff and moved to his horse. "Let's go home, boys," he muttered through clenched teeth. He glanced over at Norah.

"You coming, Norah?" he asked, forcing a calm tone into his voice.

Norah looked at her uncle, then over at the sheriff. He took off his hat and nodded at her. "Ma'am," he said.

Norah nodded, then walked back to her horse and mounted. She didn't want to aggravate her uncle any further by talking to this sheriff, who had just backed him down in front of his men. She had a feeling it had humiliated him.

The Circle L crew mounted and rode back toward the ranch. Norah rode in the middle of the bunch, staying clear of her uncle. She hadn't liked what she had seen yesterday, and this morning was worse. What had she gotten herself into?

They had crossed the creek and started through the last pasture before they reached the house when Norah thought again about the sheriff. He had stepped in when her uncle threatened. And, he'd called her *Ma'am*. That wasn't something she'd heard in New York. A small smile crossed her face for the first time that morning.

———

I watched them ride off. *Who*, I thought, *was that girl*? Lynch had called her part of his family, but I was sure I'd never seen her around here. I was still watching the horses moving away when I realized Hostler had drifted over to stand by me. I looked over at him.

"Thanks for covering me, Pard," I said. "That foreman looked like he had him an itchy trigger finger."

"Yup," Hostler said. "Why'd you say that about the cows? Lynch looked like somebody'd put a cattle prod down his britches."

I grinned. "He did, didn't he?" I agreed. "I'm just thinkin' Mr. Lynch over there don't seem to welcome the law around his property much. If he's just a peaceful, law-abiding rancher, why is he so prickly when we show up? I just wanted to give him something to think about."

"You did that all right." Hostler nodded. "And did you see that foreman's face? He's gonna be spillin' some beer when he swallers for a while after that punch you dished up the other day. You're not making many friends over at the Circle L. 'Cept mebbe for that Norah girl."

"Who?" I turned around to look at Hostler.

"Norah. Lynch called that girl Norah. The one you're sweet on and taken off your hat for and all that."

"Hmmmph." I looked down and saw I was still holding my hat in my hands. "I ain't sweet on her," I huffed.

"Okay." Hostler seemed to grin down at his boots.

I turned around and started for the horses. "Come

on," I said, "there's something I want to look at before we go back to town."

––––––

We kicked around in that old, ruined shack for close to an hour. I was lifting boards, moving an ancient sofa to look underneath, poking in all the corners and staring up in the rafters.

"What're we looking for?" Hostler asked. "You never told me exactly what we're looking for in this place."

We were in the old shack at the corner of Lynch's property. The one that I thought I might have spent some time in with old Jed Hardy when I was a boy. The more I hung around this place, the more familiar it seemed.

I leaned back against the wall and told Hostler about the talk I'd had with Leander McNelly. I told him how McNelly thought it was possible that Jed Hardy might have kept a journal during his last few years.

Hostler pushed his hat back and looked around. "Well," he observed, "we've looked just about every place there is to look inside. Maybe it could be outside, under some rocks or something?"

"Might as well give that a try," I agreed. We pushed through the rickety front door and stood outside, looking around. The beaten old boards were barely hanging on to the frame, and the roof sagged in two or three places. Only the old brick fireplace and chimney looked solid.

We moved through the clearing surrounding the shack, kicking aside rocks and logs after we poked around with our gun barrels first. Copperheads don't much like being disturbed if you roust 'em out too sudden.

After another half hour, I called it off. If there was a journal hidden in the shack or around it, I was out of ideas where it could be. We mounted up and rode back to Fredericksburg. They had invited Hostler and I to dinner at the McCabes' place, and I didn't like to miss those dinners.

———

Zeb and Caleb were standing in the train yard in Dallas. Zeb had just gotten done checking his pockets to see how much money they had left. It wasn't good news.

Caleb was watching his brother, not liking the expression he was seeing on Zeb's face. "How bad is it, Zeb?" he asked. They had spent two nights in a hotel on Elm Street in Dallas, but they'd also spent most of those nights in a saloon down the street. Caleb's throbbing head told him they'd spent too much time there.

Zeb shook his head. "That whiskey they've got at the saloon is way better than the rotgut we was makin' back home," he said, "but it shore does empty out a man's pockets in a hurry. We barely got enough to git to Californy now," he told his brother.

Caleb soaked up that news, shaking his head from side to side. "We shoulda quit sooner over at the saloon," he agreed. His eyes wandered over to watch livestock being unloaded from a train that had just pulled in. His eyes widened, and he pointed.

"Them geldings!" he said. "They just unloaded them geldings!"

Zeb whirled around. The words he'd started to say died out before he finished his sentence. He was pretty sure Caleb was right—those were the chestnut geldings they had stolen from Lynch.

While they watched, something even more astonishing happened. Two guys with badges walked over and grabbed the lead ropes for the chestnut geldings and took them away from the guy who was leading them off the train. A man came running in, yelling at the guys with badges. Then the guys with badges snapped handcuffs on that guy and took him away, along with the horses.

Caleb's mouth was still hanging open. "What just happened, Zeb?" he asked.

Zeb was still staring, but finally found his voice. "Looks like the revenooers knowed them hosses was coming," he mumbled. "Done took the hosses and the feller that was shippin' them."

"I'll be." Caleb finally closed his mouth. "What now, Zeb?"

Zeb watched the horses being led away, stared at the ground for a while, then checked the money in his pockets again. Then he grinned.

"They won't be lookin' for us no more, Caleb," he said. "Long as we stay away from that feller we sold the hosses to in Austin. We don't have to go clear to Californy no more if'n we don't want to. Mebbe we could even find us a job around here somewhere."

Caleb stared at his brother, nodded, then started to smile. "You was allus the smart one, Zeb," he said. "We could stay here in Texas." He looked around and saw a saloon just past the cattle pens at the train station. He looked over and saw Zeb looking in the same direction. They drifted toward the saloon.

"Just one drink, an' then we start lookin' for jobs,"

Zeb said. He looked at the saloon again. "Mebbe two drinks," he said.

On the way to the saloon, they decided they would switch to beer, on account, Zeb explained, that it didn't cost as much and they wouldn't get themselves drunk under the table so fast. To make up for it, they had bought two cigars and tried cigars for the first time. After several minutes, they had mostly stopped coughing.

Caleb stared through the smoke. There was a fistfight going on near the bar, but he'd steered around it when he brought the beer back to the table.

"What kind of work could we get, Zeb?" he wondered.

Zeb shrugged. "We're strong," he said. He took another pull at his beer. "Strong as an ox," he decided. "We could load things on the trains around here."

A man came through the smoke and stood over their table. "I'm Walsh," he told them. "Do you boys mind if I sit down?"

Zeb shrugged and pushed out a chair with his foot.

Walsh sat down and waved for some more beer for the table. "I'm buyin'," he announced. He looked from one to the other. "Where you boys from?" he asked.

"T..." Caleb winced when his brother kicked him under the table.

"Missoura," Zeb told him.

Walsh poured beer for both of them. "Okay," he said. "Never been to Missoura, but I bet I would like it." He set the pitcher down. "You boys looking for work, maybe?" he asked.

Caleb looked at Zeb. "What kinda work?" Zeb asked.

"Cowboy work," Walsh said. "We get cows down near Mexico and take 'em up the trail. Sell 'em to other folks in Texas who take 'em to Kansas. Then we go and get more cows. You boys ever herd cows?"

"Well," Zeb said. "We've had us a milk cow or two, but we didn't never do no ropin' or drivin' 'em up a trail."

Walsh nodded slowly, deciding. "We could teach you that," he announced. "First, you would work at King Simms's ranch, down in South Texas. You boys heard of him?"

They both shook their heads.

"That's okay," said Walsh. "We could teach you what you need to know. Pay is thirty dollars a month. You interested?"

Caleb gulped and stared over at Zeb, who tried to look like he wasn't interested. "We kin talk about it," Zeb said.

CHAPTER 9

TIGHTENING THE NET

I could smell the food before I rounded the bend on my way to the McCabes' house. I was a bit late. There had been a dust-up at the Main Street Saloon in town, and I'd had to go over and bust it up. Luckily, both of 'em were so drunk it didn't take much to pull those boys apart and hustle them over to the jail to cool off for the night.

Jake was out on the porch with Boone and Ike. I figured Hostler already had his feet tucked under the dinner table. I stopped off and told them how I had blown up the still. Jake and Ike laughed. Boone made a little whimpering noise, but that's all I heard from him.

Julia called us in for dinner. She gave me a kiss on the cheek on the way in. "I heard you had an interesting morning, Pike," she told me.

"Yep, we blew up that still," I said.

She smiled and whispered to me. "I heard it was an interesting morning besides the still adventure," she said.

I looked over at Hostler. He was sitting at the table, looking anywhere but at me. I knew for sure he'd been singing like a canary, telling Julia about the new girl at the Circle L.

I sat down next to Hostler. "You've got a mouth bigger than that cave we blew up today," I told him. "What did you say anyway?"

Hostler chortled and said nothing. I decided if I didn't have something better for him to do tomorrow, I was gonna make him scrub out the cells at the jail.

Jake walked over to the fireplace, took a piece of paper down from the shelf above it, and handed me the paper. It was a telegram to me, telling me that the stolen chestnut geldings had been found at the train station in Dallas. They were coming in at the station in Austin the day after tomorrow, and Lynch could claim them there.

"Lynch's gonna be happy to see that," Jake said.

"Yeah," I agreed. "He still won't like me much." I gave them my version of the morning's activities at the still. I said nothing, of course, about the girl, Norah. Hostler stuffed his face with food and said nothing.

"You could go out there with the telegram and give them the good news," Julia suggested.

"Well..." I stalled behind a cough. "If'n George Lynch or one of his people doesn't show up in town tomorrow, I'll ride out and tell Lynch," I mumbled.

Julia looked disappointed. Hostler opened his mouth to say something, but he thought better of it when I gave him an elbow in the ribs.

Dinner was breaking up, and I was getting ready to go home when I remembered how we'd searched for a journal at the old shack. I told them how McNelly thought maybe Jed could have kept a journal, but we had searched everywhere and found nothing.

Julia stood from the table, looking thoughtful, and

reached to gather some dishes. "Does that shack have a fireplace?" she asked.

"It does," I told her. "A big, nice brick fireplace and chimney. Jed must have had to bring those bricks in from Dallas or Houston."

"If you go back there, look for a loose brick in the fireplace or chimney," she suggested. "Maybe two or three loose ones. People hide things in fireplaces sometimes, then push the rocks or bricks back in. Makes a good hiding place."

I couldn't believe I hadn't thought of that myself. "First thing I'll look for when I'm out there again," I told her.

Jake followed me out to the porch. "What else did Leander McNelly have to say?" he asked.

I told him about the raids into Mexico and the bad blood building down there. I mentioned the stolen cattle and horses, and how the cows were being driven north to sell in Kansas.

Jake chewed a toothpick and thought that over. "Did you see anything funny out at Lynch's place?" he asked.

"Not many cows," I said. "His foreman don't like me much and thinks he's pretty salty."

Jake nodded and turned back to the door. "Well," he said, "Forster is kinda salty. Be careful with him. Lynch—there's something funny about him. Be careful there, too." With that, he said goodnight and went inside.

————

George Lynch noticed his niece kept some distance from him for the rest of the day, and that was fine with him. The little snip had followed him and his boys out to the moonshiners' still, and that had kept him from dealing with that uppity new sheriff the way Lynch needed to. At least, that's what he told himself.

The one thing that had stuck in his craw was the question from Pike Hardy about why he didn't have more cows. Didn't the man know it was a horse ranch? Still, Lynch knew that at any time there were several extra hands who had driven cows up from his Laredo ranch in South Texas, and Forster kept a few extra around to drive the cows over to meet up with herds going to Kansas.

Plus, he had a few gun hands. Mostly, those were King Simms's men, up from the South Texas ranch. Lynch had them around once in a while if he needed to lean on somebody. You needed to keep people in line.

It was time for another visit to the Laredo ranch. King Simms ran the place, and they divided the cows and profits, but he'd had a feeling King Simms was cheating him. He'd questioned King about that, but he had to question carefully. Simms was a fast draw and a dead shot. Lynch knew he had some skills there himself, but he didn't feel like putting Simms to the test.

Last time down, Simms had invited him to go along on the next, uh, operation down in Mexico, to see how things were done and how many risks Simms and his boys were taking to get the *wild cows* they were finding down there. Lynch had decided to take him up on it. He would leave tonight.

There were two things he needed to get done first at the Circle L. The first was the easiest. He needed to tell Forster to take the last three dozen head they had brought up from Laredo out to the ranch east of Austin, where they staged for a drive to Kansas. Today, he would do that. He didn't need stolen cows around here with that sheriff showing up every other day.

The second part was the hardest. Maribel had been following him around this morning, telling him he had been rude to their niece. Maribel expected him to make nice. Maybe even apologize. Lynch vowed he would never back down and take water in dealing with that snip of a girl.

Still, he had to make the peace, and he knew it. He didn't need her getting nosey and following him around anymore. Maribel wasn't the curious type—she left him alone to do his business and didn't ask questions. This niece of his was different. He had to keep her from getting suspicious until he could pack her off to Austin or somewhere.

Easiest job first, he decided. He knew about the poker game going on most days behind the woodshed, near the bunkhouse. Forster would likely be there, along with his sniper, Jackson. Lynch had a good idea of how the old moonshiner had died, but he didn't like to ask questions as long as things got done. Forster got things done.

Lynch also knew that Forster had been skimming a few cows every time they came in from Laredo and feathering his own nest with them. Again, Forster got things done. If he didn't get too greedy, Lynch would let it pass. If Forster got too greedy, well, maybe Jackson would like to make some more good money.

They jumped up when he came around the corner, still holding cards. There was money on a makeshift table they had set up. Forster was there, along with Jackson and a couple other guys Lynch didn't know. They'd probably come up from Laredo on the last drive. Lynch liked to keep the cows coming all the time in smaller herds.

Lynch walked into the poker game and motioned to Forster. Forster jammed his hat on his head, stuffed his cards in his pocket, and moved over to talk to him.

"How many head we got out there now?" Lynch asked. "About three dozen, right?"

"We got thirty-two head, boss," Forster lied smoothly. He knew there were exactly three dozen cows out there, but he had decided that four of them were his.

Lynch shrugged. He didn't mind letting Forster have the other four, he just didn't want Forster to know he was onto him. No telling what liberties he might take if he knew that.

"Okay," Lynch said shortly. "Get them over to Austin in the next couple days. I don't like that new sheriff sniffin' around here and asking questions. I'll bring some more up the trail maybe end of the week."

"Done," Forster said. He watched Lynch walk away, then returned to his poker game. He was up by twenty dollars today. The cows could keep for another day or two.

Leaving the poker game, Lynch knew he needed to act nice to his niece if he wanted to keep the peace around his house. He found Norah in the kitchen with his wife. He'd decided on a strategy. The girl liked horses. He would show her around. Maybe that would get Maribel off his back.

"There you are!" Lynch said, plastering a smile on his face. He looked at Norah. "You're interested in horses, you told me," he said. "Would you like a little tour?"

Norah turned around, surprise in her eyes. "Yes," she said simply. "What I would really like is to meet your breeder. I would like to breed my mare Honey to one of your stallions."

Lynch stopped short, fighting down the words that came to his mind. Breeding her mare would keep her around this place for at least a year. He'd hoped to be rid of her long before that. Still, taking care of her mare and the foal would keep her out of his hair. He glanced over at Maribel, who raised one eyebrow. He knew that look.

"Sure," he said. "Bert will be out behind the barn, watching them exercise the horses this time of morning."

He led the way, pointing out a few features of his operation to keep from talking about this morning. Much to his relief, he found Bert where he expected to find him. Lynch made the introductions.

"Norah would like to breed her mare," Lynch explained. "Maybe you could breed the mare to that new black stallion we've got out in the west pasture? What do you call that one? Sable?"

Bert took the cigar from his mouth and stared at Lynch. "Sable is back?" he asked. "The one the moonshiners stole?"

Lynch winced. Norah turned and gave him a questioning look. He had to patch it up as best he could. "Stolen? No, we were just a little mixed up about that. He had gone across the creek. Forster found him yesterday."

Lynch made some excuses and backed away. Enough of this. He needed to get down to Laredo. Maybe the girl would forget about the moonshiners and stolen horses comment. She could stay busy with breeding her mare.

———

Norah took her mare for a ride around the ranch, turning over in her mind what the breeder had said about moonshiners and stolen horses. George clearly hadn't wanted her to know that the moonshiners had stolen some horses. Coupled with his behavior when the sheriff blew up the still, she wondered what she had stumbled into at this ranch.

When she returned to the house and unsaddled her mare in the corral, she looked up to see her uncle leaving. He saw her in the corral, gave a halfhearted wave, and rode out. Norah waited a few more minutes before going into the house to talk to her aunt.

She found Maribel in the front room, reading. Maribel set down her book when Norah settled into a chair opposite her.

"Have a pleasant ride, dear?" she asked.

"I did." Norah debated for a moment whether she should bring up the subject, but she was curious of what her aunt knew, or would tell her, about the stolen horses and the moonshiners. It was clearly a touchy subject with her uncle.

Keeping her tone as casual as possible, she asked her question. "Bert the breeder said something about moonshiners and a stolen horse." She glanced at her aunt. "Did you lose some horses? I'd hate to lose my mare, Honey."

A cloud passed over Maribel's face for just a moment, then she smiled. "Oh, don't worry about that, dear," she said. "We had three horses stolen out in the west pasture, not that close to the corral where you're keeping your horse. George thinks some moonshiners out there took the horses. One came home on his own, George said. The sheriff is helping us find the other two."

Norah's mind immediately flashed on the thought that Maribel knew only what her husband told her, and had questioned it no further, even if she was troubled by any of his dealings. Her instincts told her not to ask any more questions about the horses.

Norah stood to go, then thought of something they both might enjoy. "Would you show me the way to town?" she asked. "Fredericksburg, right? That's the closest town? I would like to see it."

Maribel's face lit up, and Norah was sure the smile was genuine this time. "What a great idea," Maribel said. "Let's both go. We can hitch up the buggy and make a day of it. How about tomorrow?"

"Tomorrow is great," Norah answered. "I'm looking forward to it already." She was a little surprised to realize she was. "I'll just go upstairs and finish unpacking and arranging my things," she told her aunt.

Maybe, she thought on her way up the stairs, she should just drop the whole stolen horse and moonshiner subject. She had only arrived yesterday and had no idea what she would do if she wore out her welcome this soon.

————

I swung my feet off the desk and got to my feet when Leander McNelly came through the door. I hadn't known he was in town. Jake McCabe came in right behind him. McNelly waved me back into my chair and took a seat himself. I just waited for him to tell me what this was about.

"Found your geldings," he said. "I guess you got a telegram from our guys about that?"

"Got it," I nodded. "If I don't see Lynch or one of his guys in town today or tomorrow, I'll ride out there and let him know."

McNelly nodded absently. His mind seemed to be somewhere else already. I knew he'd get around to what was on his mind, so I just sat back and watched him.

McNelly glanced over at McCabe. "Jake tells me they took those stolen horses from a horse rancher out there on the Pedernales. Fella by the name of George Lynch. You had any dealings with this Lynch guy?"

I let out what probably sounded like a grunt and shifted around in my chair. "Couple times," I said. "Neither of 'em whatcha would call neighborly visits. He's loud, pushy, and rude." I opened my mouth to say something else, then thought better of it.

McNelly studied my face for a minute. "Go on, out with it," he said. "Jake don't seem to like him much either."

I leaned forward. "He's hiding something," I told McNelly. "Sure as I'm sittin' here, he's hiding something, and I bet it ain't all that legal, whatever it is. He's as edgy as a long-tailed cat in a room full of rocking chairs, every time I show up out there. He tries to cover it up by being all bossy and pushy, but I think he's scared I'll see something he don't want me to see."

McNelly grinned, then let out a long, slow chuckle. "That's pretty much how Jake described him," McNelly said. "Except for mebbe the part about the long-tailed cat and the rocking chairs."

He went over and helped himself to some coffee, then came back and sat across the desk from me. "Here's what's going on," he said. "There's a ranch down on the Mexican border near the town of Laredo. My boys and I have gone down and checked it out. It's run by a bad'un name of King Simms. They're stealing cows and horses in Mexico and murdering whoever gets in their way. They take the cows for drives to Kansas an' sell the horses wherever they can."

McNelly stopped to let that sink in. "Here's why I'm tellin' you," he went on. "I think George Lynch might be tied in with that bunch. Somebody with some money is in on this. There's cows comin' into a ranch east of Austin, most of 'em direct from Laredo. There's some more coming in from the west. I think Lynch might take some cows for himself and he lets Simms have the rest for running his place."

McNelly drank his coffee, made a face, and set the mug down. "I got no proof, but my boys have done some scouting around, and that's what we think." He looked over at McCabe. "Boone thinks he remembers an old trail that they could use to take the cows from Lynch's horse farm to Austin."

He stopped and waited for me to put it together. I stood up and paced around. "Hostler and I could look for that trail," I said. "See if we can catch 'em red-handed with stolen cows from Mexico. Fresh brands and all that."

McNelly grinned, stood up, and held out his hand. "Exactly what I hoped you'd say," he told me. "My Special Force and me are going down to Laredo to see if we can make it uncomfortable for 'em. If you can tie it in to Lynch, you and Hostler are welcome to join us." He grinned again. "As I recall, that feller Hostler can shoot a cannon."

"He's got himself another one," I said.

McNelly chuckled. "We might just find some use for it," he said.

I sat for a while after they had left. Hostler and I

would look, and I had a feeling we were going to find that trail. That's why I never saw many cows at Lynch's place. He probably just held stolen cows for a few days, then drove them over to Austin for sale.

CHAPTER 10

TWO DISCOVERIES

Maribel had the buggy hitched up early in the morning, and Norah's spirits rose as she dressed for the trip to town. Things had gotten better, she had to admit, since her uncle had left for a visit to his other ranch. She got along well with her aunt, and Bert the horse breeder tolerated her. Forster, the foreman, was a different matter. He ignored her, and that was fine with Norah. She still wondered what had happened to his face.

They set out for town and chatted about what they might want to do when they got there. Norah's wardrobe, though she came from a horse farm up north, wasn't really suited for the Texas hill country. Maribel knew of a couple shops that could help with that.

It surprised Norah to learn that the trip to town would take about three hours. "Round trip?" she asked. Maribel shook her head.

"Three hours each way," she told her niece. "We usually make a list of what we need in town so we don't have to go too often." She glanced sideways. "I'm thinking, though," she told Norah, "that it might be a lot more fun to come to town more often. I'm excited about showing you around and introducing you to some people today."

Norah found herself thinking she would like Texas better if her uncle weren't around, then immediately felt guilty for thinking that way. She turned the conversation back to what they planned to do around town when they got there.

They rolled into Fredericksburg in mid-morning, thanks to the early start they'd gotten. Maribel steered her niece to a dress shop run by a woman named Clara, where she was fitted for several new dresses. Coming out of the store, Maribel told her niece they needed to visit the café.

Moving down the street, Norah looked up to see the sheriff moving toward them. She slowed her pace, interrupting Maribel's flow of chatter. Maribel stopped and looked at Norah.

"What," she asked. She followed Norah's gaze and saw Sheriff Hardy walking up to them. He stopped and took off his hat.

"Ladies," he said, sounding a little stiff.

"Sheriff," Maribel said pleasantly. Norah only nodded, still unsure what she thought about this man. He had stepped in to defend her from her uncle, which she liked. But why, she wondered, had he blown up the still? It seemed a little excessive. She had seen the looks of hatred that Forster shot in the sheriff's direction. Her instincts told her Pike Hardy had something to do with all the bruising on Forster's face.

The sheriff was fishing around in his pocket, coming up with a sheet of paper, which he handed to Maribel.

"We, well, I mean the Texas Rangers, have found your two chestnut geldings at the train station in Dallas. They sent the horses down to Austin. You can claim them there any time after today." He stopped talking, fiddling with his hat, glancing at Norah from time to time.

Norah read the note over her aunt's shoulder. It was a telegram, telling them what the sheriff had said. They could claim the horses in Austin.

Maribel thanked the sheriff and steered Norah on toward the café. She caught Norah looking over her shoulder as they walked. Maribel grinned. "That sheriff caught your eye, didn't he?"

Norah turned her attention forward and followed her aunt into the café. "Well..." She didn't want to tell Maribel about what had happened with George out at the still. The more she floundered, the more the smile widened across her aunt's face.

"Okay," Norah finally admitted. "I think he's handsome. And he's a gentleman, but I don't understand why he blew up the still. Wouldn't two axes and a few swings have done the job? Also, why doesn't Uncle George like him? And I think your foreman, Forster, hates him. It all makes me wonder."

Maribel nodded, and Norah saw a shadow of sadness pass over her face. She regretted what she had said, but Maribel reached out to pat her hand.

"Forster," Maribel said, "is a very hard man. I don't know why George hasn't dismissed him. He seems to hate a lot of people. I don't like him. George, well, George is very, uh, determined to build a successful ranch and breeding operation. He resents anybody he thinks is interfering with him."

Maribel stopped to sip the coffee she had ordered. "I

like that sheriff," she said suddenly. "He had been kind to me, and I think he works hard to be fair and do his job. Like you said, he is a gentleman. I wouldn't worry about him not getting along with George. I trust him. Sometimes George is just hard to get along with."

Surprised, Norah covered her reaction by reaching for the muffin and tea in front of her. She almost blurted out the story about how George had threatened her at the still, then thought better of it. "Okay," she said finally. "I'll remember what you have said."

She felt better now about living with her aunt and worse about living on her uncle's ranch. *One thing at a time*, she told herself. *Figure it out one thing at a time.*

———

I walked back to the sheriff's office feeling a little flustered. I had delivered the telegram like I'd wanted to, but I couldn't make head or tails of the look on that Norah girl's face. It reminded me of the couple of years that old Jed Hardy had made me go to school.

The schoolmarm would stand over my desk with her arms crossed, watching me work at all the ciphering and spelling and the like. I had a late start compared to the other kids, but I could do it well enough. I was picking up what I needed to. The thing is, I always wanted to be out with Jed, fishing or hunting or learning how to read signs in the woods.

That schoolmarm, Miss Albert, would shake her head. "I can't quite figure you out, Pike Hardy," she would say. "I think you're pretty smart and you can do better than average, but you never do."

I stayed about average until Jed let me quit school.

After that, I went to the army. Well, that Norah Lynch looked at me about the way Miss Albert did. Like she couldn't quite figure me out.

I reached the jail and found Hostler leaning against the door, staring down the street where the ladies had gone into the café, with his arms crossed. He had that silly grin on his face, and I didn't want to hear about it.

"Don't you have some stuff to do?" I growled on the way in. Hostler dropped the grin down a couple notches and trailed inside behind me.

———

It was a full two-day trip down to the Laredo ranch, and it was a pure aggravation to George Lynch. Still, he reminded himself, it's where most of his money came from, and he needed to see what was going on down here.

The trip to Laredo had been made a lot easier after the International-Great Northern Railroad had completed the tracks from Austin through San Antonio through to Laredo. It was still a two-day trip with the ride to Austin to catch the train, but it was easier and faster than it had been before.

It was no accident that Lynch had bought the property near Laredo. They'd been building those tracks for a while. Lynch considered himself to be a great businessman who could see opportunities.

After getting off the train in Laredo, he collected his horse from the train and a drink from the saloon, in that order. The heat in Laredo always made him thirsty and short-tempered.

After twenty minutes in the saloon, he mounted and

pushed on. He wanted to catch King Simms by surprise and see how many cows Simms had on hand right now. He suspected Simms was smarter than Forster. And greedier.

The shadows were getting long when he turned in the gate, but there was still time enough to check the herd. He could see King Simms coming out of the barn when he pulled up. If Simms was surprised, he didn't show it.

"Weren't expectin' you," Simms said, shooting a critical glance at Lynch's horse. "We can rustle up some chow for you. I expect you're hungry."

"Chow can wait," Lynch blurted. "I wanna see the herd."

Simms showed surprise for the first time and took a half-step back. "Plenty of time for that in the mornin'," he said.

Lynch shook his head. "Want to see the herd now," he insisted. "I rode a long way. Take me out there now."

Simms shot another look at Lynch's horse. "Yer hoss isn't the kind of hoss you usually ride," he observed. "We got a better one if'n you want it."

Lynch swung down. "So get me another horse," he said. "I know I've bought you plenty of 'em to use, and I'm sure you stole a few more down south."

Simms's mouth closed into a hard line and he swung around to bark an order. A hand came out of the corral a few minutes later, leading a dapple-gray mustang. "He don't look like much," Lynch growled.

"He'll go all day," Simms said shortly.

Lynch turned his head and studied Simms for a second. He was a big, rangy man, and he wore two guns tied down. From what Lynch had heard, Simms was lightning with those guns and not shy about using them. Lynch decided not to push him any more tonight. He followed while Simms took him out to see the herd.

Just like Lynch had expected, there were about twice as many cows as Simms had reported to him. Simms had been short-changing him for a while now, as far as Lynch could tell.

————

King Simms leaned on the porch rail, feeling the morning sun on his face as he stared sourly across the yard toward the barn. His arrangement with George Lynch worked just fine for him when Lynch was in Fredericksburg. Now he was here, breathing down Simms's neck and obviously suspicious.

Simms fished around in his shirt pocket for a partly-smoked cigar, jammed it into his mouth, and scratched a match on the porch rail to light it. He could hear Lynch in the house behind him, ordering the cook to get him more coffee. Simms would have to decide how much he would put up with where Lynch was concerned. There were lots of ways to take care of this if Lynch pushed too far.

Hoofbeats by the corral got his attention. Simms swung his gaze to the corral, where he saw his man Walsh, with two guys Simms had never seen before. Walsh was his troubleshooter. If somebody became too much of a problem, Walsh was the guy who...removed the problem.

This time, he had sent Walsh up to Dallas on the train to sell off some horses they'd stolen in Mexico and didn't need. He had also told Walsh to find more hands up there. He'd lost several men on the raids into Mexico.

Walsh crossed the yard with two men who looked like brothers. Probably early twenties, Simms guessed. He puffed on his cigar and waited for Walsh to introduce the new recruits.

Walsh pushed the new guys forward and pointed in the direction of the bigger one first. "Zeb," he said. He pointed at the other one. "Caleb." Walsh didn't bother with their last name because Simms wouldn't even remember the first names.

Simms grunted and nodded. "Can you boys ride?" he asked. Both nodded. "Rope?" Both heads shook. "No," the bigger one said. He cleared his throat nervously. "We can shoot rifles real good, though."

Simms squinted through the smoke. "What kinda rifle you boys been usin'?" he asked.

"Henrys," said the big one. The other one just nodded.

"Walsh," Simms said. "Fix these boys up with a couple Henrys and take them out to the shootin' range. See how they do."

Half an hour later, Walsh came back with his report. "They're real good," Walsh said. "I think those boys could pick a fly off a tree branch at fifty yards. Almost."

Simms grunted in satisfaction. "Just what we need." His day was starting to look better. "We'll take 'em along tonight," Simms murmured. "We might need to pick off a couple varmints out there if anybody gets a notion to shoot at us when we take the cows."

———

Zeb and Caleb looked around the bunkhouse Walsh had taken them to. It was huge, compared to anything they had seen. Caleb bounced up and down on a bunk, then pushed his bag underneath it.

"Zeb," he said, "why do ya think they was mostly interested in how we can shoot?" It's a cattle ranch, ain't it? Why do ya think they didn't care about how good we was at ropin' and ridin' herd and such?"

Those things were bothering Zeb too, but he didn't want his little brother to know he was worried. Besides that, Walsh had said they were gonna take a little trip down south tonight. Zeb was pretty sure that meant they'd be in Mexico. Why were they going to Mexico? Why at night?

Zeb shook his head and tried to sound confident. "I expect they've got varmints botherin' the cows," he said. "Coyotes and such. They probly want us to shoot the varmints."

———

I had told Hostler that we would be riding out to the Lynch ranch this morning. Actually, I had told him we would scout for a trail toward Austin that Boone had said might be there. It would be a small trail, but I hadn't seen many cows on the Lynch place. Maybe they only ran a few smuggled head at a time. Maybe we would find them making a run with stolen cows.

I hadn't mentioned it, but I suspect Hostler knew I also wanted to look for a loose brick or two on the fireplace, like Julia McCabe had suggested. We mounted up and rode out of Fredericksburg just as the morning rays were creeping in from the east.

Neither of us had any idea if we would run into Lynch or Forster, but it seemed likely, so we dropped down south to the Pedernales and worked our way to the west. I wanted to catch them by surprise if we could. When we had been in the saddle for a couple hours, I knew we were getting close. We watered our horses in the Pedernales, then I turned Hank to the north. We had to go around the Circle L.

It was guesswork how far north we needed to go, but I knew Lynch had a rail fence running pretty much all the way around, so after a while, I let Hank drift to the west. When a rail fence showed up after topping a small rise, we kept the fence in sight and went north again. We saw no one.

We kept moving north until we reached the cover of some scattered post oak trees, then went west again. After a mile of doing that, we spread out and began cutting back and forth, eyes peeled for anything that looked like a trail. I kept checking over my shoulder at the Lynch pastures, but there were no cows. I wondered if we might have just missed a drive to Austin with the cattle they had on hand.

After another fifteen minutes, still drifting west, I heard a low whistle from Hostler. In another minute, I saw the same thing he'd seen. There was a small, thin trail running through the trees, maybe no more than ten feet wide. It was enough to run a few dozen head through. Something else caught my eye. Actually, I smelled it before I saw it. I dismounted and followed the trail on foot for a few yards. There were fresh piles on the trail.

I squatted and stared east. Hostler came around a

bend and joined me to ask the question we were both wondering about.

"How old do you think them patties are?" He pulled his horse to the side as I walked the trail a little farther.

I shrugged, trying to make up my mind on what to do. "I'd say a few hours," I told him. "They might have left for Austin around the time we left Fredericksburg. They've probably got about a three-hour head start on us."

"Can we catch 'em?" he wanted to know. That's what I'd been wondering about. Finally, I shook my head, frustrated.

"I don't think so," I said. "They've probably got too big a lead." I put my hands on my hips and stared down the trail. We had likely proved McNelly's guess to be true, but we were just a few hours too late to get them red-handed.

I walked back to where I'd left Hank and mounted up. "Maybe McNelly's got somebody watching that can pick 'em up on the other end," I said. "Let's you and me take another look at that old shack."

Hostler knew what I was talking about and fell in behind me on that narrow trail. It ended in the pasture just west of Lynch's ranch. It was only a little south and another hundred yards east to the shack.

I didn't waste any time kicking around in the boards or wandering around outside. We'd already looked through all that stuff. Hostler just watched while I tested all the bricks within my reach, starting on my right and working to the center, then left.

When I reached the far-left edge, I felt a little disappointment creeping in. Maybe, I thought, there was no journal at all. I worked from the top edge down, pulling and pushing on the bricks. When I got down on my knees, working on the last few, I felt something give. I pulled a loose brick into my hands. To the side and below it, several more slid out.

I reached into the hole I had created and felt a box. I reached inside and lifted it out. Hostler was watching, staring at the box. I carried the box out into the light and tugged at the lid. It slid open smoothly.

CHAPTER 11

RAID IN MEXICO

They gathered outside a hacienda-style house that looked like a fort. Lynch remembered the house as one of the things he'd liked about this property when he bought it. They had set the adobe house on a small hill, no doubt to repel attackers. Lynch wondered idly who the builders had been defending it against.

Men began mounting up, and his attention snapped back to the mission. The sun would set in another half hour. Simms had made it clear this was a raid across the border to steal cattle. His men had been scouting places for several days. Their prior raids had caused peasants to pool their cattle together. It gave them more firepower against the raiders.

The good news was that the pooled herds gave the raiders a bigger target. Lynch looked around and counted the number of men saddling up. There were twelve of them—far more than they needed to herd a hundred cows fifty miles or fewer back to the ranch. Lynch knew most of these men were coming for the firepower they could supply. He realized with a faint shock that this was likely to be a bloody raid. He'd never seen this end of the operation before.

Simms led the way south. Lynch looked around—everybody there wore a pistol and carried a rifle in the scabbard. After they swam the horses across a river, he knew they were in Mexico. They passed through a few small villages near the border. Children came out of the huts to stare at them. Parents dashed out and yanked them back inside.

Darkness was setting in. Simms waved two men to the front of the column. Lynch took those to be the scouts. He realized it was no mistake that they had a full moon tonight. They needed some light to get home, but not enough for the stock herders to see them coming.

The riders in front of him slowed and gathered around Simms in a circle. Simms was talking in low tones with his scouts, then the two scouts dropped back to join the circle around Simms, who pulled his Winchester from the scabbard.

"There's likely to be some shots fired," Simms muttered. "If you see anybody comin' at you, shoot first and ask questions later. And shoot to kill. We take the cows, we git outta here. Don't nobody want to be spending time in a Mexican jail."

They spread out into two lines and advanced into a small valley. Lynch could see well enough in the moonlight to make out the cattle grazing in the valley. Simms's estimate of a hundred cows seemed about right. Lynch carried his Winchester in his left hand even though he was right-handed—he felt a lot more confident in his skill with the Colt. He stayed behind two men who carried old Henry rifles like an extension of themselves.

The men in front split and began circling the herd.

Driving them north without a stampede was the goal, but that would be hard to pull off if shots were fired. If they stampeded, every man knew to close in on the sides and keep them moving north. The night was silent, and Lynch's hopes rose for a quick in-and-out mission.

There was a single shout in front of them, and then gunshots tore the night open. The line in front of Lynch broke left and right. They fired as they laid low over the sides of their saddles. A figure rose ghost-like in front of them. The man in front of Lynch levered his Henry and fired from the hip. The ghost-like figure crumpled to the ground.

The man who'd fired the Henry reined his horse around and stared at the figure on the ground. "Zeb..." he said in a pleading voice. Even in the moonlight, Lynch could see the pale face and stunned look.

"Sshhh!" came the urgent answer. "Keep riding, start herdin' those cows back north. He come at you and you done what you had to do!"

It was a stampede now. Lynch reined sharply to the right and put the spurs to the mustang. The animal leaped and carried him out of the way. Then he felt a vicious punch to his left shoulder. The Winchester clattered to the ground, and he spun out of the saddle.

The cattle thundered past him as he lay on the ground, gasping for breath. Lynch gritted his teeth and came to his knees. The mustang had trotted away. He found the Winchester lying on the ground and used it as a crutch to get to his feet.

Lynch moaned as he moved toward the mustang. He reached for the reins, but the horse snorted and moved several steps farther from him. Lynch leaned on the Winchester and cursed at the horse.

Hoofbeats thundered up to him. A man dismounted, grabbed Lynch by the collar and the seat of his britches, then shoved him up onto the mustang. Lynch moaned and swayed in the saddle. A rough hand grabbed his arm to steady him.

"Do you need me to tie you in the saddle?" a voice growled roughly. It was Simms.

It took a second to find his tongue. "N...no," he answered. Simms shoved the Winchester back into the scabbard, and Lynch grabbed the saddle horn with his good arm. A wave of dizziness swept over him, but he hung on.

Simms had already remounted. Lynch realized the echo of gunshots had died away. There were several limp, crumpled figures lying on the ground. Simms moved out, not bothering to look back to see if Lynch could follow.

The need for silence was gone. "Keep 'em together, keep 'em runnin' for the Rio Grande," Simms barked. Then he was gone. Lynch had just enough strength to rein his horse around and follow the others. The thought about Mexican jail was enough to keep him in the saddle.

One of Simms's men came alongside and used one hand to steady Lynch when he wobbled in the saddle. The pain in his shoulder was more than he thought possible from a gunshot wound. He mumbled to himself and thought of nothing but staying in the saddle.

Lynch had no way of estimating how much time had gone by. A sparkle ahead of him, reflecting the moonlight, told him they had finally reached the Rio Grande. The man next to him held on to Lynch's arm as the mustang swam the river and emerged on the other side.

Lynch gathered himself on the Texas side of the river.

He could hear Simms barking orders and urging the stragglers out of the river. Another wave of pain and dizziness passed over Lynch, and he felt someone come alongside and reach out to steady him. He slumped against the arm that was holding him until everything went dark.

———

Zeb unsaddled his brother's horse for him, watching as Caleb stumbled off into the darkness near the bunkhouse. Zeb gave each animal a brief round of brushing, led them to the water trough, then tethered them. He trotted off into the darkness, following where he had seen Caleb go.

Zeb found his brother squatting on his heels, rocking back and forth and shivering, even though it was a warm night. Zeb squatted down next to Caleb, who stared at him blankly, shaking his head.

"I shot him point-blank, Zeb. I'm pretty sure I kilt him. That Henry just blew him off'n his feet. He didn't move. I think I kilt him, and he was just protectin' his cows."

Zeb shook his head. "It's like I tole ya, Caleb," he said, looking around to be sure they were alone. "It was kill or git kilt. He woulda plugged you with that rifle of his. You was just faster, that's all."

It didn't seem to have any effect. Caleb kept rocking on his heels, staring at nothing. "We got to git outta here, Zeb," he said. "Let's saddle up and git outta here tonight. We can steal a couple hosses and just let 'em go when we git down the road a ways."

"Cain't do that, Caleb." Zeb was shaking his head

back and forth, not sure if his brother was even hearing him.

"Why not, Zeb?" Caleb pleaded.

"'Cause these here are some hard men, Caleb," Zeb hissed. "They'd catch us an' stretch our hides without askin' no questions. They don't care nothin' about killin' a man, couldn't you see that tonight?"

Caleb only nodded and went back to rocking on his heels.

"We'll take our time and do it careful, that's what we'll do," Zeb continued. "We'll git outta here, but we got to look for our chance." He looked toward the corral, where men were gathering around Simms.

"They're havin' some kind of meeting over there, Caleb," he said. "You've got to git yoreself together and we've got to go over there."

Caleb pulled in a long, shuddering breath and struggled to his feet. Zeb picked up his brother's hat and settled it on his head. "Like nothin's happened, Caleb," he warned. "That's how we've got to act now."

They walked over and stood at the outside of the group huddled around Simms, who gave them a sharp look but said nothing. Then he gave orders about taking care of men who got injured, and what to do with the stolen cattle.

———

I sat down on a log outside the shack and stared at the wooden box in my hands. It was too little to have a journal in it, I figured. I was almost scared to open it. Hostler stood across the clearing and watched me.

Finally, I slid the lid off the top and reached inside.

There was a piece of paper all folded up on the top. I unfolded the page and read what was at the top:

My Will
Jed Hardy

I took a deep breath and kept reading, holding it up to the light to make it out. The writing was a little faded and smudged.

I, Jed Hardy, bein' of a sound mind and a body that ain't too stove up yet, do leave everything I got to Pike Hardy who ain't my real son but to me he is.

I leave Pike Hardy this here shack and anything he can find in the shack. Mainly I leave him my land. The deed is in the box too. This here deed says I own a section of land on the Pedernales River.

Pike, boy, I hope you find this box someday. I don't know if I can keep the varmints away that wants to take my land. If I can't and you find the box, I hope you kin take the land back. It is yourn to do with what you want.

Good luck, Pike. Yore my boy.

I just sat there and stared at the ground and wiped at my eyes a couple times. Hostler was decent enough to stay over at the edge of the clearing and leave me alone.

Finally, I opened the next thing in the box, which turned out to be the deed to the land.

I read it a couple times, trying to make sense of what it said. Like Jed had said in the will, the deed was for a section of land. There was some more stuff that didn't make much sense to me. It had a map attached, so I studied that.

The land was here on the Pedernales. That's what the will said too. The drawing, though, showed the river and what looked like the creek that flowed past the shack to the river. The drawing showed land on both sides of the creek. Some of that was Lynch's land now. I shook my head when I thought about that.

"Everything okay, Pard?" Hostler had come over. I passed the will and the deed to him, saying nothing. I waited while he sat down on the log and read them.

Hostler read them both. He studied the map and the deed for a while and let out a low whistle. He passed them back over.

"That deed and the map look like some of the land Lynch is claimin' rightfully belonged to your pa," he said slowly.

"Yup. I read it the same way," I told him.

"How much is a section?" he asked.

"Six hundred forty acres," I answered. I'd remembered that from school. The schoolmarm, Miss Albert, would be proud.

Hostler stood up, shaded his eyes, and looked around. I reached into the box and pulled out a few pieces of paper, all folded up. They were the last things in the box. It was written by hand, like the will, but there were three pages of it. I opened them up and settled down to read again.

June 2

It ain't the same around here with Pike gone. I keep meanin' to go and visit him in the army, but I ain't done it yet. The shack is purty quiet without him around. I bought the land around it though, an' it's peaceful. I'm gonna live out my days here.

I got me a new naybor since the last time I come out here. Purty high and mighty if you asked me. He come from back east somewher, and he's got him a bunch of horses. He rode up yestiddy and asked if I wanna sell. I tole him no. He didn't take to it much. Got red aroundthe gills and rode off.

This mornin' they started to building a fence twixt our land. I rode out to see what was goin' on, and found that Mr. High and Mighty had him a mean foreman. Kinda narrow between the eyes, he is. Reminds me of an ornery bronc or two I've had. They tried to bite you when you wasn't lookin' at 'em.

Anyways, this ornery foreman tole me the fence was to keep me offa their property. I told him I didn't see why we couldn't be good naybores and I had no intent on g'ttin' on their land. He patted his six gun and tole me to be sure I don't.

June 5

I'm afeered things could be g'ttin' ugly with the naybores. I rode into town and got me some vittles yestiddy. It was g'tting' dark when I got back. I tied off ol' Dusty and was carryin' the vittles in when somebody taken a potshot at me. They wasn't tryin' to hit me, I don't think, but they was close enuf.

> *Today, Mr. High and Mighty come back over, nice as you please, and asked about buyin' my land agin. I tole him No agin. He got all red in the gills and rode off.*

June 12

> *It's g'tting' ugly now. They got me all holed up in the shack. I snuk out the back yestiddy after dark to get me some water at the crick, and they winged me tryin' to get back in. Stove up my leg purty bad. I'm runnin' out of vittles and I got to make anuther run into town. Don't know if I can get past 'em. Might take one or two down with me.*

I passed the pages over to Hostler and stayed on the log with my head in my hands while he read them. He passed them back over when he was done and just waited to see if I wanted to say anything.

I got up and started pacing around. I stopped and turned around to look at Hostler. "They killed Jed and stole the land," I said flatly.

Hostler just nodded. "That's the way I read it too," he said. "What do you want to do about it?"

I slumped back down on the log. "I don't know," I admitted. "That letter doesn't prove much. They could say he was just a crazy old hoot owl, just ramblin' on about nothing when he wrote those pages."

I picked up a stick and started whittling it. Sometimes, it helps me think when I do that. "I've got the deed, though," I said. "I need to take that to somebody to see if it's legal. Then I'll have to see how much of Lynch's land rightfully belonged to Jed."

"Belongs to you now," Hostler put in.

"Right." I tossed away the stick, got up, and started pacing again. "First thing though," I told him, "is I've got to do my job. Somebody took some stolen cattle down that trail over there." I pointed. "You and me are gonna meet 'em when they come back down that trail and ask some questions."

"Okay." Hostler nodded. "What are we gonna do if we meet them comin' back down the trail?"

"We're gonna ask some tough questions," I said. "We're gonna put 'em on the spot. You know me, I like to make folks nervous and watch which way they jump. It gives me a good idea what they're up to."

"You do like to put 'em on the spot," Hostler agreed. "When do you want to come back and see if we can meet them on the trail?"

I thought for a second. "Well, they left this morning," I said. "It's probly a day and a half to get to Austin with cows. Then they've got to sell 'em and start back. We'll look for them partway down that trail day after tomorrow."

We stood and went over to mount up. Hostler swung aboard and looked over at me. "We going back to town now?" he asked.

I nodded, but then another thought struck me. "You go on home and look in at the office," I told him. "I'm going over to Crabapple to look for an old codger who spends his time in what passes for a saloon over there. I'm gonna see what he remembers about all this."

We started back the same way we had come, swinging around the Lynch property. I wasn't ready to brace him yet on the things I'd found in the box. Hostler and I parted ways on the other side of the Circle L and I rode on into Crabapple.

I nodded at the old guy who ran the general store and pushed on through the doors to the saloon in the back. I didn't need to worry that it was too early. Old Herbie was right there in his usual spot.

CHAPTER 12

STANDOFF

Herbie watched me as I came over to his table. That's not exactly a surprise—we were the only two people in there. There was an empty beer glass in front of him, and I thought he should stick with the beer. I needed him to stay awake for as long as he could. I was afraid it was almost time for his midday nap.

The general store owner stuck his head in and asked what I wanted. I told him to bring a pitcher to the table. Herbie brightened up and stared at me. His glance slid down to the badge on my chest.

"Yeah, I remember now," he mumbled. "Sheriff, over there to Fredericksburg."

"Yup." I waited while the guy set the pitcher down on our table and picked it up to fill Herbie's glass. He drew down half of it with a loud slurping noise and wiped his mouth with the back of his sleeve.

"What kin I do fer ya, Sheriff?" he asked. "Did Boone come with ya?" He looked around.

"Boone didn't make it," I said. "Maybe next time."

"Okay." His eyes were on the pitcher, but he waited for me to say something.

"I came to ask you a little more about old Jed Hardy. The guy with the shack out there next to the horse ranch. He was like my pa when I was a kid, ya know?"

Herbie's arm stopped halfway to the pitcher and his eyes swam for just a second before they focused on me.

"No, I dint know that," he said. "Me and old Jed were kinda friends. We split a few pitchers back here in the saloon. Some whiskey, too." He looked around hopefully.

"When did he go away?" I asked. "I mean, when did you stop seeing him in the saloon?"

Herbie's forehead got a big furrow in it while he tried to think back. "I cain't remember exackly," he said. "Sorry. It were a few years ago." He poured himself another glass.

"I rode out there one day to look for him, I did." Herbie was staring at the wall, like he'd almost forgotten I was there. "That nasty foreman o' his run me off. Ordered me outta there with his pistol out an' everything."

Herbie's head was slumping down toward the table. "I dint even get close to the shack afore they run me off," he mumbled. "I wonder why they tore the fence down."

I had just stood up to go. Herbie was headed for a nap. I turned back around when he said that last sentence.

"What was that about the fence?" I asked.

Herbie's chin had just about reached the table, his lids half-mast, but he focused on me again. "That fence, a big, long split-rail fence. Jed was mad they'd put it up, but when I rode out there that day, they had done torn it down."

Norah finished riding her horse and walked down to the barn and the exercise yard, looking for Bert, the breeder. She found him in the exact same place he'd been when she had met him a few days ago.

Norah could tell he'd seen her coming out of the corner of his eye. He turned and glanced at her. "Time to bring your mare down?" he asked.

"Not yet," was her answer. Bert grunted and went back to watching the horses in the exercise yard.

"The sheriff told us they found the two chestnut geldings that had been stolen," Norah said, watching for his reaction.

Bert turned to face her. "Found 'em where?" he asked.

"Sheriff Hardy said the Texas Rangers found them at the train yard in Dallas," she said. "They've been sent back down to the train station in Austin. He said we can get them today or in the next few days." She looked around for Forster, feeling more relieved than anything else when she didn't see him.

Bert grunted again and went back to watching the horses. "Geldings got nothing to do with me," he mumbled. "Lynch likes to train some of 'em and sell 'em for racing. I heard those two were pretty fast."

Surprised he'd had that much to say to her, Norah stood beside him for a minute. The black stallion was in the corral now. Bert was watching him closely. When they led the black away, Norah looked around her again.

"George has gone away on a trip," she said. "Would Forster or a couple of his hands be the ones to go to Austin and get the geldings?"

Bert glanced at her sideways. "Lynch sent Forster on a

business trip," he said. "I'm not the one to ask about pickin' up the geldings." He ended the conversation by walking toward the barn.

Norah walked back to the house, an idea forming in her mind. She found Maribel sitting on the porch in the morning sun, so she walked up the steps and joined her aunt on the porch, settling herself onto a porch swing.

"There's nobody to go get the geldings," she told her aunt.

Maribel gave her a blank look.

"The chestnut geldings Sheriff Hardy told us about," Norah explained. "Uncle George has gone on a trip, so I asked Bert the breeder if Forster or a couple of his men could get the geldings. Bert said Forster is on a trip, too."

Maribel nodded. "Oh, right, the geldings," she said absently. She looked a little puzzled, Norah thought. "And Forster is gone, too?" She stared out across the yard. "I guess we could just wait until either George or Forster gets back. I'm sure they can hold the geldings for us."

"Or we could hitch up the buggy and get them," Norah said. "We could tie them on the back of the buggy and bring them back. We could make it a two-day trip."

Maribel's eyes lit up at the thought of a trip to Austin. "That sounds fun!" she exclaimed. A slight shadow crossed her face. "I don't guess George would mind," she murmured. She appeared to shake off that thought, and a smile returned to her face. "Let's do it!" she said. "We can leave tomorrow and I can show you around Austin."

Norah watched as Maribel went back into the house, glad that Maribel was excited about the trip. One thing Norah felt sure of: whatever strange things were going on around this ranch, her aunt knew nothing about them.

They'd had their morning chow and were sitting outside the bunkhouse at the Laredo ranch. Caleb looked around him before talking to his brother.

"Zeb, have ya done any thinkin' on how we're gonna get away from this place?" Caleb spoke in a whisper, even though there was nobody else in sight.

"Been thinkin' on it." Zeb nodded. "We gotta git outta here without getting ourselves hung as hoss thieves, and we gotta git someplace in a hurry to where they cain't find us. Or cain't come after us..."

Zeb's voice trailed off, and he stared into the woods. "Cain't come after us," he repeated.

"You done said that once," Caleb pointed out.

Zeb stood up and looked over at the makeshift corral Simms's men had built to hold a few mustangs they had swept up in the cattle raid the day before last. He started walking toward the corral and motioned over his shoulder for Caleb to follow.

When they reached the edge of the corral, Zeb pointed at two gray mustangs they had swept up, maybe a little tamer than the others, or that's how it looked to Zeb, anyway.

"If we take a couple hosses they ain't branded yet and get caught with 'em, nobody can accuse us of bein' hoss thieves," he pointed out. "Simms wouldn't wanna claim those hosses, else he might have to explain how he got 'em. So, maybe we feed those hosses a little extra grub and they come along with us, without tossin' and buckin' and such."

"Okay," Caleb agreed. "That makes sense. But you said somethin' about them not being able to foller us."

"Yeah, this next part is gonna sound crazy, but you gotta hear me out," Zeb told his brother. Caleb nodded and waited. Zeb took a deep breath.

"We git outta here on them mustang hosses, and then we turn ourselves in to the law. Tell 'em what we know about this place."

Caleb's jaw dropped, and he stared at his brother. "You done gone plumb outta your mind, Zeb," he announced.

Zeb shook his head. "These are hard men," he reminded his brother. "They ain't gonna let us outta here without tryin' to track us down and stretch our hides. The law don't know we stole them chestnut geldings from Lynch. We tell 'em how to find this place, they'll go easy on us, mebbe let us go. All they'll know we done is join on a couple raids. And we was forced to do that."

Zeb glanced at his brother, who was shaking his head and rolling his eyes. "Just think on it, Caleb," Zeb said. "Promise me you'll think on it."

Zeb reached down and gathered some long grass from the field. "Let's try givin' them mustangs some grass," he said.

Caleb did likewise. They waved the grass at the mustangs until they ambled over and snatched the grass from their hands. "I think it's workin', Zeb," Caleb muttered.

"You boys like them hosses?" The voice right behind made both of them jump. They whirled around to see King Simms standing there.

"Yeah, boss, we like 'em," Zeb said, scuffing his boot in the dirt. He searched for something else to say. "On account," he added, "that we don't got no hosses on our own."

"Oh yeah," Simms said. "Walsh found you boys at the train station, didn't he? Where was you goin'?"

The brothers glanced at each other. "We thought maybe Californy," Zeb said. "We wasn't really sure."

Simms chuckled, and the brothers relaxed. "Well," Simms said. "You handled yourselves real well the other night." He glanced at Caleb. "I seen you take out that feller that come up on you sudden. You boys can use them Henrys." He turned to go. "You boys can have them two hosses if you want. You got saddles?"

They shook their heads.

"I'll tell Walsh to leave them two hosses unbranded for you boys," he said. "And tell Walsh I said to give you two old saddles we got lying around." With that, he walked back to the adobe house.

Zeb and Caleb heaved a sigh of relief in unison.

George Lynch heaved himself off the sofa where he'd been lying all night. The pain was still intense, and he'd had little sleep the last two nights. King Simms had an army vet who had worked as a medic during the war, and that guy had checked to make sure the bullet went clear through. That was about it though. The shoulder was bandaged, but none of this was doing anything to help the pain.

Lynch shoved out to push himself off the sofa, allowing himself a quick yelp of pain, since there was nobody around to hear it. He dragged himself toward the kitchen. At least, he thought, he could smell bacon and coffee.

Two guys stood aside to let Lynch get in line first. He

dished up some eggs and five slices of bacon, then moved toward the coffeepot. He grabbed the biggest cup he could see on the counter and didn't bother to look at whether or not it was clean. After pouring the coffee, he moved to a long table in the next room.

Lynch was staring down at his plate, but could sense that someone had seated himself at the bench on the other side of the table. He glanced up and saw it was Walsh, Simms's guy he used to *fix problems*, as Simms had described him.

Walsh took one look at Lynch's face, reached into his pocket, and passed a flask across the table. Lynch opened the flask, took one sniff, and poured generously into his coffee cup before passing the flask back to Walsh.

Nothing was said, but Lynch took a noisy slurp of the coffee and nodded to Walsh, who passed the flask back. Lynch poured some more into his coffee and handed it back.

"I could take you to Austin an' git whatever you need for that shoulder," Walsh mumbled in low tones. "Git you some laudanum, probly morphine if you need it. Want me to git you a decent doctor to take a look?"

Lynch's head jerked up to stare at Walsh, then his eyes narrowed suspiciously. "Why would you do that for me?" he asked.

Walsh shrugged. "I know who's got the money behind this here cattle operation," he said. "I know who Simms is tryin' to keep happy, leastaways he's tryin' most of the time. It wouldn't do me no harm to have somebody who knows I can be his friend." He took a slurp of his own coffee after lacing it with the whiskey. "Friends is a good thing."

Lynch thought about it for only a moment. "Where's Simms?" he asked, swinging around to check the room.

"Let me do it," Walsh said. "I kin talk Simms into lettin' me do most things. He likes the way I make things work out." He stood and walked across the room to where Simms was standing. They talked for a few seconds.

Simms looked past Walsh to stare at Lynch. He turned back and talked to Walsh for a moment more, then nodded his head and walked away.

Walsh returned to the table and sat down to finish his breakfast. "We kin go tomorrow mornin'," he murmured. "We'll leave right after chow."

———

We had one lawyer in Fredericksburg, so I stopped off at his office before Hostler and I were ready to check the trail for cattle smugglers coming back to the Circle L from Austin. I dropped into a chair and handed him the will and the deed with the map. I'd kept the three pages of the journal Jed had written.

He picked up the will and read it, grinning a bit at the part where Jed said his body wasn't *too stove up*. He set it aside and glanced up. "Looks like the will is legal," he said. He reached for the deed and the map.

He studied both for a while, then set those to the side with the will. "It's a legally recorded deed," he said. "That's the real thing." He picked up the map again. "I haven't been out there, and I couldn't tell you exactly what you have out there, and what you don't." He shot a sharp look at me. "Do you think you have one or more neighbors who might claim this land after all these years?"

I just nodded.

He sat back, folded his hands, and thought for a while. "Best thing you could do," he said, "is find the deeds office in Austin where they record these things. They could study your deed and the deed for your neighbor's land and tell you what's yours and what's his. Or," he said, "I could go out and research it for you if you want."

I shook my hand and reached out to pick up the will and the deed. I folded them and tucked them into my pocket.

"Not right now," I said. "I've got a couple things to take care of first."

Hostler was ready to go when we got back to the office. I noticed he had his Winchester and a shotgun loaded up and ready to go. I didn't figure we'd be close enough for shotgun work if things got ugly, but I had to admit there's something about hearing a shotgun being racked that can back a man off.

We got away around mid-morning, and a steady ride would get us out to that trail a little after noon. I thought that was about right. They would have left Austin this morning, probably early, but even without the cattle, it would be several hours to get close to the Circle L. I planned to meet them down the trail a little. I didn't want them getting reinforcements, coming up behind me.

We reached the trail right about when I thought we would. We dismounted and walked back and forth, looking for tracks and manure. Since we had been here two days ago, there had been no traffic.

We remounted and started working our way east on

the trail, slowing a lot around the bends and keeping our ears open. We needed surprise on our side, both for our own safety and because I wanted to make them jumpy.

"Do you think there's gonna be shootin'?" Hostler blurted.

I looked over at him and nodded. "I think it's likely," I said. "If we see them comin', you get off and stay covered in the brush. If they've got more firepower than us, lever your Winchester and mebbe rack the shotgun, too. They won't know how many guns they've got trained on 'em."

We rode for another hour until we came to a sharp bend in the trail. I stopped and looked around, then looked back behind us.

"Let's set up here," I told Hostler. "They'll come up on us kinda sudden when they come around this bend. You'll have plenty of cover off to the side. I'll be there in the middle of the trail."

Hostler nodded. "You gonna be mounted or on foot?" he asked.

"Mounted," I said. "Otherwise, they could spur their horses right into me."

We moved into our positions and waited. At least an hour went by with nothing to see and nothing to hear but the birds singing. I was wondering if maybe they wouldn't show, and we had wasted a whole trip. Then I heard voices. I motioned at Hostler to be ready, held the reins with my left hand, and kept my right hand near my Colt.

They came around the bend, and I'd caught them off guard, for certain. It was Forster and two other guys. I was pretty sure I'd seen one of the two at the Circle L. I wasn't sure about the other.

Forster stared at me, then his lips split into a thin,

cruel smile. He looked at the guy on his right. "Lookee here, Jackson," he said. "We got us a duck just a-sittin on his hoss."

Jackson chuckled and leaned over to spit. "Looks like," he agreed.

Off in the brush, Hostler levered the Winchester, making some noise while he did it. All three looked off in that direction, seeing nothing.

"Gotcha a spotter in the trees over there, do ya?" Forster asked. His two guys split out a little wider on each side.

Hostler racked the shotgun, and they looked a little uncertain for the first time.

"Bunch of cows came down this trail, day before yesterday," I told Forster. "Funny how I never see many cows at the Circle L."

Forster's eyes narrowed and his right hand dropped down close to his waist. "Nuthin' illegal about takin' cows to market," he said. "That's all we done."

I nodded. "If we was to go on over to Austin and find the cows you sold," I asked, "how many of 'em would have brands so new they've not even healed over yet?"

Forster's face went a shade paler, and he sat very still on his horse. Jackson wheeled his horse slightly to face the spot where he'd heard Hostler rack the shotgun.

"What would you say," Forster asked, "if I tole you I've seen a lot of greenhorns like you, think they're tough 'cause they've got theirselves a badge? What would you say if I was to tell you I've taken down a couple of them guys?"

I returned his stare and leaned forward just a tad. "Well," I said, "I'd say it's time for this guy you're talking about now to stand his ground."

Forster's eyes dropped ever-so-quickly to check my gun, then his right hand flashed to draw his own.

CHAPTER 13

CALLED OUT

There was no time to wonder if I'd pushed Forster too far. No time to wonder if I should even be here, if I should have handled all of this differently. No time to wonder if Hostler could get a shot at that third gunman after dealing with Jackson. The only thing I could think of now was what I'd said to Forster: I had picked my spot, and I had to stand my ground.

Jackson's rifle was coming up on my right and the guy's hands on the left were moving. I couldn't worry about those things either. Forster's hand was on his gun and it was coming out of the holster. Mine was already out. I fired as he tried to level his gun and he slumped back, then rolled off his horse. There was a thumping noise when he hit the ground. He was trying to roll to his feet. Hostler's rifle blasted at the same time as Jackson's went off. I swung to cover the guy on my left, but his hands were in the air. Nobody likes to face a shotgun, and Hostler was still over there.

I came back to Forster. He was still on the ground,

struggling to rise. He still had his gun in his hand and he lifted it up. It was wobbling, but it was still deadly.

"Don't do it," I said.

He did. I fired again and nailed him dead center as his shot whined angrily past my ear. Forster's horse bolted into the brush. Hank was snorting and pulling away while I tried to keep my gun lined up. I swung down and looked to my right. Jackson was down and he wasn't moving. Hostler was coming out of the brush with the shotgun in his hands.

"Get down and lie on the ground. Face down," I barked at the guy on my left. He did what he was told, and I saw Hostler advancing toward him. I approached Forster. He was down on his back and he wasn't dead yet, but he wasn't going to make it, I could see that right away. I kicked his gun away and knelt down beside him while Hostler dealt with the third man.

Forster was glaring at me. His face was a mask of hatred. His lips were flecked with blood and he struggled to breathe. He didn't seem able to move at all.

"Jed Hardy," I said.

Forster swung his eyes to look at me. A look of confusion replaced the mask of hatred.

"Old guy living in a shack on the hill above the creek," I said. "Several years ago, maybe when you and Lynch first came to this area."

His face changed again, and I knew he remembered now. He knew who I was talking about.

"Did you kill him to take his land?" I asked, trying to keep my voice low and calm. I needed an answer while there was time.

"N-No, I didn't kill the old man." My eyes bore into his face and he returned my glare for a minute. Then his face relaxed a little. I knew the end was near for him. I think he knew it, too. He rolled his head a little and stared at the sky.

"He's a coward anyway," he growled. "Treats me like…" There was a short, explosive cough. "Treats me like I'm garbage. Lynch shot the old man. Dry-gulched 'im. Wanted the water…" There was another cough. "Wanted water for the back pastures without driving 'em to the river."

His head rolled to the side, and his chest stopped heaving. He was gone. I stood and looked around again. Jackson was dead. The third guy was lying face down on the ground with his hands tied behind his back. Hostler was staring around him, his eyes wide, then he looked back at me.

"Let's go," I said. "We've got two guys to bury and another one to haul to jail. We're done here."

———

George Lynch, seated inside a run-down shack at the edge of town in Austin, stared around him. It didn't look like any doctor's office he'd ever seen, but Walsh had promised him this guy could solve his pain better than any doctor Lynch could possibly find.

The glass on the table in front of him was half full. Lynch picked up the glass, took a sniff, and looked suspiciously at the guy across the table from him. This guy didn't look like a doctor any more than the shack looked like a doctor's office.

"If you ain't a doctor, what makes you think you can fix this bullet hole in my shoulder?" he demanded.

The guy across the table, who hadn't given his name,

shrugged. "Drink what's in the glass, give it fifteen minutes, an' tell me if you don't feel just a heap better," he said.

Another stab of pain shot through Lynch's left shoulder. He grimaced, toyed with the Colt on his right hip, then reached out and downed the liquid in the glass with one gulp. It tasted like it smelled—strong whiskey.

The guy got up and stepped toward the door. "Where you goin'?" Lynch demanded.

The man half turned to look at Lynch, a thin smile on his lips. "I'm goin' to get you more of what you just drunk," he told Lynch. "Trust me, you're gonna want more. Jest sit back and relax."

Lynch sniffed at the glass again, sat back, and waited. After a while, he had to admit, the shoulder wasn't throbbing like it was before. He felt relaxed, maybe felt the best he'd felt since they had shot him during that raid.

The guy came back and thumped a bottle in front of Lynch. He took another bottle just like that one and stuffed it in a drawer at the back of the room.

"What's that shhtuff you gave me?" Lynch asked, trying to get control of his tongue.

The guy grinned at him. "Laudanum," he answered. "I'll sell you that bottle for ten bucks. Last you for a month if you go easy on it. Your shoulder can heal up by then."

"Ten bucks," Lynch said. He started to complain about the price, then forgot what he wanted to say. He was feeling pretty happy about things. He fished in his pocket and put fifteen dollars on the table. "That bottle an' the one you just tucked in that drawer for fifteen," he announced.

The guy squinted at him, thought things over, and countered. "Seventeen for both," he answered.

Lynch stared at him for several seconds, grinned owlishly, and dug in his pocket for another two dollars, which he thumped down on the table.

The guy took the money and went to get the second bottle. He put both bottles into a burlap sack and shoved the sack across the table at Lynch, who rose to his feet and swayed back and forth.

"I thought laudanum was real bitter," he said with a frown. "That's what they always told me."

The guy chuckled and shoved the money into his pocket. "It was real bitter before I put the whiskey and sugar in there," he answered. He frowned when Lynch lurched toward the door. "Go easy on that stuff," he warned.

Walsh met him when Lynch emerged onto the street. "I'm ready for a drink," he bellowed.

Walsh took his arm to steady him and walked him down the street, pointing at a sign on one building. "I booked you a room in Thompson House, there," he said. "It ain't but noon. Why don't you just sleep that off for a while, then I'll come and get you for a drink."

———

Maribel was showing Austin to Norah, and she was seeing more and enjoying it a lot more than she had when her Uncle George was giving her the tour. They drove down Congress Avenue and Guadalupe Street before Maribel found the train yard and the chestnut geldings.

To Norah's eye, the geldings appeared to be in good

shape. She had no doubt they were of good breeding. Maribel took delivery of them, read a brief note the stable hand gave her, then led the horses out. Norah tied them to the back of the buggy. She pointed at the note, curious about what it said.

Maribel shrugged and passed the note over. Norah saw it was an order to have the two chestnut geldings, Circle L brand, to be shipped to Austin and held for George or Maribel Lynch. She read the name at the bottom and passed the note back.

"Who is Captain Leander McNelly?" she asked.

Maribel shook her head and put the paper in her purse. "I guess he's a Texas Ranger," she said. "Sheriff Hardy said the Rangers found the horses and had them sent back."

They climbed back into the buggy and pulled out of the train yard. Maribel hesitated when they reached Lamar Street, looking up and down the street and reading signs. She found what she was looking for and clucked to the horses, moving down to a livery stable.

"We'll leave them here for a while and we'll look at some shops," she explained.

Norah waited outside the livery stable, looking up and down the street while her aunt arranged to leave the horses and buggy. When a man came out of the saloon down the street, she stared, not believing what she was seeing. It was her uncle, moving unsteadily out to the street. A second man came out of the saloon, taking George Lynch's elbow.

"Uncle George!" Norah shouted, waving. She was certain it was him, but he was supposed to be way south of there, down at his ranch near the border. She shouted his name again, and she started down the street toward

him. As she drew closer, she thought he looked confused
and a little shaky on his feet.

———————

We were the center of attention when we rode into
Fredericksburg. Forster was slung over his saddle and
tied onto it. There was no doubt he was dead. The man
who had surrendered was riding next to me with his
hands tied to the saddle horn. Hostler was leading
Forster's horse. Jackson's horse was tied behind Forster's.
I rode on in to the jail with the prisoner while Hostler
arranged to have Forster and Jackson buried.

I wasn't too sure if I had anything to charge the prisoner with. He gave me the name Webster. I took him in
and locked him up in the jail. I figured I would see
whether I could tie him to stolen cows sold in Austin. If I
couldn't, I would have to let him go. He'd not put up any
fight when we stopped them out there on the trail.

When Hostler came in, Jake McCabe was with him.
Jake parked himself across the desk from me. "Heard you
had a little dust-up out there," he said.

I told him the story. I asked him to go back and tell
me if he'd ever seen the man I had in the cell. He came
back and dropped into the chair again, shaking his head.
"Never saw him," Jake said, "but it always seemed to me
Lynch had a lot of hands coming and going out there.
This one is new, I guess."

He stopped and gave me a look across the desk. "First
man you've had draw on you, ain't it?"

"It is." I stared out at the street. "It's different from the
guys I shot in the army. That was war. I didn't think he'd
just haul his smoke wagon like that." I shook my head.

"If he'd dropped his piece when I told him to, before that second shot, he didn't need to die..." My voice trailed off.

"You did your job," Jake said. "You won't forget it, but you don't need to fret over it, either. You never know which way a man's gonna jump when you start askin' questions. Sometimes, a guilty man comes up shooting like that."

Jake picked up his hat and moved across to the door. "You know you can stop at the house and join us for dinner tonight." He waited while I raised my eyes and nodded slowly. "I'll let Julia know," he said. Then he put on his hat and left me there in the office, wondering if I'd ever have to draw on a man like that again.

———

Lynch was in a saloon with Walsh. He'd slept off the laudanum for a couple of hours. When he'd come out to the street, Walsh was waiting for him, and he'd trailed along with Simms's *fix-it man* for a drink.

His shoulder was only throbbing a little now, to go along with the throb in his head. All things considered, he felt better, but Lynch promised himself to go easy on the laudanum. He liked to keep a clear head.

That's why he was drinking beer while Walsh was downing whiskeys over there. Lynch knew the man couldn't be trusted. Even so, he stopped with his beer glass halfway to his mouth, realizing Walsh had just asked him a question he hadn't expected.

Lynch brought the beer glass back down on the table, searching his brain to remember what Walsh had just asked him. Walsh was watching him, all sharp-eyed over there, waiting for an answer. Lynch couldn't quite remember the question.

He returned the stare and picked up his beer for another pull. "Whaddya mean?" he finally asked.

"Just what I said," Walsh answered, still watching him the way a coyote watches a rabbit. "Don't it bother you that Simms steals all them cows from you? Don't you wanna do something about it?"

Lynch eyed Walsh over the beer glass, taking his time while downing two or three swallows. He set the glass down. The part of his brain that wasn't mush was trying to choose his answer carefully.

"I know he steals," Lynch answered. "I haven't figured out how many he steals."

He stared back across the table, curious to see what Walsh would have to say. Walsh slugged down his whiskey and waved for another.

"What's it supposed to be?" he asked. "Fifty-fifty split?"

Lynch nodded and waited.

"You ain't seein' close to half them cows," Walsh said. He stared at the table, thinking. "I'd say for every ten cows we rustle down in Mexico, you see mebbe three," Walsh finally said. "An' Simms keeps the other seven. Somethin' like that, I'd say."

Lynch nodded again. He needed to know what Walsh wanted. He decided to draw Walsh out. "I'm guessing you're gonna tell me what you can do to help me with that," he said.

Walsh slugged down the fresh shot and nodded heavily. "I kin tell you what to do if you want yer cows back," he agreed. "Simms don't pay his boys enuf. They ain't happy about it. You pay 'em more, and I can get 'em workin' for you instead of Simms. You just take all the cows he has down there now, and you'll be about even. Send Simms packin'."

Lynch toyed with his beer glass. "And you can make this happen, is that what you're telling me?"

"Durn tootin, I can!" Walsh had a gleam in his eyes now. Lynch had heard enough. The rest would have to wait. His brain was still foggy from the laudanum. He stood, surprised to learn that he was still wobbling a little.

"Let's talk more tomorrow," he said. He lurched toward the door.

Walsh left some money on the table and moved out to the street. Walsh was mad, Lynch could see that much. He'd expected to close this deal. He could smell the money, Lynch could tell. Walsh crowded his elbow and Lynch pushed him away.

Somebody was shouting at him. People were staring. Lynch hated to draw attention. He stared into the sun. Somebody was coming at him, calling his name. It was his niece. Lynch looked around, relieved when he didn't see Maribel. What was this fool of a girl doing in Austin?

His brain whirled, trying to make sense of this. Lynch looked down at his shoulder. Maribel didn't know about any of this. If she found out, this sweet little operation with stolen Mexican cattle might all be over. "Can't let my wife find out," he blurted to Walsh.

Lynch knew that Walsh was moving away, circling behind the girl.

———

Norah glanced behind. Maribel hadn't come out yet. Her uncle was standing there, staring at her. The closer she got to him, the more she realized his eyes were glassy, and he was working at standing up straight and keeping his feet under him.

"Uncle George!" she exclaimed. "What are you doing in Austin?" Her eyes dropped to his injured shoulder. "What happened to your shoulder?" She turned, looking for her aunt. "Maribel!" she shouted. "George has been hurt!"

Norah swung back around to look at her uncle. He was looking over her shoulder. He shook his head back and forth, but said nothing. A shadow moved up alongside, and she heard a footstep behind her. When the butt of the gun handle came down on the back of her head, the world went black.

CHAPTER 14

GATHERING STORM

Maribel emerged from the livery stable, puzzled when she didn't see her niece. She had expected Norah to wait for her at the entrance. She shot glances up and down the street, seeing nothing at first.

When she turned for a second look to her right, Maribel watched, confused, as a man she didn't know seemed to help a woman into the back of a cart. Recognition of what she was seeing came in two stages. First, she recognized the red dress Norah had worn today. Second, she realized the woman was being loaded into the wagon, not helped. The woman wasn't conscious!

"Norah!" Maribel yelled the name as she ran toward the wagon. The man who was trying to stuff her in the back of the wagon dropped her, jumped in, and picked up the reins. Maribel looked to the right side of the wagon, where a man was staggering to climb in opposite the driver.

A second wave of shock passed through Maribel, even more powerful than the first. The man on the right was her husband. Maribel's lips moved, but she didn't seem able to say any words.

The driver pulled the man into the wagon. The passenger glanced backward as he settled into the seat. He stared for an instant, then reached to pull his hat low over his forehead and jerked around to face the front. The driver whipped the horses, and the wagon lurched out into the street, picking up speed quickly.

Maribel slowed down and stopped in the middle of the street as the wagon pulled away. "George," she whispered. She stared as the wagon turned a corner and disappeared. Her eyes dropped to Norah, who was down at the side of the street and not moving. Maribel ran to kneel beside her niece.

A man and woman passing by came to kneel beside Maribel. The woman reached out to take her arm and guide her out of the street. The man tipped his hat to Maribel and lifted Norah, moving her to safety. He asked his question twice before Maribel turned and focused on him.

"Ma'am," he said, "can we help you?"

Norah moaned and stirred. Maribel helped her to a sitting position, then turned and stared at the man who had asked the question. Several seconds passed while the couple waited for an answer.

"We need a doctor first," Maribel said decisively. The couple helped her lift Norah to her feet. They stayed with Norah and Maribel, steering them to a doctor's office and waiting while the doctor checked the wound, bandaged her head, and told Norah she would need to rest for several hours before moving.

Maribel looked at the man and woman, who had

waited in the office when Maribel had asked them to stay just a bit longer.

"Do you need the sheriff?" the woman asked.

Maribel nodded, then shook her head and began digging in her purse for the note they had given her in the train yard when she had picked up the chestnut geldings. She opened the note and read it, her eyes coming to rest on the name at the bottom of the page.

"Texas Rangers," she murmured. The couple stared at her, not sure they'd heard correctly the first time. Maribel cleared her throat and said it more forcefully. "Take me to the Texas Rangers' office," she told them.

———

George Lynch held on to the edges of his seat as the wagon careened around corners. They finally reached the edge of town and took the trail south. Lynch couldn't really process in his head what had just happened. He looked into the back of the wagon. There was blood at the edge where Walsh had tried to load Norah into the back.

Maribel had looked right at him, but he wasn't sure she had recognized him. She had said nothing other than to yell Norah's name, he'd heard that. She had stared right at him, but had said nothing. He had pulled his hat low and had turned around in a hurry. Maybe, he thought, she didn't know it was him.

They had almost kidnapped Norah, though. He still couldn't wrap his head around that. How much trouble was he in here? Walsh had hit her in the back of the head with his gun butt and had nearly thrown her into the cart before Lynch even knew what was happening. The laudanum, he thought bitterly, had messed him up.

What would he do now? He glanced sideways at Walsh, who was still driving the wagon as fast as it would go, looking over his shoulder now and then for signs of pursuit. Walsh knew as well as he did what they would do to a man who hurt a woman in Texas. The end of a noose was likely waiting. It all depended on whether anybody could tie him into this. How much did Norah know? She would remember somebody had hit her while she was talking to him.

Lynch said nothing. Walsh was still whipping the horses to put some distance between themselves and Austin, and that was fine with Lynch. He stared at the trail in front of them and came to his decision quickly. He would have to clear out of Texas. There were a couple of things to do first though.

Lynch had no intention of going along with any plan Walsh might have. He needed two things before he cleared out of Texas. First, he was pretty sure he knew where Simms hid his money. Lynch had bought that adobe house and had taken a tour before Simms moved in. There was a basement with a hidden entrance. He'd seen Simms coming from that direction in the early morning hours once or twice. That's how he would get even with Simms for stealing from him. He would clean out Simms's stash in the basement.

Second, Lynch stashed his money at his bank in Austin, but he didn't deposit it with the bank. Too many prying eyes could figure out how much he had. Maribel might find out, and he had no intention of sharing with her.

Lynch's banker had come over from London ten years

earlier, and he had installed twenty iron boxes inside the safe. He called them safe boxes, and he sealed them with a key only the customer had. The boxes were inside a safe that used the new timer locks. Only Lynch could get to the money, and nobody knew how much was in there.

Lynch's lips curved into a cruel smile as the wagon bounced down the trail. Simms was a fool for putting his money under the adobe house. Lynch would have his own money AND Simms's money before he left Texas. He had to do something about Walsh, too. What he'd done to Norah would probably get both of them hung if anybody figured it out. Satisfied with his plan, Lynch reached into his bag and pulled out the laudanum. His shoulder was hurting again.

———

Maribel stopped inside the door of the Texas Ranger offices. It was a little bigger than she'd expected, and she realized for the first time that Leander McNelly might not even be there. Who would she ask for if he wasn't there?

A man looked up from the desk closest to her. "Ma'am," he said. "Can I help you?"

Maribel found her voice. "Leander McNelly," she said firmly. "Is Captain McNelly here? My name is Maribel Lynch."

"Wait here," the man told her, then disappeared into the back of the room. He came back a minute later, followed by a man of average height with dark hair. He was younger than Maribel had thought he'd be.

The man extended his hand. "I'm Leander McNelly, ma'am," he said pleasantly. "Follow me."

They went to a small, cramped office littered with

paper. McNelly dusted off a rickety camp chair and offered it to her, then sat in a chair just as rickety behind a battered old wooden desk.

"Sorry," McNelly said. "I don't get many visitors back here. Did you get the horses I had sent to the train station here?"

"We did, thank you," Maribel told him. "Now I've come about something else." She told McNelly the story of how they'd come to Austin and how someone had attacked her niece. She finished by telling McNelly how she had seen her husband get into the wagon with the attacker.

McNelly listened without interrupting until she had finished, then leaned back and formed a steeple with his fingers while he thought about it. He leaned forward to ask his question.

"You said the man who hit your niece pulled your husband into the cart, that your husband looked a little wobbly. Was he dragging your husband in the cart when he didn't wanna go, or was he just helping your husband get it?"

Maribel bit her lip while she thought about it. "I don't know for sure," she admitted, "but it didn't look like George was trying to fight him off."

"Mmmm." McNelly went back to making a steeple with his fingers. He glanced across the table at her, then asked a very direct question.

"You and your husband have a horse ranch, I know, out past Fredericksburg," he said. "We've been told there are a lot of stolen Mexican cattle coming up the trail to be sold in Austin for the drives to Kansas. Have you noticed some cows passing through the area, or have you seen a lot of extra hands coming and going from your ranch?"

Maribel stared at the table, feeling a slight flush climbing up her cheeks. Finally, she nodded. "We don't have many cows," she said, "but I think George keeps some on the pastures at the very back of the property. And, we seem to have a lot of hands I've never seen, staying for a few days and leaving. George says they work for him on our ranch down in Laredo."

McNelly sat up straight, grabbed a pencil and some paper, and got ready to take some notes. "Tell me about the ranch at Laredo," he said.

Maribel had a sinking feeling her husband was in the cattle thieving business and she was turning him in to the authorities. Part of her didn't want to believe it, but she had looked the other way long enough. She had to admit that several things seemed funny about George's activities.

"I have only been to the Laredo ranch once, several years ago, when George first bought the property," she said. "I'm afraid I don't remember much. I know it's near the Mexican border and there are a lot of pastures. The house is hacienda-style, a big adobe building. Looks solid as a fort." She paused, trying to think of anything else she knew, then shrugged and stopped, waiting for any questions he had.

McNelly didn't seem to have questions. He picked up the paper with his notes and tucked it into his pocket. Then he took another sheet of paper and made a few notes. He handed over the paper to Maribel.

"I'm going to have one of our Rangers escort you back to your ranch," he told her. "How is your niece?" he asked.

"The doctor says to leave her there at his office until

tomorrow," Maribel answered. "Then he says we can go home."

McNelly pointed at the paper he had just given her. "I need you to give this paper to Sheriff Hardy when you get to Fredericksburg," he said. "You know Sheriff Hardy, right?"

Maribel nodded.

McNelly stopped at the door with her, running his finger over the notes he had made. His hand stopped moving while he re-read the part about the adobe house. "One more thing," he told Maribel. "Tell Sheriff Hardy to bring Napoleon when he comes to meet me. He'll know what I mean."

————

"Look, Zeb, I can rope the fencepost 'most every time!" Caleb walked over to the fence post to loosen and retrieve his lasso. "Mebbe we could get work as real cowboys when we get outta here!"

Zeb lifted the brim of his hat and watched while Caleb roped the fencepost again. "Shore, mebbe we could," Zeb agreed. "Only the fencepost don't move when yore tryin' to rope it. You've got to allow for that."

Caleb nodded his head thoughtfully. "One thing at a time, Zeb, one thing at a time." He eased himself slowly to a sitting position beside his brother. The soreness from riding horses all day was easing up slightly.

Caleb looked in all directions and lowered his voice. "Speakin' of one thing at a time, when do you figger we can get out of here, Zeb?"

Zeb pushed himself up to his elbows and shook his head. "I wanted to git out afore they have another raid into Mexico," he said. "But now they're sayin' we're goin' down there agin by end of this week. I don't think we can get out without 'em noticing before then."

Caleb slumped down, disappointment etched on his face. "When, then? We almost got ourselves shot on that last raid."

"Mebbe we get out during the raid." Zeb glanced over to get his brother's reaction.

Caleb stared blankly. "How do we git away during the raid? Won't they notice we're not there?"

Zeb shook his head. "Too much stuff goin' on, Caleb. Folks were riding and shootin' the whole time. It took a while to sort out the cows and settle 'em down when we got back. We just hang back, like, when it starts heatin' up. When the shootin' starts, we light a shuck outta there. We take a different trail, circle around Laredo, hit the trail for Austin."

He stopped to let his brother soak up the idea. Caleb looked hopeful and scared all at once.

"They'll be lookin' for us though," Caleb protested. "Won't they be lookin' right away?"

Zeb shook his head. "There's so much going on, they might think we got shot durin' the raid," he answered. "They won't send anybody back to look—you know they're just tryin' to get those cows to the Laredo ranch. They'll ask around, sure, but if we get away from the raid with nobody seein' us, I think we can make it to Austin."

Caleb nodded slowly. "Do you still wanna turn ourselves in when we git to Austin?" he asked doubtfully.

Zeb nodded. "I don't want that there Simms guy or George Lynch follerin' me for the rest of my life," he announced. "We won't be confessing to nuthin' that's against the law. We tell 'em they forced us to go on the raid."

The brothers turned to look at two men coming into the yard in a wagon. When the dust settled a little, they recognized Walsh and Lynch.

"Do ya think Lynch ever recognized us, Zeb?" Caleb asked.

Zeb shook his head slowly. "I don't think so, but I ain't willing to take a chance for much longer," he answered. "Let's put by a little grub to stick it in our saddlebags. Stuff that'll keep. Enough to get us to Austin. We'll be ready to go when they send us on that raid." He looked at Caleb, who nodded.

"End of the week," Caleb agreed.

———

By the following morning, the doctor assured Maribel that Norah could travel home if they didn't push the pace. "Stop whenever you need to, make sure she gets her rest when you get home," he told Maribel.

After an hour on the trail, Maribel realized her biggest challenge would be in getting Norah to rest at all. She rode along for two hours before Maribel insisted on stopping for water and a little food. The Ranger sent by McNelly dismounted and joined them.

When the Ranger moved away to look after the horses, Maribel raised the question for the first time about what Norah remembered from the day before in Austin.

Norah seemed to choose her words carefully. "I saw Uncle George coming out of a saloon," she started. "He has an injury to his shoulder, I think. There was a sling around it—I think it could have been a gunshot wound, because I could see a bandage below his collar."

Norah stopped and glanced uncertainly at Maribel before continuing. "He was wobbly. That's the best way I can describe it. Not drunk, I don't think, but like he couldn't really focus on me. He seemed to want to push me away. Then I saw a shadow come up from behind and I blacked out. Somebody hit me from behind."

Maribel nodded, then spoke softly, almost as if she were talking to herself. "I saw George," she said. "He looked like you described—wobbly. I know he saw me, but he pulled his hat down and tried to climb into the wagon, like he didn't want me to see him. There was a guy trying to put you in the back of the wagon. He dropped you and hauled George in when I ran over there."

Maribel stopped, staring at the blanket. "I...I don't know what to think about all of it," she said finally. "Captain McNelly at the Rangers gave me a message to take to Sheriff Hardy." She sighed and gathered up the remains of the food they'd been eating. "I'm going to see what Sheriff Hardy thinks about all this."

They traveled several more hours, then made an early camp. To Maribel's relief, Norah seemed to feel fine the next morning and insisted on riding straight through to Fredericksburg. Maribel agreed on the condition that Norah would see the doctor in town right after they went to the sheriff's office.

Given the length of the journey, Maribel decided to stay at the boarding house in town that night and made arrangements at the livery stable to care for the horses, including the chestnut geldings. It was a short walk from there to the sheriff's office. The Ranger tipped his hat and left them at the edge of town.

———

I was sorting through a few posters and some mail when the door swung open and Maribel and Norah Lynch walked in. I stared for a minute, I'm afraid. Norah had a bandage wrapped around her head. I'll have to admit that my first thought was how pretty she was, even with the bandage.

After that, my manners kicked in, well, as much as I have manners. I jumped up and grabbed a chair for Norah to sit in. She shook her head and laughed, but sat in the chair.

"Don't fuss over me, Sheriff," she said.

Maribel Lynch had already found the other chair. I ran my hand through my hair and looked over at the coffeepot. "I'd ask you ladies if you want some coffee," I confessed, "but Boone came in here and made it a while ago, and it ain't...isn't...fit for ordinary humans to drink. Hostler and me, well, we're already used to army coffee."

They both laughed, but then I thought they both looked tired, or strained, or something like that. "You don't need to entertain us, Sheriff," said Maribel Lynch. She pushed a paper across the desk to me. "This is a note Captain McNelly asked me to bring to you," she said.

Surprised, I took the note, opened it, and read:

PIKE

I ASKED MARIBEL LYNCH TO BRING YOU THIS NOTE BECAUSE I NEED YOUR HELP. I'M PRETTY

SURE GEORGE LYNCH IS BEHIND SOME CATTLE
RUSTLING COMING OUT OF MEXICO. HE'S USING
A SECOND RANCH HE'S GOT IN LAREDO, RIGHT
DOWN THERE AT THE BORDER.

I'M GOING AFTER HIM. BRING HOSTLER
SOON AS YOU CAN. I ENCLOSED MONEY FOR THE
TRAIN. I'LL MEET YOU AT THE STATION IN
LAREDO.

LEANDER MCNELLY.

I looked up at the ladies, not sure what to say.

"Oh," Maribel added, "he said something else. He said for you and Hostler to bring Napoleon. He said you'd know what he meant."

CHAPTER 15

FOLLOWING THE MONEY

My brain was pretty much spinning around. Hostler came in and I passed McNelly's note to him. His face lit up when he read the part about Napoleon. That boy just lived his life to shoot a cannon. Me, I was still trying to figure out what to say to the ladies.

Maribel solved my problem for me. "Sheriff," she said, "tell me what you think about this. I think I deserve to hear the truth."

I brought my eyes back to look at each of them. "Yes, ma'am, you do," I admitted.

"Maribel, not Ma'am," she corrected. "Do you think my husband is rustling cattle in Mexico and bringing them up here?"

I nodded. "That's what I think. Cap'n McNelly thinks so, too."

Maribel kept coming. She wasn't going to leave me any wiggle room on this. "Why do you think so?" she asked.

Time to put the cards on the table. "You don't have

many cattle, I noticed that right off," I told her. "It's a horse ranch, of course, but there were an awful lot of hands for just the horses I saw. That started me wondering. Then, of course, it was the look of a lot of them hands...those hands."

I don't think Maribel had even blinked yet. I looked over at Norah, she was leaning forward with those blue eyes just boring into me.

"A lot of those boys don't look like they would know one end of a cow from the other," I explained. "But they know a lot more than that about guns. Double-tied-down pistols and such. Hard edge to 'em. Starting with that foreman, Forster. He is...was a hard man."

A look of confusion passed over Maribel's face. "What do you mean, he was a hard man?"

I went back to looking at the desk. I looked up at Norah. "We—I mean Hostler and me, we braced Forster and two of his men on a trail to Austin. Some cows had been driven up that trail just a few days ago—from your ranch to Austin. We braced Forster and his boys on the way back, asked 'em where they'd been and such."

It got quieter than a church in there. "Forster, he hauled out his pistol on me. I shot him. He's dead. A man he called Jackson tried to throw down his Winchester on Hostler. Jackson's dead too. We've got the third man in a cell in the back."

I waited for somebody to say something. Maribel was sitting real stiff in her chair, but she nodded. I looked over at Norah. I couldn't imagine what this would sound like to a girl from back east, like her. She looked a little pale around the gills, but it wasn't as bad as I thought it would be.

Maribel stood, a little color coming back to her

cheeks. "You did what you had to, Sheriff," she said. "I'm going to go home now and look for what I can find in George's study. Papers or whatever else he had."

I tipped my hat, and she left. Norah stayed, looking at me, real curious, I'd say.

"You're getting to Laredo on the train?" she asked.

I nodded. "We'll have to ride over to Austin, but from there we can take a train down to Laredo and get out to his ranch."

"Why do you do it, Sheriff?" she asked. "You blew up that still to get Uncle George riled, you confronted Forster in the trail, like you said. Why do you handle things that way?"

I picked up my hat and shuffled it around with my hands. "The man who was like my pa to me, name of Jed Hardy, told me a story one time I never forgot. Jed was an old mountain man, up Colorado way. One time, he was on a narrow ledge and came face-to-face with a mountain lion. Jed said, 'Pike boy, there was two things I could do. I could ignore him and hope he'd go away. That don't never work, so I puffed up my chest and spread out my arms and looked as big as I could, hopin' he'd go away. That didn't work neither. He didn't like me on his ledge, so he gathered hisself up to jump me. That's why I carry my old buffler gun. Only one of us come down off that ledge.'"

She studied my face for a while. "So, you're saying you had to face up to it right away, because avoiding things wouldn't have worked?"

"That's it, ma'am. I saw that when I was in the army, too. A man shows his colors when he's pressed. Better to know what you're dealin' with right away."

"Norah," she corrected. She stopped at the door and

looked at me again. "Aunt Maribel says you're a good man, and she trusts you," she said.

I nodded, still spinning the hat around in my hands.

A tiny smile spread across her face for the first time since she had come in with her aunt. "I think Maribel has good judgment," she said. Then she was gone.

Hostler came around the desk to stand next to me. "Are you ever gonna tell them that George Lynch killed your pa?" he asked.

I shrugged. "I don't know," I told him. "I just don't know."

————

I studied the old Napoleon cannon Hostler had bought and hauled out to Jake's ranch. I had to admit, it looked like the Napoleon cannon we'd had out at the fort in New Mexico, and I knew what Hostler could do with it. If King Simms was forted-up in an adobe house, for sure I didn't want to charge the house and draw their fire.

Jake McCabe was with me. Boone was prowling around somewhere.

"What do you think?" I asked Jake. "Are the trails good enough to haul Napoleon over to Austin and take the train to meet McNelly?"

Jake nodded. "No problem if you take the main trail to Austin, not the one you followed Forster on. I don't know anything about the trail from the Laredo station to his ranch at Laredo." He waved an arm at Boone, then passed the note over to Boone.

Boone looked it over. "Yep, I'd say you kin do it. Just foller the main trail to Austin and then git on the train." He grinned. "You'll get some attention, haulin' old

Napoleon through Austin. You got hosses that can pull a cannon?"

"I have a couple of plow horses he can use," Jake answered. "They're not fast, but they can get it there."

Boone nodded and wandered over toward the corral. I watched him go, then asked Jake the question that was really bothering me.

"Do you think Maribel and Norah are safe?" I asked. "What if Lynch thinks they're on to him and comes back to the Circle L?"

Jake folded his arms and thought about that. "They might could be in some trouble," he agreed. "Maybe I'll ride out there and offer to let them stay at our place. They'd be safe here."

I wasn't quite convinced. "What if they won't come?" I asked. "That Norah's got an independent streak in her."

Jake chuckled. "That sounds a little like Julia," he said. He paused and thought again. "If they won't come, I'll ask Boone to keep an eye on 'em over there," he said. "Boone's not a youngster, but he's still tough as an old piece of cowhide and meaner than a snake with that Winchester, if he's riled. And," he added, "I'll cover the sheriff's office while you're gone."

Thirty minutes later, we had Napoleon hitched up to the plow horses. Julia gave us some food for the trail, and Hostler and I pulled out, headed east and south to meet up with McNelly near Laredo.

———

When they reached the Circle L, Maribel went directly to George's study. Norah walked in with her and watched her opening and closing drawers, pulling out papers and reading them. Norah grabbed a pencil and a piece of paper and excused herself.

She went to the kitchen and made notes about the train trip from Austin to Laredo. When she finished, she tucked the notes away in her room. Maribel was now her friend, George she didn't trust. There might come a time when she needed to go to the Laredo ranch to help Maribel claim what was hers.

When Norah returned to the study, Maribel was standing in the middle of it, staring around her with tears forming in her eyes. "I didn't really find anything," she told Norah. "I'm sure he's hiding something."

Norah walked over to put her arm around her aunt. She looked around the room, trying to think of a place Maribel might have overlooked. She walked over to the big wooden desk in the corner of the room and walked around it.

"No use," Maribel said. "I looked there first and went through all the papers. Nothing." She shook her head in frustration. "I really don't even know what I'm looking for."

On a hunch, Norah pulled out the desk chair, dropped to her knees, and looked under the desk. Looking up, she saw a piece of paper tacked to the underside of the wood. She reached up, pulled it free, and brought the paper to Maribel. They studied it together.

"It's for a bank," Maribel murmured. "Texas State Bank in Austin, it says." She stopped and glanced at Norah. "We don't have an account there," she explained. She pointed to the bottom of the page. "It's a receipt of some kind—for something called a *safe box* with a number on it." She turned the paper over. "There's no key or anything. Why doesn't it have a key?"

Norah went back and crawled under the desk, feeling carefully for anything hidden there. She crawled out and shook her head. "Nothing else there," she informed Maribel. "If there's a key for this *safe box*, he must have it on him."

Maribel nodded, thought for a moment, then started for her room. "Pack up a few things," she said. "I think Sheriff Hardy needs to know about this box. We might be able to catch him. And," she said, "we might need to take another trip to Austin."

———

"Sheriff," Maribel said on her way through the door. She stopped short when she saw it wasn't Pike Hardy. "Oh," she said, realizing it was the former sheriff, Jake McCabe. "I found something at the house, and I thought Pike Hardy might need to know about it."

McCabe stood and extended his hand. Maribel shook his hand, then Norah's hand. There was a noise from the back, and Boone came out, carrying an empty food tray.

"For somebody that whines about the food all the time, he shore cleans his plate," Boone observed.

McCabe pulled up chairs for the ladies, then sat behind the desk. Boone took a seat on his haunches in the corner. "Pike left town about an hour ago," McCabe said. "I'm covering for him while he's gone. What can I do for you?"

Maribel hesitated for a moment, then pulled a sheet of paper from her bag. "Do you know about our trip to Austin and the note Leander McNelly sent to Pike?" she asked.

McCabe nodded. "Pike came by our ranch before he

left, and I know everything he knows about the cattle rustling and the ranch your husband runs down south," he said, extending his hand for the paper.

Maribel handed him the paper. "It's a receipt for something called a *safe box* at a bank in Austin. We don't have an account there that I know of. Do you know what a safe box is, Jake?"

McCabe shook his head, stood, and reached for his hat. "I don't," he said, "but we can ask Mark Hayes over at the bank here in town. Maybe he's heard of it."

———

Hayes came from his office when McCabe asked for him. He studied the receipt Maribel gave him. He glanced up, nodding slowly. "I've heard of them," he said. "They started in London, and a few banks use them back east. Haven't heard of 'em in Texas, though."

He handed the receipt back. "Usually," he said, "they build a row of boxes in the safe—iron boxes, I think. The bank manager has to let the customer into the vault, then the box owner uses his key to put things in or take 'em out. Nobody else really knows what's in the box, and it's just about as safe a place to put cash or valuables as you can get."

Maribel put the receipt back in her bag. "Would the manager let me in that box?" she asked. "I'm his wife. Would the manager have a key?"

Hayes shrugged. "Don't know the answer to either question, ma'am," he confessed. "It all might depend on the bank manager as to whether he'll let you in. He probably won't have another key himself, but he could likely get one made."

Maribel turned to Norah. "Let's go to Austin," she said. Norah followed her out.

"Ladies," McCabe said as they reached the street. "You could both come and stay for a few days with Julia and me. Just until we know things are safe for you. Maybe make the Austin trip after a few days."

They glanced at each other and shook their heads in unison. "I'm sorry, Jake," Maribel said, "but I've got to know what this is all about." They walked down the street, climbed into their buggy, and drove away.

Jake McCabe turned and looked at Boone. "They might be in over their heads," he told Boone. "George Lynch is about to be a cornered rat. No tellin' what he might do. Tail 'em from a distance, make sure they stay safe over there in Austin."

Boone nodded, retrieved his Winchester from the sheriff's office, and fell in behind the buggy, letting a little distance build up between them.

———

King Simms sat with Walsh in the den at the back of his adobe ranch building. He handed a bottle of whiskey to Walsh, who poured himself a double shot and leaned back to enjoy it.

Simms waited for just a minute, then leaned his elbows on the desk in front of him. "Well?"

Walsh stared into the bottom of his empty glass. Simms passed the bottle to him, and Walsh poured a shot even bigger than the first one. He gulped it, set the glass down, and wiped his mouth with the back of his sleeve.

"It's like you thought, boss." He nodded. "He knows you've been takin' more than half the cows we steal. I tole him like you said to, that him and me should team up to get even. He didn't say yes, but I think he's in."

Simms leaned back and stared out the window. "Anything else happen in Austin?" he growled.

Walsh shrugged. "I sent him to get some laudanum. He had hisself a heapin' shot of that, just about passed out in the saloon after. He taken some more on the way home. I think he likes it. He won't be no trouble when he's slugging down that laudanum."

Simms was still staring out the window, only half-listening. "We're going on another raid in Mexico tomorrow night," he said.

Walsh nodded.

"Lynch went on the first raid and got hisself shot in the shoulder," Simms reminded him. "Get him to go again tomorrow night. Make sure he gets taken care of permanent this time."

Walsh stared, then nodded his head, got up, and left. He had learned not to ask questions when Simms gave orders. Asking questions would be a good way to turn up dead on the raid himself.

Simms drummed his fingers on the desk for a while, then leaned over, opened the bottom drawer of the desk, and pulled out a money belt. He couldn't trust his hiding spot with Lynch around. Simms put on the money belt, stood, and walked to the far wall in the den and pulled back a bookshelf, exposing a door.

Simms opened the door and descended the stairs into the basement. He pulled a bag from beneath the table in the center of the room, opened it, and counted his money. Eight thousand dollars. That was the part he hadn't spent already. He grinned at the memories.

Simms counted out six thousand dollars and stuffed it

into his money belt. If Lynch found the rest of it and stole it, he was welcome to the money for as long as he could live. Simms didn't figure that would be for very long. He would hunt Lynch down like a dog and kill him if he touched any of this money. That's assuming he survived tomorrow night's raid, Simms reminded himself.

———

Lynch opened one eye as Walsh passed him on the porch. He kept on snoring. The bottle of whiskey and laudanum was on the ground beside him. Walsh paused, hovering over him, then snorted in disgust and walked away.

Lynch kept up the snoring noises for another thirty minutes, then got up and left the porch, carrying the laudanum and whiskey bottle with him. He walked to the room he was using at the back of the adobe house, opened the bottle, and poured the contents out the window.

Rustling around in his bag, Lynch pulled out a bottle of watered-down whiskey and poured some into the bottle he'd just emptied, stopping when it was about halfway filled. He walked over to the window and looked out, thinking things over. He was satisfied with his plan. They needed to think he was in a laudanum-induced stupor when they left on that raid in a few days.

CHAPTER 16

SOUTH TO THE BORDER

Norah stayed in the bank lobby while Maribel went back to meet with the bank manager. They had tried to turn Maribel away—it was only after Norah's insistence that the manager came out to quiet things down in the lobby.

When she saw Maribel's face coming out of the office, Norah knew Maribel's request had been denied. Maribel's face was flushed red, and she ignored the manager's outstretched hand after he had escorted her back to the lobby. Norah followed her outside.

Maribel blew out a noisy, miserable breath and stared down the street. "He wouldn't even admit George has an account here until I showed him the receipt," she said. "Then he had to admit that much, but he insisted the account is only with *Mr. Lynch* and not me."

Customers were stopping to look at them on their way into the bank. Norah steered her aunt down the street. They ducked quickly into a café and ordered coffee. Norah waited while Maribel vented her frustration. Finally, she ran out of steam.

"What can we do now?" she finally asked.

Norah shrugged and waited while the coffee was being served. "Our original idea was to get to Pike Hardy and give him the information," she reminded her aunt.

"How are we supposed to do that?" Maribel asked. "I don't even have the train information anymore, and anyway, how safe would it be for us to go?"

Norah stared out the window. "I don't know, either," she said, her voice trailing away. Suddenly her eyes widened. "I don't believe it!" she exclaimed. "Wait here."

Norah dashed outside to confirm what she thought she had seen. Boone had walked past, glancing into shop windows as he went. In an instant, she realized that McCabe had sent Boone to watch over them, and Boone had lost the trail when they ducked into the café.

Boone was facing the other direction, so Norah walked up behind him. "Hello, Mr. Boone," she said sweetly. Boone jumped visibly and wheeled around.

He stared at her, then slowly broke into a grin. "Well, you caught me," he admitted. "Jake sent me to keep an eye out and keep you ladies safe. I lost you when the two of you come out of the bank."

"We're in the café," she said, pointing. "Come and join us. I have a proposal to make to you." Boone followed warily.

Norah sat down opposite Maribel and Boone pulled up a chair to join them. "Do you want some coffee, Boone?" Maribel asked.

"Well, it's probly too weak, but I'll try some," Boone sniffed. He was still watching Norah out of the corner of his eye.

Norah got right to the point. "We have some information we need to get to Pike Hardy," she said directly. "I want you to take me down to where he is."

Boone shook his head immediately. "Cain't do it, ladies," he protested. "I don't even have a copy of that there stuff that Cap'n McNelly gave him." Norah reached into her bag and pushed the information she had written down across the table.

Boone looked at the paper, then looked up at Norah. "Yore a cagey one," he said. "I reckon that's why Pike is sweet on you."

Norah's mouth dropped open. She looked at Maribel, who just smiled and nodded. Norah decided she had to get things back on track. "With that train information, Mr. Boone, she said, you could escort me down there."

"I cain't take you ladies down there where a fight is fixin' to break out," he protested. "Jake would tack my hide to the wall. Then he'd take me down an' shoot me."

Maribel jumped in to help out. "I'll go home to the Circle L," she said. "You'll only need to take Norah down there."

"I ain't too sure it's safe for you at the ranch, neither," Boone protested.

That surprised Maribel, but she had an instant answer. "Then I'll go and stay with the McCabes," she answered. "They invited me to stay there until Jake thinks things are safe."

Norah could see Boone was weakening, so she pressed her advantage. "If you say we're getting into a dangerous spot, I'll stop where you say to stop," she said. "I'll do whatever you say. Just get me down to see Pike Hardy."

Boone threw his hands in the air and slurped some coffee. He made a face and put the cup down. "Too weak, jest like I said," he mumbled. He looked across at Norah. "Okay, I'll do it," he mumbled. "Jest do what I say." He took another slurp of coffee and made the same face. He looked at Norah again, and a grin spread across his face. "You are a cagy one," he told her. "I'm expectin' you to pay for the train tickets."

————

Old Napoleon hadn't slowed us down as much as I thought, but the trip to Austin wasn't exactly a piece of cake. Rolling Napoleon through Austin had raised a few eyebrows, but McNelly had left word with folks at the railroad, so no problems when we got there. They loaded up old Napoleon and strapped 'er down with no questions asked.

We were several hours down the line, bouncing around a turn in the tracks, when Hostler sat straight up and slapped his forehead. It made me jump, on account that he'd been asleep and snoring just a minute before.

"Cannonballs!" he said. "Powder! All we've got is the cannon!"

I chuckled and shook my head. "I sent a telegram to McNelly before we left and told him he would have to bring those," I said. "Getting Napoleon there is our part of the job." The smile faded from my face. "Nobody wants to charge a house that's pretty much a fort with guns trained on us," I said. "That's why McNelly wants the cannon. We've just got to get it there."

Now, I knew we were finally getting close. I was counting on McNelly having a man there to meet us at the station in Laredo. Despite that, I was getting a little jumpy. You can't exactly ride up to a forted-up house with a cannon and think folks won't see you coming.

It turned out I didn't need to worry about meeting McNelly. A guy in buckskins with squinty eyes and an old Henry resting in the crook of his elbow spotted us just as soon as we stepped down from the train.

"McNelly sent me," he said. "I'm here to guide you boys in." His eyes traveled back behind me to look at Napoleon, being offloaded from the train. "It wasn't hard to find you," he told us, "even without the cannon, you fit McNelly's description."

I joined McNelly in a small café and had a cup of coffee while he brought me up to date on things.

"We're less'n a half-day's ride from their ranch," he told me. "We've been scouting the place for a couple days now. There ain't a lot of cover, just some mesquite trees and prickly pear bushes, so my boys have mostly been using field glasses to check things out from a distance. We'll have to bring the cannon up at night. They don't post scouts, so we can do it."

He stopped and waved his arm. "We have fourteen men out there, plus you two," he said. "They've got about the same, but we'll take 'em by surprise. They like to get pretty likkered up at night, so that'll help with a dawn raid."

"You're sure they're raiding into Mexico and stealing the cattle?" I asked.

McNelly nodded. "Yup." They've got a lot of cows down there, but they're not set up to keep 'em around permanent. Not enough grass to support what they've got. We've been watchin' and I think they're gonna stage one more raid before they drive these cows north. We might just catch 'em red-handed."

McNelly told me we would move up closer and set up camp again. "They're not expecting anybody," he said. "We'll get close enough to move in on 'em under cover of night and be good to go by first light the next morning."

McNelly looked like he had a few more things to say, but he was interrupted when one of his men walked through the saloon doors and approached the table. "Need to talk to you for a minute, Cap'n," he said.

McNelly moved away and they talked in low tones for a few seconds. Then McNelly turned around to look at me. "Boone just showed up," he said. "Turns out he was on the same train as you, just caught it as it was leaving the station in Austin. Didn't know he was on the same train, but he knew my man at the station here in Laredo. Sounds like he's just as ornery as I remember him." McNelly shook his head and told me the next part. "He's got a girl with him. She's asking for you."

————

Zeb and Caleb shuffled into the big adobe house, holding their hats in their hands and looking around uncomfortably. It was the first time they'd been in the house. They didn't really want to go in, but they'd been told King Simms was going to give them their pay.

They waited in line behind two other hands, trying not to fidget and scuffle their feet. It was a relief when Simms motioned them forward. He handed them each a pay packet. They had already agreed not to look inside until they got out of the house.

"Good job, boys," Simms said. "Walsh said you did a good job last time. We go tomorrow night. You boys ready?"

"Yessir," Zeb said. Caleb nodded his agreement. Simms looked behind them, done with them already. They wasted no time getting out of the house.

On the porch, they walked past George Lynch, who was snoring loudly in the porch swing. An empty bottle lay next to him, and they could smell the whiskey from two feet away. Walsh came out of the house and walked past them, shaking his head as he went.

"Useless," he growled. He shot a glance at Zeb and Caleb. "Let that be a lesson to you young fellas," he said. "Lay off the laudanum. It'll turn you into somethin' like Lynch over there. He don't know what day of the week it is anymore."

Simms came out of the house, followed by another two hands. "Come on, boys," he said. "We'll go out to check the herd we have and I'll tell everybody about what I expect from you tomorrow night." He turned to look at Lynch, snoring loudly on the swing. His nose wrinkled in disgust. "He's useless," Simms told them. "We'll let him sleep it off. He's gotta run out of laudanum sooner or later."

————

Lynch waited until the hoofbeats died away before raising up to check the ranch yard. It was empty. He reached down to the whiskey bottle at his feet and poured off two inches' worth of his cheap whiskey onto the ground at the edge of the porch.

Getting to his feet, he tiptoed into the house, listening for anybody who might have stayed behind. All was quiet. Just to be sure, he moved to the kitchen door and looked in. Even Cook had gone with Simms.

Lynch made his way around the corner and found Simms's study without any trouble. It was as he remembered it. He looked around, his eyes stopping at a bookcase on the far wall, across from the desk.

He moved over to the bookcase. Every moment counted. No telling when they would come back from Simms's little meeting, and he had to be snoring on the porch again when they got here.

The bookcase moved away from the wall easily. The door to the basement swung open without a sound, and Lynch trotted down the stairs. He struck a match and looked around in the darkness. There was a large canvas bag under a table in the center of the room. Lynch chuckled. Simms hadn't even tried to hide it.

It took only a few seconds to toss the bag on the table and open it. Lynch struck another match and felt around inside the bag. He lifted the contents out and examined them in the light of the match. He made a growling sound, followed by several seconds of heartfelt cursing. It took only another minute to count the money.

"Two thousand dollars," he muttered between more oaths. What had Simms done with the rest of the money? Lynch had ten times that amount in his safe box in Austin.

After his anger cooled a bit, Lynch put the money back in the bag. Simms either had more money on him, or he had moved it somewhere else. Lynch couldn't afford to have Simms on his trail for only two thousand dollars. He would have to move on without it.

Two minutes later, the basement door was closed and concealed and Lynch was back on the porch swing. He would still have to take care of Walsh before he left. He couldn't afford to leave that undone. When Simms and some hands returned to the house a half hour later, Lynch was snoring loudly on the porch swing.

———

I stared at McNelly. "Norah Lynch is here?" I asked. McNelly's mouth started to twitch at the corners.

"Yup," he said. "But I didn't tell you it was Norah Lynch. How did you know?"

I ignored him and started to move past, toward the saloon doors.

"I'll have a man at the train station after you talk to the lady," he said. "He can show you and Boone where my camp is outside of town." He was grinning at his boots now.

I ignored him again and went outside. Boone was standing there. Norah was a few feet behind Boone.

Boone looked at me and shrugged. "Jake told me to keep an eye on her," Boone explained. "She's uncommon, strong-willed, and cagey, that one. I figgered the only way to keep an eye on her was to bring her down here like she asked."

"It's okay," I told him. "You can meet me at the train station after I've talked to her. McNelly's man will show us where his camp is. You wanna help go after the cattle thieves?"

"Wouldn't miss it." Boone grinned.

Norah surprised me by linking her arm through mine and steering me down the street. "Boone got me a room at a boarding house," she explained. "We can sit on the bench across the street and I can tell you what we learned about George."

She sat me down on the bench and sat next to me. I

was extremely aware she was sitting very close to me. I gotta say it didn't occur to me to complain. I was starting to hope this would be a long conversation.

She started by telling me they had seen the cannon on the train. "I had no idea you were on that train with the cannon. We got on the train at the last minute and were just a couple of cars behind you, I guess."

"That's Napoleon," I explained. "Hostler can do some amazing shootin' with Napoleon. McNelly told us to bring it."

"The real reason I came," she said, "is that we found out that Uncle George has something called a safe box in a bank in Austin. Do you know what a safe box is?"

I shook my head. "Never heard of it," I admitted.

She explained what it was and how Maribel had no idea it existed, or even that Lynch had an account at that bank. She explained how Maribel had tried to get into the box, but the bank president wouldn't let her. Norah figured George Lynch had paid the banker some extra money to keep his mouth shut about it.

"You think he's going back there to get the money," I guessed. "If he's been storing money from the stolen cattle there, he might have quite a pile in the safe box. Can't just walk away from it."

"That's what Maribel and I think," she agreed. "Maribel is trying to keep an eye on the bank. Hopefully George hasn't sneaked in there and gotten the money." She leaned into me a little closer. "Are you sure he's down here?" she asked.

I swallowed hard a couple times and found my voice. "Pretty sure," I said. "McNelly thinks he's here and plans to raid the ranch house in a couple days. We'll know for sure by then." I thought for a second. "I'll have McNelly telegraph back up to Austin," I said. "He can have a guy watch the place and arrest Lynch if he shows up."

Norah slipped her arm back through mine. "I was hoping you could do something like that," she said. "Boone was moaning all the way down here, but I think he kinda enjoyed the trip."

We stood and she moved around to face me. "Maribel was right," she said. "You're a good man. A strong man." She leaned in closer and my tongue couldn't find one single thing to say. We stood there for a minute, then she pulled my head down and kissed me.

I think I mumbled something, but I'm sure I couldn't tell you exactly what it was. I remember moving across the street to the boarding house with her and saying goodnight. She moved down the hallway and around the corner.

I turned to go outside and bumped into a door behind me. I heard the clerk snickering at the desk, but I was in too good a mood to go over and straighten him out. I just went down the street, moving back to the train station.

CHAPTER 17

DEADLY DAWN

I t was a full moon as twelve riders moved toward the Rio Grande River. Zeb and Caleb started the trip in the middle of the pack of riders, but were able to fall back toward the rear when they crossed the river.

Emerging on the other side, Zeb glanced around to see if all of King Simms's men were there. As they assembled on the Mexican side of the Rio Grande, he leaned toward Caleb to tell him who was missing from the party.

"Lynch ain't here," he whispered.

Caleb glanced around, then nodded. He wasn't sure if that was good news or bad news. He'd never seen a man do that much sleeping, laudanum or no laudanum. They hadn't really expected him to come.

Simms pointed the way forward and took the lead. It was obvious to Zeb and Caleb they were headed more to the west than last time, that made sense. They'd already taken all the cows near the border in this location last time.

Zeb reined in his horse and dismounted to adjust the stirrup, or at least that's what he wanted it to look like.

Caleb reined in to wait for him, and they had fallen to the back of the group by the time Zeb remounted. Walsh, their minder, cast a sharp glance at the back but said nothing.

For twenty minutes, they could hear nothing but the creak of saddle leather and an occasional coyote howl. Caleb wiped his sweaty palms on his pant leg. He was anxious to drop farther behind the group, but he knew they would have to wait until the rustlers started rounding up cattle. A gunshot or two would help cover what they did, Caleb just didn't want the shots aimed at them.

Simms reined in up front, turned around, and began dividing his men so they could circle both left and right. They could hear the cattle now, and as they moved forward, they could see a small herd in a valley in front of them. Zeb guessed there were about two hundred head.

Zeb and Caleb both rode with the column on the left. Walsh moved his horse over to join the same column. He was riding directly in front of the Tennessee boys. That made them both nervous.

The pace quickened as they circled to the east and the cattle started to move. Zeb and Caleb dropped off the pace, but only slightly. They couldn't afford to make Walsh suspicious. Finally, they got the break they were hoping for. Gunfire sounded in front of them. Walsh pulled his Winchester from the scabbard and spurred his horse forward.

Zeb slowed his horse and moved to the east. Caleb followed, and they drifted until they reached a small group of mesquite trees. The boys dismounted and peered out into the valley. They could see four or five riders and the occasional muzzle flash as the riders exchanged shots with the vaqueros.

Zeb moved to remount his horse and ride away, but he was stopped by a gasp from Caleb. He swung around to look at his brother. Even in the moonlight, he could see Caleb had gone pale. Caleb pointed a finger toward the valley.

"Walsh is comin' back!" he gasped.

Zeb whirled to look at the valley. The gunfire had died down and the Circle L riders had moved in to head off a stampede. They swung the lead cows and got them running in a circle. Walsh had turned and was retracing his path, head swinging left and right to pick up a trail.

It was obvious to Zeb that Walsh was looking for them. Now he had to face the question he'd been asking himself for almost a week: Was he willing to kill Walsh in order for him and his brother to get away?

While he watched, Walsh lifted his Winchester and levered it. The answer to Zeb's question turned out to be easier than he thought. He had to kill Walsh before Walsh killed them. Zeb reached back and slid his Henry from the saddle.

"Zeb!" Caleb squeaked, his eyes big as dinner plates.

Zeb laid the Henry across the mustang's back and sighted in on Walsh's chest. Before he squeezed the trigger, a gunshot rang out from behind them and to the west. Both boys jumped and whirled to look.

Walsh fell backward off his horse and lay still. The horse snorted and raced away.

Lynch only stayed in the swing for a few minutes after the raiding party left. He couldn't afford to stay there much longer—if they got too far out in front, he would have to abandon his plan to take out Walsh. That would leave loose strings, and Lynch hated to leave loose strings.

When he was satisfied they were out of sight, he sprinted to the corral and saddled up the dapple-gray mustang he'd been riding since he'd come here. Well, at least he'd ridden the mustang until he started spending his time snoring in the swing.

He had to admit, the mustang had some staying power. It wasn't the quality of horseflesh he was used to, but he could ditch the mustang later on tonight and not worry about it. He couldn't do that with the expensive horses he bred at home.

For the first several minutes, he had to use his ears more than his eyes. Even with the full moon out, they had left at a sharp pace and he had some catching up to do. He heard them first. When he made visual contact with them, he eased the mustang's pace and concentrated on keeping a constant distance behind them.

When the raiders swam the Rio Grande and met up on the other side, Lynch had to wait. He paced and cursed, watching them through the field glasses he had stolen from somebody in the bunkhouse.

Simms remounted and led them out. Lynch sprang back into the saddle and swam the mustang across the river, but he had trouble finding them on the other side. When he couldn't hear them after a few minutes, he swung the mustang back and forth, trying to find tracks as best he could in the moonlight.

He struck the trail farther west than he'd expected. He

made a mental note that he would have to come east on the way back. After shooting Walsh, he had no intention of stumbling into the Circle L Ranch yard.

Lynch caught up with them just in time to see Simms splitting his riders, moving them east and west. He grabbed the field glasses and squinted at the riders, trying to identify Walsh.

There! He saw Walsh moving to the left with half the riders. Walsh was at the back. The two yokels from somewhere in the hills back east were lagging behind. Walsh was just in front of them.

Gunfire sounded ahead, and Walsh urged his horse forward. Lynch followed, then reined in when he realized the two yokels were dropping out of the chase. Puzzled, Lynch reined his horse wide. He dismounted, swinging the field glasses from the hillbillies to Walsh, trying to keep track of both.

The gunfire died out and Lynch felt a surge of excitement when he saw Walsh returning. Lynch watched Walsh, leaning over the saddle to look for tracks, then sweeping his gaze left and right.

Lynch's lips split into a sarcastic grin. He got it now. The hillbillies wanted to quit, and Walsh was looking for them. Well, he thought, no matter to him if the hillbillies quit. It made his job easier.

Lynch braced his Winchester up against a mesquite tree trunk, took careful aim, and squeezed off his shot. Walsh jerked backward, then tumbled off the saddle. Lynch couldn't afford to stick around and make sure Walsh was dead. He jumped into the saddle and spurred the mustang north and east. After a hundred yards, he stopped to see if the hillbillies were following. They weren't. Lynch spurred the horse again. He hoped to make Laredo by sunrise.

———

Zeb's head jerked up, and he stepped back from the Henry. Walsh was down, but Zeb was certain he hadn't fired. He turned to look at Caleb, who froze, staring at the body of Walsh.

"Who shot him?" Zeb hissed.

Caleb recovered enough to turn and look for the source of the gunshot. There was motion over there, then he could hear hoofbeats. He ducked and watched as a dapple-gray horse raced past, not fifty yards away.

"Lynch," Caleb said. He looked over at his brother. "Lynch was ridin' a dapple-gray hoss, at least he was afore he took to drinkin' that laudanum all the time. It was Lynch that shot Walsh!"

It was true, Zeb remembered Lynch on a gray horse. The sound of people shouting and moving in their direction got Zeb moving. He jumped on his horse and hissed at his brother. "Mount yer hoss! They're comin' this way!"

Caleb came out of his trance and swung in behind his brother. They raced away, counting on getting enough distance between themselves and the Circle L riders without overtaking Lynch, somewhere out in front of them.

They ran the horses hard for about a mile. Zeb concentrated on holding a little west of the direction taken by Lynch, moving mostly north toward the river. He slowed the pace a little after the first mile, but kept moving at a fast trot. Relief flooded over him when he caught the sparkle of moonlight reflecting from the Rio Grande.

They swam the horses across the river before letting them water and rest for a few minutes on the other side. The night was quiet as the brothers looked anxiously across the river, dreading the sight of Circle L riders.

Caleb moved his horse alongside Zeb. They spoke in whispers, even though they could hear nothing around them.

"Where do ya think we are, Zeb?" Caleb asked anxiously. "I mean, I know we're back in Texas, but where d'ya think the Circle L is from here?"

Zeb pulled an old compass from his pocket and stared at it in the moonlight. He returned it to his pocket, then lifted his hand to scratch his head for a moment. He shrugged. "I think," he said finally, "that we crossed the river over thataway." He pointed west. "And," he continued, "I think Lynch crossed it over yonder." He pointed in the other direction.

"That's good, Zeb," Caleb murmured. "Mebbe we could go past Circle L to the east of it. Ya wanna go over to Laredo? We could hit the trail up to Austin from there."

"Yep, that's what I'm tryin' to do," Zeb agreed. "I dunno if we can find the trail to Laredo in the dark. It ain't much of a trail. But I don't wanna hang around here neither. We've mostly got to keep movin', the way I see it."

Zeb pulled the compass out again and set their direction to due north. "I'm jest hopin' we crossed the river east of the Circle L," he explained. They walked the horses, more worried now about direction than speed. Forty-five minutes passed before Caleb gasped and pointed to his left. They could see the adobe house, standing out clearly in the moonlight.

They swung the horses to the east and moved out at a trot, not daring to say anything while they got clear of the Circle L Ranch. Finally, they slowed and stopped. Zeb dismounted and led his horse forward on foot, pointing north again.

"Let's look for that trail to Laredo, Caleb," he said over his shoulder.

They were so intent on finding the trail that neither of them saw two shadowy figures rise from the ground. The sound of a rifle being cocked stopped them in their tracks, and they raised their hands slowly into the air.

"That's good, boys," said a voice in the night. "We're Texas Rangers, and we're taking you in to see our captain. Don't try nothing funny if'n you expect to see sunrise in the mornin'."

We had broken camp west of Laredo shortly after darkness fell, moving toward the Circle L. McNelly had his scout out in front and we followed slowly. We didn't have McCabe's plow horses to pull Napoleon anymore, but we had four horses supplied by McNelly and we switched them out every couple hours. Luckily, there weren't many obstacles and Napoleon rolled along the trail without giving us much trouble.

McNelly said we were a half-day's ride from the Circle L Ranch, so I knew it would take several hours to get there at this pace. The plan was to be in place at sunup, with Napoleon zeroed in on the adobe house. Hostler couldn't wait for it, I could tell. That boy loved to shoot the cannon more'n just about anything.

When McNelly called a halt, I guessed we were several hours short of sunrise, and I was pretty good at guessing the hour after all the patrols I had led in Injun country with the army. We could see the adobe fort/house off in the distance. Hostler told me we were in range, and I helped him position the cannon.

McNelly came up to me, watched while we finished getting old Napoleon ready, then told me his scouts had brought in a couple of riders. "Come with me and we'll talk to them," he told me. "You too," he said to Hostler.

We found a couple of guys, maybe around twenty, sitting on the ground with their hands tied behind them. They wore some homespun clothes, and when they talked, everything about them said *mountain boys* to me.

"Where you from?" McNelly said for openers.

They looked at each other. "Missoura," one of them said.

The other one nodded.

"That's funny," I said. "I've got a good friend from back in the hills of Kentucky, and he sounds a lot like you. Matter of fact," I said, "we've got an expert on this sort of thing with us." I turned around and waved. "Hey, Boone," I said, "come over here."

"Tell Mr. Boone here where you're from," I told them.

They looked at each other, then the same one said "Missoura" again.

Boone pulled at his beard for a minute and started laughing. "Way up from the hills in Tennessee, sure as shootin'," he said. He looked at the two prisoners. "Way I know that is that's where I'm from," he told them. Then he walked away, still laughing.

"Now we've got that out of the way," McNelly said, "why don't you boys tell me the truth about why you were out there, skulkin' around in the middle of the night?"

They looked at each other again, then they started talking. This time, it sounded like the truth.

"Tell us your names," McNelly said.

One of them said his name was Zeb, the other was Caleb. It looked like Zeb did all the talking for them.

"We was in Dallas, on our way from…Tennessee," Zeb said. "Then somebody come up to us at the train station, said we could learn to be cowboys down here. Said his name was Walsh. We taken the train down here with Walsh, met a guy named King Simms, boss of this place."

Zeb looked over at Caleb. "And we did learn some cowboyin', didn't we, Caleb?"

Caleb nodded.

"But then," Zeb continued, "they started makin' us go on cattle raids, down to Mexico. Nearly got kilt down there a time or two. They went down last night, and we stayed at the back and snuck outta there. We was headed to Laredo when your scouts stopped us."

Caleb found his tongue for the first time. "That guy Walsh, he got kilt down there tonight," Caleb blurted. "Got hisself dry-gulched by a guy named Lynch. Shot him dead, right outta the saddle."

I leaned forward. "Lynch?" I asked. "George Lynch?"

Zeb took over again. "Yep, that's him. Ever'body thought he was outta his head on laudanum all the time, but he shore enuf got off the porch and come down and kilt that guy Walsh tonight. Got himself outta there, probly headed to Laredo or someplace east."

I pulled McNelly away. "I've got to get Boone back

over to Laredo to watch Norah Lynch," I said. "He's got to go now."

McNelly nodded. "Sure. Do you want one of my scouts to go with him?"

"Naw," I answered. "Boone always claims he could track a rattlesnake over bare rock, and he just about can. He'll find it by himself."

After I sent Boone back to Laredo, McNelly was asking about the cattle. "Where do they bring 'em to, where do they graze them?" he asked.

Zeb pointed north. "They've got a pasture, kinda fenced with rails. The pasture ain't much, but it can hold 'em for a couple days. They'll drive those cows right betwixt where you are and the house, though. You'd best pull back a bit if'n you don't want 'em to find you."

———

We pulled back a couple hundred yards, taking Napoleon back with us. We were out of range now, but we could move it back and get it zeroed in again later. McNelly positioned his men and walked around to check everybody.

"Now," he said, "we just wait."

Hostler crouched down beside me. "Do ya think those Tennessee boys could be a couple of the ones that took potshots at you and stole the geldings?" he asked.

I nodded. "It's for sure possible," I said. "I been thinking about it." I shrugged. "Maybe they just need a second chance. We'll see."

We could hear the cattle and feel the ground shaking when they got close. The herd trotted past, with three or four riders on each side and a couple more riding drag. One guy peeled off and went to the house.

After half an hour, the riders came back. They hit the whiskey pretty hard, I'd say. There was a lot of yelling, a fistfight or two, and guys falling down outside the bunkhouse. Finally, they quieted down. We moved back and took up the position we'd been in before. Hostler assured me that old Napoleon was zeroed in. The first shot was to hit just in front of the house.

McNelly moved past me to talk to two of his guys. "Can you boys sneak in there, open the corral, and drive the horses out without anybody the wiser?" he asked.

I couldn't see his scout grinning, with it being dark and all, but I could hear it in his voice. "With as much as those boys have had to drink," he said, "we could empty out that corral if it had elephants in there without them wakin' up."

"Get to it," McNelly told him.

Chapter 18

Hearing from Napoleon

We watched while McNelly's two men finished moving the horses out of the corral, then crept back to our lines. McNelly reached into his bag and pulled out a long, circular tube. It looked like it was made of brass, or something like brass. I stared at it.

McNelly grinned. "I had an uncle in the navy during the war," he explained. "This here is a speaking trumpet." He put it to his mouth and turned toward the adobe house.

"Hello the house," he shouted. "We are the Texas Rangers and we have you surrounded. Come out of the bunkhouse. I wanna see hands in the air!"

"We don't have it surrounded," Hostler mumbled to me. "We're just a-settin' over here."

"They don't know." I grinned. "And it ain't gonna matter after you introduce those boys to Napoleon."

There was no sound from either the house or the bunkhouse for a full minute. McNelly turned around to look at Hostler.

"Touch 'er off," he said.

Hostler lit the fuse on Napoleon. There was the crash of the cannon firing, then the unmistakable noise of a cannonball headed in. It landed about twenty feet to the left of the house, just where Hostler had aimed it. The noise was deafening, even at this distance. Dust and sparks billowed up from the crater it dug in the ground.

It took only a few seconds for the men to come spilling out of the bunkhouse, some of 'em still in their long johns. They all held their hands in the air. No signs of weapons anywhere.

"Nobody wants to argue with Napoleon." McNelly chuckled. He got back on the speaking trumpet. "Come this way and keep those hands in the air," he shouted.

They did as they were told, marching into our lines, where McNelly's men took them prisoner, tying their hands behind their backs. Then they tied the ankles together. They weren't going anywhere. There were eight of them. McNelly turned, looking for Zeb and Caleb. "Is that everybody?" he asked.

Zeb shook his head. "It's everybody except King Simms," he answered. "And you already know George Lynch ain't there."

McNelly clasped his hands behind his back, staring at the adobe house while he thought things over. Finally, he turned back around to Hostler. "Can you put one into the wall?" he asked. "Not enough to take the whole house down, but maybe cave in one wall? I wanna take him alive if I can."

Hostler nodded and went to work. After a couple of minutes, he was satisfied. He loaded up another cannonball and fired. It was perfect. The cannonball crashed into the eastern side of that adobe fort, the side facing us, and the wall collapsed. When the dust settled, the rest of the house was still standing, but I gotta say it didn't look too good.

————

King Simms was getting drowsy, but even the second glass of whiskey hadn't put him to sleep just yet. Somebody had gunned Walsh down out there tonight. At first, he was sure it had been the two yokels who'd shot him, but when they all got back to the house, Lynch wasn't there. That made Lynch the most likely shooter in his mind, even though the boys from the hills hadn't come in either. Simms scowled and cursed himself for letting Lynch fool him with that laudanum act. He reached for the whiskey bottle again.

Simms dropped the bottle and staggered out of his chair when he heard a voice coming from outside the house. Even in his present condition, he knew those thick adobe walls kept him from hearing much from outside. He walked to the front door and opened it. All was quiet now.

Simms shrugged and headed back to his study to see if he'd spilled all the whiskey. He had another bottle if he needed it. He picked up the bottle and grinned when he saw he had at least half of it left. That's when he heard a sound he'd not heard since the war. He dropped the whiskey bottle again.

Incoming cannonball!

There was a deafening explosion outside, and the house shook from the blast. Simms staggered and fell against the wall. Dust and debris from the ceiling showered him. He clawed his way back to his feet, choking in the dust and trying to understand what was happening.

His brain told him it couldn't be possible this was what he thought it was, but his reflexes and awful memories from fifteen years before kicked in. He was under artillery attack. Simms lurched to the back wall. He pulled out the bookcase and opened the door leading down to the basement.

Adrenaline started to clear his fuzzy brain. Simms hurried over to his desk, where he picked up the lantern, burning to light the study. His Winchester was leaning up against the wall at the corner of the room. He picked that up, too, and took them downstairs, taking his time not to trip on the stairs.

Simms climbed back up the stairs and looked around the study. There wasn't anything else he needed in the house. He would ride this one out in the basement. He pulled the bookcase back to the wall, covering the secret passage. Just as he was closing the door behind him, he heard that awful sound again.

This one was a lot closer. Simms turned to hurry down the stairs when the explosion hit. The stairs trembled under him as he clapped his hands to his ears. He took a step down, missed a stair, then fell and rolled to the bottom, striking his head on the hard basement floor. He blacked out.

————

McNelly stood in the early morning light and looked at the adobe house through his field glasses. He grinned and handed them to me. The eastern wall of the house had collapsed. The rest of the house was standing, but it looked kinda off-center here and there, plus there was a lot of debris inside. Dust hung heavy in the air. I could see no activity anywhere.

"Great shot, Hostler," I told him. I gave him the glasses to have a look at his handiwork.

McNelly assigned two men to guard the prisoners and told Hostler to make sure nobody made off with Napoleon. That left ten men, now that Boone had left. He called five of them and told them to hustle around the back of the house double-time.

"Make sure nobody's getting away through a window on the other side," he told them. The five hustled off in a circle around the house.

McNelly arranged for the other five to form a skirmish line to advance on the house. "Any fire from the house, you drop and return fire," he told them. "Shoot to kill. If it gets too hot for us out here, we'll pull back and have Hostler over there give 'em another taste of Napoleon." He grinned at me. "Let's go see what we've got," he said.

I looked over at Zeb and Caleb, still tied up. "Keep an eye on those boys too," I told the guards, then advanced on the house with McNelly.

It stayed quiet all the way to the house. There was no sound or any sign of movement. We met up with the five men McNelly had sent around the house. They'd seen nothing, either. It was puzzling. One man had peeled off and gone into the house when the cattle rustlers first came back from Mexico. That man was probably King Simms. Where, I wondered, had he gone?

We entered through the blown-out eastern wall and stayed spread out, advancing at the same pace through the house. We didn't want to get caught in a crossfire with each other. I had my Colt in my hand, just like the others, and we left nothing untouched, checking each room and kicking through the debris.

After forty-five minutes, we'd found nothing. At last, we called a halt and gathered around McNelly in the ranch yard. He shook his head. "Best I can tell, two of 'em got away from us," he said. "Bad luck for us, they were the two biggest fish."

He looked over at me. "I expect you'll want to get on into Laredo, Pike," he said. "I know you'll be lookin' for George Lynch. If you find him, handle the best way you see fit and I'll back your play."

McNelly looked over at the empty corral. "If Simms got away from here, he must be on foot, 'cause we emptied that corral." He thought for another moment. "We'll round up them cows out there and get 'em back to Mexico," he said. "Those Tennessee boys can come with us and see if we can't get the cows back to their owners. If Simms wants to steal a horse, the fastest, easiest place is probly Mexico. We'll keep an eye out."

He looked at me again. "We'll get Napoleon back to Austin," he said. "Can we keep Hostler for the trip back to Austin, just in case we need to use the cannon again?"

I nodded and went to talk to the Tennessee boys for a minute.

I found Zeb and Caleb where we'd left 'em, which wasn't much of a surprise. They were trussed up like turkeys.

I squatted down next to them. "What are you boys gonna do after McNelly's done with you?" I asked. I explained McNelly wanted them to guide him back to Mexico to return the cows, then they would be free to go where they wanted.

They looked at each other. I didn't figure they had any

idea what they wanted to do, they'd been too worried about how much trouble they were in.

I was thinking about the land left to me by Jed Hardy. It seemed pretty clear that George Lynch was either going for a stretch in prison or might just wind up getting his neck stretched, depending on where he was going and what he planned on. That meant the land in the will was mine with no problems, and I could run some cows on it.

"I believe in folks gettin' a second chance," I said. "You boys learned a little about cowboyin' down here, right?"

Zeb was the one to speak up, like always.

"We did." He nodded. I could tell he liked the part about a second chance.

"You know the area around Fredericksburg, or Crabapple, or the Circle L Ranch?" I asked.

They looked at each and went to crawfishing around, as best they could when they were all trussed up like that.

Finally, Zeb decided to stick his neck out. "We been there," he agreed.

"Well, the thing is," I said, "I've inherited some land next to the Circle L. Fact is, I inherited part of the Circle L itself. I'll explain that some other time. What I want to do is to run some cows on that land. I don't have much time for it, so I thought mebbe I could hire a guy or two to run those cows an' look after the place. You boys interested in that?"

They stared at each other, then stared back at me. "You'd hire us to do that?" Caleb asked.

"I would," I said. They were still staring at me. "I think you boys have learned a lot in the last few months, about life, I mean, not just about cowboyin'. You would be honest and work hard for me, I think. I'm willin' to take that chance on you."

"We would," Zeb blurted. "We sure would."

"Okay," I said. "It's a deal. You boys have any money to get back to Fredericksburg after McNelly's done with you?"

"We got paid a few days ago," Caleb said. "We ain't had a chance to spend it anywhere. We can get to Fredericksburg."

"See you there," I said. I threw a saddle on Hank, mounted up, and turned toward Laredo. Lynch had a head start on me, and I didn't like it. He had some things to answer for, and I was just the one to ask the questions.

———

McNelly walked over to cut Zeb and Caleb loose. "I want you to guide us, returnin' them cows," he told them.

"We know," Zeb said. "Pike Hardy told us. They've stole cows from two different spots since we been here. You wanna take 'em all back to where they stole from last night?"

McNelly nodded. "These are those folks' cows, so we'll take 'em back there. Maybe they'll share some with the other people that've been robbed." He turned to look at them. "What else did Hardy tell you?" he asked. "Any idea what you're gonna do when we're done here?"

"Hardy done hired us to hep him start up a ranch," Caleb said.

McNelly stared at them, then chuckled. "I am only a little surprised," he said. "Pike Hardy's a good man, and you boys are lucky."

"We know it," Zeb assured him.

Simms was dimly aware of sounds above him in the house. His ears were still ringing from the cannonball blast, but he could hear voices and footsteps. His eyelids fluttered and came open slowly. The lantern was still burning on the table, but the flame was running low. He struggled to hear the conversations upstairs, but it was too muffled.

Simms pushed himself to a sitting position and suppressed a groan. He shot a glance up the stairs, the door was still shut. He struggled to remember if he had pulled the bookcase against the wall before closing the door, he was pretty sure he had.

He struggled to his feet and suppressed an oath when the pain shot through his head. He reeled over to the table and made sure he had the Winchester rifle handy. Then he reached down and pulled the bag with the money up to the table. He half expected that Lynch had stolen the two thousand dollars in there, but found it was all still in the bag.

Simms pulled the money out of the bag and stuffed it into his money belt. Then he turned down the lantern until the light went out, picked up the Winchester, and cradled it in his lap. He had no intention of being taken prisoner by the army or whoever it was out there that had a cannon. He would go down shooting.

Sitting there in the dark gave him a lot of time to think. He would still even things with Lynch, but now he had other things to worry about first. Somebody had come after him with a lot of firepower. The adobe house was probably a wreck up there, and whoever had attacked the house had probably taken the cows and arrested his hands.

That meant all he had left was the money in his belt. There should have been a lot more money left, he knew that, but the women and whiskey in Mexico just came too easy. Still, he had eight thousand dollars to start over, and that would have to be enough.

After some time passed, he realized he wasn't hearing voices or footsteps upstairs anymore. They might have left, but he couldn't take chances. With his luck, if he climbed the stairs and opened that door, they would have a shotgun pointed at his head like a gopher coming out of a hole. He resolved he would wait for two hours.

It was hard to measure time in the dark. After a while, he laid down on top of the table, laying the Winchester down next to him. It wasn't comfortable on the hardwood of the table, but he somehow drifted off to sleep in the dark.

When Simms came awake, he was disoriented and lost. He rolled to one side and fell off the table, cursing in the darkness. He laid on the floor, remembering slowly where he was and how he'd gotten there.

There was no way to know how long he'd lain there in the dark, but he knew he was done hiding out in his own basement. He had to know what was going on up there and who was in his house.

Simms found his way to the stairs and climbed them slowly. He opened the door, keeping the Winchester handy, and blinked painfully at the sunlight coming through the window in his study. All was still quiet.

Simms shoved the bookcase aside and emerged into the study. He set the Winchester down and pulled his pistol, slowly advancing through the house, room by room. After ten minutes, he was satisfied the house was empty. When he came to the eastern wall, he found only open space, looking out over the ranch yard and pasture.

He climbed through the wreckage and looked around the yard and the surrounding pastures. Whoever they were, they had left. Simms walked out to check the bunkhouse, noting a vast crater where the first cannonball had landed. A quick check told him none of his men were here, either dead or alive.

Simms returned to the house and made himself a pack with the food he could find in there. He looked around the house for anything else we wanted to take with him. He found some ammunition in the study, shouldered the Winchester, and left the adobe house. He wouldn't even bother checking the cows. Even if they were still there, he had no one to help drive them.

He stood in the ranch yard and made his decision. It would be easiest to steal a horse in Mexico, but that was going out of his way. He would take the road to Laredo and steal a horse along the way to town. He would let the horse go before he got to Laredo and take the train north if it looked safe.

Simms knew he would be back in Texas, but for now, it was time to get out. The Nation, that's where he needed to go right now. He could lose himself up there pretty easily. He could pay for what he had to pay for and steal the rest. After some time went by, he'd be back in Texas. A man could make a lot of money in Texas.

He shouldered the Winchester and started walking east toward Laredo. Hopefully, he'd find a horse to steal pretty soon.

CHAPTER 19

THE BOONE DILEMMA

George Lynch pushed on toward Laredo. He had to admit it was lucky that he'd found the trail during the night, with only moonlight to guide him. Still, he'd done it. His shoulder ached, as it had ever since he'd laid off the laudanum. He still had a bottle of the stuff and he would take it again if the shoulder didn't stop throbbing.

He would use it, that is, when he had the money from the safe box in Austin in his money belt and he was headed out of Texas. Unlike all the other idiots he'd met lately, Lynch didn't want to go west. With the money he had in the bank, he could make a nice start on a horse ranch in Virginia. He would be a society man. A single man. Nobody out there knew about Maribel. He would just move on from her, too. The thought brought a smile to his face.

Lynch stopped to water his horse when his path crossed a creek. He walked around to check the horse's flank while he watered—no brand. Simms must have picked it up on a Mexico raid. Lynch could sell him in

Laredo, maybe at a livery stable. He could use the cash to get to Austin on the train.

He flexed his left arm and swung it in a small circle. The pain was still there, not crippling like before, but still there. Lucky it was his left shoulder where he'd taken the bullet. Lynch stepped away and practiced drawing his gun. The right arm was good.

That reminded him he'd be going back east without ever having used the gun skills he'd spent so much time practicing out here in Texas. That seemed like a shame. Maybe he would still have a chance. He wasn't in Virginia yet.

Lynch remounted and struck the trail again. By his estimation, he would reach Laredo just before dawn. He didn't plan on riding through town that early. One or two early risers would be out, and he didn't want to be seen and remembered. He would lie over before he got there, take a nap, then ride to Laredo. He could blend in with folks going to the shop or headed for breakfast at the café. His stomach growled at him, and he decided he would be one of the folks in the café.

Funny, Lynch thought, about those hill country boys during the raid last night. Simms paid well and had people who didn't mind stealing cows and shooting anybody who got in their way. Those boys had run away, no stomach for it. They had looked a little familiar at first, said they were from Missouri, which Lynch didn't believe.

Still, he had checked his back trail a few times, and they hadn't followed him. No skin off his nose, he reminded himself, if they quit on Simms. He was sure he had slipped away without being seen or recognized after shooting Walsh, that was the main thing.

A thought sparked in his brain and Lynch reined in his horse and cursed so loudly that the gray pranced sideways and tossed his head. The moonshiners! He'd seen them in Crabapple, all down-at-the-heels, riding crowbait horses and selling moonshine in the alley behind the general store. They had shaved their beards and cut their hair, but he knew they were the ones he had seen in Crabapple. They must have known who he was!

Lynch urged his horse forward again and turned this over in his head. He hated loose ends, and these boys were both loose ends. The problem was, what could he do about it? He didn't dare turn back. The only path was forward. In the end, Lynch decided the only answer was to stay in front of everybody. In front of Simms, especially if the Tennessee yokels told Simms what they knew. Get to the bank in Austin and get out of Texas.

Lynch pushed on for another hour, then guided the horse a good distance off the trail and into a gully behind a stand of mesquite trees. He couldn't afford to be seen by anybody, and it was time to get a little sleep before riding on into Laredo.

He had to stake out the mustang at the bottom of the gully, away from any grazing, but it couldn't be helped. He muzzled the horse and shook out his bedroll. Sleep didn't come—he kept thinking about the moonshiners and how much they knew or might tell. On top of it, he couldn't find a comfortable position for his shoulder.

Finally, Lynch kicked aside the bedroll and took the whiskey bottle out of his bag, then opened the second bottle of laudanum he'd gotten from that quack doctor in Austin. Just a touch of laudanum and whiskey to get to sleep wasn't going to be a problem, he told himself.

Boone pushed hard through the night, knowing how worried Pike Hardy was about Norah. Boone didn't consider it likely that Lynch would go after her—how could he even know she was in Laredo? Still, Laredo was the closest rail stop, so if Lynch wanted to get out of town as fast as he could, the train station in Laredo was a likely place he'd go.

By the time he rode into Laredo, Boone was trying to remember the last time he'd eaten. "Got my gun belt rubbin' up against my backbone," he mumbled to himself. He tied his horse to the rail outside the first café he came to, casting his eye down the street. Norah was in a boarding house just down the street, but she was an eastern girl, wasn't she? "Probly not up yet," he told himself.

Turning from the hitching rail, Boone froze in place. Norah Lynch was coming out of the café. Not only was she up, she'd already had breakfast. Boone pulled down his hat and moaned. Breakfast would have to wait.

For a moment, he considered walking over and telling her he was here to protect her from Lynch. He decided against that for several reasons. First, she was so independent, she might just flare up at the idea of being watched over. Boone couldn't deal with that.

Second, he thought he could do a better job of watching out for her if he trailed along behind, keeping an eye out for Lynch if he showed up and made a move. Third, if she didn't want him around, she might just make it her mission to shake him off her trail. Like he'd already found out, she was a cagey one, Boone told himself.

Boone moaned again when he caught the scent of fresh rolls wafting out of a bakery. He pulled down his hat, crossed the street, and followed Norah as she walked down the street, passing by her boarding house and going into a bakery.

———

Norah had been thinking about the bakery since she got up this morning. After a small breakfast at the café, one of those sweet rolls at the bakery was just what she needed. On her way to the bakery, she stopped to look at the dresses in the window of a dress shop.

Something in the window's reflection caught her eye. She stopped and studied it, being careful not to turn around. The image she saw made sense now, she grinned when she saw who it was. Boone was watching her from across the street.

Norah kept grinning. If Boone was watching out for her, Pike must have sent him back because Pike was worried about her. She liked that idea. Watching Boone, it occurred to her that he could track people or wild animals in the woods with the best of them, but he was terrible at following a girl around in town without being noticed. The thought made her chuckle.

Norah continued down to the bakery, pausing at the door to see if Boone was following. He was. She chuckled again. Maybe by lunchtime she would tell him she was on to him and ask if he wanted to join her at the café for lunch.

———

I didn't need to worry about finding the trail to Laredo. For starters, the morning sun had broken through some clouds and I had plenty of light. Besides that, old Napoleon had left some deep ruts in the ground when we'd hauled him through last night. A blind man might have been able to follow those ruts out to the trail to Laredo.

Lynch had me worried, especially since Zeb and Caleb had told us how Lynch had murdered a guy named Walsh down there, south of the border. He had murdered at least two men now, counting Jed Hardy. I had to believe there had been a few more in between. It was hard to know what he would do to Norah if he knew she'd trailed him down here.

Jed had told me how you never knew what the frontier would do to a man. *"Pike,"* he'd told me, *"it's funny what a man can do when he ain't livin' with laws and police and judges and such to tell him what to do. Some men, they learn how to make their own way, but they look out for others, make peace, and hep others. Some take what they want and turn into bad 'uns when there's nobody tellin' how they oughta act."*

Lynch was, for sure, one of the guys who took what they wanted. He might have settled down for a while at his ranch, once he'd taken that from old Jed, but something had gone wrong with Simms at the ranch down here at the border, and he was on the run. That made him even more dangerous.

I reached the trail to Laredo and settled Hank into the best pace I thought he could keep all the way to town. I glanced at the sun overhead and figured we should strike town in Laredo a little before noon. Lynch would have a head start of several hours on us. At least, I thought,

Boone was probably there by now. That thought made me feel better.

———

Lynch woke up with the sun shining in his eyes. It took a moment to remember where he was. He shoved his bedroll aside and staggered to his feet, rubbing his eyes and staring around in astonishment. Then he remembered, cursing for the first of many times that morning.

"Laudanum," he growled. "And whiskey." He swiveled around to look for his horse—the gray mustang was still there. Lynch lost no time saddling the horse and stowing his bedroll and rifle. As they moved back out to the trail, he glanced overhead. He wasn't an expert at reading the time, but he knew from prior trips he was about an hour out of Laredo. He would be lucky to get there before ten o'clock.

His luck changed a little for the better when he saw the livery stable just outside of town. He'd forgotten it was there. He knew there was a sharp-eyed old geezer who owned the stable. Lynch was pretty sure he could sell his horse to the old geezer and walk into town.

Lynch rode into the stable and swung down. A quick glance told him he was alone with the old man.

"I'm sellin' my horse," he announced. "Gonna make you a good deal on him."

The old man circled the horse, checked the gray's teeth, then walked back around him, stopping for a minute when he saw there was no brand. He gave Lynch a sharp look, then stepped back.

"I'll give ye fiddy dollars fer the hoss," he announced.

Lynch stepped back like someone had struck him

across the face. "Fifty dollars!" he barked. "Fifty dollars? He's worth twice that."

The old man shrugged. "Not to me, he ain't. He ain't got no brand. How do I know he ain't been stole?"

Lynch spluttered, feeling a red flush crawling up his cheeks. The old man was no fool. Lynch had lost control of this right from the start. "He ain't, hasn't, been stolen," he hissed.

The old man shrugged. "If'n you say so. Still only worth fiddy dollars to me."

Lynch was in a hurry. Fifty dollars was still something. Simms had probably stolen the horse in Mexico, anyway. "And the saddle. Saddle too."

The old man gave the saddle a sharp-eyed glance. He had this guy over the barrel. "Sixty dollars with the saddle," he announced.

Lynch's protests died in his throat. For all he knew, the train for Austin was about to leave. "All right, sixty," he growled. He waited an eternity for the old man to walk into what passed for an office and return with the money. The old man started to count it out, but Lynch just grabbed the money and stuffed it into his pocket, then took his bedroll and Winchester from the saddle.

There was nothing to do now but walk to the train station. Lynch had made this trip many times, but this time he didn't want to be seen. He quickly reached the town, then dropped down near the Rio Grande to avoid the busier areas north of the river. He jogged north to reach the train station on Farragut Street.

His luck took a turn for the better when Lynch found out there was a train leaving for Austin at three o'clock and arriving tomorrow morning. He bought a ticket and asked the clerk to store his rifle and bedroll until he returned. The clock on the wall told him it was now almost eleven o'clock.

Feeling bolder, Lynch stepped out of the train station. A growl from his stomach told him he was starving—he hadn't eaten since last night. His favorite café in Laredo was on Houston Street, just a few blocks away. His original plan was to avoid the main streets in town, but his stomach won the argument over what to do next. Lynch headed for the café.

Lynch rounded the corner onto Houston Street and froze. The old deputy to Jake McCabe was lounging across the street, propping himself against the wall and watching people moving in and out of the shops across the street. What was that guy's name? Boone, that was it.

Lynch pulled back and watched Boone. If Boone was in town, Lynch's gut told him this was about him. Now, when he was so close to getting away with his money. He had to take out Boone before the train left.

———————

Boone was pretty sure Norah had seen him, and he didn't really care anymore. He'd traipsed around after her all over town, and it was time to get something to eat. He ducked into the bakery she'd left just about twenty minutes ago. The smell of the sweet rolls was overpowering.

Boone looked at the sweet rolls and patted his stomach. His wife Alice would get after him for eating sweet rolls, but Alice wasn't here. He grinned and ordered two of them. While they got his order ready, he watched through the shop window. Norah had gone into the general store across the street.

After paying for the sweet rolls, Boone stepped outside the shop and walked to the corner, with the main street in front of him and an alleyway behind him. He leaned up against the wall of the bakery and belted down both sweet rolls.

———————

Lynch pulled back around the corner and slumped onto a bench. His mind was racing. His gut told him he was in trouble here. The first thing to do was to get rid of Boone. He couldn't shoot him in the middle of town—he had to silence Boone until he could get himself out of town on that three o'clock train.

A sign on a building two blocks back, on his way over from the train station, flashed through his mind. Lynch sat up straight on the bench, then leaped to his feet. There was no time to lose.

A quick stop in a feed store was the first thing to do. Lynch bought a four-foot length of rope, then had the proprietor cut it in half. Lynch grabbed the ropes and dashed out the door, headed for the doctor's office he had seen before.

A quick glance through the window told him the doctor was in there by himself. Lynch's luck was holding. Dropping his ropes outside the door, he then threw it open and dashed in. He shouted, "Shooting! There's been a shooting!"

The doctor whirled around and stared at him. "Where?" he demanded.

Lynch pointed out the door. "Other side of town!" he shouted. "Over on Water Street. Hurry!"

The doctor stared a moment longer, then grabbed a

black bag and rushed out the door. Lynch ran out behind him, then stopped to watch as the doctor trotted around the corner and out of view. Lynch dashed back inside, yanking open the door to a supply cabinet he'd seen when he first ran into the office.

Lynch ran his finger up and down the shelves, searching for one thing in particular. His finger stopped halfway along the second shelf. His lips twisted into a smile. "Chloroform," he murmured to himself.

Taking the chloroform bottle and grabbing a couple of rags on his way out, Lynch was in business. He had seen the vets use chloroform on his horses a time or two, and he knew it worked on humans as well. They'd been using it since the Civil War, or so he had heard. He picked up the ropes he'd left outside and dashed down the street.

It took only minutes to race back to where he had seen Boone before. Lynch circled and came in from the alleyway behind. Boone was still there, arms folded across his chest, still watching a general store across the street. Lynch didn't have time to worry about who Boone was watching over there.

He unscrewed the top on the chloroform bottle and shook several drops onto one rag he had taken from the doctor's office. He closed the gap to where Boone was standing, moving slowly and silently. There was no one watching on the street. Lynch grinned. He could do no wrong today.

Boone heard only the last step or two as Lynch lunged in, reaching around and clamping the rag over Boone's mouth. The old man was surprisingly strong, shaking back and forth and clawing at the hand over his mouth. Lynch hung on grimly, dragging Boone backward into the alley.

After several seconds, the resistance became more and more feeble until Boone sagged back limply against him. Lynch hurried to drag Boone out of view, hauling him to the back of the alley and behind the store next to it. He stood back and looked at Boone. There was no movement.

Lynch hurried to retrieve the ropes he had dropped and trussed up Boone's wrists and ankles until he was sure the old man couldn't free himself. He took the other rag from the doctor's office and stuffed it into Boone's mouth, then stood back to admire his work.

Satisfied Boone was out of the way, Lynch walked briskly to the front of the alley, getting as much distance from Boone as he could as quickly as he could. Turning the corner onto Houston Street, he came face-to-face with his niece, Norah Lynch.

His reaction was pure panic.

CHAPTER 20

THE STREETS OF LAREDO

W hen Norah left the general store, she was looking for Boone. She'd seen him through the window of the store, eating something he had just bought at the bakery. He had been following her around all morning, and obviously, the man was hungry. She would just put him out of his misery and treat him to lunch at the café.

The trouble was, Boone wasn't there when she came out of the store. She crossed the street to the corner next to the bakery, and he wasn't anywhere to be seen. Puzzled, she turned slowly, looking for him. When she came full circle and started to cross the alley next to the bakery, she ran into her uncle.

"George!" she exclaimed, surprised and scared at the same time. That was when she saw the crazed expression on his face. She tried to step back, but he jumped forward, wrapped one arm around her neck, and started to drag her into the alley. She dug an elbow into his ribs, loosening his grip for a moment, and ran toward Houston Street.

He caught up in an instant and wrapped his arm around her neck again. Norah dug in her heels so he couldn't drag her back toward the alley. That was when she saw him pull his gun from the holster. He held it against her temple.

People had stopped in the street and were staring, but nobody moved to help her after he pulled his Colt. Norah was still struggling, sure he wouldn't fire in the middle of a busy street. She heard hooves pounding and lifted her gaze. Her eyes widened in surprise.

Pike Hardy, on horseback, was thundering down Houston Street at a full gallop.

Hank and I cantered into Laredo a little before noon, by my reckoning. The sun was high overhead and I was starting to feel better about things. McNelly had probably rounded up King Simms by now. Lynch had gotten away, but he knew better than to come back to my neck of the woods near Fredericksburg. Boone was here to watch out for Lynch and keep him away from Norah.

I rounded the corner onto Houston Street, heading for the boarding house where Norah was staying. Then I saw a ruckus going on, several blocks down the street. A man had his arm wrapped around a woman's neck and she was struggling to get away from him.

I leaned forward and stared. The woman was wearing a green dress, and I knew that green dress. It was the same one Norah was wearing the day I met her. Her hat kept me from seeing the man clearly, but I was ready to bet every dollar I had that George Lynch was the man who had her wrapped up.

I put the spurs to Hank, and he leaped forward. I yelled at the top of my lungs for folks to stay out of my way. I could see people leaping back up to the boardwalk as we came down the street full tilt.

I could see that Lynch had his pistol against her head, but I knew he was bluffing. If he shot a woman in the street like that, he would swing at the end of a rope before sundown from the nearest tree. As I closed the distance, he turned the gun toward me. We were only a block away now.

His first shot went wild when Norah lunged back against him. I leaned over the side of Hank so only my left leg and shoulder were targets and began reining Hank in as we got closer. He fired again and I felt a burning stab across my left shoulder.

I rolled across Hank and dropped to the ground on my right, but I had only a second of cover as Hank plunged forward for several more steps. I rolled up to my knees and saw him bringing that gun to bear on me.

Norah lifted one foot and slammed it down on the inside of Lynch's ankle. Then she bent her head and sank her teeth into the arm he had wrapped around her neck. Lynch howled in pain, cursed, and lost his grip. Norah wrenched free from him and dove to the ground.

She had thrown his aim off, but he was bringing the gun around again. I came to my feet as I drew my Colt, but I was off balance and staggered as I came up. That probably saved my life. His shot whined past my left ear, then my gun was clear and I fired. He staggered back.

I felt my mouth pull back into a snarl of pure rage as I walked in on him, firing again and again. My second shot struck him full in the chest and he went to his knees. The third shot cut right through his heart. By the time my brain told my fist I didn't need a fourth shot, he had slumped sideways to the ground.

I moved to check on Norah, but the rush was gone and the pain from the gunshot was setting in. My legs didn't seem to be working right. I dropped to one knee to let the dizziness pass.

"Pike!" Norah was up and running toward me. She stopped when she saw the blood, then ran up to drop beside me. "You're shot!"

"Yeah," I said. I tried to think of something else to say, but I couldn't seem to think of anything.

"Come over here," she told me, clearing a path and sitting me down on the boardwalk. She looked at my arm and tore a sleeve from her dress to wrap it up. "Somebody get him a doctor," she yelled.

The next few minutes are still a little blurry. I remember hanging on to Norah and clenching my teeth when a doctor showed up and poured something over the bullet wound. "Just grazed," he said, wrapping it back up. The doc tilted his head at the body of George Lynch. "He's a lot worse off," he told me.

"He'll be fine," the doctor told Norah. He got up and moved the people back who had gathered around. "Give him some air, folks," he said. They pulled back, leaving Norah and me still sitting on the boardwalk.

When some quiet settled in, we started to hear an odd thumping noise. We stood and looked around. The noise wasn't coming from inside the bakery, but it was close by. We rounded the corner and the thumping got louder.

"Boone," Norah exclaimed. "Boone was standing right here right before George attacked me!"

We found Boone behind the bakery, tied up good and madder than a hornet with a sore stinger. I cut him loose and he came up with fire in his eyes. "Somebody knocked me out with some stinky stuff on a rag," he roared. "I'm gonna kill him!"

"I beat you to it, Boone," I told him. We walked back out to Houston Street, where they were loading Lynch's body onto a wagon. "Go see for yourself," I said.

Boone moved stiffly over to the wagon and watched as they loaded up what was left of George Lynch. Boone turned around and got some cussing out of his system. By the time he walked back to us, he had calmed down some.

"I'm goin' to get some chow at the café," he mumbled as he walked past us. A few steps later, he stopped and turned around. "You didn't leave nuthin' for me, Pike," he grumbled.

Norah linked her arm through mine and we followed Boone down to the café.

———

THREE WEEKS LATER

We spread out the picnic blanket right where the properties met. Things had gone surprisingly fast after we came back from Laredo. The deed and Jed's will made it pretty clear that I owned a section of land on the Pedernales. A trip to the land office in Austin had confirmed it. The creek I had first seen when I came out to investigate the theft of George Lynch's horses split my land down the middle.

Maribel hadn't fought it at all. She had welcomed me as a neighbor. I might put up a fence someday to divide the land from my neighbor on the west side, but Maribel and I had decided we didn't want or need a fence on this side.

Norah laid out the food on the blanket. All my favorite things were there, including the chocolate cake she saved for the end. I ate until I couldn't hold any more, then I sprawled out on my back and stared up at the blue sky. Norah laid down and used my good shoulder for a pillow.

"Maribel has invited me to come and live at the house with her," she told me. "What do you think of that?"

I turned that one over in my head. "Well," I said finally, "it's a great place for you to live. Only trouble I see is that I wouldn't get to see you too often. It's a couple hours to get to Fredericksburg. I'll be coming out once in a while to check on my property, but Zeb and Caleb will run the cows for me and live in Jed's old shack." We could hear them hammering once in a while up there— the shack needed some fixing up.

Norah rolled over so she could look me in the eyes. "I thought of that," she said. "I want to see you more often too, so I can divide my time."

I sat up, puzzled. "Divide your time?" I asked.

She smiled. "Julia McCabe told me I can stay in an extra room at their place whenever I want," she said. "I'm even thinking about taking a teaching job in Fredericksburg. If I do that, I would just be out here on weekends. Maybe you could stay with us on weekends."

A grin spread across my face. I'd say it pretty much ran from one ear to the other. "Now that," I said, "is what I call a plan."

We laid back and just enjoyed the afternoon for a while, until Norah suddenly sat straight up. "What about

King Simms?" she asked. "Did they ever catch King Simms?"

I shook my head. "I got a telegram from Leander McNelly yesterday," I told her. "They didn't find him. Not in Mexico and not in what was left of that old adobe house. McNelly said they found a basement room in that house. Simms could have been hiding out in there when we attacked."

Norah sat up and leaned on one elbow, looking troubled. "So, he's still out there somewhere," she murmured.

"Don't worry," I told her. "He's never operated around here, except through George Lynch. He's got no reason to come around here now. He might even leave Texas 'cause he knows McNelly's still after him."

She nodded and leaned in to give me a kiss. "Let's go see how the boys are doing with that shack," she said.

———

We found them sawing some boards behind the shack. A look inside showed they had patched up the cracks in the walls and replaced the boards that had rotted out. Things were coming along.

"Remember my rule for working on my ranch," I said.

They both nodded their heads. "No moonshine," Zeb said. "We won't make no moonshine. We jest take care of the cows."

"Right," I said. "I've got some cows coming in next week. I'll be back then."

Norah and I loaded up the buggy and started back to town. We were invited to dinner at the McCabes' place. It was the first time we were all getting together since the adventure down at Laredo.

We found them all waiting for us on the porch. We joined them there and I told them about my new place and how things were shaping up out there. "Zeb and Caleb just about got that old shack fixed up enough for 'em to live in," I finished.

Boone's eyes lit up. "You've got them boys livin' out there by the crick?" he asked.

"Yeah," I answered, "but they know I'll fire 'em the minute they make a drop of moonshine. If I see any shine out there, those boys will be looking for another job, somewhere else."

"Oh." Boone slumped back down in his chair. His wife just shook her head and smiled. If anybody could get used to Boone, she was the one who could do it.

Julia McCabe chuckled and stood up. "Come on, everybody," she said. "Dinner's ready." She held open the door and waved everybody in.

We stood and went to the door. Julia cast a shrewd glance at us as we went past. We stepped inside and Norah wrapped an arm around my waist. I put my good arm to use, wrapping it around her shoulder.

"I think," Julia said to nobody in particular, "that my work here is done." Then she followed us into the house.

PART TWO

THE SHADOW OF SAM BASS

CHAPTER 1

SALOON SETUP

FREDERICKSBURG, TEXAS, 1878

Buster's Saloon on Third Street was new in town, and I had a bad feeling about it the minute I pushed through the doors and stepped inside. I'd been told the whiskey was nasty—this guy Buster probably cooked it up out back himself. I knew the drill. Start with straight alcohol and add some water. Hopefully, it was fresh water. Throw in a plug of tobacco for some color and a bar of soap to give it a bead. Roll it out and start serving.

Looking around, I saw the owner had quite a few folks drinking his nasty brew. The bar, which was nothing but a board running down the back wall of the place, was full of guys bellied up and belting it down. There was a sharp-eyed man with a mustache running from his lip down the sides of his face to his chin, pouring the drinks. He told me his name was Buster. I had a feeling that's not what his momma had called him.

I swung my head to take in the rest of the place.

There was a poker game going on in the corner. I saw the dealer raise his arm and shake his sleeve a little. He stopped shuffling and put his arm back down when he saw me watching him. He glanced at my badge and dealt off the top. I had a hunch he didn't do a lot of that when nobody was watching.

There was a thug over in the corner, sizing me up. He was the muscle in this place, no doubt. He glanced at the badge, then looked down at the sling I had wrapped around my arm and shoulder. That was a keep-sake from a shootout down in Laredo a couple weeks ago.

My friend Jake McCabe, the last sheriff around here, had told me about guys like this. Taught me how to whip them in a fight, too. These guys liked to load up and swing a haymaker that started down around their knees and ended up on your chin. I knew I could take this guy, but not in the shape I was in right now. That was some-thing to think about.

There was movement to my left, and I finally saw a friendly face in the crowd. Boone was Jake's old deputy, back when he was the sheriff. He was an old man with a lot of bark on him, and he was playing poker at another table. He nodded his head toward the dealer at the side table and pointed at the guy's boot when he moved his hand to pick up his cards.

Hideout gun in the boot. That's what Boone was telling me. Good to know. I looked back over at Buster, who had stopped pouring and was staring across the saloon at me.

"Kin I hep ya, Sheriff?" he asked. "Want some whiskey, *Sheriff*?" He drew out that word sheriff, like he was baiting me to lock horns with him. He glanced at

Muscles, over in the corner. Muscles came off the wall and rolled up his sleeves.

Another glance told me the dealer's hand was sliding down toward his boot. Buster stepped closer to the bar. It didn't take a genius to guess he had a double-barreled shotgun under there. This was a setup if I'd ever seen one, and believe me, I'd seen a couple before today.

"That stuff?" I snorted. "I ain't had rotgut like that since my army days. Did you throw in one plug of terbacky or two when you cooked up that batch?"

Buster's eyes narrowed. He took a step toward the bar and my hand dropped to my Colt. "Take another step," I advised him, "and I'll have to take you down to the doc's office to plug up some leaks."

The dealer's hands had dropped to his boot. Boone drew his gun, cocked it loudly, and laid it on the table in front of him. The other players at his table scattered and the dealer froze.

"That goes for you too, Magic Fingers," I told him. "Only, I'll have the doc plug ol' Buster's leaks first. He might not get around to you in time."

That left Muscles, who was just holding his ground over there near the wall. He sneered at me.

"Didn't nobody ever tell you not to bring a gun to a fistfight?" he snarled.

"Well now, that plumb surprises me," I told him.

He dropped the sneer, glanced over at Buster, then back at me. That had thrown him for a loop. "What?" he asked. "What're you surprised about?"

"Well," I said casually, "I wouldn't of thought you were so yellow as to pick a fight with a man when he's stove up." I glanced down at the sling. "Or," I said, "mebbe you're all muscle and no fight."

He started for me. "Fred!" The shout came from behind the bar. "Leave it alone." Buster stared in my direction. "For now," he said. "Leave it alone."

"Good choice, Buster," I told him. "I'd hate to close this place down for a couple of weeks while I investigate things. You never know how many laws could be gettin' broke in here."

He nodded, watching me like a rattler. I could feel Muscles, or Fred, or whatever his name was, just staring pure hate in my direction. I drifted to the door. Boone picked up his six-shooter and joined me outside.

When we reached the street, Boone chuckled and dropped his Colt back into the holster. "You could always make friends in a hurry," he observed. "They couldn't decide which one of 'em wanted to stretch your hide first in there."

"Yeah," I agreed. "That's a pack of rascals if I've ever seen one. No good's gonna come from that place."

Boone leaned up against a hitching rail and shook his head at me. "You don't got no deputy since Hostler left," he reminded me. "Jake and I been takin' turns tryin' to help you out."

I nodded. Hostler had been my deputy up until a couple of weeks ago. Then he got a telegram from home, saying his momma was sick, and he'd moved back from where he came, back to East Texas.

"I know," I said. "I didn't expect to walk into a loaded deck like that. I'll be more careful next time." I massaged my shoulder a little. "I at least need to get my wing back in shape before I tangle with Muscles in there."

Boone grinned and patted me on my good shoulder. "Let me know afore you tangle with him," Boone said. "Let me get some bets down first. I know who taught you how to fight." He unhitched his horse and swung aboard. "Got to git home to the missus," he said, then he reined his buckskin around and trotted out of town.

———

After telling those boys in the saloon about taking them down to the doc for some patching up, I remembered I was supposed to go in and get my shoulder checked. Going to the doc isn't my favorite thing to do, but I figured to get it over with as soon as possible.

My name is Pike Hardy, and I've been sheriff in Gillespie County, Texas, for a little over a year. After mustering out of the army, I thought it would be a little more peaceful around these parts than it had been in the army. The first year didn't turn out that way, and today wasn't off to a very good start with that new saloon in town. Still, I like to grab the bull by the horns. I would keep an eye on those saloon boys.

I let old Doc Freeman poke and prod me for a while. Then he rotated my arm a couple times and I yelped.

"Good," he said. "It's healing."

"Well," I mumbled. "At least it was until you got holt of me."

"Still ornery, too," he said. "There's another good sign."

I got away from the doc as fast as I could and went looking for my girl, Norah Lynch. Norah and I had been through some tough times together, but things were looking up now. I had inherited some land right next to a spread owned by her Aunt Maribel. I'd been thinking lately that I could hang up my badge one day and be a gentleman rancher out there. A man's got to have a plan.

She'd said she would be at the dress shop down the street. I moved in that direction. Today was bound to get better.

———

Latigo Smith relaxed his gun hand slowly and moved it away from the holster. He'd sat with his back to the wall, like he always did, just out of habit. Most times, that came in handy. He could see if anybody came through those batwing doors looking to lift his scalp. This time, though, it had left him in a bad way.

The dealer had been cheating for at least half an hour, no doubt about that. He'd dealt from the bottom three times that Latigo had noticed. There was something going on up that sleeve of his, too. Just about the time that sheriff had come in and called the dealer Magic Fingers, Latigo had decided to do something about it. Now he didn't have to.

Now, he just cashed in his chips and moved over to the bar, thinking about how close he'd come to getting into another gun fight. How many had there been? Four or five, depending on how you counted them. He tossed off a shot of really nasty whiskey and thought about something his ma had told him.

"*Lat,*" she'd said, "*a man needs to avoid trouble whenever he can. You ain't never got the hang of that. You don't go lookin' for trouble, but you don't seem to stay away from it, neither. That's gonna be what they put on your gravestone if you ain't careful.*"

"What's yer name, stranger?"

The voice startled him, and Latigo looked up into the sharp, shifty eyes of the guy pouring that gut killer he called whiskey. It wasn't an unfriendly question, but Latigo wasn't looking to make friends in here either.

"Latigo," he said shortly.

The barman snorted. "That's a long handle," he said, still staring with those beady eyes. "What do yer friends call you?"

"When I've got friends, they call me Lat," he answered, stepping back from the bar. It all of a sudden seemed a little close and stale in here. He dug into his pocket, tossed a coin on the bar, and moved toward the door. When he looked back, Beady Eyes was still staring at him. A quick glance told him that Muscles hadn't moved away from the wall and Magic Fingers was paying him no mind.

Lat leaned against the wall outside of Buster's Saloon, still a little worried about how close he'd come to drawing down on Magic Fingers in there. That made twice he'd almost gotten himself in serious trouble since coming to Texas. And, the thing was, he'd come to Texas to get out of trouble and lead a peaceful life. Well, more peaceful than it had been anyway.

The trouble had really started with that yellow-haired girl back in Leadville, Colorado. Lat had been younger then, and he had to admit, pretty dumb where that yellow-haired girl was concerned. Up until then, he hadn't got himself into anything too serious. Ma had told him he needed to walk away from fights sometimes, but that just didn't seem to be in the cards for him.

They'd come west on the Santa Fe Trail, Lat and his ma and his pa. They had California in mind, but Pa had come down sick with cholera after they stopped at a bad watering hole. He'd died out there on the trail, and Lat had settled down with his ma in Santa Fe.

They'd done okay there, too. They had kept body and soul together anyway. Ma had taken in washing, done some cooking and cleaning, whatever she could do to keep food on the table. Lat had gone to school for a while when she insisted, then when he got a little older, he'd taken a job at the livery stable, then at the blacksmith shop.

After that, Lat had taken a job at the saloon. Ma hadn't liked that, but he could make a lot more money by pouring drinks and throwing out the trash than he could at the livery stable. That's what Bert, the old guy who owned the saloon, called it. When those mining boys got rowdy, Lat had to take out the trash. By that time, he was twenty-one years old, six-foot-two, and two hundred pounds of muscle. Lat had gotten some welts and bruises on him a couple times, but he learned fast.

Lat grinned when he remembered. Bert liked to say that *"when Lat thowed somebody out, they stayed thowed out."*

Ma hadn't objected too much until he'd bought his first Colt 45 and strapped it on. Then he'd practiced until he was good with it. Really good. That's when Ma had really started to worry about him.

Then two things happened that changed his life. First, Bert died, and his widow had no use for Lat. Two months later, Ma had died. It had come on sudden, and it took Lat by surprise. After her funeral, he'd seen no reason to hang around Santa Fe. He had drifted around New Mexico for a while, then he'd heard about getting rich in Leadville, Colorado. That had sounded good to him.

When Lat got to Leadville, it was 1874, and he was almost twenty-five years old. He'd been in a lot of fights and carried a few scars to prove it. He also had a nasty scar and gash across his right ribcage. That's where a kid with a smokewagon on his hip and an itching for a reputation had called him out one night down in Trinity. It was the first man he'd killed in a gunfight, and he'd wanted no part of it.

Lat signed up with a mining outfit in Leadville, and they'd put him to work cleaning the heavy black sand out of the sluice boxes. It was hard, dirty work, and he was ready to move on when somebody found out that the heavy black sand was rich with silver.

Lat had worked a little claim at a place called California Gulch for a year and he'd struck a little color. Then he found out he could make more by riding shotgun on the wagons carrying the silver to Denver. He'd had a nice setup for another year and made some good money until the day two highwaymen had stepped out of the trees with the idea of robbing the wagon.

Lat had drawn and dropped them both before they could throw those Winchesters down on him. They had loaded the bodies into the wagon and they drove on to Denver. The driver had warned Lat he might have trouble with the sheriff in town.

That sheriff had one good eye, a nasty scar across his right cheek, and an attitude. He'd dragged Lat off to jail with hardly a question asked. Luckily, there was a judge in town who'd held a trial after Lat had spent two days in jail. The judge let him go after the driver told his story.

It turned out that both the highwaymen were cousins to the sheriff, and it was his gang doing the robberies. If Lat had been smart, he'd have left town and moved on right away. The trouble was, he'd met that yellow-haired serving girl down at the Dry Gulch saloon.

That girl, she'd made nice to him like he was something special. He had spent too much of his hard-earned money on the beer and whiskey in that saloon. He didn't much like the whiskey, but that yellow-haired girl brought it to him every time and told him how handsome he was.

One night, she had asked him to go to the back room with her and help her lift a keg of beer and bring it in. When they got to the back room, she pointed at the keg, then stopped him when he bent down to lift it. She'd picked up his hands in hers and kissed them both. Then she'd spun him around and pinned his hands behind his back.

"I've got him," she yelled.

The back door popped open and that one-eyed sheriff came in. He was holding his six-shooter in his right hand, but his arms were crossed and he was laughing. "Good job, Myra," he told her.

"You kilt my cousins out there, ya know," he told me. "If'n that old judge wasn't so soft, I'd have stretched yore neck by now." He laughed a mean, ugly laugh. "I'll just have to do this another way." He chuckled.

Lat yanked his right hand free, drew his Colt, and shoved that yellow-haired girl away from him, all in one move. The sheriff's one good eye got real big, and he tried to bring that gun around and line it up on Lat.

It was too late. Lat drilled him dead center with one shot, turned around, and grabbed the rope away from the yeller-haired girl that she'd been fixing to tie him up with. He tied her hands and feet and stuffed his bandanna in her mouth. He needed the time to get away from there.

Luckily, there were gunshots going off all the time in Leadville in those days. Nobody bothered to see what was going on behind the saloon. Lat ran down to the livery, forked his bronc, and got out of town. That's when he had come to Texas. So far, he had stayed out of trouble down here. Just barely.

Lat heard a horse trotting by and came back to the present. He looked up to see the sheriff trotting past him, headed out of town, it looked like. Lat tipped his hat to the sheriff, pushed away from the saloon wall, and walked in the other direction. He had nothing against this sheriff, but then again, he'd not had much reason to trust a man with a badge up to now.

Lat had seen a sign for a café earlier today, and he walked along the street for another two blocks before he saw the sign again. He took off his hat and stepped inside. Maybe the café would be a friendlier place than Buster's Saloon.

CHAPTER 2

KING IS BACK

Boone dropped into my office the next morning, just as I was planning to ride out to my property. I was more interested in seeing Norah than I was in seeing the property. Boone thumped his boots on the top of my desk. I glared at him and he dropped them to the floor.

"Word is," he announced, "that there's some horse racin' going on up north of here." He squinted at me to get my reaction.

I leaned back and stared at him. "Betting?" I asked.

Boone took a toothpick from his shirt pocket and started chewing on it. "Probly," he said.

"Ya think they've got stolen horses running? And where is the track?"

He answered the questions in reverse order. "Up north and east. Ain't close to any towns that I know of. Folks have just found it. Don't know about stolen hosses, but I'd say there's a good chance of it."

"Hmmph." I leaned back and started to put my own boots on the desk, but I didn't want to encourage Boone to do it. I stared out the window. "I guess," I said, "I'll check on that when I get around to it. Got other stuff to do first."

Boone nodded and chewed on the toothpick some more. "Word is," he said, "it's run by that feller with the new saloon in town, Buster. He's got a couple thugs fixin' the races and robbin' folks."

Well, that was different. I leaned forward and put my elbows on the desk. "You know how to find this place?" I asked.

He shook his head. "Don't know, myself. Heard from that new feller in town, Latigo Smith. He knows. Don't know if he'd show you, though. Plus, you gotta be careful. Those boys would probly just as soon dry-gulch you as say howdy if you showed up out there."

I heaved a sigh and went back to staring out the window. "This Latigo Smith," I said. "What's his story?"

Boone shook his head again. "Don't know much," he said. "Guy keeps his mouth shut. I get the feelin' he's been on both sides of the law. I'm guessin' he mostly wants to come down on the good side, now, but don't expect him to do you no favors. Just my hunch, that's all."

Boone stood to go. "Want me to make you some coffee before I go?" he asked.

My stomach growled, just thinking about it. I waved a hand in the air. "Nope," I told him. "Thanks for the info, though."

Boone shoved the toothpick in his mouth and turned for the door. "I'll go with you if'n you want," he said.

———

I reined in when I reached the edge of my pasture land and watched my cattle coming to water in the Pedernales

River. I had about forty head now. I had bought most of them from my friend Jake McCabe. They were mostly longhorns and some other mixed breeds that had come up from Mexico.

The longhorn was a great breed for trail drives, but I didn't think the drives would last much longer. The railroad was changing everything. I was sure there were other breeds better for ranching and beef cattle. I'd heard a lot about the Hereford cattle that had just come to Texas. I couldn't get my hands on any of them yet, but I would keep my eyes and ears open.

I rode up to the shack at the northern edge of my property. I had inherited it, along with my land, from the old mountain man who had raised me. The Hall brothers, Zeb and Caleb, were running things for me out here. I hadn't been able to pay them much, but I had an idea about how to make things better. I wanted to talk to them about that today.

Zeb and Caleb had been moonshining and getting themselves in some trouble when I crossed paths with them. I had given them a second chance and things seemed to be working out. I glanced at the shack as I dismounted, it looked about the same. Then again, the only solid thing about the whole shack seemed to be the fireplace and chimney. Maybe it was too much to expect them to rebuild the thing.

The boys came around from the back when they heard me. They had a little vegetable garden going in the back, and I knew they could bring in plenty of deer meat around here. They were crack shots with those old rifles of theirs.

They had hammered together what passed for a few chairs out on the porch, and we took a seat out there. The crick flowed past, just a few feet away, and I could remember fishing in there a time or two as a boy.

They made their report on the ranch—three new calves since my last visit. They talked about buying a dog to help guard the herd from varmints at night, and I promised to look into it. I paid them what I could for the last two weeks, they shoved the money into their pockets without looking at it.

"Would you boys like to buy into the herd?" I asked. "I haven't been able to pay you much, and you're growing and shooting your own food around here. I could hold a couple dollars a month from what I've been paying and you could consider you each own one of those new calves out there."

Their eyes lit up. I don't think they'd even considered it before, but they had been used to living on almost nothing, out there in a shack and cave just west of my property.

"You mean it?" Zeb finally said.

"Sure," I said. "Folks feel more like working at some-thin' if it belongs to them. We could kinda partner up at the ranch."

I don't think they knew exactly what to say. I glanced back at the old shack they'd been living in. It had been in pretty bad shape for a long time. I didn't need it fallin' in on them some night. I pointed off to the east, where Norah lived with her Aunt Maribel.

"Maribel Lynch, over there," I said, pointing again, "lost several hands after her husband got arrested and his cattle thievin' operation got busted up."

They nodded—these boys had helped us bust up the cattle thieving. It's why I had given them this second chance. They waited for me to say something else.

"What I'm saying," I told them, "Is that she's probly got several cots open in her bunkhouse right now. Maybe you boys could stay over there if you maybe helped her now and then with some repairs and such around her ranch."

They looked at each other and said nothing. I waited for somebody to speak up. Finally, Caleb cleared his throat and leaned forward.

"They would be plumb nice," he said. "We done thought of that a time or two, but we was scared to ask or even bring it up." He glanced over at Zeb, and I thought both of them looked a little puzzled.

"The thing is," he continued, "is that we was told Maribel is sellin' the ranch and movin' back east." He looked over at Zeb again, then looked at his feet. "We thought mebbe you knowed about it already," he said.

I stared at them. I'd heard no such thing. "Who told you?" I asked. "When did you hear about it?"

Zeb took over. "Just yestiddy," he filled in. "We was gonna make sure you knew, about it, we was plannin' on talking about it just as soon as you come out. It was one of their hands that tole us about it yestiddy." They both fell silent.

That one set me back. How long had this been planned? I hadn't seen Norah in several days now, maybe it had been a surprise to her too. I had to find out. I stood suddenly and they both stood, fiddling with their hats. They looked nervous.

"You done...did the right thing, telling me," I said. "I've just got to go over there and find out what's happening." I mounted up on my horse and looked back over at them. "Don't forget," I said, "pick out a calf apiece out there. I'll hold back a couple dollars next month to start paying for them." I wheeled my horse around and set out for Maribel's place.

———

We sat on the front porch after dinner. Maribel sat in the swing on one side, Norah and I sat in chairs on the other.

"Sorry to spring it on you both so suddenly," Maribel said. "Once George got killed, and I had this ranch to myself, I knew my heart wasn't in it. Coming west to have a horse ranch—that was always George's idea. I was always perfectly happy back in New York. When I got the offer for this place at a good price, I just decided to move on it."

I wanted to ask if she was sure—did she know she had enough to go back east and move on? She seemed to know what I was thinking.

"It wasn't just the money from the sale of the ranch," she said. "George had hidden some money away in a box at that Austin bank, remember?"

Now I remembered. George had taken some of his money from his horse ranch and maybe from cattle rustling and hidden it away in a private metal box in an Austin bank. Something new, called a safe deposit box or something like that. Maribel probably had plenty of money.

The sound of the swing squeaking seemed loud. I glanced out into the afternoon sun, not sure what to say. I wanted to ask Norah what she planned to do now, but I would wait until Maribel left.

"Who's going to buy this place?" I asked. "It's a pretty big place—not many folks around here are likely to have the money."

"It's a man from Virginia," Maribel answered. "Some-body George's horse breeder knew. He came out on the train last week to take a look at the place. He won't live here, but he wants the ranch. He made me a good offer. I didn't accept until three days ago."

I glanced over at Norah. She reached out to take my hand. "I just found out yesterday," she said. "I was plan-ning to ride into town tomorrow to tell you."

I nodded. It got even quieter on the porch than before. Mostly, I could just hear that swing squeaking. After a while, Maribel got up to go inside. "I'll let you two figure things out," she said.

I waited until the front door swung shut. "What are you going to do?" I blurted. I'm not a guy who waits to find out how things are.

"I'm staying," she said. "I like it here, and you're here."

I felt a pretty fair amount of relief washing over me. "You gonna move into Fredericksburg?"

She shook her head. "I'm going to buy a place," she said. "Not this place, but I'm going to buy some property."

She had told me she had some money she'd inherited, but she'd never told me how much it was. I just waited to hear more.

"I can't afford Maribel's place, or I would have bought it myself," she said. "It'll have to be a smaller place, but I want a ranch."

"We won't be neighbors," I said, feeling let down.

Norah got up, took two steps, and sat in my lap. "We can talk about that," she said. "I've heard that Stonewall, a little town east of here, is a good place to buy some land. There's not much to the town, but we'd just want the land anyway, right?"

I tossed that name around in my head for a while. It sounded a little familiar, but mostly I came up empty on where that was.

"Still in this county," Norah said. She grinned. "You're sheriff over there, too. It's closer to Austin and the railroad, and that's a good thing. Easier to move horses and cattle. I have enough to buy a smaller place over there."

Well, I thought, at least she wasn't leaving the county. My place out here didn't seem like home sweet home anymore, though. I stared glumly over the porch rail. "We won't be neighbors," I repeated.

"Maybe we could be," she said.

I stared at her. "How?"

"The man who bought Maribel's land is still in Austin until the end of the week," she told me. "He asked about your land, too. You have the stream running through there. It would make a nice addition to this place. You could sell to him, and we could both buy land near Stonewall."

A grin spread slowly across my face. "We'd still be neighbors," I said.

She leaned over to give me a kiss. "Yes, we would," she told me.

"I think it's about time I got up there to Stonewall to take a look around," I said. "After all, like you said, I'm sheriff over there, too."

———

King Simms leaned back in his chair and watched carefully while the man across the table dealt the cards.

The man was cheating, that much was for sure. The thing is, he hadn't cheated Simms yet. He'd dealt a card or two off the bottom to two of the other players, but not to Simms.

The man picked up the deck, shuffled it, and started dealing. There! One card came off the bottom to the man to Simms's right. Simms moved his hand down to rest at his gun belt, where his well-used Colt .45 rested comfortably. The dealer noticed and hesitated. Simms's card came off the top, just like it should. Simms nodded at the dealer and relaxed.

An hour later, Simms cashed in. He was up by thirty dollars. Enough to have made the last two hours worth his while, but not enough to get the other players riled when he cashed in. Simms took his money and bought himself one more whiskey. It was only another half hour until he met his buyer.

Simms had made some good money down in Texas, stealing Mexican cattle and selling the cows to folks making the drive to Kansas. The thing was, he didn't have much of his money left, and some more of it had been stolen. Simms growled under his breath, just thinking about that.

Then, his ex-partner, a man by the name of Lynch, got himself shot by a sheriff down in Laredo. Simms's ranch house had gotten blown up by the Rangers, and there wasn't anything left for him down in Texas. He'd ridden to the Nation.

Now he was in a little one-horse town called Cameron, down at the southeast corner of the Nation. It had taken a little while to get an operation going, but it seemed to work now. Simms had run across a guy who just went by the name of Skinny, who had gotten things going.

Skinny had himself a plan to steal horses from folks up there on the Santa Fe Trail, then bring the horses down here to the eastern part of the Nation to sell. From there, the horses could disappear down into Texas or over into Arkansas. Skinny promised there was some good money in it. Mostly, Skinny just wanted a good gun hand to back him up if things got rough. That's where Simms came in. Simms was just the man for that.

Simms stepped out to the porch and leaned back against the wall of the saloon. Skinny was already at the livery stable to meet the buyer, and Simms planned to join him. He would be there for sure when the money changed hands. Simms didn't trust anybody else with his money.

Still, Simms waited a little longer. He was a cautious man. Skinny claimed to have sold to this guy before and promised things would be smooth. Simms dug into his shirt pocket, came up with a cigar, and struck a match.

A man walked down the street and into the livery stable. Simms paused with the match in the air, stared, then lit his cigar and shook out the match. The guy who had just gone into the livery was black. Simms shrugged. There were some black cowboys around, some of 'em good trail hands, he knew. Still, he didn't figure this guy for the buyer, so he waited a little longer.

An old man stumbled out of the bar behind him, clutching a whiskey bottle. He popped the cork and took a long swig, his Adam's apple bobbing up and down. "Trouble over there," he slurred.

Simms pulled the cigar from his mouth, blew a smoke

ring, and fixed a stare on the old drunk. "What kinda trouble?" he growled.

The old man pulled the cork again, making a loud popping noise. He shrugged. "Don't know exackly," he admitted. "But that there was Deppity Marshall Bass Reeves, so it's trouble for somebody in that stable." He drained the bottle in one long swig.

Simms swung his gaze to the livery stable. "That guy was a Deputy Marshall?" he snorted. He went back to watching the livery stable. "He's black."

The old man chucked the empty bottle into an alley, where it shattered. He stumbled back toward the saloon door. "Don't make no difference what color he is when he thows down that Winchester on ya and ties up your hands, marches you down to Ft. Smith," he explained.

Simms threw out a hand to stop the old man before he disappeared into the saloon again. "What's in Ft. Smith?" he demanded.

The old man snorted and wiped his nose on his sleeve. "'T'ain't what, it's who," he slurred. "Isaac Parker is in Ft. Smith. That's where Bass Reeves is gonna take somebody. To see Judge Isaac Parker. Don't nobody want to go see Judge Parker."

The old man started to move on, but Simms stopped him by placing a hand on his chest. "Hold on, old timer," he said. "Why don't nobody want to go see Judge Parker?"

The old man stared at him. His eyes seemed to swim in and out of focus. He belched. "You ain't from around these parts, then," he decided. Simms shook his head impatiently.

"Judge Isaac Parker is known as the Hangin' Judge," the old man said. "You can probly figger out why."

The door to the livery stable opened and Skinny rode out first, his hands tied to the saddle horn. Bass Reeves rode out next. Seeing Reeves from the front, Simms could see the badge on his chest. Reeves held a Winchester across his lap.

Simms turned to face the other way as they rode past. Maybe, he decided, stealing horses and selling them up here in Indian Nation wasn't as good a deal as Skinny had told him it was.

CHAPTER 3

REVENGE PLANS

I got a buggy at the livery, hitched up my horse, and
headed east from Fredericksburg. Norah had done
some checking on what we might find out there. I
listened as we rode toward a place called Stonewall

"The place I want to look at is only about fourteen or
fifteen miles from Fredericksburg," she told me. "Closer
than the property you had down there to the west on the
Pedernales. This is east of town, closer to Austin, still on
the Pedernales River."

I nodded. I had made the trip to Austin yesterday, and
Maribel's buyer had made me an offer on my land, right
there on the spot. He had seen it when he bought Maribel's place. He had no questions, and he had a lot of cash.
I liked him right away, of course. I would be flush with
the money in my bank within a couple of days.

We went past a place called Enchanted Rock, which
was a popular site for folks to picnic. I hadn't thought of
Texas as a place for caves, but we saw some rock forma-
tions, and Norah said there were caves in the Stonewall
area.

I kept the river on my right, but started to wonder if I was getting us lost. I asked Norah if this path looked familiar to her.

She grinned. "The river will work as a landmark for us. Just hold it on your right, like you're doing. The place we might buy is still a few miles east of here. It's a section of land. Between the two of us, I think we could buy it."

I did the arithmetic in my head, just barely. Six hundred forty acres for the two of us. That sounded pretty good to me. Especially the part about this property being closer to Fredericksburg. It was a full day just getting out to my old place and back. I clucked at the horses to keep them moving, then stole a cookie out of the picnic basket. Norah pretended not to notice, but I saw her grin.

"How'd they come up with the name Stonewall?" I asked.

"Named after the Confederate general, like you'd expect," she said. "Somebody established a stagecoach stop there a few years ago. Now some families have settled around the area."

I looked at the land as we were rolling on to the east. I could see a lot of grassland, looking pretty rich. I was guessing the soil was a mixture of clay and sand, which wasn't bad. There were stands of trees—mostly post oak and cedar elm, from what I could see. The rich grass would make for some good grazing land.

Norah knew the asking price, and between us, we could pay it. Zeb and Caleb were in favor of moving out there with my cows and working for me at the new place. We knew we would need a few fences before Norah brought any horses, but this seemed like something that could fall right into place for us, other than that.

Water was always something to consider. We'd been told there was a stream running across the land, feeding down into the river. We would need to see if it had enough water moving through it to water cattle and horses. The Pedernales River was a water source, of course, but the stream running north and south would be a big help. We also had to allow for drier times in the height of summer. Norah had been told the settlers had dug a well on the property and put up a log cabin. We would check out all of that today.

I kept the river on my right, and I knew we were getting close to the place. I was hoping it would be everything we were hoping for. Norah reached out to me. I held her hand and kept the other hand on the reins. We rolled on toward what we hoped would be our future.

———

Arthur Engels was the name he'd been born with. His little brother had hung the name Buster on him. He hadn't much liked it at the time, but after a while, he didn't mind it. It was better than Arthur. Buster had drifted south and west from Ohio, and he liked the money he could make in Texas. Most of it wasn't legal, but that didn't bother Buster.

The saloon in Fredericksburg was working out pretty well. Watered-down homemade whiskey, a poker game that lifted money from the pockets of anybody dumb enough to play—that made for a good start. A barmaid who could pick a few pockets from drunk customers, and shortchanging them at the till helped as well. Still, the best money was being made at the racetrack.

Buster was a little surprised at how fast the word had

spread about the horse races he held every Saturday morning. His little homemade track was out there in the middle of nowhere, but they came anyway. The closest town was Willow Creek, formed by some folks who didn't like the Germans settling in the area. Lucky for Buster, outlaws seemed to like Willow Creek. Between the outlaws around Willow Creek and Buster passing the word quietly at his own saloon, the little track was a busy place on Saturdays.

The races themselves were a great way to sell the stolen horses Buster kept in a nearby canyon—Balcones Canyon. Sure, Buster did some betting on the horses. He had a couple of guys who watched the horses in the canyon and brought them to the races on Saturdays. Buster had ways to make the horses look good when they raced. His handlers volunteered to take care of all the horses brought to the races. A little too much food and water for the other horses before the race usually made Buster's horses look good when they ran.

The outlaws and saloon regulars who came to the races were always looking for fast horses. Buster's stolen horses didn't always win, but they usually did. Then, they brought a good price after most races.

The railroads brought the horses. Houston and Texas Central Railroad brought the horses down from the Nation, or brought them from the rail yards at Austin, Houston, or Dallas. A few dollars here and there, and it was surprising how many horses just didn't get to their destination. It went without saying that Buster's customers at the races didn't worry too much about brands on the horses.

There was just one thing that was troubling Buster about his overall sweet setup in this county. That one thing was the sheriff, who was sticking his nose in the saloon every day or two, poking around, asking questions. Buster didn't need a nosy sheriff hanging around. He stepped to the door of his office, yanked it open, and bellowed.

"Fred! Get in here!"

Fred wasn't really the bouncer's name, but it was the name Buster used when he couldn't remember somebody's name. He'd found people usually answered when he paid them enough. Buster had found Fred hanging around the train yard in Austin, robbing the bums of whatever change they had in their pockets. He made much better money working for Buster.

The bouncer showed up at the door, wiping the beer away from his mouth with his sleeve.

"What've you done about that sheriff hanging around here?" Buster demanded.

Fred, or Muscles, as the sheriff called him, stared at Buster blankly. "He's been wearin' that sling on his arm," Fred/Muscles reminded him. "I was waitin' for it to be a fair fight. Then I was gonna bust him up a little, kinda discourage him." He flexed and swelled up a little. "I don't mind spendin' a couple nights in the jail for it. I hear the food is pretty good."

Buster's eyes narrowed as he squinted through the smoke from his cigar. "He weren't wearin' that sling the last time he poked around in here, was he?"

"No," Fred/Muscles admitted. "He just got out of it a day or two ago, I think."

Buster shrugged. "Long enough. Start some fisticuffs the next time he shows up. See if you can get him to throw the first punch," Buster advised. "Then hurt him enough to keep him away from here. Extra five bucks in it for you."

The bouncer's eyes lit up, and he flexed again. "Can't wait," he said. "I'll bust him up good. You'll see."

Buster was already looking at some papers on his desk. He waved the bouncer away and didn't even hear the door when it closed.

———

King Simms stood on Sixth Street in Ft. Smith, Arkansas, and stared at the two-story brick building in front of him. A few people scurried in and out in Sunday-go-to-meeting clothes. Simms figured those were the lawyers, or judges, or some such. He'd been watching for about half an hour, and he'd seen one man going in there in shackles, but it wasn't Skinny.

Simms wasn't even sure why he was here. There was nothing he could do for Skinny. Maybe he felt a little guilty that Skinny was on trial and he wasn't. Not that he had any ideas about joining Skinny. Especially not with this Isaac Parker guy as a judge. Simms felt himself gulp a couple of times. Finally, he worked up the guts to walk into the courthouse. Skinny was going to be tried today, that's what he'd heard.

Simms walked into the courtroom and took a seat on a hard wooden bench. He glanced left and right. He wondered why these other people were in here to watch a trial. The guy on his left looked like a farmer—what was he doing here? Simms didn't feel like asking.

The first case was a guy on trial for killing a deputy. The judge read that part out loud and the farmer on

Simms's left started shaking his head. "Kilt a deppity," the guy mumbled.

It didn't seem to take very long. Some guy said he saw the deputy get shot when he tried to bust up a poker game, and it was the guy on trial who had done it. A couple lawyers got up and said some things that didn't make a lot of sense to Simms, and first thing he knew, the judge sentenced to guy to "hang by the neck until dead."

"Yup," said the old farmer next to Simms.

Simms felt the sweat breaking out on the back of his neck. Then they brought Skinny in and announced he was on trial for stealing horses.

"Hmmm," said the old farmer next to Simms. Finally, he had to ask the guy what he thought. Would they hang Skinny for stealing horses?

The old man looked at him funny, then shook his head. "Naw," not for stealin' hosses," the old guy said. "If a few folks caught him an' decided to skip bringing him to the law, they'd have a necktie party for him, fer sure. Not the judge in court, though."

Simms felt a little better. The black Marshall came in an' said how he'd found Skinny in the livery stable with a bunch of horses. He knew the horses were stolen, the Marshall said, on account of the brands and the horses already being reported stolen.

This one seemed to go faster than the first one. After a while, the Hangin' Judge hammered on the desk and announced that Skinny was going to jail for fifteen years for stealing the horses.

Simms got up, bolted past the old farmer, and felt Skinny's eyes on his back as he slipped out the back door. He was sweating pretty much from top to bottom now, and he was in need of a saloon and some whiskey. He found both within five minutes.

It was getting on toward noon, and the saloon was crowded. Simms elbowed his way into the long, knotted board serving as a bar and ordered a whiskey. He tossed it down and made a face, then ordered another. He'd had worse. He needed to feel numb.

"That'll tie yer brisket in knots if you keep it up," somebody said.

Simms glanced to his left. There was a guy with his hat on a leather string hanging down on his back. He stared into the bottom of his empty glass.

Simms tried to ignore him, but the stranger was downright chatty. Simms ignored the question about where he was from. The stranger tried again.

"Here and there," Simms finally said. He looked around, but there was no place to sit and no other spots at the bar. He waved for another whiskey.

"Knots in yer brisket," the stranger said, nodding. He picked up his glass and stared into the bottom of it.

Simms got his third round and took a little more time with it. He didn't have enough money for too many more. Might as well take his time.

"Where ya goin'?" was the stranger's next effort at a conversation.

Simms glared at him. "How d'you know I'm goin' anywhere?" he growled.

The stranger shrugged. "I don't know nobody who hangs around here for long," he observed sadly. "They're generally going up to the Nation, or down to Texas. Maybe to N'awlens."

"That's it." Simms said, hoping to shut the guy up. "New Orleans, I think."

The stranger brightened up. "You know Jack Davis?" he asked. "Used to ride with Sam Bass? I used to ride with Jack for a while myself, afore he threw in his hat with Bass."

Simms felt interest for the first time in this pest leaning on the board next to him. "Sam Bass?" he asked doubtfully. "The guy that robbed the train in Nebraska, stole all that gold an' got away?"

"Yup." The stranger nodded. "They caught a few of them boys, but not Jack Davis. He got away to Californy, folks say, then come back to N'awlens. Got him a saloon or a poker game or both, folks say." He stared into the bottom of his glass again.

Simms waved for a round for both of them and waited until the glasses were full. The stranger downed his with the loudest slurp Simms had ever heard. "Bass got away too, right?" he asked.

The stranger shook his head sadly. "Fer a while is all. They kilt him down in Texas just a month or two ago. Texas Rangers got him."

"Oh." Simms lost interest again and looked around for a table with an empty seat. Still nothing. He reached for some money to pay.

"Funny thing about Sam Bass's gold, though," the stranger said, holding on to the bar like the room was spinning.

Simms's ears picked up again. "What about the gold? What happened to the gold?" He waited for an eternity as the stranger's chin slid down to the bar. With an effort, he straightened up and looked over at Simms.

"Folks don't know what happened to all his gold," he slurred. "All that money—it don't seem like he had time to spend it. None of it never turned up. Thatsh a lot o' gold. Don't nobody know what he done with all of it."

The stranger grabbed the bar and managed one last sentence before sliding down toward the floor. "I'd ask ol' Jack Davis about it if'n I got down to N'awlens." There was a thump as he landed on the floor. Simms laid some money on the bar, stepped over the stranger, and found his horse, tied up in front of the courthouse. New Orleans might be just the place for him to go. Anything was better than here.

———

I was sitting in my office, testing my wing. The doc had taken off my sling yesterday and told me to go easy for a couple more weeks. The gunshot wound had healed. I swung the arm around slowly, surprised to find most of the pain gone. Maybe that nasty-smelling stuff the doc smeared on there had helped.

I thought about how the doc had told me to take it easy, then I thought about Muscles, down there at Buster's Saloon. I maybe needed to wait a few days before I checked that place out again. I had a feeling Muscles was just itchin' to take me on. I just needed a few more days, I thought.

The office door opened and closed. I looked up and was surprised to see a guy in a badge walking toward me, holding out his hand. I stood and saw the badge was the Texas Ranger badge. He gave me a firm shake.

"Richard Ware, Rangers," he said.

I introduced myself. That name was just a tad familiar, but I couldn't seem to remember where I'd heard it. I pointed him toward the empty chair in front of the desk and took a seat myself. I waited to hear what he'd come for.

"You heard that Sam Bass was killed about six weeks ago, Sheriff?" he said for openers.

Now he had my attention. I nodded, and now I knew where I had heard his name. "I did," I said. "I heard that you're the one who shot him."

He shrugged and looked at the floor. "He was retreating toward the livery stable and shooting at us," he explained. "There were a couple of us shooting back. I'm not sure which one of us fired the shot that took him down."

Now I remembered that nobody really wanted to be the one who shot Sam Bass. They were a little afraid he still had a gang that would come back and get revenge. I just let that one go and waited for what else he had to tell me.

He looked back up at me. "Have you heard of Frank Jackson?" he asked.

I shook my head. That didn't sound familiar at all.

"Frank Jackson was one of the Bass Gang," he explained. "Bass was pretty much shot to doll rags, but Jackson got him bandaged up and got him out of town. Left him outside of town at the cemetery. Bass said he told Jackson to go. He rode away during the night, I expect."

"I guess he's got some sand," I said.

Ware nodded grimly. "The thing is," he said, "is that we think Frank Jackson has come this way lately."

Now he really had my attention.

CHAPTER 4

DEALING WITH BUSTER

I leaned forward and searched my brain for what to ask Ranger Ware. "What makes you think he came this way?" was what I finally came up with.

"Because," he said, "a shopkeeper out east of here in a little town near Austin says Frank Jackson bought supplies there a few days ago. Says the guy was headed this way, maybe east of here."

I gotta confess, I might have gone a little pale around the gills for just a bit. Norah and I had been out to Stonewall just yesterday. We were buying property there. I didn't want to think that one of the Sam Bass Gang was hanging his hat in the area.

My brain finally started working. "How does this shopkeeper know Frank Jackson or what he looks like?" I asked. "Lots of folks might start thinking they've seen him if he's the only one of the gang to get away in one piece."

Ware nodded. "Yeah, I was asking about that myself. It seems that this shopkeeper, name of Wagner, was in business in Denton, up north of Ft. Worth, a couple years ago. Jackson was up there at the time, probly partnered up with Sam Bass right around then. The Bass Gang was up north and robbed the train in Nebraska just before they came to Denton and met Jackson. After they came to the Denton area, they wound up in Round Rock. That was when we shot Sam Bass."

I leaned forward on my elbows. "I guess he might know him on sight," I admitted. "I don't guess anybody has any idea what Frank Jackson would be doing out here?"

Ware shook his head. "Nobody knows." He took a piece of paper out of his pocket, unfolded it, and passed it across the desk. I could see it was a sketch.

"This is what Jackson looks like," he said. "I think it's pretty close. I got a look at him real fast when the shootout happened." He stood up and held out his hand. "Be real careful if you see him," he warned me.

Nobody had to tell me that. I stood up and shook his hand. "Can I get a telegram to you if I have to?" I asked.

He nodded. "Telegraph the Ranger office in Austin. They'll know how to get in touch." He pulled the office door shut behind him.

Lat Smith wasn't sure why he liked to hang out in Buster's Saloon. The whiskey was sure to rot his belly, the guy running the card game cheated when he dealt, and the bouncer didn't like him. Lat decided he liked it because he was around trouble all the time, but so far had stayed out of jail here in Fredericksburg.

He knew the whiskey would kill him if he kept pouring it down, so he stepped up to the knotted plank that served as a bar and ordered a beer. It was, he reflected, hard for a saloon to mess up beer, so far as he knew.

Lat sucked the suds off the top of the brew and watched curiously through the door leading to the back area of the saloon. Buster was over there talking to the guy who ran the card game. They seemed to be jawing quietly back and forth. Lat drained half the glass and kept watching. He saw the card player draw his pistol, check the chamber, and stand back against the wall. The pistol was in his right hand.

Lat drained the rest of the beer in one gulp and looked around the bar. The bouncer was standing in the far-right corner with another guy Lat had seen here in the saloon a lot. Both of 'em looked like they were practicing taking swings at each other.

Lat looked around at the front door, where a guy was ready to dash out the door. He was looking at Buster, like he needed a signal before he went. Lat dropped a coin on the bar and slid out the door. This was more trouble than he wanted to be around. They were setting up that new sheriff, sure as shootin'.

Lat looked up to see Pike Hardy, the new sheriff, ambling down the street. Behind him in the saloon, he could hear shouts and the sound of tables and chairs getting knocked over. The guy who had been waiting by the door rushed out into the street, looking around wildly.

"Sheriff!" he yelled, waving at Pike Hardy. "There's a bad fight in there! You've got to come quick!"

Hardy's head came up, and he trotted down the street. The man who had been yelling dashed back inside the saloon, waving for Hardy to follow. No doubt, Lat Smith thought, he was letting Buster know that the number one target in Buster's shooting range was about to walk in the door.

Lat stepped over and held up a hand as the sheriff got close to the saloon. "You don't want to go in there, Sheriff," he warned. "Leastways, you don't wanna go in the front door. They'll shoot you down like a turkey before Sunday dinner. The bouncer has a fake fight goin' and the poker dealer is waiting in the back hall, pistol out and ready."

───────

I stopped where I was, eyeing this guy I'd only seen in town once or twice, wondering whether or not to believe him. My gut told me he had no reason to be lying to me. I glanced up and saw the guy who'd been hollering for me to come into the saloon. He looked out, saw me watching him, and ducked back inside.

I looked back at the man standing in front of me. "Latigo something, right?"

He nodded. "Latigo Smith. Lat."

"Thanks for the tip, Lat. Could you do one more thing for me?"

He didn't answer, just watched me.

"Could you go to the café around the corner?" I asked. "Boone is sure to be in there, having breakfast. Could you tell him to get over to Buster's Saloon and come in the back door when he gets there? Tell him to come in quiet."

Lat Smith thought it over, nodded, and moved past me.

"Hey!" I said. He turned back. "Why did you do this for me?" I asked. "Just curious."

He shrugged. "Every man deserves a fair fight," he said. "What they've got set up in there is nuthin' more than a bushwhacking. Ain't nobody deserves that."

I watched him move off, then moved over to the alley next to Buster's Saloon. I walked on cat feet to the back door and eased it open. I had to hope it didn't squeak. The door opened quietly, and I slipped inside. So far, my luck was holding.

I was breaking a little sweat when I stuck my head around the corner and checked the hallway leading into the saloon. The card dealer was standing there, back to me, watching the front door like a hawk. His pistol was out and up.

I glided forward, taking my time, worried a little about the squeaky boards under me. I drew my Colt, and when I got close to him, reversed the grip. I heard a whisper of sound behind me. I had to trust that it was Boone, coming in the back door.

I held the Colt by the barrel and took the last step to come up behind him. "Pssst!" I whispered. He wheeled around, and I sledged him over the head with the Colt. I grabbed his collar as he fell, but the pistol slipped from his hand and clattered on the floor.

Boone leaped past me and levered his rifle, aiming it at the bar. "Hold on," he said. "If yore next move ain't to lean down and put that shotgun back under the bar, it's gonna be just about the last thing you ever do, Buster."

I moved past Boone and took in what was happening inside the saloon.

Buster had his hands on the bar. I stepped around, pushed him back, and came up with a shotgun, lying on a shelf underneath. I tossed it over to Boone, and he caught it with one hand.

Muscles and some other guy I'd seen hanging around the saloon both had their shirts off and their fists up in the air. There was some busted furniture on the floor around them, but I didn't see a mark on either one of 'em. Muscles looked over at Buster as I came up from behind the bar. Everybody was so quiet, you'd have thought we were in church.

Muscles looked over at me. He was itching for trouble, no doubt about that.

"You got yer sling off now," he said. "Cain't hide behind that sling no more, sheriff."

"Who's hiding?" I asked. "You staged a fake fight in here while there's a guy waitin' in the back to bushwhack me. Buster, over there, was gonna take me down with a shotgun if the first guy missed." I looked over at Buster. "You've got two hours to get out of town. If I see you after that, I'm comin' for you."

I looked back at Muscles. "Same goes for you," I told him. "And your bushwhackin' poker player buddy after he wakes up."

Muscles seemed a little less sure about things now. He looked at the Colt in my hand. "You got a gun, sheriff. That don't look like a fair fight to me."

"Outside," I told him. "I'll give you your fair fight. Then you'll leave town." I looked at the guy who'd been staging the fight with Muscles. "Git," I said. He left.

I motioned for Boone to follow me out the front doors. Muscles left first. When I stepped outside, folks were forming a circle in the street. I handed my Colt to Boone and stepped off the boards outside the saloon, following Muscles toward the middle of the circle.

He stopped in front of me, set his feet, whirled around, and busted me with a punch right to the gut. I could feel the air whooshing out of me and staggered back. Muscles charged me in a bull-rush, hands out and getting ready to claw my eyes.

I managed to sidestep and trip him. He went down in a heap, but then I saw him grab a fistful of dirt and push himself off the ground. I jumped forward and slammed his head back down into the street, then I backed off and circled him, feeling the air moving back into my lungs. I'd figured he'd use every dirty trick he knew, but I hadn't expected that one.

He pushed himself back up, and he was moving a little slower. There was a trickle of blood coming from his nose, and his eyes glittered with anger. He charged again, throwing a left and a right. I ducked under both punches and shoved him away, but he landed a glancing blow to my ribs. I had to admit, this boy could punch.

His face twisted with an evil smile. "You ain't throwed a punch yet, sheriff," he taunted. "You sure you can?"

He rushed me, swinging a wild, looping right fist. I sidestepped to my right and leaned away from it, then stepped in and swung a straight overhand left, smashing him right in the mouth. He staggered back and landed in the dust. Blood started from his mouth and he spat out a tooth.

Muscles came off the ground with a roar and tried to smash me in the belly again, but I'd seen that one already. I jabbed him on the eye with a hard right. When he kept coming, I smashed him again in the same spot. His eye started to swell, and he pawed at it with his fist. He was breathing in jagged gasps.

"You don't sound none too good, Muscles," I told him. "You been swillin' too much beer in the saloon?"

He snarled something at me, but his mouth was so swollen up I couldn't tell what he said. He rushed me again, then stopped, ducked, and lifted his boot to smash it down on the inside of my ankle. I stepped away, and he was down low and off-balance, trying to land that boot down on me.

I grasped my fists together and swung my arms like a club, connecting with the side of his head. It sounded like the butt-end of an axe hitting a log. He dropped to the ground like a sack of potatoes.

I looked at a couple of the saloon regulars, who were staring at Muscles. He hadn't moved yet. "When he wakes up," I said, "tell him I'll give him till sundown to get out of town now, on account of him takin' such a beating. Not a minute longer."

I turned and got my Colt back from Boone. From the side of my eye, I saw Latigo Smith collecting money from several people and stuffing it in his pockets. He looked at me, cracked a smile, and tipped his hat. Then he turned and headed up the street.

I chuckled. Can't hold it against a man for making a little side money taking bets when he gets a chance.

———

I sat where I'd been many times before—on the porch of the big stone house owned by my friend Jake McCabe and his wife, Julia. Julia's parents had lived here before, but just lately they had moved into town. The big house and ranch were getting to be too much to keep up with, they said. Now that Jake had retired as sheriff, he and Julia could take over the ranching.

Boone was leaning back in a rocking chair in the

corner. He and his wife Alice had built a line cabin out west of the main house. Boone owned a share of the cattle on the place. He stuffed a big, foul-smelling cigar in his mouth and set it on fire.

"I didn't know you smoked cigars," I told Boone. He blew a smoke ring in the air and grinned. "Got it fer free," he explained.

"Boone," came a voice from inside the house, "I can smell that cigar. You said there weren't any more!"

"Last one, dear," Boone said, looking cautiously over his shoulder. "I tell ya," he said, "that woman's got a nose like a bloodhound."

"I heard that!" came the same voice from inside the house.

Boone shrugged and hunched over. "An' ears like a coyote," he whispered.

Jake chuckled and looked at me across the porch. "Boone tells me you didn't make no friends at the new saloon today," he said.

"Yep," I agreed. "They would have dry-gulched me if I'd walked in the front door. The guy in the back hall who was gonna do the shooting, he'll be in a bed at the doc's office for a couple more days. I fetched him a clout on the noggin with my pistol. That bouncer that I had a fight with will be eating scrambled eggs and applesauce for a few days. I've already run Buster and the bouncer out of town. The dry-gulcher will be leavin' when his headache lets up."

Jake nodded. "Well," he said, "you always did like to meet things head on. Maybe it's best you did. Better keep an eye out for a while though," he advised, "just in case they're hanging around outside town somewhere, wantin' to even the score with you." He stopped and watched Boone stub out the last of that evil-smelling cigar.

"You still need a deputy," he reminded me. "Gotta have somebody to watch your back, like Boone always watched mine. Boone can only help out sometimes."

I nodded. "I know," I said. "Still looking." That reminded me of the guy who had warned me not to go into the saloon today. "Have you met a Latigo Smith?" I asked.

Jake shook his head and looked over at Boone. Boone nodded thoughtfully.

"He's the one who come and told me you needed help at the saloon," Boone remembered. "Did he warn you not to go in?"

"He did," I said. "He's hard to figger. He told me they had set up a dry gulch in there. Said he thought everybody deserved a fair fight." I grinned a little. "I think he made a few dollars bettin' on my fight with the bouncer."

Boone's face lit up with a smile. "He's not only salty, he's a smart man!" he boomed. Then his face clouded over. "I didn't get no chance to make any bets, not with havin' to watch yore back and save yore hide today."

"I'll buy you a beer next time you're in town," I told him.

Boone folded his arms across his chest. "Seems to me that was worth at least two beers," he bargained.

"Done," I said. I turned back around to Jake. "Something you probably don't know," I said. "There was a Ranger in town today, the one that shot Sam Bass over in Round Rock. He said that one of the Bass Gang, a guy named Frank Jackson, was seen in a town east of Austin, headed this way a couple days ago."

Jake's feet came down off the porch rail and he sat up

straight. "That's the one that got Bass out of town and stayed with him at the cemetery, that's what I heard," he said. "Why would he be over in these parts?"

I shook my head. "Ranger Ware doesn't know. Doesn't know if he's from around here or just got away from Round Rock, picked this county for no reason. Do you know of a family named Jackson from around here?"

Jake stared up at the porch roof, frowning. "Nope," he said finally. "Don't believe I do." He looked over at Boone.

"You've been around here longer than me," he said. "Is there a family named Jackson out that way?"

Boone shook his head. "Ain't too many settlers out that way to start with," he pointed out. "I don't remember nobody named Jackson."

Jake looked at me thoughtfully. "I expect you'll want to go over and check that out," he said. "But you gotta be careful about this one, too." He shook his head. "You really do need a deputy," he repeated.

Norah came out to announce that dinner was ready, so we dropped the subject and followed her inside. I tucked into Julia's delicious dinner and said nothing more about it. It was plenty to think about though. I wondered if Latigo Smith might want a deputy's job.

CHAPTER 5

RACETRACK

Frank Jackson crawled through the tent flap, stretched, and scratched himself while he stood in the morning sun. He'd been here near a tiny town called Stonewall for about two days. Partly, he was just staying out of sight after Sam Bass got himself shot. Partly, too, he was trying to follow up on something Sam had said, just before Jackson left the cemetery where he had taken Sam Bass. Sam had died just after what Jackson had heard there, right outside of Round Rock.

Jackson stared south, remembering Sam Bass lying against the tombstone where Jackson had propped him up. Both of them had known Bass had only a short while to live. His breath was coming in short, ragged bursts as he pleaded with Jackson to leave.

"I'm done," he said. "They done fetched me. Nothin' you can do for me here. Ride out whilst you still can."

Jackson only glanced at Bass's face once in a while. They had joined up north of Fort Worth after the big train robbery in Nebraska. Since then, Bass had seemed like the dad Jackson had never had. He stayed where he was, listening for sounds in the night.

Sam Bass reached up with a sudden burst of strength, grabbed Jackson's collar, and pulled him down close. "I hid most of my take from the Nebraska job," he whispered hoarsely. "Spent some time down here several years ago, an' I stumbled across a cave. Robbed a few banks, down south of here, stashed some of that money in a cave. Place don't look like nothin' but a sinkhole."

Bass stopped, gasping for air. Jackson passed him a waterskin and helped him tip it back. Bass swallowed, spat, and passed the waterskin back. "I put most of the gold from the train robbery in there, too." He shook his head and started to laugh. A coughing spasm took over, and he laid back against the headstone to gather his breath.

"I was allus afraid I'd run out of money. That's what happened ever' time. So I jest kept on robbin' after I come back from Nebraska. Trains and banks, mostly. You know. You was in on most of those. Anyways, I never spent most of the gold from that Nebraska robbery."

Bass dropped his head and stopped moving. Jackson dropped down to check, Bass was still alive.

"It were a mistake, you know. Plumb accident about that gold."

Jackson stared at him. Bass gave another short, harsh chuckle.

"Them boxes of gold coins weren't even in the safe. Just sittin' on the floor. I kicked at one of 'em on my way out of the express car. Buncha gold coins jest spilt out all over the floor."

Bass pulled himself together one more time. "Anyways, you gotta git outta here and go find the gold. It's your'n. You stuck by me when nobody else did." He slumped down to one side and propped himself on one elbow.

"It's in them rollin' hills out there. Betwixt a town called Stonewall and another town called Boerne. Ride on a line between them two and keep your eyes peeled for a cave on your way. Closer to Boerne than Stonewall."

Bass gave another sharp chuckle. "Crazy town, Boerne. Buncha German settlers. They walk around talkin' Latin or some such. They'll leave you alone, though." He waved a hand in the air. "That's it. Git. Leave a man to die peaceably."

Jackson had arranged the waterskin and pistol next to Bass, caught up his horse, and left. He had almost expected to hear a gunshot, with Bass taking himself out the easy way. He rode away without hearing it.

Now, stretching in the morning sunshine, he stared down a faint trail that would take him from here, near Stonewall, to Boerne. He had decided to make camp in a little valley near the stage trail. Drawing a crowd was the last thing he wanted.

Jackson made a small cooking fire and put on the coffee pot and a skillet for some bacon. He walked over to saddle up his horse. He would leave his tent up for a couple of days while he searched for the cave. He would give it three days. If he couldn't find Bass's gold stash in three days, he would move on to New Orleans and look up Jack Davis.

———

I puttered around the office for a couple hours. My swollen knuckles had gone down to normal and my shoulder was feeling better again after my fight with Muscles a few days ago. I'd been putting off going out to Stonewall and that area until I felt a little better. If I ran into Frank Jackson, he sounded like a pretty salty customer to tangle with, and I needed to be at my best.

I stepped outside and loaded my Winchester into the saddle. Before I mounted up, I saw Norah coming into town with Julia McCabe. Norah had been staying out there with the McCabes since Maribel sold the ranch. It would be several more weeks until Norah had a livable place at the new property out in Stonewall.

We stopped off at the café for a while. Norah was excited about the new place, and she would be shopping for a few things she could use in the house, once we had one up and going at the ranch. We kissed goodbye outside the café and I walked back to mount up, then saw Latigo Smith walking down the boardwalk on the other side of the street.

On a hunch, I walked over to thank him again for tipping me off about the bushwhack setup at Buster's Saloon. It was all boarded up over there, and they were looking for a new owner.

Latigo nodded and tipped his hat at me. He looked me in the eye, but only for a moment. "Don't nobody deserve to get dry-gulched like that," he said. Then he shook my hand and moved on.

Funny, I thought, as I watched him walk away. He kinda acted like a man who'd been on both sides of the law in his past, just like Boone thought. Suspicious but friendly, all at the same time. I knew that was a pretty common story for a western man who has moved around a lot. I had a feeling Latigo Smith was one of those.

I walked back to the office and mounted up on Hank,

my horse. It was time to get out to Stonewall and look around.

The ride was about two hours, so the sun was climbing overhead when I got there. There wasn't much to Stonewall, just a general store, blacksmith, and feed store. I stopped at both the general store and the feed store. Only the owner of the general store nodded when I showed him the sketch.

"Couple days ago, I'd guess," he said, pulling at his beard and looking at me just a tad suspiciously. He peered at my badge. "You live over to Fredericksburg?" he asked.

I told him I would be out here to start a ranch, and my lady friend was moving out here. He brightened up a little. I could see he was counting on some sales. "I'll drop by when we need things," I said.

He pointed south and a bit west. "He rode off thataway."

I looked in the direction he had pointed. It was right in the direction of the property I had bought with Nora. Nothing more to do in this little town, so I rode out to the property to look around.

We'd seen the property when we rode out just a few days ago. The wildflowers were dying out for the season, but the grass was springing up. There would be grazing for my cows and Norah's horses when we were ready to move them out here.

A ten-minute ride around our ranch showed nothing I hadn't seen a few days ago. There were no tracks, although the ground was a little dry right now. I rode in a line along the direction the shopkeeper had pointed out because I had no better clues to follow. When I topped a rise, I stopped and looked around with my field glasses.

I proceeded for a short while, topping rises and checking with the field glasses. It didn't seem like I needed to spend any more time on this. If Jackson were here, he'd probably have ridden on at least two days ago.

I topped one last rise and looked around. There was something flapping in the breeze at the bottom of a small valley. I locked in on that spot with the field glasses and saw what looked like a small tent. I put the field glasses away and rode in cautiously, circling the spot a little, looking for any movement.

I moved in and dismounted, looking around. It was a tent, all right, and there were signs of a small campfire. I tested the coals, this fire had been out for at least a couple of hours. I rose and looked inside the tent—nothing there. I moved back toward my horse, looking around me. When I saw the glint of sun reflecting off metal, I dove behind a rock.

It was none too soon. The crack of a rifle shot echoed in that small valley. Hank ran a short distance and stopped. My rifle was in the scabbard. No chance I would expose myself to get the Winchester. Nothing to do but wait it out. I could only hope they wouldn't shoot Hank.

———

Frank Jackson lifted his eyes from the Winchester's sight and cursed under his breath. Something had tipped the guy off at the last minute. Jackson glanced overhead. Probably a glint off the rifle barrel. He hadn't taken the time to set up his shot more carefully. No time now. He needed to get away from here before anybody else came looking for him.

Jackson shoved the Winchester back into the scabbard and led the horse away, staying under cover provided by trees and rolling hills where he could. After twenty minutes, he mounted and rode straight for the Pedernales River, wading the horse in and riding along the bank for another twenty minutes.

He swam the horse across the river and emerged on the other side, then struck a path due east. He wanted to be in New Orleans in a few days. Enough of looking for a treasure that might not be there. Sam Bass could've been out of his mind, the shape he was in. Time to start life over. Maybe Jack Davis would have some ideas for him.

———

I'm not a patient man, but I can be when my hide is maybe gonna get shot. I stayed down for a long time, risking a peek over the rock from time to time. When I felt sure this guy was gone, Frank Jackson, or whoever he was, I whistled for Hank.

Hank came over, and the first thing I did was to get my Winchester in my hands. I mounted and circled around to where I'd seen the glint of sunlight. I found his rifle shell lying in the grass. He'd fired only once, I remembered.

There were some faint tracks. I followed them slowly, letting him build up a little distance, wary of any place where he might take cover and wait for me. It was late afternoon when the tracks led me straight into the Pedernales River. No point in going any further. I turned Hank around and headed back for Fredericksburg.

———

Buster wasn't the name he preferred—it had just sounded like a friendly name to use when he had opened the saloon. Now that the saloon was closed, he would have preferred a different name, but he didn't much care to be called Art, either—that was his given name.

Buster scowled and cursed under his breath as he looked at the horses he had hidden in the Balcones Canyon. Not that this wasn't a pretty sweet setup—it was. It was just that he'd been driven out of Fredericksburg, where he preferred to stay. The canyon and his race track weren't really his style. And that little town near the track, Willow Creek, mostly had a bunch of outlaws and pickpockets lounging around. Buster preferred to be the one who did the fleecing, not the one who got fleeced.

Buster watched as his horse handlers moved the horses to some new grass. Those guys were replaceable, but they could use their pistols if they needed to, and they didn't seem to be too greedy. Buster's card dealer and bouncer were here now, too.

Buster cursed again when he thought about being driven out of Fredericksburg. That sheriff, Hardy, was way too high and mighty to suit Buster. He would pay. Buster had his doubts about Latigo Smith, too. Somebody had tipped off Hardy, and it was Latigo Smith who left the saloon right before Buster's plan fell apart.

Buster yelled at his card dealer and bouncer to help with the horses. The dealer had a ridge across his head where Hardy's pistol had landed. Buster figured he could use that to his advantage. The bouncer, on the other hand, the one Hardy called Muscles, was pretty useless now. He reminded Buster of a whipped dog, ever since Pike Hardy had given him that beating.

Buster looked at the horses. They were mostly

mustangs and had some decent speed. He could sell most of them at the next race. There was a black stallion out there that he had stolen from a ranch in central Texas and used for breeding. He had four colts and two fillies from that stallion. Those, he could get a good price for. Maybe he would do that and move on after he'd settled his score with Pike Hardy.

————————

Lat had heard about Saturday horse races on some little track near the town of Willow Creek. It hadn't taken long to find out where Willow Creek was, and he figured if he rode out to that area in the late morning on a Saturday, it wouldn't be hard to find the races. He'd found that a man could make some money at these little illegal horse races. Lat figured he could use the cash.

The best way to make money was to bet on the horses owned by whoever had set up the races. Lat knew it wasn't exactly right to say the horses were owned by whoever set up the races—they were most likely stolen. Still, these guys had a way of winning their own races.

The first thing to do was to get a look at this guy's horses. In this case, the horses were *owned* by Buster, the guy who just got his saloon shut down. Lat was pretty sure they wouldn't remember him or pay any attention if he came to the races. Still, he was a careful man, and he planned to look things over today. Maybe he would come back in a week and make some bets.

An early start had him close to Willow Creek by about ten o'clock in the morning, at least according to the hand-drawn map Lat had with him. He was just starting to doubt the map when he saw a man coming down the road, riding one horse and leading another behind him on a rope. Lat pulled over to let them pass on the trail, then risked asking his question.

"Comin' from the races?" he asked.

The man nodded, spat, and cursed, in that order. "Crooked races, them's crooked races," he snarled.

Lat nodded. He knew that part already. "Straight ahead?" he asked.

"Jest foller the trail." The man spat again and rode away, his back stiff with anger.

The sounds of the races guided Smith before long. The first thing he heard was a gunshot, probably the start of a race. As he drew closer, there were a lot of cheers and curses to guide him in. He spotted an oval as he rounded a bend and saw horses running. Nobody paid any attention to him as he dismounted and stayed back on the edge of the crowd, which he guessed to be around fifty people.

A roan mustang on the small side won the first race. Lat watched closely as money exchanged hands after the race. Muscles, the bouncer, as Sheriff Hardy called him, seemed to hold the money. Buster, the bar owner, collected most of it from the bouncer after the race, as far as Smith could tell. That was exactly what he'd expected.

The next race was won by a lineback dun that looked a little bow-legged to Latigo. The owner was a loud, bearded man who was wobbling a little as he collected his cash. You have to let 'em win a few to keep 'em honest, Smith thought cynically. He noticed Buster didn't seem to have placed any bets on this race.

Another of Buster's horses won the last race, a chestnut gelding. Just about everybody else had left the races by then, so Smith mounted up and faded off into a stand of burr oak trees near the track. He waited until Buster and his party left, leading five horses and moving off to the northeast. Smith waited until they had moved out of sight, then followed the tracks.

Intent on the tracks, the canyon appeared almost out of nowhere and took Latigo Smith by surprise. He had been tracking for about an hour. When he topped a rise and saw a canyon opening up in front of him, he pulled off the trail immediately, afraid they had seen him. If they had seen him, he didn't want to run into a welcoming party.

After staying down and out of sight for several minutes, Latigo Smith set off on foot, leading his horse and keeping his eyes peeled for the edge of the canyon. When the edge came into view, he tied off his horse and edged forward, peering down.

The rifle shot came without warning. Smith felt the blow to the side of his head and dropped to the ground. He never heard the echoes of the shot bouncing off the canyon walls.

Chapter 6

New Orleans

He was completely clear on what Buster had told him to do, he just didn't like it. Buster just called him Dealer, and the sheriff had called him Magic Fingers, but he preferred to be called Ace. Somehow, Buster had pegged him as somebody who would just dry-gulch a man and never think about it twice, but Ace didn't feel like going along with that.

Back there in the saloon, he'd been told to shoot the sheriff when he came through the front door, and Ace had to admit that would have been a dry-gulching. But he had no doubt Buster would have shot him with that shotgun under the bar if Ace hadn't done it. Ace touched the ridge on his head he'd gotten from the sheriff. He wondered if that would ever go down.

Now, Buster had told him to wait at the top of the trail to Balcones Canyon and shoot anybody who might try to follow them in. Ace hadn't really thought there was much chance of that, he'd been checking the back trail all the way in and had seen nobody.

But then, right after everybody else had ridden in and

gone down to the floor of the canyon, somebody had shown up. Ace recognized him as a customer from the saloon. He didn't know the guy's name, but he'd been in the saloon several times, and he was sure enough trailing them into the canyon.

Ace scooted down to take cover behind a fallen log. He propped his rifle over the fallen log and watched as the guy pulled off the trail and dismounted. Ace followed him through his rifle sights as the saloon customer, whoever he was, moved up to look over the canyon rim. The guy peeked over, then pulled back. It was decision time for Ace.

This was a cold-blooded murder. Ace's mama wasn't that proud of him, but she'd raised him better than this. Sighting down the rifle, Ace aimed to graze the guy's head. If he missed just a little left, the guy was dead, but Ace wouldn't think about that. He would try to graze the man's head, and he could tell Buster he'd killed the guy. Buster was too lazy to check it out for himself.

Ace aimed carefully, drew in his breath, and let it out slowly as he tightened up on the trigger. The rifle boomed, and he watched as the man dropped and the horse bolted off into the brush. Ace stood and glanced down into the canyon. Everybody was looking up at him. Ace held up his hand to let them know he had things under control, and they all went back to what they were doing.

Ace hopped down from his perch and crossed the trail, moving carefully to find the guy he had shot. He lay where Ace had dropped him, with a bloody furrow across the side of his head. Ace dragged him back into the brush. He looked over to see that the horse hadn't run too far.

That was all he could do for this guy. He would tell Buster he had killed somebody and buried him in a shallow grave. Ace let a little time pass by, then led his horse down into the canyon to report to Buster.

———

It was hot, and the sunlight had found an opening in the oak leaves above him. Latigo Smith's eyes fluttered open, and he moaned, rolling to the side. The movement brought another moan from him. He reached up and explored the pain at the side of his head, his fingers came away bloody. He tried to remember what had happened, but his mind was blank. The furrow in the side of his head must have come from a gunshot.

Smith struggled to a sitting position. It cost him all the strength and energy he had at the moment. After collecting himself for a minute or two, he noticed a rustling noise. His hand dropped to his belt, and he pulled his Colt. Strange, he thought, that he still had his gun.

Gritting his teeth against the pain, he turned his head to locate the source of the noise. It was his horse, grazing in the bushes. Latigo heaved a sigh of relief. He clucked to his horse, and the animal came over. Latigo used the stirrup to pull himself to a standing position. He reached for his waterskin and counted himself lucky again—it was still there. He drained the water, wondering what kind of bushwhacker would leave him with his horse and gun intact. Not to mention the water.

Smith put his foot in the stirrup, then waited for a wave of dizziness to pass. He heaved himself into the saddle, slumped over the horse's neck, and guided him back to the path he had followed in, but this time, he headed away from the canyon. Water was what he needed now, both for himself and the horse, and he was sure there was a stream down there in the canyon. Why would they hold their horses down there otherwise?

The trouble was, there would have to be a guard or two posted to guard the horses. Smith was in no shape to face up to anybody. He had crossed a stream on the way up here from the horse races. He struggled to remember how far back down the trail that was. He stayed down, slumped over the saddle, rousing himself just enough to urge the horse on when the animal stopped to graze.

Evening shadows were falling across the trail when he heard the burble of a running stream. When they reached the water, Lat guided his horse down the trail and out of sight in the bushes. He fought the pain and nausea as he tethered the horse and pulled his Winchester from the saddle. Then he walked back to the stream, set the rifle down, and laid on his belly, splashing water on his face and the wound on his neck. He cupped his hands and drank deeply, then went back to lead his horse to the water.

Smith picked up his rifle and staggered over to the horse, plunging one hand into the saddlebag, looking for food. He came up with two small pieces of beef jerky, which he devoured on the spot. He followed the stream for several feet, scouting for deer tracks. When he couldn't find any fresh tracks, he moved away from the stream and slightly uphill.

Settling down into a thicket overlooking the stream, Smith sighted down the barrel of his rifle. He glanced overhead—maybe a deer would come to find water as it got closer to sundown. He leaned back against an elm tree and waited. Somewhere along the way, he dozed off to sleep.

Lat Smith sensed it was shortly before dawn when he woke up. Nothing was moving—it was an absolutely still morning except for the slight rustle of leaves from a northerly breeze. His Winchester had slipped down to the ground beside him. Smith picked it up and watched the stream as gray light began to filter through the leaves.

When a small four-point buck came to the stream to drink, Smith dropped him with the first shot. He pulled his knife from a loop in his belt and moved down toward the deer. His spirits rose. He now had food, water, and a place to rest while he recovered.

Two days later, he left his camping spot. One shirt sleeve now made a bandage around his head. The pain and dizziness had passed. Smith decided to return to Fredericksburg, where he would plan what to do next.

———————

Things had been quiet around town for a few days, and that's the way I liked them. I hadn't seen anything of Buster or any of his crew. Without a saloon to operate, they'd probably just moved on. That's what I was thinking when I kicked him out of town. No point in staying around if there's no money.

I was walking down to meet Norah at the café when I looked up to see somebody with a bloody bandage wrapped around his head. He was staggering down off his horse in front of Doc Freeman's office. I couldn't get a good enough look at who it was, so I stuck my head in the café just long enough to tell Norah I'd be back in a few minutes.

I pushed into the doc's office and watched while he unwound the bandage. It was Latigo Smith, the guy who had tipped me off that I was gonna get bushwhacked at the saloon. He looked at me, then looked away. It wasn't friendly or unfriendly. I just couldn't figure that guy out.

Doc Freeman looked my way and snorted. "This ain't more of your work here, is it?" he barked.

"C'mon, Doc," I huffed. "You know the bouncer picked that fight."

"Yep," Doc agreed. "You sure enough left him all stove up, though." He wagged a finger at me. "Busted nose, two teeth missing, two busted ribs and a knot on his noggin the size of an egg."

"It was him or me," I said. I looked over at Latigo Smith. "I'll wait," I said, "until the doc's done with you. I'll be outside."

I took myself outside and parked it on a bench. Latigo Smith came out about ten minutes later. "Doc says I'll live," he said. "I guess you wanna know how this happened, huh, Sheriff?"

"I do," I said. "I thought I'd run the troublemakers out of town."

He said nothing, so I just waited. "You did me a good turn, Lat," I reminded him. "I need to know if there's trouble in my county."

He stared down the street for a while, then turned to face me. "There's a horse race runnin' every Saturday, up near Willow Creek," he told me. "It's run by that Buster feller, his dealer, and the bouncer you busted up. Couple of other guys, just handlin' the horses. I got dry-gulched up there." He thought for a minute. "Somebody could've kilt me, easy, but he didn't. Don't know what to think of that."

I asked him questions for a few minutes. He told me about the race and following the horses and crew to the Balcones Canyon. I thought about that for a couple of minutes. The track was in my county, but Balcones Canyon wasn't. Didn't matter, I decided. I would have to check it out.

"Could you show me where to find 'em?" I asked. He said nothing. "I would make you a temporary deputy," I said. Now he stared at me.

"You'd make me a deppity?" he asked. "You don't know me, Sheriff."

"I'm thinkin' I know you well enough for this," I answered. "Plus, it's just temporary."

He kept staring. "I been on both sides of the law," he said shortly.

"Lots of folks have, out here in the west," I said. "Sometimes a feller gets in a bad spot. It don't mean he's a bad man. I reckon I would trust you to do this."

He opened his mouth and closed it a couple times without saying anything. I stood and patted his shoulder. "You just think on it," I said. "You know where my office is."

I went back to the café, found Norah, and told her about my talk with Lat Smith.

She listened all the way through and thought it over. "What makes you think you can trust him?" she asked.

"For one, he saved my bacon back there at the saloon," I said. "It's a hunch, but I think I have pretty good hunches about people."

She reached across the table and patted my hand. "Yes, you do," she said.

———

King Simms crossed Canal Street, thinking this must be the widest street he had ever seen. He paused and looked off to his right—he was only two or three blocks from the gulf. Somebody driving a cart yelled at him, and Simms guessed he had just been cursed in French. He raised a fist in the air and shook it, which produced another volley of words that sounded French.

Simms ignored the cart driver, but turned partly and parked one hand on the Colt that was turned toward the street. The yelling died out. Simms grinned to himself. Funny, he thought, how many arguments he had settled with his double-tied-down Colts. He reminded himself to go easy for a while here in New Orleans. The sheriff of whatever parish he was in right now might come down pretty hard on shootings.

The sign on the building in front of him was what Simms had been looking for. The saloon was called the Aces High Saloon. A sign stuck in the window promised fair, legal poker games every night. King had been told this was the saloon belonging to Jack Davis. According to the old drunk in Arkansas, Jack Davis had ridden with Sam Bass. Davis, Simms reasoned, might just know something about what became of Sam Bass's gold from the Nebraska train robbery.

Simms pushed through the doors and stopped to let his eyes adjust to the dim light. He checked the watch in his pocket—three o'clock in the afternoon. He had timed it to be late enough that he hoped Davis would be in here, but early enough that Davis wouldn't be too busy. Simms hoped to get himself hired at this saloon. It would take a while to find out anything about the gold. He could work at the place meanwhile.

Running a poker game, that's how Simms hoped to go

to work for Davis. Before his cattle thieving days, Simms had considered himself the best card sharp a man could find in Hell's Half Acre, back in Ft. Worth. He was a master of the bottom deal, the ace-up-the-sleeve, and the marked card. He would play the game honest here, though, at least until he had the trust of Jack Davis. Just a little information, that's all he was after.

Simms looked around the room. He could see things more clearly now. There was a game of cards going on in the corner, there were two or three customers at tables, and another two at the plank bar that ran down the side of the room. There was a bartender back there polishing some glasses. Simms gave him a sharp glance. This guy was too old to be Jack Davis. He would ask for Davis at the bar.

Simms stepped to the bar and ordered a whiskey. He tossed it down when it came, telling himself he couldn't spit it out in here, no matter how bad it was. To his surprise, the whiskey was good. He ordered another.

When the bartender brought the second glass, Simms asked if this was Jack Davis's saloon.

The man gave him a sharp glance while he polished the bar with a towel, then nodded. "It is," he said shortly.

Simms nodded. "I been lookin' for some work," he explained. I can serve up drinks, run card games, anything he might need. Is Jack Davis here?"

The bartender polished for a while longer, giving Simms another hard look or two, then made up his mind. He pointed at the card game going on in the corner. "Over there," he muttered. "Jack Davis is the dealer."

King picked up his second glass of whiskey and drifted toward the poker game. He stopped behind an empty chair and waited to catch the dealer's attention.

Jack Davis, a sharp-eyed, husky man in his mid-thirties, pointed at the chair and nodded. Simms took a seat.

For the next thirty minutes, Simms said little, playing an honest game and losing a little money on purpose. He kept an eye on the dealer, and to his surprise, Davis was running an honest game. Simms played for another half hour, getting a little more aggressive and winning back what he had lost. When he was up ten dollars for the game, he cashed in and moved back to the bar.

When the game ended about two whiskeys later, Jack Davis moved over behind the bar, taking some orders and cleaning up. King Simms decided this was his chance. "Mr. Davis," he began.

Davis cast a quick glance in his direction, then removed the cigar from his mouth. "Jack," he grunted.

"Jack," Simms corrected. "I've worked in saloons since I was just a pup, and I'm hopin' you might have something for me here. I see you been runnin' your own card game. I could do that for ya, or serve drinks or whatever you need."

Davis ran his eyes up and down Simms, resting them briefly on the double-tied-down Colts. "Where you from?" he demanded. "What's yer name?"

"Simms," he said, answering the second question first. "King Simms. From Texas. Just got in town this mornin'."

Davis glanced at the guns again. "You always wear 'em double-tied-down?" he asked.

"Always do." Simms nodded. "Just to defend myself, mind you. There's bad folks out there. Sometimes a man has to defend himself."

Davis shoved the cigar back in his mouth and nodded.

"I'll give you a try," he said. "I know you can play poker. Ever dealt?"

Simms nodded. "Done it a lot," he agreed. "I always run a fair game," he added. "You could ask anybody who knows me back in Texas."

"Don't know nobody back in Texas," Davis lied. He pulled the cigar and blew a cloud of smoke at the ceiling. "Okay, I'll give you a try," he said. "Be here at twelve o'clock noon tomorrow. We close at one a.m." He stepped from behind the bar and disappeared into the back without waiting for an answer.

Simms left the Aces High, turned, and walked two blocks to the French Quarter. He planned to make some good money on poker while he was here, but he would do it in some different saloons here in the Quarter. He would keep it clean at the Aces High. At least, he decided, for a while.

He was really looking for a card game where he could make some money, but he detoured into a bakery there on Canal Street. He had to admit, the bakeries in New Orleans were the best of anyplace he had ever been to.

CHAPTER 7

DEPUTY LATIGO

I was already sorry I'd offered to buy breakfast at the café for Latigo Smith. I had thought my old deputy, Hostler, could shovel down the groceries, but he couldn't hold a candle to this guy. It might be a little dangerous, I thought, to ask questions with all that food going down his gullet, but I had to try.

"Uh, Lat, what did you find to eat out there at the canyon? After you got shot, I mean?" I ducked a little sideways after I asked. I didn't wanna get sprayed when he started talking.

I was relieved when he swallowed first and came up for air. "Shot me a deer and had some of that deer meat," he said, reaching for his coffee. "Backstrap, mostly. Found me a few berries, too." The server brought a second breakfast, and he reached for his fork again.

I pointed at the furrow on the side of his head. Doc Freeman had wrapped it up in a fresh bandage. "How's the head?" I asked. "Did Doc say how long before you could be up and around again?" I started to say that clearly nothing had affected his appetite, but I needed him to come out to the canyon as my deputy.

"Doc says I got the hardest head he's ever seen," Lat told me. "Said it's even harder than your'n." He grinned a little and went after the fresh order of bacon. "Told me don't lift anything too heavy and said not to get shot again for a few days. I figger I'm good to go."

Well, that sounded like the doc I knew. I waited for him to clear his plate. I'm thinking that took about a minute, but it might have been two.

He knew where I was headed. "You still wanna know if I'll be your deppity and go after the outlaws up there in the canyon, right?" he asked.

I nodded.

"I'll do it," he said, pushing his plate aside and reaching for his coffee.

"Good." I thought for a second and looked at him curiously. "You didn't sound too sure at all yesterday," I reminded him. "What made you decide?"

He stopped with the coffee cup halfway to his mouth and looked at me over the top of it. "One thing," he said, "is I guarded some gold shipments up Colorado way. I got me a powerful dislike for anybody that'll take a potshot at folks from behind trees and logs and such. That's what these folks did."

He took a gulp of the coffee and set the cup down. "Other thing is, you trusted me," he said. "Not a lot of folks have done that in my life."

I nodded. "I trust what my gut tells me," I said. "There's one other thing I want to ask though. You said you've been on both sides of the law. When were you on the other side?"

He stared at the tabletop, then looked up. "I left home

at sixteen," he said. "Didn't know nothin' I needed to know. Jest thought I knew everything already. I got pretty hungry. Stole me some food outta a few gardens and some fruit off people's trees. Even took a hoss, rode to the next town, then turned him loose. The law was lookin' for me for a while after I took the hoss. I got away, didn't never steal a hoss again."

"Fair enough," I said. "Sounds like those days are over." I changed the subject. "When we get out there to those races," I said, "and maybe follow those folks to the canyon, how many shooters are we gonna be dealing with? Guys that can likely really handle a gun?"

Lat Smith leaned back and thought that one over. "Three," he said. "The card dealer might shoot from behind some cover, and the bouncer just wants to use his fists. I don't count them. Both hoss handlers carry a Colt, and I think they can use 'em. Not real dangerous, I'd guess, but I wouldn't count 'em out."

I waited. "Then there's Buster, the guy that runs things," Smith said. "He didn't wear a smokewagon when he was in the bar, but he does out there at the races and in the canyon. I'm guessin' he's pretty good with it. Likes other folks to get their hands dirty instead of him, but you'd want to think twice before you call him out."

"So," I said. "Three shooters. I'm thinkin' we need three guns and a little surprise on our side to have 'em covered."

Just then, Boone came in, spotted us, walked over, and pulled up a chair. "What's for breakfast?" he asked. "The missus only made me one breakfast before I come to town."

"You're just in time," I said. He looked hopeful.

"Nope, you got to buy your own breakfast," I told him. "But we could use your help."

———————

Frank Jackson reached New Orleans, with nobody following him, at least as far as he could tell. Spending most of the last year robbing trains with Sam Bass had left him pretty jumpy. Seeing a badge near the place where Sam said he had left the money had convinced him to move on, but now he was having second thoughts.

Jack Davis had been with Sam for a short while after coming back from the Nebraska train robbery, but then he'd disappeared. Sam had thought maybe Jack Davis would wind up in New Orleans, and now Frank had found him. He stared up at the sign for the Aces High Saloon and wondered if Jack would recognize him. Time to find out.

He pushed through the doors and saw Jack Davis right away, pouring a drink behind the bar. Davis pulled a cigar from his mouth and nodded briefly when Frank Jackson walked up. Jackson couldn't tell if Davis recognized him or not. He parked himself on a stool at the bar and ordered a whiskey, which Davis served up.

"Frank Jackson," he reminded Davis, who just nodded.

"I remember," he said shortly.

Jackson nodded. "Sam's dead," he said abruptly.

Davis studied the glowing end of his cigar, then parked it in a dish on the bar. "I heard," he said. Davis shook his head. "Sam didn't have no sense," he growled. "He should have taken that money and lit a shuck out of Texas. Had to keep robbin' trains instead."

Jackson took a sip of his whiskey. "We robbed some trains, Sam and me and some others, after you left."

"Game for idiots," Jack Davis growled. "Too many Pinks around now. Guards and such."

Jackson's brow furrowed for a moment. "Pinkertons, you mean."

"Yup." Davis glared at a man rubbing a cloth over the bar, standing close enough to hear the conversation. He pointed at a table in the middle of the room. "Guys waiting for poker over there," he barked. "Git over there and deal."

The man walked away and sat down to deal. Davis watched him suspiciously, then looked back at Frank Jackson. "Take my advice," he said. "Train robbin' days are over if you're smart. Sam and me, we just got lucky in Nebraska. Just about everbody in the gang is dead now. Railroads don't take kindly to folks stealin' their money."

Frank Jackson absorbed that information and stared into the bottom of his empty glass. Sam Bass had told him another idea about making money in Texas, but Jackson decided not to bring it up. Davis refilled his glass. "On the house, kid," he said.

"Sam told me he buried some of his gold, jest before he died," Jackson blurted. "Do you think that's true?"

Davis pulled his cigar from the dish and took a puff, staring at Frank Jackson. "Mebbe," he said finally. "Sam went to robbin' trains as soon as we got back to Texas, so I can believe he didn't spend it all." Davis shook his head. "Sam gave a lot of it away, though. Buyin' drinks for everybody in a bar and so on. Didn't have no sense about money. Mebbe he buried some of it." He gave Jackson a sharp glance. "He tell you where?"

"No," Jackson lied. "Probly ain't worth it, anyway. He

probly spent most of it, some way or another." That much, he decided, was probably true.

Jack Davis reached into his pocket and pulled out several gold coins, which he slid across the bar to Frank Jackson. "That's for watchin' out for Sam," he said. "I heard what you did for him. Stick around New Orleans for a while, figger out what you wanna do."

Jackson pocketed the money and finished his drink. "Thanks," he said simply, and walked out. Maybe, he thought, that was good advice. He knew he wasn't going back to Texas right away. Jack Davis had managed to disappear in New Orleans. A man could do worse. He turned and walked toward the French Quarter.

———

A quick glance out the door told King Simms the kid was headed toward the French Quarter. He had to get back to dealing the poker game if he wanted to keep his job with Jack Davis, and he wasn't ready to move on yet. Davis suspected him now that he'd tried to eavesdrop on that conversation, but that was all right. He had a feeling this kid headed toward the French Quarter could tell him more than Davis could anyway.

Time dragged until Davis came over to take over from King Simms. Simms knew the big money games started around ten o'clock and Davis didn't trust him yet with the big money gamblers. When he got his chance, he would take some money from those guys. For now, he gave his seat to Davis and slipped out the door, turning toward the French Quarter.

He found the kid he was looking for in the third saloon he tried in the Quarter. The kid was sitting by himself, and looked like he'd been working on the whiskey for a while, which was good. Whiskey loosened tongues.

Simms sat down at the bar next to his target and said nothing for a while. After about ten minutes, he offered to buy the next drink. The kid shrugged and nodded. "Frank Jackson," he slurred.

Simms shook his hand and waved for another round. "King Simms," he said. "From Texas."

Jackson brightened up. "Just come from Texas," he said. He opened his mouth to say something, then changed his mind.

Simms changed the subject. "Saw you in the Aces High today," he said. "Just started working there. You a friend of Jack Davis?"

Jackson nodded. "Yup. Kinda. We used to ride with the same crew." His chin slid down toward the bar. He pushed himself off the stool and moved toward the door. "Thanksh for the drink," he said.

Simms nodded. "Come and see me at the Aces High," he said. "We can have a drink and play some cards."

Jackson waved over his shoulder and wobbled out the door.

Simms watched him go, then waved for another whiskey. He had a feeling this kid knew some things that Simms could use to make money. For one thing, he knew that name. Frank Jackson had ridden with Sam Bass, was with him at the end. Simms would be patient. The kid would open up and talk before too long. Sam Bass had taken a lot of money off that train in Nebraska. Maybe some of it was still around.

———

The three of us—Latigo Smith, Boone, and I—were on our way to the homemade race track when the sun came up. I wanted to be there and in place before the races got started. The track was in my county, but Balcones Canyon wasn't. That was one reason for the early start.

The other reason was that guy Buster. He was a canny one, I had to admit. He was the kind of guy who always had an ace up his sleeve. Always had more than one plan. He had it in for me, too. He would want to stretch my hide if he could. He had set up one ambush already. I had to keep that in mind.

Of course, there's always something you don't figure on that comes up. My old captain back at the fort in New Mexico, he talked about plans of mice and men. That never made much sense to me. I've never seen a mouse make a plan myself. I knew what he meant though.

Today, for instance, we were out to the edge of town when we ran into Miss Clarabelle, out walking her dog. Miss Clarabelle never missed a chance to tell me about the evils of drinking and how I needed to do something about it. Explaining the law to her didn't slow her down at all.

Today, though, she had to tell me how she'd heard about me closing down Buster's Saloon, over there on Main Street. Turns out she was plumb proud of me for doing that, and she expected me to close down the other three saloons.

I couldn't close down the other three, of course, but I saw no reason to interrupt her when she had a full head of steam. She was mostly happy, so I was ready to just wait her out and go my way. It was working, too, because she had let go of my sleeve and taken a step back or two. Her nasty little dog had quit nipping at my horse's feet.

Then she turned toward Boone and pointed a finger at him. "What about YOU, Mr. Boone?" she hollered. "You agree with me about the evils of demon rum, don't you?"

I closed my eyes and hoped for the best. Boone looked at her, cocked his head to the side, leaned over the saddle and spat. It missed her dog, but not by much.

"Certainly, Miss Clarabelle," Boone said solemnly. "I can't abide that nasty rum." He paused and stared down the road. "I'm a whiskey man, myself," he said. "Much better than that demon rum."

Well, that set her off. I'd have moved on out and promised to talk to her later, except she had hold of my sleeve again. I couldn't just drag her down the road. What I'm saying is, we lost about half an hour before we got past Miss Clarabelle.

What with the early start and the overcast day, the light wasn't as good, and Lat missed the trail, such as it was, a time or two. We had to backtrack and lost more time. We still got to the racetrack before they got started, but Buster's people were there and setting up.

We had come in from the west side, so we spread out and watched while they got things ready. Two rough-looking characters packing pistols on their hips herded five horses into a little makeshift corral. The dealer, the guy I'd called Magic Fingers and busted over the head a little while back, was walking around the track, tossing away rocks and sticks and such.

Muscles sat himself down behind a little board stretched atop a couple of big rocks. That was where folks placed their bets, it looked like. I put the field glasses on Muscles for a minute and grinned to myself. He had some nasty yellow-colored bruises on his face, still healing up. I figured he was still working out how to eat with those missing teeth. He was another one who had it in for me.

I swung the field glasses back and forth. The one I couldn't see was Buster, and he was the one I really had to find. Forty-five minutes went by and some people started arriving. They left their horses in the corral and went to talk to Muscles. Some money changed hands.

I swung the field glasses up a little to look at the ground to the east of the track. There was a gradual rise to a bluff that ran for maybe one hundred yards on that side. That troubled me. That was a natural defensive position, and I was afraid Buster was up there, commanding an excellent field of fire.

I eased my way out of my position and worked my way around to find Latigo and Boone. I found Boone first, then Lat cat-footed over to join us.

"I can't find Buster," I said. "Either of you seen him?"

They both shook their heads. "Mebbe he just skedaddled out of yore county, like you told him to do," Boone offered.

I shook my head slowly. "That's not like him, I don't think," I said after a while. "He might get more careful, but it doesn't sound like him to turn tail and run." I looked up at that ridge on the east side. "If I had to guess," I said, "he's up there, forted-up and watchin'."

I glanced over at Latigo. "He knows somebody trailed them up to the canyon last time," I reminded him. "We already know from the dust-up there at the saloon that he'll let his boys take the fall for him if he can."

Nobody disagreed with that. We watched them as the horses lined up for the first race. Magic Fingers fired a gun to start the race. A skinny gray mustang won.

Muscles paid out some money, but I was pretty sure Buster and his boys kept most of it.

I pointed at the makeshift corral, where the two horse handlers were taking horses back and forth. "Lat," I said, "can you work your way over to that corral and get the drop on those two?" He nodded. "They're not thinkin' about a fair fight," I said. "You know that from last week. Do what you have to do."

"Boone," I said, "that leaves you with Magic Fingers and Muscles. I don't think Muscles is armed, but the other one ain't above a hideout gun, I'm thinking."

"Got it," Boone said. "You goin' up to that ridge to look for Buster?"

"I am," I told him. "Just let them finish the races now, move in on them after they're done and packing it up down there. If Buster's up there on that ridge, he won't be gettin' any shots off in your direction."

I eased away from them and circled the track. I was raised by Comanches, so I knew how to use cover and stay quiet out there. If Buster was there, I would see him before he saw me.

CHAPTER 8

A DAY AT THE RACES

I had to pull back into the cover of the oak and pecan trees before circling around Buster's homemade horse track. They had felled some trees to clear the area surrounding the track, and I didn't feel like showing myself in Buster's sights while I circled. I had no doubt he would pull the trigger if he could get a bead on me.

When I reached the north side of the racing oval, still hanging back to take advantage of the cover, I pulled out my field glasses. Stopping in the shade of a big live oak tree, I scanned the eastern slope in front of me. There was a slow rise broken by occasional brush and trees, stopped by a limestone ridge running north–south for about one hundred yards. Then the gradual rise continued again, cresting a hill that commanded a good view of the track and the surrounding grounds. If it were me out there, I would take a position up at the top.

I swung the field glasses back and forth uneasily, letting them pause on the limestone ridge. It offered a good field of fire and an easier, shorter path to the trails leading out of here, but I didn't trust it. My days in the army told me that higher ground was always better, and there was a crest above that ridge.

I put the field glasses away and led Hank forward on foot, still staying back where the tree line was thicker. If Buster was out there, he had to be north of me, but I wanted to climb up most of that rise before I moved in toward him. Stopping to scan every few yards, something caught my eye on that limestone ridge, and I pulled up again to use the field glasses.

There appeared to be a rifle barrel lying across the ridge! I focused in and steadied myself against a tree while I studied it. Something narrow and straight lay across the ridge, with a blanket or something tossed over most of the barrel. I moved the glasses to the right to see a figure hunched behind the ridge. There was a hat, I could see that clearly. A blanket or serape covered the figure kneeling there. There was something unnatural about the whole setup, but I couldn't quite put my finger on it.

Several seconds dragged by, then a minute or two. That figure hunching behind the ridge hadn't moved. That seemed a little strange—I would have expected him to shift a little. I swung the glasses back to the left and studied where the barrel protruded from the blanket. There was no shine reflecting off the barrel, even though an inch of it was in the sun.

It was a setup! He had rigged up a dummy in a serape, hunched over a straight stick. If I showed myself by moving in or gave away my position by firing at it, no doubt, Buster would take me out from the top of the hill. I grinned to myself a little. He didn't know what an old campaigner he was dealing with here.

The trees thinned out toward the top of the hill, so I

left Hank tied up and worked my way to the crest. I then crawled slightly over the other side before I worked my way north, keeping my eyes peeled and my ears perked up for any sign of Buster. The cover was a little scarce now, but I couldn't take too much time. My job was to cover Latigo and Boone when they moved in down below. I had to be in place when they did.

He had his back to me when I spotted him. He was hunkered down at the top of the hill, watching that dummy he had set up to draw me in. He might know his way around saloons, I thought, but he was a bit of a tenderfoot to have his back to me. He should have guessed I would circle around and come in on him from this side. He looked like a sitting duck now.

I cat-footed it to about thirty yards away from him and settled down behind a small boulder at the top of the hill. I squatted down and planted myself with my Winchester laid across the top of the boulder. The footing was a bit dicey there at the top of the hill, but I had a good position and view of Buster. It turned out that the footing was a little worse than I thought. It almost cost me.

I'd gotten there just in time, I could see that. No sooner had I settled down when I saw him shift his attention from the dummy on the limestone ridge to the track down below. Boone and Latigo must be moving in, I figured. When I saw Buster shift his rifle and come up a little for a shot down toward the track, I gave him his one and only chance to change his mind.

———

Boone and Latigo Smith moved slowly toward what Buster's crew was using for a betting table. Boone and Lat had both stowed their Winchesters in their scabbards—they needed a little surprise on their side when the odds were two against one for both of them. Carrying rifles would draw too much attention. Boone slowed down while Latigo prepared to circle the table and approach the makeshift corral. A horse race in progress had everybody's attention.

The horses were neck-and-neck and rounding the bend, then the race finished, followed by two rifle shots sounding from the ridge. All eyes turned up the hill, searching for the source of those shots. Boone took two or three quick steps and covered Muscles with his Colt. "Hands on the table," he snarled. Muscles did so and sat stock-still. The dealer, though, looked a little fidgety.

"Hands up," Boone barked. The dealer was hovering to Muscles's right. Reaching with his left hand, Boone pointed at Latigo Smith. "Deputy Marshall over there," he shouted. "Everybody, stand right where you're at. Anybody got any ideas about fetching his iron, you'll have extry holes in you. Don't nobody need that."

The dealer's hands were dropping. Boone swung to cover him. "Hands!" he shouted.

Boone saw the dealer's hands come up, but the right one wasn't empty. *Hideout gun!* Boone's brain screamed, and he fired just once.

Latigo Smith sprinted for the corral as Boone moved to look at the dealer. He hadn't moved since he dropped, so Boone circled to keep Muscles covered while keeping the track in front of him.

There were two horse handlers/gun hands in the corral as Lat closed in. The first moved toward a

Winchester propped up against the railing. Lat Smith put a bullet at his feet and the man froze.

"Hands in the air," Lat shouted. Gunshots echoed behind him. The first man froze as ordered. The second, partially screened by a post, clawed at his pistol as he dropped to one knee. Lat's first shot caught him in the shoulder and he spun away, still trying to clear his gun. The second shot drilled him through the heart. He sprawled on the ground inside the corral. A strange silence fell over the racetrack.

A quick glance told Latigo there was no point in inspecting the man on the ground. He marched the second horse handler out toward the track, having barked at the man to empty his holster. A brief look at his friend told the second horse handler he needed to do just that. He walked quietly in front of Lat Smith.

Boone nudged the dealer on the ground, there was no response. He tossed a pair of handcuffs at Muscles. "Put those on," he ordered. Lat Smith marched the second horse handler out of the corral and held his gun on the crowd while Boone tied the man's hands behind his back.

"Races are over," Boone barked. "Everybody get the hosses he come in with and move out." Within ten minutes, the racetrack had emptied except for Boone, Lat Smith, and the two prisoners.

Boone glanced at the two dead men. "Ain't got no shovel," he grumbled. He glanced up toward the ridge. They'd heard nothing else since the two gunshots.

Boone glanced over at Lat Smith. "I kin keep these two varmints quiet," he offered. "Mebbe you need to check on Pike. Awful quiet up there."

Lat nodded, then walked over to mount his horse. He squinted at the hillside in front of him. No telling if there was a wounded man up there, and it might not be Pike Hardy. He reined his horse to the right and prepared to take the long way up the ridge, checking for tracks as he went.

When Buster moved and swung that rifle, I had to stop him from getting a bead on Boone and Lat Smith.

"Buster!" I boomed. "You're in my sights right now. Drop the rifle!"

He froze where he was, then shrugged. It looked like he was dropping the rifle, but then he grabbed it, swung it toward me, and dove sideways. A wild shot went over my head, but he was gathering himself for another, and now he could see my position.

I shifted and moved my Winchester, but there was loose dirt under my left foot. I slid as I triggered the shot. I knew I'd hit him—I could see him spin, but his second shot was so close there were rock fragments flying in front of me. I ducked, then my foot went out from under me and I rolled down the hill.

I tried to hold on to my Winchester, but I came up against a cedar tree and got the wind knocked plumb out of me. I rolled up and sucked wind, trying to find my Winchester. It was down the hill, maybe fifteen feet below me. I half-slid, half-rolled down to it, grabbing it and rolling over to look up the hill.

I felt relief flood through me when I couldn't see him. I crawled up to the shelter of the tree that had stopped my fall, taking glances around it from time to time. I tried to locate Buster while I let my breathing come back to normal.

Finally, I climbed to my feet and started up the hill, Winchester at the ready. I crested the rise and looked over toward where he had been. He was gone. I moved down to his position—there was blood there, a lot of it. There was a trail of blood leading away that ended near an oak tree. Horse tracks led down and away from there.

It was clear he'd been able to mount up and ride out. I heaved a sigh of frustration and began walking back to the spot where I had tethered Hank. I had to find Buster before the trail went cold on me.

————

Three days passed before Frank Jackson drifted back into the Aces High Saloon. King Simms, dealing poker at the time as he usually was, had almost given up on talking to Jackson again. Simms was getting more and more curious about that Nebraska gold Sam Bass might have left behind. That was easier money than rustling cows out of Mexico like his last setup, which had been pretty easy, he had to admit.

Simms couldn't call a halt to the game, like he wanted to, and go over to loosen Jackson's tongue with whiskey. Not with Jack Davis watching him like a hawk. He had to settle for keeping one eye on Jackson, over at the bar, while the poker game thinned out a little. Simms bottom-dealt a few times to encourage the players to move on.

There were two other players left at the table when Jackson moved over to join the game. Simms nodded at him. He was pretty sure Jackson remembered him, even though Jackson had been pretty drunk that night in the French Quarter.

One player dropped out and Simms watched for a

chance to drive the other out of the game. He waited for the man to bet heavily against Jackson, then Simms dealt him a deuce off the bottom. The man cursed under his breath, took the money, and left the game, then stalked out of the saloon. He stopped at the door to glare at Simms, who held the man's gaze. Simms's hand dropped to his hip. The man moved on.

Simms pointed at the bar and motioned to Frank Jackson. "Buy you a drink?" he offered.

Jack Davis watched while Simms rose from the poker table, then looked around and shrugged. There was nobody else playing cards at the moment.

Davis served them both a whiskey when they took stools near the bar, then disappeared into the back.

Simms decided to come straight to the point. Coming at things sideways wasn't his way of doing things, and who knew when Jackson might show up in the saloon again? "I know you rode with Sam Bass," he blurted.

Jackson stopped with the whiskey glass halfway to his mouth, then stared at Simms with narrowed eyes.

"What makes you think that?" he demanded.

Simms shrugged. "Your name has gotten around," he mumbled. "Everbody knows you stayed with Bass till the end. Showed you got a lot of sand. Plus, you said you rode with Jack Davis for a while. Lots of folks know Davis rode with Sam Bass." He tipped his whiskey back and waited.

The suspicion faded from Jackson's eyes and he slowly relaxed, then tipped back his drink. "Sam Bass was a good partner," he snarled. "He didn't deserve to git shot up by no Texas Rangers."

Simms waved for more whiskey. "Were you with him

in Nebraska?" he asked, even though he knew the answer already.

"Nope," came the quick reply. "Robbed a couple of trains with him in Texas, but I wasn't with those boys in Nebraska." He pointed toward the back room. "Davis was with him," he said. He looked around the bar and waved. Simms got the point. That's how Davis had paid for this saloon.

"Some folks say Sam didn't spend all that gold afore he died," Simms ventured. "Mebbe there's some it left somewhere."

Frank Jackson's head came up and whipped around. He drained another whiskey and relaxed. "I dunno about that," he said. His head slumped a little.

Simms decided that was a lie, but he changed the subject. Plenty of time to come back and talk about the gold later. "Robbed a couple of trains with him, though?" he asked, pretending to be impressed.

"Yup." Jackson frowned down at the bar. "Sam says there ain't no money in train robbery no more," he said, slurring slightly. "So does Davis." He shook his head sorrowfully. He glanced around the room, then dropped his voice to a whisper.

"Stagecoaches, thatsh what Sam wanted to do next," he slurred. He stared into the bottom of his empty glass.

Simms waved for another, but couldn't keep the doubt out of his voice. "Stagecoaches?" he asked, eyebrows shooting up. "Stagecoaches are dyin' out. Trains been takin' their place. Who'd want to rob a stagecoach anymore?"

"San Antonio to El Paso stage. Thatsh the one you kin still rob." Jackson stared around the room again, whispering in a still softer voice and getting drunker by the minute. "There's still money in that one, Sam said. No trains down there yet. Runs clear across the south of Texas, it does. Some folks are goin' clear to Californy. Carryin' money, Sam says."

Simms racked his brains, remembering his time in South Texas. He'd been down near the border, but still... He knew there was a stage line all right, but remembered army bases and forts being built to protect it. "Forts," he told Jackson. "Army bases all over the place. How you gonna rob that?" he asked scornfully.

Jackson's chin rested on the bar. He pawed to pick up his whiskey glass. "Out west," he explained, still in a whisper. "Thatsh where they built them forts. To protect against Injuns an' such. You got to hit it a lot closer in— close to San Antonio. Thatsh where you hold up that stage. Lotsh of money on it, Sam said."

Simms turned that one over in his head. It was possible the kid knew what he was talking about. Simms glanced over at Jackson, who was fading out fast. There wasn't much time left for this talk. He would have to pick it up later. Davis would come back out and bark at him to get another game going.

Simms nudged Jackson, who propped himself up and stared owlishly at Simms. "We got to talk about this some more," Simms said. "Two days from now, about eight o'clock," he said. That would be his night off. He could make some plans by then. "Over in the French Quarter, where we were before."

Simms nudged at Jackson again, who waved a head in the air. "Right," he mumbled. "Two nights from tonight."

Simms looked around—there were gamblers gathering around the table over there. By the time Davis came through the back door and glared at him, he was already moving in that direction.

"Gentlemen," Simms said, pointing at the table. They circled the table and sat down.

These were some of the bigger gamblers. Davis was starting to trust him more with the money games. Things were coming together. He might need a stake for this stagecoach idea. He could take it from these guys. He just had to plan it right. New Orleans would be too hot for him if he robbed this set of gamblers. Time to get back to Texas after that.

CHAPTER 9

THE BASS PLAN

I wove a path between the trees on the way back to my horse. I knew my quarry could still be up on that hill-crest, ready to fire at me. I reached Hank, untethered him, and swung into the saddle. I could feel the sting in my face for the first time. When I brushed at it with my sleeve, it came away bloody. Rock chips. No time to worry about that now.

Swinging the horse around, I retraced my steps to the place where Buster's bloody trail ended and the horse tracks began. They led straight down the hill and toward town—Willow Creek. He wasn't wasting any time or trying to cover his tracks. When I leaned over to check the ground, I could see drops of blood on the grass. He'd been hit pretty hard.

I wove around on a dim trail, in and out through the trees, still wary that Buster had enough left in him to set up an ambush for me. I eased Hank around the bends and kept an eye out for a rise in the trail where he could lie in wait for me.

Rounding a bend and entering a straight stretch on

the trail, it startled me to see a horse grazing at the side of the trail. His saddle was still on him, and his reins were trailing in the grass and brush. I pulled up and took out my field glasses—now I could see a shape lying on the other side of the horse.

Pulling the Winchester from the scabbard, I rode in slowly, keeping the rifle trained on the figure in the grass. I dismounted and walked in, still alert, but by the time I came around his horse and had a clear look at him, I relaxed and lowered the Winchester.

Buster was lying on his back at the side of the trail, eyes open and staring at the sky, but he couldn't see anything anymore. My shot had taken him on the right side of his chest. I wasn't sure how he had managed to come this far before falling off his horse. I knelt and closed his eyes, then led his horse over and went to pull a rope from Hank's saddle.

Buster was no lightweight, and dead bodies are heavier than you'd expect, anyway. I struggled to get him up and put him face-down over his horse. I tied his wrists and ankles underneath for the trip back to Fredericksburg.

I heard a voice and whirled around, then recognized it was Latigo Smith. He was still a little way off, but I guess he knew I'd be a little jumpy right now. He rode in slowly and eyed the dead man, slung over his horse.

"That makes three," he said.

I knew right away what he meant. "Which ones?" I asked.

Lat leaned over and spat. "The dealer—the one you called Magic Fingers—pulled a hideout gun on Boone. He's dead. Then one of the horse handlers drew on me.

That just leaves Muscles and the other horse handler. They didn't draw on us."

I nodded and led Buster's horse over to mine, tying them together. I mounted up.

"I guess Boone's got an eye on those two," I said. "Are they back at the track?"

Smith nodded and fell in behind me. It didn't take long to join up with Boone. I stared at the two prisoners and thought things over.

"Neither one of 'em drew on you boys?" I asked Boone and Latigo. They both shook their heads.

I scratched my head and thought about it. "I don't know if I want to bother bringing in two guys for helping at an illegal track," I mumbled. I looked over at the makeshift corral and decided.

"Okay," I said, "You're both more trouble than you're worth. I'm going to give both of you a better deal than you've probably got coming. Both of you get on a horse over there, and you'd better get on your own horse, not a stolen one. Once you're astride, get out of my county. If you come back, I'll make you sorry."

I nodded at Boone to take the cuffs off Muscles while I cut the ropes on the horse handler. They both headed to the corral at a trot, saddled up, and took off without looking back.

Once we'd loaded up the corpses on spare horses, there were still five horses in the corral. Too many, I decided, to bring back, with each of us leading a dead man's horse back to town.

"They got water in that corral?" I asked.

Lat Smith nodded.

"Okay, I'll come back to get 'em tomorrow. They're probably all stolen. I'll have to see if I can get 'em back to their owners." I looked at Lat. "Come with me?" I asked.

He nodded again. We set out for Fredericksburg.

King Simms made it a point to get to the saloon in the French Quarter earlier this time. He also made it a point to buy beer for Frank Jackson instead of whiskey. He needed the young man sober for this little talk. Simms wanted to loosen his tongue just enough to talk more about the stagecoach route.

When Jackson came in, he approached the table from behind and surprised Simms by pulling out a chair and dropping into it unannounced. Simms shoved a pitcher of beer and a glass at him. Jackson pulled a face, then shrugged and filled up his glass.

"What d'ya wanna talk about?" he asked.

Simms picked up a faint smell of whiskey and thought this probably wasn't Jackson's first stop tonight. Still, he seemed willing to talk.

Simms took a long pull at his beer, then launched right into it. "Tell me more about this stagecoach from San Antonio to El Paso that Sam Bass wanted to rob," he said.

Jackson shot him a sharp glance over his beer, then shrugged again and set the glass down. "First leg runs from San Antonio north and west to Fort Concho," he said. "Runs through a town called Boerne, makes a stop there, then runs west of Fredericksburg to the Fort. Hooks up with another stage line there and runs out to El Paso. One of the few lines that ain't been replaced by the railroads. Yet."

"You're sayin'," Simms interrupted, "that Bass wanted to rob it afore it gets to Fort Concho. After that, there's more forts, and army and such."

Jackson slurped loudly, put his glass down, and filled it back up. "Yup," was all he offered.

Simms scowled. "What's on that stage worth robbin' anyway? Who's on the stage? Why did Bass think it was worth robbin'?"

Jackson shot him another sharp glance. "Why?" he demanded. "You wanna rob it?"

Simms took his time answering that one. "Mebbe," he said. "Why didn't you try to rob it yourself if'n you think it's a good idea?"

Jackson shook his head. "I cain't make plans and organize folks and stuff the way Sam did," he admitted. "Might take some money to set things up, I ain't got none of that neither. Sam thought mebbe we could get away in another stagecoach. The law wouldn't think of lookin' in one of those. I ain't got money for that." He glanced away. "I just tole you about this because I thought maybe you would want to do some of that. I'm more of a guy who can handle a gun an' do what he's told."

Simms leaned back and thought things over. This might shape up the way he'd hoped. He leaned forward again and put his elbows on the table. "You didn't tell me what Bass thought was worth robbin'," he reminded Jackson.

Jackson slurped loudly and set the glass down. "Well," he said, "for starters, there's folk movin' west that got their money and valuables and such with 'em."

Simms shook his head and started to get up.

"Plus," Jackson said, "the stage brings the mail for

Fort Concho and some other forts out west. Sojers got to get paid sometimes, don't they?"

Simms sat down again, a quick smile crossing his face. He waved for another pitcher. He didn't really care if Jackson got drunk now. He'd made his decision.

"Okay," Simms said, "listen up. I'll get the money and run the gang, just like you want. You can join me. We'll split the money," he lied. "I think mebbe we only need two, but I'll get somebody else if I think we need him."

Simms paused, thinking fast. He had a poker game tonight and Jack Davis wasn't going to be in the saloon. He had to strike tonight and get out. He stopped Jackson's hand as it reached for the new pitcher.

"Listen good for just a minute, then you can have the beer," he ordered.

Jackson sat back to listen.

"I'm gonna leave New Orleans tonight," Simms told him. "I'll meet you in this town called Boerne."

Jackson nodded.

"Four days from now," Simms said.

Jackson nodded again.

Simms stood and left abruptly. Jackson was perfect, he was thinking. He would do what he was told, and Simms would put him in front of the bullets. They would pull a few robberies, then Simms would clear out. Maybe he could come back to New Orleans and open his own saloon.

Jackson watched him leave, then reached for the pitcher again. Tomorrow was soon enough to leave New Orleans. He would help Simms with a robbery or two. It would give him a chance to look for Sam's gold some more. If he found it and there was enough money, he would clear out and go back east. Nobody would be looking for him out there.

———

The poker game was shaping up just about the way King Simms wanted it. His plans were set for a return to Texas. He just needed to get himself a stake before he left, and tonight was the night. He had four players at the table with him. Three of them had played here before, and Simms had set them up for this on previous nights. He had let them win some house money and made sure the drinks kept flowing. They should be pretty easy pickings tonight. The fourth man Simms had never seen before. He'd laid a stack of money on the table, so that got him into the game. Simms figured if he could take that money before the night was over, he'd be ready to leave New Orleans. The man had a gold watch in the vest pocket, so Simms thought of him as Gold Watch for the rest of the night.

All four agreed to straight poker, which was the game Simms preferred to play. He was just about as good at cheating at draw poker, but not quite. He could control the deal a little better with straight poker. Simms was adept at shuffling some higher cards to the bottom of the deck, where he could deal them to himself. He'd found that players who were suspicious they were being cheated watched pretty carefully when he dealt to them, but not so much when he dealt to himself.

Simms also had a king in one coat pocket and a queen secreted in a vest pocket. Aces looked too suspicious, besides, Simms was pretty good at dealing those off the bottom. Just in case, he had a stacked deck in his boot he could use in a pinch.

After the first hour, they were down to three players, plus Simms. Both Simms and Gold Watch were up by about a hundred dollars. One of the original four had started with some bad luck. When it came down to just Simms and that guy still in on a hand, Simms dealt himself two aces off the bottom and finished him. That left three plus Simms.

Two more hours went by. Gold Watch had stopped drinking, and worse, when he leaned forward to collect some winnings, Simms spotted a pistol in his waistband. Simms had one himself, of course, even though the town laws prohibited concealed weapons. Shootings weren't nearly as common in New Orleans as they were in Texas and the frontier. Simms considered for the first time that he might have to draw his gun before the night was over.

Not that King Simms was worried he wouldn't come out on top. He had practiced and used that cross-draw from his waistband. That wasn't the problem. He would have to get out of town in a hurry before the law came. He began to work out an escape route in his mind.

Two hours later, Gold Watch and Simms had both folded on a hand, the remaining two kept raising until one of them went all in. Simms didn't care which one won. It was past midnight already, and this was certainly going to come down to Gold Watch and himself. The one who'd gone all in lost—that took it down to three players.

Simms steadily cheated the third player until he had about half the man's money. The man stood abruptly, cashed in with a curse, and took what he had left. Gold Watch was eyeing Simms sharply. Simms was pretty sure

Gold Watch knew he was cheating. That would make things tougher.

A quick glance at Gold Watch's stack of money told Simms there was probably about $1,500 over there—roughly the same size as Simms's stake in this game. For two hours, they played to a draw, with no significant amount of money changing hands on either side. A small crowd gathered around to watch. Simms wondered idly how these people didn't have something else to do at two o'clock in the morning.

Gold Watch had those keen eyes on Simms all the time. Simms didn't dare use the face cards he'd hidden on himself. It wasn't just Gold Watch—there was a crowd watching. Simms was determined to walk away with the money tonight, but he couldn't seem to make any progress. The more time that dragged by, the more he saw his chance slipping away. Finally, he got the break he was looking for.

Just as Simms finished shuffling, there was a crash from the bar area, where the bartender had dropped a pitcher and several glasses. A few curses followed the sound of the breaking glass. All eyes turned for just a few seconds to look at the bar. In a flash, Simms exchanged the deck he'd just shuffled for the one hidden in his boot. He dealt slowly and carefully, sensing this was the hand that could end it.

Gold Watch looked at his cards without expression—Simms knew he was looking at two pair, aces over sevens. Simms waited while Gold Watch opened with a small bid. Simms saw the bid and raised slightly, drawing him in a little at a time. Several raises later, Gold Watch pushed his pile to the middle. When it was time to show the cards, Simms laid down a full house, tens and fives.

Gold Watch shot a deadly glance across the table. He stood slowly, and Simms did the same, reaching to rake in the money from the middle of the table. He was careful to use only his left hand, his senses on high alert as Gold Watch took a step or two back.

"Cheater." It was one of the few words Simms could remember hearing from his opponent all night, and it came out as a low snarl. When Simms saw the man's hand flash toward his waistband, Simms was ready.

The cross-draw came out just the way he'd practiced it a thousand times. Simms's first shot went into Gold Watch's belly, the second went into his chest as the man staggered backward. There was no third shot. The small crowd backed away from the table, stunned and keeping their hands in sight.

Simms finished raking the money into his hat and dashed out the door. He knew he had just a few minutes to get out of New Orleans.

———

Latigo Smith stirred some sugar into his coffee at the Main Street Café in Waco and gave me an uneasy look across the table. We had dropped off the dead bodies for burial yesterday, and my jail was empty. That's the way I liked it.

I wasn't sure why Latigo was giving me the look I was getting right now, but I was real happy with his help at the racetrack, so I was pretty sure he was barking up the wrong tree. I just sat and waited while he whipped that coffee around with his spoon.

"He was fixin' to throw down on me with that rifle of

his, ya know," Smith announced. "I didn't have no choice but to stretch his hide."

So that was it. He thought I was going to tell him he had to answer to me for killing one of those stock handlers at the track.

I nodded my head up and down several times. "I know it," I agreed. "If you and Boone hadn't taken care of those boys, they'd have come after me. I asked you to come an' cover me out there, and that's what you did. Couldn't be happier."

The look on his face changed from suspicious to confused. "Okay," he said, still stirring.

"You're gonna turn that into butter if'n you keep going," I said, pointing at the coffee.

He grinned for just a second, took a big slurp, then sat back to see what I wanted.

"Jake McCabe and Boone keep reminding me I got no deputy," I said abruptly. "That, and they keep reminding me I've got some enemies out there. I thought mebbe you could see your way to helpin' me out with that problem."

His coffee stopped halfway to his mouth. He put it down, but his mouth was still wide open. Reminded me of the largemouth bass I'd caught at the property last week.

"Yore askin' me to be yore permanent deppity."

He didn't really ask the question, just said it like he couldn't quite believe it. "Why me? You still don't know much about me."

I shrugged and watched the waitress bring us breakfast. "I've seen you're a man who can handle things," I said. "I think you're a man to ride the river with. I've got a hunch I can trust you."

He shook his head for a while, then finally laughed.

He stopped and stared across the table at me again. "What enemies?" he asked.

I stared out the window. "I think Frank Jackson, from the Sam Bass Gang, might be fixin' to operate around here," I said. "And there's a guy named King Simms might show up in this county, too. I killed a partner of his a little while back. Got a bad feeling about Simms."

I explained a little more about both of them.

He shook his head for a while. "My mama used to tell me I don't have no sense sometimes," he said. "I guess this could be one of those times." He held out his hand.

I shook his hand, then reached into my shirt pocket and pushed a badge across the table. He put it on and we both dug into breakfast.

Chapter 10

Discovery!

There was an extra guest on the porch at Jake and Julia McCabe's house when Norah and I got there. Norah went on inside while I introduced my new deputy, Latigo Smith, around the group. Boone knew Lat, of course, but Jake didn't, and Jake's special guest hadn't met him.

I took a minute to say hello to Captain Leander McNelly of the Texas Rangers. Jake, Boone, and I had been on a little excursion, I guess you'd say, to No Man's Land up in the Nation. I had arrived with my troops from the fort in New Mexico just in time, and Jake and Leander still seemed plumb grateful for it.

We talked for a while about those times, plus a couple of dust-ups Jake and McNelly had been into before my time. Then McNelly surprised us by telling us he was retiring from the Texas Rangers. I guess I should say it surprised me in particular. Jake was nodding his head like he understood. I'd been hoping McNelly would be there for me if I got into a nasty scrape. The man was tougher than boot leather.

McNelly looked over at me after a minute. "I've got to warn you about a couple guys you might run into, Pike," he told me. "They're pretty salty. You've got to keep your head up." He nodded over at Lat Smith. "You'll want to remember these names too," he said.

McNelly stopped to light a cigar and looked at me again. "First name is Frank Jackson," he said. "That sound familiar?"

I nodded slowly. "There was a Ranger Ware that came by last week," I said. "He told me Jackson was a member of the Sam Bass Gang when he got shot over there at Round Rock. Ware thought Jackson might have come this way, but I've not heard anything else about it. You still think he might operate around here?"

"Yup." McNelly paused to think about it. "Ware is the one that shot Sam Bass," he started. "Nobody wants one of that Bass Gang paintin' a target on his back, so we've kept that part quiet. Thing is, Bass had a few ties in that area, includin' an old boy who spends most of his time in the saloon over there. Name of Dunwiddie. Dunwiddie don't like talking to Rangers or sheriffs. He knows more about what Bass was doin' around here than anybody. And Frank Jackson was the last one to see Sam Bass alive.

McNelly looked back over at Lat Smith. "It seems to me," he said, "that if a brand-new deputy that nobody knows is a deputy over there in Round Rock, he could find Dunwiddie. And that old boy might get downright talkative if he took a shine to you. Might help you trace Frank Jackson."

Well, that made sense. I looked over at Lat, who nodded. "I can leave in the mornin'," he said. "I'll find this Dunwiddie and grease his throat a time or two."

McNelly looked satisfied, then looked back at me. "The other name I think you should keep track of," he said, "is King Simms. We busted up his cattle rustling operation in Mexico, I'm sure you ain't forgettin' that. I don't think he was too fond of his partner, but you did kill that partner when he drew down on you."

I was a little puzzled now. You can usually tell when my forehead gets all wrinkled up and I move my mouth without saying much. "King Simms never saw me, and I didn't see him," I reminded McNelly. "He cleared out before we breached that fortress of his. I don't even know if he's ever heard of me."

McNelly flicked some ash from his cigar over the railing, then put his boots up. "He knows," McNelly said. "I made it a point to track him after we busted up that operation. I don't like leavin' any loose ends out there, and Simms is a big loose end."

The cigar left a little trail of sparks when McNelly waved it around in the growing darkness on the porch. "Simms went north to Dallas and Fort Worth for a while. I tracked him to the White Elephant Saloon in Hell's Half Acre. He did some talkin'. He wants to get even with you and me. So yeah, he found out about you, Pike."

McNelly put his boots down and leaned forward. "He's left Texas, I'm pretty sure. At least for now. Dunno where he is right this minute, but deep down, I'm sure he's gonna come back to Texas. He's an outlaw through and through, and he's a Texas boy. He'll be back."

Norah came out to tell us dinner was on the table, and we all stood and moved to the door. McNelly placed a hand on my shoulder and left me with one last thought. "Some men just carry a grudge, Pike," he told me. "That's something I've seen a lot of in my time with the Rangers. I think King Simms is one of them."

———

I sat on the porch after dinner. Jake and Boone stayed inside with the ladies while I thought things over. Lat Smith came out and paused on the porch steps. "I can ride for Round Rock tomorrow," he said. "You got somethin' else you need me to do here?"

I waved a hand in the air. "No," I said. "I'd like you to get over to Round Rock and see if this Dunwiddie guy can get his tongue loosened a little. I don't want no surprises if Frank Jackson is operating in my county."

I watched as Lat mounted up and rode out. It still seemed a little unlikely to me that King Simms knew anything about me and wanted to carry a grudge. I had to remember, though, Leander McNelly was one of the best, and he'd been at it a lot longer than I. I'd best watch out.

I stood and walked back inside to see if Norah was ready to go. It was a long ride to our property in Stonewall, and I sure wasn't going to let her ride it alone after dark. Frank Jackson or no Frank Jackson. And King Simms, I reminded myself. I couldn't forget about him.

———

Frank Jackson pushed through the doors at the Suds Saloon in Round Rock. He had vowed never to come back here—it was too dangerous. Greed won out. He had to admit—greed usually won out. He might have a deal with this King Simms to rob a stagecoach, but if he could find Sam Bass's money, that was faster and less dangerous. Except for this first part about showing up in Round Rock again. Maybe things had settled down by now.

Dunwiddie was sitting in his usual spot at a table by the window. He was by himself this time. Jackson had seen Dunwiddie with Sam Bass over there a few times. Jackson figured it was worth his while to stop off on his way to meet up with Simms in the town of Boerne. Maybe Bass had told this guy Dunwiddie something. They had seemed to know each other.

Jackson pulled out a chair and sat down abruptly across the table from Dunwiddie. The old man looked up and lurched a little. Those eyes were clear, though— Jackson had the feeling the old man kept a clear head and just pretended to be drunk. A man could learn a lot that way. Maybe get some free drinks, too.

Dunwiddie watched him, then pushed an empty whiskey glass to the center of the table. Jackson shook his head.

"Beer," Jackson said. "That's all I'm buyin'."

Dunwiddie shrugged. "Better'n nuthin'," he agreed.

The server came and left. Jackson poured them both a glass, then settled back. Dunwiddie slurped loudly at the beer, but those eyes peering at him over the top of the glass were sharp.

"Sam Bass," Jackson said suddenly. "You knew him."

The old man shrugged and stared out the window. "Knowed him a little when he were a boy. Afore he got hisself in so much trouble." He paused and looked at Jackson. "Mebbe Sam come in and talked a little the night before he got shot." Dunwiddie poured another beer. "I've seen you before, too," he said. "You was with Sam."

Jackson sat back, feeling his stomach knotting up. He

started to deny it, but those eyes weren't buying what he was selling right now. He changed his mind and reached for the beer.

"Sam's dead," he said.

The old man nodded. "Everbody knows that in these parts," he said.

Jackson changed the subject. "Where did you see me before?" he asked. "I didn't come in here with Sam."

Dunwiddie shook his head. "Nope, t'weren't in here. I seen yer pitcher on the wall over to the sheriff's office and post office."

Jackson set the beer down and watched the old man. "I was with Sam, right till the end," he said. "I was Sam's friend too."

The old man shrugged. "Whaddya want from me?" he asked.

The saloon was filling up, and Jackson needed to get out before anybody recognized him. He decided to get right to the heart of things. "Sam told me, just before he died, that he might've hid some of the Nebraska gold," Jackson said. The old man was watching keenly. "Probly enough to share," he lied. "Sam tell you anything about it?"

Dunwiddie reached for another glass of beer. "That pitcher down at the sheriff's office, it says I could get me a hunnerd dollars if I turn you in," Dunwiddie mumbled. He looked up at Jackson, then his eyes got round when he felt the barrel of a Colt 45 in his ribs under the table.

It amazed Jackson how Dunwiddie collected himself and kept on pouring the beer. "I'm too old to go sashaying around them hills lookin' for treasure. It seems to me what Sam told me might be worth, say, fiddy dollars to you. I'll jest stay here, and you can look for that gold. If'n you find it, it's yours."

Jackson sat back, then slowly put the Colt back into the holster. He reached into his pocket for fifty dollars and placed it on the table, but kept it covered with his hand.

"Tell me what you know," he growled. "I'll give you the fifty if I think it's worth it. You try to turn me in, you'll be dead before you know it."

"Sam liked his whiskey," Dunwiddie observed. "Din't care that much about the money. Kinda funny that way. Liked the robbing part better." Jackson's hand moved toward his gun belt again, and Dunwiddie skipped ahead to the part Jackson was waiting for.

"Kep' some of it, Sam did," Dunwiddie said. "Figgered he might get to settle down with it someday, but he couldn't quit robbin' banks and trains. Anyway, he said he found a cave between towns of Stonewall and Boerne. Burried it there."

Jackson picked up his fifty and stood. Bass had told him all this himself. Dunwiddie raised a hand to stop him. "Right along the stagecoach line betwixt them two towns. In a cave in the cliff walls. Didn't get off the trail no more'n a hunnerd yards, that's what Sam said. Told me he marked it in plain sight, that's what he said. That's all I know."

Jackson stood where he was, fingering the fifty-dollar bill. He'd traveled between the towns, but not along the stage line. Marked in plain sight, that could mean anything. He challenged Dunwiddie on that. Dunwiddie shrugged. "Didn't say no more. You kin take the fiddy dollars or leave it, but that's what I know."

Jackson drummed his fingers on the tabletop, then

shoved the fifty across the table at Dunwiddie. It was more than he knew before. He had to get out of this town.

_____

A day later, Frank Jackson took only a minute in the tiny town of Stonewall, Texas, to make sure there was actually a stagecoach stop in town. The owner of the stop told him in a thick German accent that it would be two more days before a stage came through. Jackson left town quickly, seeing no one but a lady coming into town. He nodded and tipped his hat on the way by.

Satisfied he was on Sam's trail, Jackson found some wheel ruts heading southwest out of town. With no stages coming, he stuck tightly to the trail. He wound through stands of live oak trees broken by meadows thick with grazing grasses. As the sun climbed on his left, he could feel beads of sweat trickling down his back.

After an hour, Jackson could see limestone cliffs rising to the north. He reined in and tried to guess the distance to the cliffs. He decided they were too far away and continued along the trail. His hopes rose as the trail seemed to move closer to the cliffs. Dunwiddie had said cliffs. A cave into the side and beneath a limestone cliff seemed a lot more likely than a cave opening up in the middle of the meadow.

When he judged the trail to be within one hundred yards of the cliffs, Jackson reined his horse over and rode along the side of the cliffs. "Marked in plain sight," he muttered to himself. That's what Sam Bass had told Dunwiddie. He had no idea what that meant.

Rounding a bend, Jackson had to rein in sharply to

keep his horse from running into a boulder lying beside the cliffs. He skirted the boulder, glancing up the cliffs and still muttering to himself. A man could get killed if one of those boulders rolled down on top of him.

Glancing down as he resumed a path along the base of the cliffs, he reined in suddenly again, then turned his horse and retraced his steps to the boulder. He dismounted and studied the face of the boulder. It was faint, but there was no mistaking an arrow scratched into the top of the rock!

Being an outlaw had taught Frank Jackson to be careful. He squatted beside the boulder and studied his back trail. The limestone cliffs leaned inward from the top down, so he wasn't visible from the top. Looking back and over to the east, though, he wasn't as happy about his position. There was a large stand of live oak trees atop a small rise back there. It wouldn't be hard for someone to watch him from concealment.

Time was the most important factor, he decided. Jackson rose and hobbled his horse, then came back to study the face of the limestone. Directly behind the boulder, there was an opening in the rock! He knelt and peered into the crevice. There was a narrow, rocky path leading into the cliff, sloping downward.

Moving back down the trail to a small stand of trees behind him, Jackson gathered some dry sticks. He came back to his saddlebag and pulled out a box of matches. He hadn't thought to bring a lantern, which caused a quick round of cursing, but there was nothing he could do about that now. He moved back to the face of the cliff and moved inside, finding enough space to build a small fire just inside to give him light.

Carrying a small spade from his saddle, Jackson

hunched over and followed the trail around a bend inside the cave. He didn't have to go far. Half-buried under some dirt against the cave wall was an old box. Jackson guessed it to be about two feet by three feet. A few quick thrusts with the spade unearthed it. He dragged it to the cave mouth and kicked out the small fire he had built.

There was no lock on the box, just a wax seal. He shook his head in disbelief. What was Bass thinking? That wouldn't keep anybody out. Jackson squatted on his haunches and threw the lid open. Even in the dim light of the cave mouth, the shine from the gold coins was clear!

He sat against the cave wall and stared at the money, then crawled out of the cave and got to his feet. He didn't know how much money was there, but it looked like more than he could carry in his saddlebag. That meant two trips, or maybe three. He had to hurry. Somebody else might stumble across that boulder at the base of the cliff.

Jackson reached his horse and had to walk around him to reach the saddlebag. As he moved to untie it, a glare reflected from the trees to his east. That was the spot he'd worried about. Somebody was watching from the trees, probably with field glasses.

Frank Jackson pretended to untie the saddlebag, watching the trees and slowly pulling his Winchester from the scabbard. There! He saw the flash of light again. He threw the rifle over his saddle, sighted down the barrel, and pulled the trigger. He lifted his head slightly and stared into the trees. Somebody was moving. He had them on the run!

Wasting no time, Jackson pulled himself into the saddle, keeping his hold on the Winchester. He put his boots to the horse and took him toward the live oak trees, straining to catch movement in there. As he reached the edge of the tree line, a rifle blast startled him, just as a bullet whined past his head. Tree bark dug into his cheek.

He swore and dove out of the saddle, hitting the ground and diving behind a large live oak to his right. He stared at the ground where he had first landed when he dove. His Winchester was lying on the ground there. He didn't dare crawl over to get it. Jackson cursed under his breath and pulled his Colt from the holster. He settled down to watch. The hunter had become the hunted.

Chapter 11

Dunwiddie

Frank Jackson lay flat against the trunk of a live oak, keeping the tree between himself and the stand of oak trees fifty yards to his north and east. The rifle shot had come from there, with an open grassy area between the stands of trees. Blood still dripped from his cheek onto his shirt. He pressed some moss and dead leaves together and packed it onto his cheek to stop the blood. He would have to wash it out later. For now, he just wanted to make the bleeding stop.

Minutes crawled by. He had a hard time estimating how long he'd been trapped here. Looking around, he found a dead tree limb within reach. He pulled it to him, then stretched it out beyond the tree trunk. A rifle shot echoed and the tree limb snapped in half. Jackson yanked what was left of the branch behind the live oak, startled and scared. Somebody over there could shoot. And he didn't even know how many of them were in those trees.

Jackson lost track of time, but by the time dizziness had set in and thirst had left his tongue feeling like a dry stick in his mouth, he knew he had to get out. He pushed the broken remains of the tree limb out again, making sure the live oak tree still covered his hand. There was no shot this time.

Rising to a crouch, he estimated the distance to his horse. Thankfully, the animal hadn't strayed far. Lunging out from behind his cover, Jackson stumbled and almost fell. He regained his footing and ran to the horse, grabbing the saddle horn and lifting himself up. He felt the blow in his shoulder before he heard the shot.

His left shoulder went limp, but Jackson grabbed the saddle horn with his right, leaned over, and slammed his boots into the horse's side. Startled, the animal shot forward, dodging trees on the dead run. A second shot slammed into a tree trunk behind him, then Jackson was out of the tree line, hanging on and trying to guide the horse with his knees. They were moving away from the shooter, that's what really mattered.

He saw the ravine approaching, but had no way to stop his horse. He gathered his strength and held on when the animal leaped the ravine and landed on the other side. Pain shot through his shoulder and all the way down his side, but he stayed in the saddle.

They covered several miles while his horse calmed and slowed down to a trot. The jolting gait was almost as bad as a gallop, but Jackson wanted to keep moving. When he saw a ribbon of water shimmering up ahead, he knew they had reached the Pedernales River. The horse waded the river at a shallow point, and Jackson stopped him on the other side.

Jackson rolled off the horse on the far bank, leaving the animal ground-hitched. There wasn't much choice—

he needed to get to the water. Jackson fell face-down into the river and cleaned his cheek, then splashed the cool water over his aching shoulder. He ripped the sleeve away and looked at the wound. It was raw and oozing blood, but the bullet had passed through.

The outlaw tore off the sleeve that was still intact, dipped it in the river, and bandaged his left shoulder. He moved back to his horse and drank deeply from his waterskin. He hadn't even thought about water when he was running from that rifleman back there. He knelt to refill the waterskin. Finally, he led his horse to a stand of oak trees, tethered the animal, and spread out on his bedroll. He needed to rest and heal. The gold would have to wait.

———

Norah stayed behind the rock she'd been using as cover for the last two hours. She wasn't sure this had been a good idea, but what was done was done. Pike had told her someone had fired at him when he was down in this area, just beyond the property the two of them had purchased for a ranch.

When she had seen the stranger in Stonewall this morning, her instincts had told her he was trouble, so she'd followed. She knew, like anybody else, her instincts weren't always right, but she usually wasn't sorry when she trusted them. She had what she needed with her—Winchester rifle, field glasses, and some water.

This guy had traveled along the stagecoach route. It didn't seem that strange at first, so she had almost gone back to the ranch. But then she noticed he moved over to the limestone cliffs when those appeared on the north side of the route. He definitely seemed to look for something along the cliff wall.

When he had dug into the face of the cliffs, then disappeared inside, she was very curious, and she had to admit, she had gotten a little careless. She had pressed closer to see what he was doing, and when he came out and went to his horse, he had spotted her. Probably, he had seen a reflection of her field glasses.

When he fired, it had come uncomfortably close. Things could have ended there, but he jumped on his horse and charged in her direction. That's when she had pulled out her Winchester and returned fire. The first shot had missed, she was pretty sure, but she might have hit him with the second.

Norah was still here, waiting, because she wanted to be sure he didn't return. Also, she needed to know there was nobody else waiting out there—somebody who might follow her back to the ranch. Her house there wasn't complete yet, and she often camped out. She wasn't sure if she could feel safe doing that again.

Finally, Norah stood and swept the area below with her field glasses. There were a few things she could do now, and she had to choose. She could search the area where she'd fired on him and see if there was blood. She could go down to the cliffs and try to find what he'd been after down there. Or she could go back to Fredericksburg now and tell Pike what had happened.

Eventually, with no movement or signs of life down below, she decided to do all of it. She saddled her mare and rode to the stand of trees where the guy had holed up under her rifle fire. It wasn't hard to find where he had been. There was blood on the leaves in there, and not a small amount of it. She shaded her eyes and looked off to the west where he had ridden. Nothing.

Norah shrugged and rode down to the place where he had been digging at the cliff wall. It didn't take long to find what she was looking for down here, either. There was a boulder, a lot of footprints, and a small fire was still smoldering just inside a crevasse going into the cliff wall. Norah stopped, checked the surrounding area carefully, then ducked and crawled into the cave.

Around the first bend, an old iron box lay open. Norah crawled to the box and, not trusting her eyes, dragged it back into the light from outside. No doubt he had built the fire to give a little light, but it wasn't helping now.

Daylight fell on gold coins, and there were a lot of them. Norah gasped and sat back against the cave wall, staring at the treasure. Questions poured through her mind, one after the other. Where had it come from? How had this stranger known about it? Was there more, deeper in the cave?

Norah had a feeling that the man she had shot wasn't in much shape to come back for the gold. Not right away. There was a lot of blood in that stand of trees. Greed, though, was something to think about. Maybe the guy could fight through a lot of pain for this much money.

She debated what she should do now, but caution finally won out. If she spent time pulling this treasure out and making trips to carry it off, this guy could come back. He might not have gone far. Worse, he could come back with a bunch of his buddies. She was a sitting duck in this cave. She needed a lantern to look for more gold deeper in the cave. It was, she decided, time to go.

The garden she had planned on planting this morning

was the last thing on her mind now. She climbed up on the mare and struck the trail for Fredericksburg, following along the Pedernales River. The Winchester stayed on her lap the entire way. Norah's family was from the east, but her father had taught her how to shoot. That had come in handy today.

Latigo Smith pushed into the Suds Saloon in Round Rock and looked around. He'd been in a thousand places like this one, it felt like. He'd been in a couple of knuckle-and-skull fights and one shootout he couldn't avoid in places just like this. Luckily, the sheriff in the shootout town had seen it Lat's way. Now, he thought to himself, he was a deputy sheriff, but he didn't want anybody in this town to know about it.

Lat walked over to the bar and got himself a shot of whiskey, then leaned back against the bar and surveyed the room while trying not to look like he was. There was an old codger nursing a glass of beer by the window. After a couple more glances around the room, Lat decided that was probably Dunwiddie.

The trick was to get the old man into a conversation and try to get some information without the guy figuring him out. Smith drifted to the table next to the old man and then let a small wad of money show while he stuffed it in his pocket. The old man's eyes locked in on the money. He nodded and looked away.

The old man made a show of draining the last of his beer and plunking the empty glass down on the table. Lat didn't look over. He concentrated on his whiskey, which he finished, then waved for another.

"Got another chair over here," the old man offered.

Lat shrugged, then got up and joined him. "Name's Lat Smith, old timer," Lat said as he took a seat.

"Dunwiddie," was all the old man said.

Lat nodded. "How you doin', Mr. Dunwiddie?"

"Jest Dunwiddie."

Lat's whiskey arrived. He pointed at it. "One fer you?" he asked.

Dunwiddie's eyes lit up. "Don't mind if I do, young feller. What brings you to Round Rock?"

"Just driftin'," Latigo said, looking around the room. "What can you tell me about this town?"

Dunwiddie paused to suck down his whiskey in one long slurp. "Big doin's lately," Dunwiddie said proudly. "Them Texas Rangers done shot and kilt Sam Bass here, jest a couple o' weeks ago."

Smith allowed his jaw to drop and his eyes to widen. "No kiddin'? Sam Bass, the train robber? Got hisself a whole mess of gold, up there in Nebraska?"

"Thatsh him." Dunwiddie nodded proudly. "Rangers shot him down there near the livery." His fingers pointed in two or three different directions. "Then he got dragged outta town and died up in the cemetery, just there outside of town."

"Dang." Lat shook his head and stared out the window. "Sam Bass, kilt right here in Round Rock, Texas." He switched to beer for his next order. Had to keep his head clear. "I wonder what ole Sam Bass did with all that gold. Spent it as fast as he got it, I reckon."

The old man's eyes took on a crafty sheen. "Not what everbody thinks, it ain't like that." His voice dropped a notch or two. "I knew Sam Bass. Knowed him when he was still in short britches. He din't spend it all."

Lat turned to face him, he didn't have to pretend to hang on to the old man's words.

"What'd he do with it?" Lat prompted.

The old man ran a finger around the inside of his dry whiskey glass and smacked his lips. Lat waved for another whiskey.

"Burried it, that what he done," the old man confided. "There was one o' the Sam Bass Gang in here, just two nights ago, he thought so too. Paid me fiddy dollars to tell him what Sam told me." He glanced toward the pocket where Lat had stuffed his money.

Lat thought about it, then shook his head. "Ain't got fifty to spare," he said. "Still got to get me a bed for tonight, got to get some breakfast in my gizzard in the mornin', then I'm still driftin'." He looked over at the old man. "I bought you some whiskey. Don't that count for nuthin'?"

Dunwiddie waved for another whiskey and paid for it himself. "Last of my money," he announced. "You got twenny, pilgrim?"

Lat thought it over, reached into his pocket, and slid twenty dollars across the table. The money disappeared faster than Lat would have thought possible.

"Burried it, like I said," the old man told him. "Foller the stagecoach line from Stonewall to Boerne. Limestone caves along there. Inside one o' them caves. Says he marked it plain as day."

More questions brought no more information. Latigo stood to leave. "That Sam Bass Gang member that was here," he asked, "what was his name?"

The old man shook his head and refused to answer. As Smith turned to go, the old man mumbled: "They got his pitcher on the wall over to the post office. You can go an' see for yerself over there."

Smith left money on the table, then crossed the street to the post office. The first poster he saw was for Sam Bass, they hadn't gotten around to taking it down yet. He stopped at the second poster and read the name underneath: Frank Jackson.

————

Norah had been telling me about the gold treasure all the way out from Fredericksburg, but I still wasn't quite ready for what I saw. Norah stood guard with her Winchester, which she had already used a few times today, while I pulled the iron box out into the late afternoon sun.

I plopped down on the ground and stared at it, and Norah took herself a seat right beside me. I didn't know what questions to ask first. Not that there was anybody to ask about it. The guy who'd dug it out had scattered from here to breakfast, maybe packing a little lead from Norah's rifle.

I looked over at the packhorse we'd brought with us. I had a double saddlebag slung over him, plus the saddlebags Norah and I had on our own horses. I figured it was enough to pack this stuff back to Fredericksburg. I'd get it tucked away in the Fredericksburg bank and maybe then I could start working on who it belonged to.

"Let's count it," I said. I glanced around. "There's nobody around. We can count while we put it in the saddlebags."

They were twenty-dollar gold pieces, and they looked

like they'd come straight from the mine somewhere. We counted almost five hundred of them. Norah spared me the trouble of getting out pencil and paper to do the ciphering. It was just short of ten thousand dollars, she told me. I guess that back-east schooling came in handy that day.

When the horses were loaded up, I pointed to a stand of oak trees east and north of us. "Is that where he holed up after you shot 'im?" I asked.

She nodded. "He charged me after he took the first shot," she said. She pointed to a bigger stand of trees farther west. "I was in there, watching him through the field glasses, like I told you at the sheriff's office. He shot back, then jumped on his horse and came after me. He had just reached those trees when my first shot took him off his horse."

I found some blood where Norah pointed it out. No doubt there had been more of it earlier, but several hours had gone by since she'd been here. I found it drying on some leaves and some of it was smeared on a tree trunk. What was on the tree trunk was high up, though. I figured he'd been bleeding from his face to leave blood this high.

"You maybe hit him twice," I told Norah. "How many times did you fire?"

"Three times," she said. "The last one was just to keep him moving."

I nodded. "That's some good shootin'," I said. "Remind me not to get you riled up at me."

I looked at the trail of hoofprints leading out of the woods. "Let's follow that for a while," I said, glancing overhead. "We don't have much time before we have to get this gold back to town, but maybe the trail will tell us something."

————

It didn't take long to see he was heading for the Pedernales River, and unless he was a total tenderfoot, he'd have smarts enough to use the river to cover his trail. We stopped tracking and turned toward Fredericksburg. I'd feel better when this money was in a vault at the bank. This much gold brings out the worst in some folks. We'd seen some of that today already.

I'd told the bank president I would need him there after closing time today. He'd said I could find him at the bank or the café. We found him finishing up some supper at the café, and he came with us to stow the gold in his vault at the bank. I put the receipt in my pocket and walked with Norah down to the office. She put on some coffee while I put my feet on my desk and stared at the ceiling.

"Those gold pieces were new," I blurted. "They were all stamped 1877, right?"

Norah came over and set my coffee cup down in front of me. "All of them I saw," she agreed.

"Huh," I said, and went back to staring at the ceiling. The door opened and closed, and my new deputy, Latigo Smith, came into the office.

He helped himself to coffee and slid down to sit on his haunches against the side wall. "Had an interestin' trip to Round Rock," he started.

"I'll bet it wasn't as interesting as our day," I said, and then I told him about the hidden gold we had brought in.

He stared at us. "You found it near the stagecoach trail between Stonewall and Boerne, right?" he asked.

I looked over at Norah and nodded. "Yep, that's about where it was," I answered. "How did you know?"

Lat pushed himself to his feet and set his coffee cup on my desk. "I know whose gold that was," he told us. "And I got me a good idea who was after it."

Chapter 12

Making Plans

Main Street in Boerne, Texas, was a lot wider than King Simms had expected. He supposed that was good. Lots of room to maneuver a stagecoach past any buggies and other whatnot that could clog up the street. The stage stop was at the end of Main Street. It was a little bigger than what he'd expected, it seemed to be combined with a hotel. He could work with that.

No, the real problem was the size of the town. Some guy at the post office had told Simms proudly that more than one hundred people lived in this town. That was too many. Simms needed to slip in and out of town without too many folks getting a good look at him. He needed less than half a hundred.

Simms slumped into a chair in a café and stared at the courthouse across the street. The building was almost new. He hadn't been expecting a county seat like this one, either. That brought lots of folks doing business. Lots of lawyers. Simms growled under his breath, startling the girl who had come over to take his order.

Music sounded from down the street and Simms

stared at some people playing instruments under a large shade tree. "What kinda music is that?" he demanded.

The girl backed up a step. "It's a polka, sir," she mumbled. "We have a German band that plays every day."

Simms slumped forward and slurped from the coffee she had put down on the table. German bands playing polkas in the middle of Texas? He was starting to hate this place.

The girl left with his order and Simms tried to shut out the music noise. North of Boerne somewhere, was almost the perfect spot to hold up a San Antonio stage bound for the west. It couldn't be near the town, like he'd planned on before. Except for that, things were looking good. He would just have to pull the holdup north of town somewhere.

He had stopped off in San Antonio to look things over, and things looked fine there. The stage stop was busy, of course, and the town was much bigger than Boerne, but he saw what he wanted to see. There were stages leaving daily, and he had followed one west for a short distance. There were just a few passengers and some luggage, but the soldier who had taken a seat on top with the driver told Simms what he wanted to know. He didn't even have to ask. The army had an interest in what was on that stage, and Simms was betting it was payroll money. Just what he had hoped for.

Simms still liked the idea Jackson had mentioned. Actually, he'd said it was Sam Bass's idea, but it was a good one. Rob the stage, then make your getaway on another stage. Posses and sheriffs didn't chase stage-coaches, did they? Simms had never heard of it. That reminded him of his other problem. Where was he going to get hold of a stagecoach? Where would he hide it after the robberies?

The fresh cup of coffee and the hot apple pie cheered him up a little, but he still had a couple of problems to solve. He would have to take them one at a time. He would hold up the stage near Boerne, but not too close by. Maybe up the trail to the north. He could scout that area after he met with Jackson. He pulled out his pocket watch and looked. Jackson was supposed to meet him here in twenty minutes, just outside the café.

Simms wandered down the street to the stage stop and watched them loading up a stage. When the stage left, Simms stepped over to a man who'd been handling luggage and horses.

"Hello." At least Simms was pretty sure that's what he had said.

Simms was getting more and more irritated at the German accents, but he plastered on a smile and pointed at the departing coach.

"Whaddya do with them coaches after you're done with 'em?" he asked.

The man looked confused. Simms wasn't sure if he couldn't understand the question or if he just couldn't understand the English language.

Finally, the man shrugged. "We always fix them. I fix them," he said, pointing proudly at his chest.

Simms's smile faded. "You don't never sell an old one?" he asked hopefully.

The man looked at him like he was crazy. "Nobody buys an old stagecoach, I tink," he said, then walked stiffly away.

Simms cursed under his breath and started back toward the café. He pulled out his pocket watch again and checked the time. Jackson was late, of course. That produced another round of cursing. Simms ducked into a saloon to find a beer. The Germans had beer, didn't they? They'd better not serve it with polka music, he growled under his breath.

———

Frank Jackson spent a day and a half in the spot where he had stopped on the north side of the Pedernales River. He shot a rabbit for some food to go with the jerky in his saddlebag. The bullet had passed through his shoulder. It wasn't festering, and he was regaining some movement. Even so, a wave of nausea passed over him when he pulled himself into the saddle.

Today was the day he was supposed to meet King Simms in Boerne. He couldn't travel fast, not with this shoulder. He started at daylight, crossing the Pedernales and retracing his route to the cave where he'd found Sam Bass's gold. He had little hope. Whoever had shot him would most likely have ridden down and found the loot right there at the mouth of the cave.

When he got close, Jackson circled the area surrounding the cave carefully, checking both the place where he got shot and the woods used by the shooter. Confident he was alone, Jackson approached the limestone cave. He swore violently when he saw footprints and horse tracks in front of the cave.

It cost him dearly to dismount and look, but he couldn't see inside the cave from the saddle. He had to know for sure if the gold was gone. It was. Jackson sank to his knees and collapsed to the floor of the cave. After ten minutes, he struggled to his feet and went outside to remount.

It would make him late for his meeting with Simms, but Jackson had to get an idea of where the gold had gone. Struggling into the saddle produced a fresh wave of cursing. He grabbed the saddle horn and held on while he fought through the pain.

Reining his horse around, Jackson followed the tracks until they came to the trail between two towns. Stonewall was to the east. Fredericksburg was off to the west. He pulled up to study the tracks. There wasn't a lot of traffic on this trail, and more than a day had passed. Wind and a brief rain shower during that time made it too hard to tell which way they had gone.

Jackson turned and started toward Boerne. As he rode, a plan formed in his mind. Tomorrow, he would check in Fredericksburg first, although he wasn't sure what to look for. If somebody had come in and started spending a lot of mint-new gold coins, he might get lucky.

Another thought struck Jackson as he rode. Stonewall was a tiny little town. He remembered riding past a woman as he rode out. He'd tipped his hat. She couldn't have turned and followed him, could she? It was a long shot. He didn't know many women who could shoot like the person who'd plugged him. Didn't know any, actually. Still, he might try finding the tracks of whoever shot him from that stand of trees. First, he had to meet with King Simms.

———

Jackson wasn't sure how late he was when he dismounted near the stage stop in Boerne. Simms lounged against the wall of the general store across the street. His face reminded Jackson of a mama bear whose cubs had just gone missing. He crossed the street slowly, feeling Simms's eyes traveling from his face to his shoulder.

Simms stared at the cuts on Jackson's face, then lingered on the stiff way he carried his left shoulder.

"What happened to you?" Simms barked.

Jackson shrugged, then regretted the movement in his shoulder.

"Needed some cash. Held up a general store back yonder."

"Where?" Simms demanded.

Jackson started to shrug, then thought better of it. "Back there just outta New Orleans. He got a bullet in me."

"And your face?"

"Splinters," Jackson said. That part was true. He moved to a bench and sat down. "I can work," he said. He wasn't sure about that part, but he was counting on having a few more days before they made any moves.

Simms prowled back and forth, his mind racing. It might, he thought, be time for a new partner. He decided to keep Jackson in the picture for now. He might still be useful. Simms stopped and pointed across the street at the stage stop.

"Too much activity here," he announced. Jackson said nothing. Simms kept prowling. "I like the idea of carrying the loot away in another stage," he said.

Jackson left off massaging his shoulder long enough to stare at Simms. "You like that idea?"

"Think about it," Simms answered. "Nobody's going to think we're getting away on a stage. The sheriff sees a stage, he's not gonna stop it. We rob the stage on our hosses, hide the stage somewhere close by. Cut loose the hosses on the stage we robbed so nobody can follow." He paused and stared down the street. "Don't know where to get a stage, though."

Jackson leaned his head back against the wall. He was ready to find a saloon. An image came to his mind from two days before. There was a stage stop in Stonewall. A tiny one.

"Stonewall," he said.

Simms stopped pacing and stared at him. "Whattya talking about?" he demanded.

"There's a tiny stage stop in a town called Stonewall. Mebbe fifteen miles east of Fredericksburg. Northeast of here. Got one old coach in there. Place is dead. I'll bet you could even buy the stop and coach together if you've got the coins to do it."

Simms sat down on the bench. "Stonewall," he repeated. "Maybe I'll check that out."

Jackson nodded and stood.

"Where you going?" Simms barked.

"Saloon." Jackson looked back. "You wanna come?"

Simms shook his head. "I'll be back tomorrow," he said. He watched Jackson walk away. He needed another partner, he decided. Jackson would have to go. Too bad. Simms would find somebody in better shape. Somebody who knew how to shoot without getting himself all shot up.

Simms got up and stared up and down the street. A telegraph office in Boerne was too much to hope for. Beyond the hotel/stagecoach stop, a livery, a blacksmith, and a general store, there were just the usual shops, one café, and a couple saloons. He needed a gunhand to replace Jackson, and he would have to get that in person. This called for a trip to a tiny town called Stonewall. First, he would make a trip to Austin and then circle back.

Now, he had to take a look at that trail leading north out of Boerne.

————

Frank Jackson lay behind a log in the same stand of trees somebody had used to shoot him several days ago. There were a few boot prints and some broken branches around, along with two rifle shells he had found. What had really gotten his attention was the size of the boot prints. He'd been shot by a woman or a very small man. He'd been thinking about that woman he'd seen coming out of Stonewall when the movement below got his attention.

Careful not to make the same mistake the shooter had made a few days ago, Jackson stayed in the shade and laid a rag over his field glasses to watch. Somebody was looking at the cave down there and checking the tracks in the area. A glint of sunlight off the man's chest told him this was a sheriff doing the scouting. Most likely, he would come from Fredericksburg.

Whoever he was, the guy didn't stay long. He mounted and rode toward Stonewall. Jackson wasn't really interested in following. He was more interested in looking around the cave again, and then he was hoping he could track his shooter back to wherever they came from.

Jackson didn't spend a lot of time at the cave. He had some matches and used them to crawl back as far as he had the first time. A quick look told him the cave didn't extend much farther back before the walls closed in too far to allow passage. The iron box was gone. There wasn't so much as one gold coin left on the floor.

Retracing his tracks to the small boot prints in the stand of oak trees, Jackson took his time, backtracking his shooter. It didn't take long to see they had been following him, holding to the route of the stagecoach line. When he had veered off to look into the cave, his follower had moved down to the wooded area where they had swapped lead.

Jackson dismounted when he reached the trail for the stagecoach, took a drink of water, and fished in his back-pack for a little jerky. He wasn't going to stop looking for that gold. He'd never seen that much money in one place and probably never would again. He just had to decide what to do next.

He'd first thought he would ride into Fredericksburg and pick up the trail, but the little town of Stonewall was closer. Maybe he could nose around over there, seeing as how there wasn't much to it. He didn't expect Simms to be there yet, checking on that stage stop.

Jackson walked into the general store in town. There wasn't much else around. There was something that passed for a café, but it looked like somebody had just put a porch on their shack and set up shop. There was a tiny school and a few houses along with it. Probably most folks just lived around the town and came in for mail, school, and supplies. The general store was just about his only bet.

There were two guys just about his age, Jackson

guessed, picking up an order at the back. The store owner piled some supplies on a countertop. "This is what I've got for the sheriff," he announced. "How you boys coming with that house?"

"We dug the well and got 'er pumpin'," one announced in a thick accent. Mountain boys, Jackson thought. "Workin' on the house now," he finished.

They turned to go, then the shopkeeper stopped them. "Hold on," he said, "I've got some flower seeds the lady ordered."

Jackson froze where he was, thoughts running through his head. There was a sheriff, no doubt the one he'd seen, building himself a house out here, and there was a *lady* there too. Maybe the one with small boot prints.

"Help you?"

Startled, Jackson stepped over the counter. "Ammo," he said, pointing at his Colt. "Couple of boxes."

He paid, shutting down any efforts the store owner made to get acquainted. Stepping outside, he mounted and followed the two mountain boys from a distance. He had a good idea now of where to start looking for that gold.

———

Simms had heard of the Scholtz Beer Garden in Austin, but had never been there. For one thing, he'd been too busy running his cattle rustling operation down there near Laredo. For another, he favored whiskey over beer. He'd only come tonight because he needed a gunhand, and this seemed like the best place.

He took his glass and leaned back against the bar. He

had a good idea of the type of man he was looking for. A guy wearing a tied-down gun, for starters, and somebody not too drunk. A man who made his living with his gun couldn't afford to be drunk if he got called out. Card player, that was okay. If he was too good with the cards, that was a distraction Simms didn't need.

His eyes scanned the crowd, then came to rest on somebody he recognized. This guy had worked for him down near Laredo. Pretty good with a gun and didn't ask many questions, as he remembered. Funny name. Simms struggled to remember it as the guy waved and walked toward him. Got a nickname on account of his roan horse. *Blue*, that was it.

Blue came to a stop in front of Simms and tipped his hat. "Boss," was all he said.

"Blue." Simms nodded. "What're you doin' in Austin?"

Blue shrugged. "Lookin' for some work," he said. "Ain't been the same since your operation got busted up. Worked a cattle drive or two to Kansas, but that's kinda dryin' up, too. Railroads have just about kilt the cattle drives. Tire of smackin' the back of a horse all the way to Kansas, anyhow."

Simms waved at the bartender. "Lemme buy you a drink, Blue," he said. "I just might have something you'd like."

At a table in the corner, Simms laid out his plan to rob a stagecoach. "Just north of Boerne, mebbe five miles. There's a sharp slope down along the trail and a quick turn at the bottom of the hill. Excellent cover from some brush down there, too. Driver's got no choice but to slow down when he gets to the curve. We step out and rob 'em."

Blue nodded slowly. "What do I do?" he asked.

"If they've got a guard that looks like he could make trouble, you shoot 'im. If not, jest hold your pistol on 'im until we've got all the money."

Blue barely blinked at shooting the guard. Simms was feeling good about his choice. Then Blue's forehead furrowed up.

"They got enuf money in them stages to make it worth our while?"

Simms allowed himself a pleased grin. "The one we're gonna rob will," he promised. "First, we'll rob a stage just to test a couple things out, up farther north. Then we'll make some big money. I've got it planned."

Blue nodded. "I'll do it," he declared. "Fifty-fifty?"

Simms shook his head. "There might be another guy," he answered. "One-third apiece." Simms had no intention of sharing that much, but Blue didn't need to know about that.

"Meet me at the café in Boerne in two days, around noon," he said. Simms didn't wait for an answer. He was already on his way out.

CHAPTER 13

FINDING FOOTPRINTS

G etting a close-up look at the sheriff's property was turning out to be a little tougher than Jackson had expected. There was a ranch house framework going up atop a small rise on the northeast corner of the land. A well had been sunk out in front of the house. Jackson had seen a crew working there on the first day, but nobody had been back to work on the house today. Maybe, Jackson thought, they were waiting for a new shipment of lumber. Or maybe another crew would put on the roof. If there was a break in the work being done, he would have to act fast.

In any case, he wanted to get inside that house and have a look around. If the gold wasn't hidden in there, maybe he could find a clue where it was. There was also the matter of the hill country boys, who were putting up fences for livestock. There was an area of maybe fifty acres on some rolling hills that ran to the tree line on the west side. That was already completely fenced when Jackson started watching the house.

Today, they had finished a smaller fenced area on the

east side of the house. That puzzled Jackson a little. Both fenced areas were on grassy pasture—they had to be for grazing. Maybe they had both cows and horses. Or maybe some other animals, like sheep. His brow wrinkled up a little at that thought. This wasn't sheep country, so maybe horses. He knew plenty of ranchers who got downright riled about sheep coming in to take the grass.

The best spot he could find for watching the house was at the top of a small rise about thirty yards away. The rise there was about on a level with the house. It was in the large fenced pasture, so he'd had to wriggle under the fence. Jackson had heard of barbed wire, but this was the first time he'd seen it. He had the ripped britches to prove it. The grass was ungrazed, so he could wiggle to the top of the rise and watch through his field glasses. With these bumpkins from the hills hanging around, it was as close as he could get.

Now Hardy had shown up, and he was talking to the hill boys out in front of the house. It was too far away to overhear anything, of course, but Jackson clearly saw Hardy give some money to each of them. Then he pointed out toward the pasture where Jackson was hiding. He ducked away from the field glasses in panic for a moment, then reassured himself that Hardy couldn't possibly know he was out here. He resumed watching, but couldn't tell what was happening.

After they talked, the two hill boys/fencers mounted up and rode away. Hardy walked the property for a few minutes, disappeared inside the house, then came back out just a few minutes later. He walked to the well and dipped himself a bucket of water. After drinking, he mounted up and rode away as well.

Jackson stayed under cover for at least half an hour,

watching the house, feeling suspicious of a trap. Finally, he decided this might be his best chance. He rose and ran toward the house in a half-crouch. Reaching the open space where the front door would be located later, he paused, looked around, then ducked inside.

He found nothing. There were a few tools inside, but nothing else lying on the floors and no place he could see to hide anything. The floor was solid dirt—nobody had been digging there. He stood in total disappointment, swearing to himself, unwilling to leave. That was when he heard a horse approaching.

Panicked about the sheriff returning, Jackson ducked out the back of the structure and ran for the cover of a sparse stand of burr oak trees. He half expected to feel a rifle bullet slamming into his back at any moment. He counted on speed, running for cover and diving into the cover of the trees and brush when he reached it. He kept moving, ducked down, and circled around until he reached his original hiding spot.

Jackson stayed flat on the ground for several minutes, catching his breath and afraid to raise his head even enough to get a look through his field glasses. Those glasses were still at the top of the rise. He laid flat and eyed them for several seconds. Finally, he had to know what was going on out there. He raised up and pulled the field glasses to his eyes to get a look.

He immediately saw there were three horses at the house. Somebody must have ridden in on one horse and led the other two, because he saw only one rider. No wonder he had heard hoofbeats. He watched as the new arrival led the two unsaddled horses and let them loose in the smaller fenced pasture the two hill boys had just finished working on.

When the rider let the horses loose and turned, Jackson's jaw dropped just a little. It was a woman! He moved the field glasses just slightly for a better look. It was the woman he had seen leaving Stonewall just the other day! Things were making a little more sense to him. The sheriff had himself a woman. That opened up a few new possibilities, mainly because it could give the sheriff something to worry about. Jackson packed up and retreated to the tree line. He had some things to think about.

———

"You're crazy!" The words burst from King Simms's mouth and he knew right away it was a mistake. The stage stop owner in Stonewall was named Werner, but he pronounced it *Verner*. Werner's eyes narrowed, and he turned to go back inside. Simms forced himself to calm down. He reminded himself he needed this.

Seven hundred dollars for the stagecoach and the stop in Stonewall for the Harrison Stage Lines was probably a fair price. It's just that Simms was used to taking what he wanted. The cattle rustling out of Mexico, for instance—those cows hadn't cost anything except the price of the ammo. The guys that got themselves shot, well, they just went off his payroll.

This guy Werner wanted to move back to Minnesota to join some cousins. Simms had gotten that much out of him. At least, that was as much of the German accent as he could understand. He could understand the guy just fine when he said he wanted seven hundred dollars. Simms changed course and held up a hand to stop

Werner from leaving. He worked through this thing in his head.

A new stagecoach would cost at least $1,500. He'd been able to figure that much out. This coach was at least thirty years old, but he'd taken a ride in it and had to admit it wasn't bad. The wheels seemed fine, and the body of the coach seemed to be in good shape. The seats were pretty torn up and it was a rough ride, but what stagecoach didn't have a rough ride? It's not like he was going to be selling tickets unless somebody walked in and demanded one. Then he'd take their money if it didn't interfere with his plans.

Werner seemed to know that Simms wanted this a little too much. Simms didn't know how the guy knew, but Werner had Simms over the barrel. This setup was perfect. He did a little arithmetic in his head. One trial run followed by two quick holdups of stages with army payroll, and he would have what he needed. Back to Bourbon Street and his own saloon. That's what this was about.

Simms finally nodded his head and managed what passed for a smile at Werner. "Okay," he said, "seven hundred dollars, and it's a deal. You give me the stage, this stop, and write a letter to Harrison Stage Lines. Tell 'em I'm the new owner. I'll get my own hosses and a driver."

He already had a couple stolen horses for this, and Blue could drive it. Werner didn't need to know that.

"Okay," Werner said. "I'll write a letter. You haff money?" His eyes narrowed suspiciously. "Vat iss your name?"

"Uh, Perkins. Jed Perkins." Simms turned his back and pulled a wad of money from his pocket. He didn't want Werner to see how much he had. This guy would raise the price. Simms counted out seven hundred and turned to show Werner the money. He pulled it back when Werner reached for it.

"The letter," he reminded Werner.

Werner harrumphed a time or two, but moved over to a desk and took out a pen and paper. He scratched his nose a few times, then scrawled a letter and held it out for Simms to read.

Simms skimmed the letter, then stuffed it carelessly into his pocket. It wasn't much of a letter, but he didn't really think he would need one. This was just in case somebody from the stage lines came sniffing around, poking into things. Simms hoped to be out of here long before that could happen.

"Look around," Werner said. "It iss yours." He left and moved off down the street, looking pleased with himself.

Simms didn't spend much time looking around. He'd already looked at the stagecoach. There were a few tools around for working on the coach, a desk, and not much else inside. Passengers ate down the street at the café. Out back, there was a tin roof over a water trough and a hayrack. Simms had already seen that when he had tethered his horse there.

Simms turned to see Werner talking to somebody wearing a badge. He was pointing at the stage stop. Simms put on his hat and ducked out the back. He mounted up and rode away in the other direction. The last thing he wanted to do right now was to meet the sheriff. If this went well, he would never have to meet the sheriff.

———

I stepped into the stage stop with Werner, expecting to meet the new owner of the place...and he wasn't there. We stepped out the back and saw him riding away. Werner just scratched his head, looked at me, and shrugged.

"He vass here just a minute ago," he mumbled.

I didn't know what to think of it, but it didn't seem to matter a whole lot. We didn't have more than one or two passengers out of here on a full week's schedule, usually. I really didn't figure this stage stop was going to last all that much longer. Sounded like Werner had found himself a fool to part from his money.

"I'll catch him next time," I said over my shoulder as I left. The fact is, I had bigger things on my mind. I had put off something really important, trying to find just the right time, and I had to get this done. I'm talking about proposing to my girl, Norah Lynch. We had bought this land together and were building her a house, but we both knew the house was supposed to be for the both of us. I just had to get this done. I'd already thought about what I wanted to say. I just wasn't sure I would get all the words out in the right order.

I had one thing on my side to make this special. Something she didn't know about. Her Aunt Maribel had given me the wedding ring Norah's mother had worn. It was a family treasure, she said, but Norah's mother always intended for her daughter to have it. It was burning a hole in my pocket right now, as a matter of fact.

Things weren't quite like I expected when I rode up to the new house. Norah's new mare and buckskin gelding were in the corral that Zeb and Caleb had just finished fencing, but Norah wasn't out there. She was bent down in front of the house, holding her Winchester and inspecting the ground.

I rode up, dismounted, and joined her. She straightened up and gave me a quick kiss, then went back to checking the ground. This wasn't the way I'd pictured this. She was worried about something.

I didn't have to ask what she was doing. There were footprints in front of the house she wasn't expecting to find. We circled the house together and found prints leading away from the back. I followed them to a small stand of trees and some brush, but lost the trail there.

Coming back to the house, we went from room to room, but it was hard to tell if anybody had been in here. There had been a crew working on the place, and of course Zeb and Caleb had been here every day for a couple weeks until they went to get my cows from the old property. They had left yesterday.

We walked back out front and leaned up against the brick wall surrounding the well while we talked about it. Lat Smith had told us the other day what he'd found out in Round Rock. We'd agreed it could have been Frank Jackson out there in the cave, and we might have found Sam Bass's share of the Nebraska train robbery. None of us liked the thought of Sam Bass's shadow hanging over our county.

The thing is, Norah had put a bullet or two into whoever had gotten into that cave. We weren't even sure if the guy was still alive. And we didn't think he could have tracked us back to the house. We had taken the gold directly to Fredericksburg and put it in the bank. The ranch was in the other direction and several miles away.

I could see right away that I was more worried about it than Norah was.

"It could have just been some drifter looking for food," she told me. "Maybe Zeb or Caleb rode up and scared him off. I haven't been here for several days. Those boot prints could be three or four days old."

I knew she was right, but I couldn't get past the idea of an outlaw hanging around the house, possibly looking for the gold. Norah reminded me he could have already gone in there, had a good look, and realized the gold wasn't around here.

I didn't want her to come back out here without me for a while, but that Norah, she's a strong-minded woman. She pointed out that Zeb and Caleb would be back with the cows by tomorrow afternoon, and then they would all three be out here anytime she came out to work with her horses.

That settled me down on it some. We talked about the three new horses she had bought in Austin. They were being delivered later this week. I cheered up when I could picture us having a ranch here, stocked with the horses and cattle. That reminded me of what I had planned to do this evening, before the boot prints around the house had messed up my plans. That's when my palms got a little clammy.

I wasn't too sure this was the time to bring it up, but that ring from Maribel was feeling awfully heavy in my pocket. I think I went a little red around the gills and commenced to hemming and hawing. Norah, as usual, could see right through me. She didn't know about the ring, though. That was my ace in the hole.

She reached over and took my hand. She pretended not to notice how clammy it was. "What is it, Pike?" she cooed. "You've got something on your mind, I can tell."

"Well, yeah...yes, I kinda do, but I'm never too sure if I'm picking the right time to bring things up."

"Whatever it is," she assured me, "It's a beautiful evening, we're out here on the land we bought together, on the place where we've talked about making a life together. How could this not be a good time?"

Well, that one got me over the hump. I talked about how I'd first seen her and thought she was so pretty. I told her I hadn't thought she would see anything in an old country boy and retired army guy like me, but she always took me by surprise. I told her how I couldn't picture my life without her in it anymore.

Along about then, she knew where I was going, and her eyes got all big and misty. I fished that rock out of my pocket and got down on my knee, just like everybody told me I was supposed to do.

"What I'm trying to say, Norah Lynch," I finally spat out, "is that you would make me the happiest guy in the world if you would marry me." Then I opened that box and she saw the ring.

Things get a little blurry in my memory after that, but I remember she said yes, pulled me to my feet, and gave me a kiss. Then we kissed some more. I can't recollect exactly how long.

We stayed out there at the ranch until dusk was setting in, then we headed back to town while we still had a little light. I dropped her off at the boarding house, where she had a room. We agreed I would be out at the ranch early to join her while she worked the horses. When Zeb and Caleb came, I would come back to town.

She promised, and I was feeling pretty good about everything that night. It's when I woke up in the morning that I started to worry about Frank Jackson again. What if she got out to the ranch today before Zeb and Caleb got back with the cows? She was probably all eager to get the place ready for those new horses.

There was a little work to do at the office, but Lat Smith was there and told me he could take care of things. I told him about the tracks around the house, and he offered to come out there with me. I told him he would do me more good here. I usually grabbed some breakfast at the café with him, but today I just had to get moving.

I swung by the boarding house, and Norah wasn't there. The landlady didn't know where she had gone, but I knew she was eager to work those horses at the ranch. That's when I really started to imagine some bad things, so I saddled up my horse, Hank, and hit the trail toward Stonewall. I stopped off at that cave first to look for any fresh tracks. I knew now that I couldn't rest until I had checked things out a little more.

CHAPTER 14

JUST IN TIME

There were fresh tracks around the cave. The floor of the tunnel inside was too hardened and packed down to tell for sure, but I had a good idea that Frank Jackson or one of the Bass Gang had come back. If he had, he probably knew we had taken the gold. I stood and trotted back to my horse. Once he knew the gold was gone, he wouldn't be hanging around here. He'd be looking for where it went.

I hesitated while I searched the ground for any new clues. The area was trampled a little too much to tell me which way he'd headed this time. There were tracks leading to some trees to the north, but those were probably old.

I couldn't take a chance. I mounted and rode to the stage trail and struck it east toward Stonewall and the ranch I was building with Norah. First, I had to know he hadn't gone after her. Then I would worry about tracking Frank Jackson wherever he had gone.

Jackson swung around the ranch and approached as he had before, crawling under the barbed wire and moving on hands and knees. He reached the top of the small rise he'd been using to scout the house. One look through the field glasses told him he had wasted some time.

The woman was over on the far side in the smaller pasture, working with her horses. He'd come the long way around to get close to her. Jackson raised his head to scan the property. The woman was alone, but she was working one horse on a lunge line. It would be hard to approach when she circled around constantly like that.

One thing was still in his favor—she seemed to be alone. He couldn't see workers or ranch hands of any kind. Jackson dropped back below the crest and moved in a circle toward the back of the house. That would shield him while he worked closer and waited for his chance. If he got close enough, he would take her down in a rush.

Reaching the house took only ten minutes. Jackson had no choice but to wait it out from there. Movement on his part would be the fastest way to tip her off. He settled down behind the walls and listened to the steady trot of the horse on the lunge line. When the sound stopped, he risked a peek around the walls of the house.

The woman had turned her back and was brushing the horse. Jackson crouched down and moved at a steady pace toward the woman. When she turned slightly in either direction, he dropped to the ground. The gate, he could see, had swung shut, but it didn't appear to be latched. He crawled the last fifty feet on his stomach.

When he reached the gate, she turned her back and bent down to check the horse's hooves. Jackson gathered himself, sprang to his feet, and rushed through the gate, preparing to launch himself and take her down. When she swung around and threw dirt into his eyes, it stunned him. Blinded and staggering forward, he felt her boot land in his stomach. His vision blurred, and he started to fall.

———

Zeb and Caleb hadn't arrived with the cattle yet when Norah reached the ranch, she was mildly disappointed. If things had gone well, they'd hoped to be back last night. In any case, she expected them to come soon, and Pike had said he would be out this morning as well. She was eager to get started working with a mare she had bought last week. Mostly, the mare was for breeding stock, but Norah wanted to work her on the lunge line this morning.

First, she checked the tracks around the house, both front and back. They looked no different from what she had seen last night. Feeling confident that no one had been here since then, Norah walked to the newly fenced pasture, roped the mare, and began working her.

Thirty minutes later, she tied the mare to a fencepost and bent to check the hooves. Norah moved from one side to the other, satisfied until she lifted the left rear hoof and saw a small rock lodged in the hoof. As she released the leg, she saw the mare's head come up. Then her ears came forward.

Norah could hear footsteps behind her now. She had time to bend down and scoop up a handful of dirt. She wheeled and threw the dirt into a man's face as he lunged toward her. His momentum carried him into her as he cursed and clawed at his eyes. Bowled over by his weight when they collided, Norah scrambled free and aimed a kick at his ribs as he came off the ground.

She heard a grunt of pain and a gasp of air after the kick. She turned and leaped toward her Winchester, propped up against the fence just a few steps away. She wasn't quick enough to get clear of him. He dove, grabbed her ankles, and tackled her. She felt his weight come down on her and felt his hands around her neck, shutting off her air.

"Where is it?" He hissed the question at her.

Norah's eyes fluttered open at the question. Her hands clawed at him as she struggled for air. He let go of her throat and leaned in. She smelled whiskey and tobacco as he repeated his question.

"What'd you do with the gold?"

Still struggling for breath, she pushed at him and gasped to answer. Suddenly, she heard another voice. Her attacker came up off the ground, his hand sweeping down for his pistol. Two shots sounded before he got the pistol clear, then she saw him jerk backward. A third shot followed the first two. He collapsed on the ground at her feet.

———

I picked up Norah's trail after I hit the stage road moving east. The tracks were fresh, and this road had little traffic. These had to be her tracks. I picked up the pace as the sun rose overhead. The first thing I could see as I approached the ranch was that Zeb and Caleb hadn't returned with my cows. The big pasture was empty.

That was a disappointment. I left the stage road and moved in closer. The new house came slowly into view, and that was puzzling. There was no sign of Norah at or around the house. I thought I would see her there.

A rise in the ground and a stand of oak trees blocked the view of her horse pasture, but I still thought I would see her when I cleared the trees. She'd come out here to work with her horses, after all.

When I rounded the oak trees, I saw what I'd feared all along. Norah had her back to the house, working on a horse's hoof. A man was sprinting across the fenced pasture, and as I watched, he dove at her.

I put the boots to Hank, and he leaped forward, galloping toward the fenced pasture. Norah was putting up a fight. Jackson, or whoever it was, was clawing at his eyes, and I saw Norah put a boot into him. It wasn't enough. When she tried to get away, he tackled her and got on top. His hands were around her neck.

As I neared the fence, it looked like I might get there too late. Hank couldn't jump the fence, and I didn't have time to dismount, open the gate, and run inside. As they struggled on the ground, they rolled and turned in my direction. I drew my Colt and yelled at the top of my lungs.

His head came up, and he started up from the ground, pulling his gun. Now I had a clear shot. Hank had slowed as we neared the fence, but he was still moving along the fence line. I fired the first shot as the attacker cleared his holster. It wasn't a clean shot, but I got enough of him to knock him backward and throw his aim off.

I pulled Hank to a stop with my left hand and fired twice more. I probably only needed one of them. That second one took him dead center. He staggered backward and went down. As he fell backward, the third shot hit him in the neck.

I pulled my feet from the stirrups and jumped off Hank's back and over the fence. If that guy had so much as twitched, I was ready to empty my gun into him. When I neared the body, I could see there was no need. I holstered the Colt and turned to drop beside Norah as she pushed herself up to her knees. We stayed there and hugged.

I pulled back to look at the marks on her neck. Norah told me she was fine and struggled to her feet, looking over her shoulder.

"I think it was Frank Jackson," she said. "He asked me what I did with the gold." She touched the sore spots on her neck. "The gold question might have kept me alive long enough for you to get here," she said. "He knew he couldn't find it if he killed me."

I was enormously relieved and furious all at once. Relieved, of course, that I'd gotten there in time, but angry at myself for not getting there sooner. Furious with her attacker. I stared at the man lying on his back, feeling the blood rushing to my face.

"He's as dead as he'll get," Norah pointed out, "and I'm fine. You came just in time." She linked her arm in mine and walked me back to the house. We double-checked the house and property for anybody who might still be out there. Finally, satisfied he'd acted alone, I sat with her and waited for Zeb and Caleb. They rolled in with the cattle about half an hour later.

We told them the story of what had happened. I told them their number one job for the next week or two was to guard Norah whenever she was out there. After that, maybe we could all relax. The boys helped me load the dead man on his horse for me to bring him back to Fredericksburg. Norah came to town with me.

King Simms had done his homework carefully. He hadn't planned on another trip to San Antonio, but this seemed worth it. Until now, he had planned on some guesswork to know when the valuable shipments went out on the stagecoach to El Paso. That, and maybe some legwork by Frank Jackson, but he no longer trusted Jackson.

No, the best way to know what was on the coach was to have somebody here in San Antonio who he would pay to let him know. He'd found that a few dollars spread out here and there could do the trick. Amazing what folks would do for a little cash.

So, with that in mind, he'd spent some time in the café across the street from the San Antonio stage stop, watching for somebody who might tip him off for a few dollars. He had in mind somebody who wasn't too smart and who liked his whiskey, in that order. It didn't take long to pick out his man.

The guy in the best position to know would be the clerk selling tickets inside, but Simms had to rule him out right away. The clerk seemed pretty smart, for starters, and Simms had followed him after work twice. The guy had gone straight home to a boarding house, without even stopping for a beer on the way home. That wouldn't do.

Candidate number two was over there, hitching up horses and loading trunks on the top of the stage right now. Simms guessed him to be about twenty, and he was sleepwalking through the morning, as best Simms could tell. He hitched horses like he'd done it a thousand times and threw steamer trunks on top of the stage without worrying too much about breaking anything inside.

Simms had to admit, the guy didn't look curious about what was in the trunks or take much notice of the passengers, but Simms could fix that with money. The kid could get curious about those things in a hurry if he wanted to.

That was the second thing that made Simms smile. He'd been planning on following this guy after work, but he didn't have to wait that long. He trailed the kid for a couple blocks when he left for lunch until he turned onto Houston Street, then watched him go straight into a saloon.

Simms waited until he came out, which was about forty-five minutes later. He wasn't staggering, which meant he'd probably stuck to beer at the lunch hour, with maybe a sandwich to soak things up a little.

Simms strolled around town a bit, then went back to the café for some food. He was waiting when the kid left the stage stop at five o'clock. The kid went back to Houston Street, turned, and ducked into the same saloon. Simms followed with a small, cruel smile on his face. This was going to be easy.

He paused outside the batwing doors and had to squint to make out the dingy sign above the doors: *Ike's Saloon*. Simms shrugged and pushed his way inside. He might have to remember the name if he needed to meet with the kid again. He was hoping that just one meeting and a little payoff would be all it would take.

Pausing to adjust to the light, Simms picked out his stool pigeon at a table by the window. The kid stared suspiciously as Simms approached, but his expression softened when he saw Simms held a shot of whiskey in each hand.

Simms said nothing, he held out the whiskey and pointed at an empty chair.

The stage stop kid pushed out the chair with his foot while relieving Simms of one of the whiskey glasses.

"I'm passin' through," Simms declared. The kid shrugged. "You work around here somewhere?" Simms asked.

"Stage stop," the kid said. Simms stared at him long enough to make the kid uncomfortable. "Hitching horses and loading steamer trunks and like that," he added after a long pause.

Simms gave the kid a fake name of Ike Stout, borrowing the first name from the saloon. The kid said his name was Roy.

Simms waved down another server and handed Roy another shot of whiskey. "I don't guess they pay much over there," Simms observed.

Roy snorted and drowned his sorrows with the whiskey glass.

"I'm lookin' for somebody that might want to make a few extra bucks," Simms said smoothly. The kid looked up for the first time. Simms just let the words hang in the air.

"Doin' what?" Roy finally mumbled.

Simms shrugged. "Nothin' hard," he said. "I might want to know what they're carrying on the stage from time to time."

The kid stared hard at him. "I jest throw the stuff on top," he snarled. "They don't tell me nuthin' about what's inside."

Simms nodded. "But I'll bet a smart kid like you could find out if he wanted to," Simms observed. Saying the kid was smart was tough, he downed his shot to cover the laugh that had bubbled up in his throat.

"How much?" Roy asked.

Now Simms knew he had the kid. He glanced across the table—Roy was wearing rags and probably slept in a livery stable somewhere. He certainly smelled like it.

"Ten bucks a month," Simms said carelessly. "First month paid up front."

Roy said nothing. His mouth worked open and shut like a fish, which, in a way, Simms figured, he was.

"Okay."

So, Simms thought, the fish can talk. He slid ten dollars across the table. It disappeared into the kid's pocket instantly.

Ten minutes later, Simms had worked out how Roy could reach him by telegram in Fredericksburg. The kid would notify Simms what was on each stage, using the fake name Simms had given him.

Satisfied, Simms gave the kid one more whiskey shot, then leaned in uncomfortably close. "Good," he said. "I'm sure you're a kid who knows how to keep his mouth shut." He patted the Colt on his hip and leaned in farther. "If you get chatty, I'll know where to pay you a visit." The menace in his voice was unmistakable.

The kid went pale. The mouth worked open and shut a few more times. "Yes, sir," he stuttered.

Ten minutes later, Simms was on his way to scout two possible holdup locations.

———

The next afternoon, Simms followed the stagecoach route from Boerne north toward Kerrville. He was determined that the robberies would happen between those two Texas cities, or not at all. Ten miles out of Boerne, he found what he wanted.

He'd been thinking about a spot where the stagecoach had to climb a hill. With some cover at the top, he, Blue, and Frank Jackson could step out when the coach was moving at a crawl. If there was a shotgun rider on top, maybe he would be reasonable. If not, that's why he had Blue. The robbery would be easy after that.

As it was, Simms found a steep downhill, followed by a sharp turn at the bottom. Several large boulders provided cover at the bottom. The stage would almost have to come to a complete stop in order to make the turn at the bottom. They would be ready.

Scouting to the east, he found it would only be a short distance after the robbery to merge with the other coach road—the one from Boerne to his stage stop in Stonewall. Along the way, there was a stream flowing down from the Pedernales River. He might be able to drive the coach along the stream bed far enough to throw off any trackers. It was perfect. He would wait to rob the first payroll stage here.

Moving north, looking for a place to make his practice run robbery, things weren't as good. Finally, just a few miles short of Kerrville, he found a place that would work. It was an uphill climb. Not a steep one, but enough to slow the coach.

Just before he reached the climb, Simms pulled over to read a wooden sign driven into the ground beside the coach road. "Gillespie County," he mumbled to himself. He shrugged. It made no difference to him which county he was in when he robbed the stage.

Simms spurred his horse forward and looked over the

setup. Not as good as the first one, but good enough. They would have farther to go to reach the coach road from Boerne to Stonewall, so they would have to make sure there was no pursuit. Maybe he would tie a couple branches to the rear wheels of the stage to brush over the tracks.

It would do. The first robbery would be here. Now he had to connect with Blue and Frank Jackson, then wait for word from the kid at the San Antonio stage stop.

Chapter 15

Name from the Past

There were two Texas Rangers camped in my office when I arrived first thing the next morning, two days after the shooting. Richard Ware and Leander McNelly were both there. I could smell coffee, so I knew they'd made themselves useful already. I hoped they had some good news.

I stepped around the desk and helped myself to the coffee. I made a face, but at least it was better than Boone's coffee. I took a sip and got right down to it.

"I'm guessin' you boys got my telegram that I shot somebody that could be Frank Jackson," I said. They nodded. I fished around in my desk drawer and slid a photograph across the desk to them.

"My deputy, Lat Smith, is out of town for a couple days, checking the northern part of the county," I told them. "We had a little dust-up over an illegal race track a little while back. I want to make sure nobody's got the ponies running again up there. Lat saw a poster for Frank Jackson over in Round Rock, so he could identify the body if he were here."

"We've got a cabinet maker named Jeb that just gets 'em in a coffin and gets 'em in the ground at Boot Hill just as fast as he can," I continued. "This guy you're looking at went in the ground yesterday. But we've got a guy here in Fredericksburg who takes pictures for weddings and families and such. Got his start during the war. He took this picture for me."

McNelly picked it up, took a look, and passed it over to Ware, who nodded. "Frank Jackson," he said, sliding the picture back to me. I put it back in the drawer.

McNelly leaned back in his chair. "Anybody else know about this?" he asked. "I mean, does anybody else know it was Frank Jackson?"

"Only two," I said. "My girl, Norah, was the one who got attacked by Jackson. My deputy, Lat Smith, I'll have to tell him when he gets back. Everybody else, I just told 'em it was a guy that pulled his smokewagon on me when I caught 'em robbing a store."

McNelly nodded thoughtfully. "Probly best to leave it that way," he said. "We don't exactly know what's left of that Bass Gang, and we don't need to get 'em all fired up about one of their own gettin' planted on your Boot Hill out there."

He leaned forward and put his elbows on his knees. "There's something else you should hear about, Pike, although I don't expect it will affect you none out here."

"There was a shootout over to New Orleans last week. They ain't much used to gunplay over there," McNelly said. "Couple of guys got shot over what sounds like a crooked poker game. Dealer hauled iron first, accordin' to witnesses in the saloon." He stopped and looked at me. "Two reasons why I'm tellin' you this now."

I had a feeling I wasn't gonna like this, but I wanted to hear it anyway.

"The saloon where this happened is owned by a guy who ain't usin' his real name. Nothing too strange about that. Thing is, a few folks think his real name is Jack Davis. One of the Bass Gang. Can't nobody prove anything now, but some folks think that's him. Davis wasn't in the saloon when the shooting happened. His poker dealer was runnin' the place while Davis was gone. Lit a shuck outta New Orleans after the shooting, that shooter did."

I stirred around in my chair. This Sam Bass thing wouldn't seem to go away for me. That guy casts a long shadow, I thought.

McNelly watched me for a minute, then kept going. "The other thing is more about the guy that done the shooting. Pretty slick with his six-gun, folks said. The sheriff over there asked us to send a few posters if we had any idea if it could be somebody from out our way. Didn't sound like he was from around there, folks said."

I had one name that popped into my head. I was hoping it wasn't the one McNelly was about to mention.

"You told me King Simms never saw you, right? Or maybe know you came with us to shut down that cattle rustling operation in Mexico?" McNelly asked.

That was the name I didn't want to hear. I had killed Simms's partner, George Lynch, in a shootout on the streets of Laredo. McNelly and I, along with his troops, had shut down Simms's operation down there near the border with Mexico. Simms got away, though, and I remembered McNelly telling me the man carried grudges.

I thought about it long and hard. "I don't think he'd

know about me or be looking for me," I finally answered. "For sure, he never saw me. He's probly never even heard of me unless George Lynch said something before we met up in Laredo. So it was King Simms that did the shooting down in New Orleans?"

McNelly glanced over at Ware, then nodded slowly. "Two gamblers in the saloon that night thought mebbe the guy looked like the King Simms poster," he said.

I stared at the desktop and let a few thoughts run through my head. "No reason to think this has anything to do with Frank Jackson, right?"

They both shook their heads. We talked for a couple minutes, then they got up to leave. I followed them out. "Do you have a poster for King Simms?" I asked. "I can at least see what he looks like."

McNelly pulled one out of his saddlebag and handed it to me. I unrolled it, took a look, and shook my head. "Don't think I've ever seen him," I said. "But I'll be watching."

I watched them ride off, then went back into my office. I was hoping I'd seen the last of King Simms. His mug on the poster was enough for me. He could stay over there in Louisiana, as far as I was concerned. I'd had enough excitement around here lately.

———

The trick was to carry the stolen gold, wallets, and jewelry in a place where nobody could see it. Simms stood back from the old stagecoach he'd bought and looked it over. There was nobody else in the stage stop office with him, and that's the way he liked it. He knew he would have to open the place for a little while every day, or folks would get suspicious. First, though, he had to do some work on this stagecoach. The office was more like an old barn, so he'd just rolled the doors open at the back and pulled the stagecoach inside.

Simms climbed up on top and looked things over. There was a place to set a strongbox on the top, behind the driver and shotgun rider. That was too obvious. It almost invited highwaymen to rob the stage. A cruel, thin smile passed across Simms's lips. That was almost funny, the thought of shooting a guy trying to rob his stage, after he'd already robbed another stage. Nope, that wouldn't work. He planned to be the only highwayman in these parts.

He climbed down and crawled inside the stagecoach. The seat was narrow and hard, but he'd expected that. He'd rather smack the back of a horse than ride in one of these things any day. Simms got down on his knees to inspect the seats. He decided he could tear out the board with the padding and leather covering on one seat and put it back with a hinge screwed to the wall of the coach.

Simms looked carefully at where the seat was attached to the wall of the coach, running his hand along the wood. A hinge should work there. He could use the hinge to open the seat up. He would store the goods inside, below the seat—just that one addition to hold the loot. If anybody asked about it, he could say he had built in a little extra space for luggage. Simms climbed out, cracked open a bottle of whiskey on a shelf in the stage stop, and decided he'd had a good idea.

He poked his head out the back door, remembering some scrap lumber in a pile behind the stage stop. The old owner, Werner, had clearly done his own repairs on the stage. Simms picked up several boards and an old rusty saw, then carried them back inside. He set to work with the old saw, cutting down the boards to the size he needed. He could use them to make a box under the seat, big enough to hold whatever he could steal from the stages.

Simms poked around the shop, looking for any tools Werner might have left besides the old rusty saw. He found a few nails but nothing else—not even a hammer. Werner must have taken everything else with him.

Simms cursed, picked up his hat, and jammed it down low on his head. He picked up a pencil and a scrap of paper, scrawled the word *closed* on the paper, and stuck it in the front window. Then he set out for the general store down the street.

Hat down low enough to make it tough to see his face, he entered the store. Just his luck—the owner wanted to introduce himself and talk.

"Howdy, stranger, name's Elmer," he said, holding his hand out.

Simms nodded and pushed past him. He couldn't even remember the fake name he had given Werner when he bought the stage stop... Perkins, that was it. Jed Perkins. Not that he wanted to tell this nosy shop owner.

Simms found his way to the hardware, growling when Elmer offered to help him find what he was looking for. He pulled out three hinges, some screws, and a screwdriver. He picked up a hammer and a box of nails on his way to the counter.

Elmer made another try at talking to the stranger. He needed every customer he could get. "Gotta fix some things, do ya?"

Simms grunted and pushed his money across the countertop without answering. Elmer fished in an old cigar box where he kept his change. He couldn't keep himself from one more effort.

"The missus and me would be glad to have you 'n yer family over for dinner sometime."

Simms heard the words on his way out the door. He didn't break stride. When he reached the street, he vowed to buy anything he needed in Fredericksburg after this. A nosy shopkeeper was the last thing he needed.

Back in the stage stop, he left the *closed* sign in the window and got down to work. It didn't take long to remember his hands were mostly skilled in dealing cards and pulling out his Colt. The first part of his project wasn't too bad, though. He clawed out the nails and pulled the old seat out of the coach. He inspected it and set it down on the floor. He should be able to put hinges on it and attach it back to the wall of the coach.

Simms hammered together a box to put under the seat and attached it to the floor and walls of the coach with a maximum amount of effort and several volleys of cursing. The boards were old and weathered, and it made for tough going.

When the box had been hammered into place, he began screwing the hinges on the old seat. This was a fresh kind of torture. He needed a drill, but he didn't have one. He needed gloves—his hands were breaking out in blisters. He wasn't about to go back to see Elmer in the general store to ask about gloves.

Simms grabbed an old shirt out of his carpetbag, ripped it in two, and wrapped the pieces around his hands. Forty-five minutes later, with sweat coursing down his face, he had the old seat screwed back into place. He lifted the seat, peered down into the box, then dropped the seat back down to cover the box he'd just installed. He looked at his blistered hands and went looking for his whiskey bottle.

An hour later, with the level of whiskey down about two inches, he heard a rustling at the door. Hunched down against the wall, he sprang into action. Despite the whiskey and his blistered hands, he was on his feet with his Colt in his hands in seconds. When he saw Blue's face peering in through the window, he relaxed. He'd forgotten he had told Blue to meet him here.

Simms opened the door, scanned the street outside, then locked the door again behind Blue.

"You see Jackson out there anywhere?" he demanded. "Jackson was supposed to meet us here, too."

Blue shrugged. "Ain't never met Jackson," he reminded Simms. "But there warn't nobody out there lookin' for the stagecoach stop or nuthin. But," he mumbled. "There was..." his voice trailed away.

"There was what?" Simms barked. He was still in a foul mood from his carpentry work on the stage.

Blue shrugged again. "They was a-buryin' somebody out at Boot Hill, over there to Fredericksburg. I asked folks at the saloon who it was. Nobody knowed, but some of 'em think it was somebody from the Bass Gang."

Simms stood still, rooted where he was, trying to remember if anybody could make a connection between himself and Frank Jackson. He decided they couldn't, so he relaxed just a smidge. He watched as Blue looked into the coach and inspected the new box he built under the seat.

"Can anybody set on there?" Blue asked doubtfully.

A thundercloud passed over Simms's face. "Don't nobody have to set on there," he snarled. It's for storing the loot from the robberies, you idiot!"

Blue backed off a step and stood in the center of the room, twirling his hat in his hands. He set his lips in a thin line. He glanced at the Colt on Simms's hip and said nothing, but he was a man who remembered insults.

Simms forced himself to calm down. He needed Blue for now, especially if Jackson had gone and got himself killed. He hauled a couple chairs from what had served as Werner's office area and told Blue to sit down.

Simms leaned in. "Did you pick up any telegrams for me in Fredericksburg?" he asked.

Blue reached into his pocket and pulled out an envelope. He handed it over.

Simms took the envelope. "You gave 'em my fake name?"

Blue nodded.

Simms lifted the flap on the envelope. It was unsealed. He stared at Blue suspiciously. "Did you read this?" he asked, his tone low and threatening.

Blue shook his head. "Never learned to read nor write, Boss," he mumbled. He glanced up at Simms, then stared at the floor.

Simms pulled out the message and read:

Stage on Thursdy got a couple folks from back east.

lookin like they've got some jewels and watches

and such. Stop

Next Tusdy is the big one. Goin to all the forts. Stop

Simms folded up the telegram and put it in his pocket, still thinking about Blue. If Simms were in his shoes, he'd have said what Blue said about not being able to read. He would have been lying, of course. His eyes dropped to an old, well-used Smith and Wesson .44 Russian on Blue's hip. He would have to keep his eye on Blue. He'd caught the man checking out Simms's gun a couple times. There could be more to deal with than he'd thought before. Blue might wonder if he was fast enough to take down Simms and keep the loot.

"Day after tomorrow, we take out the stage, just south of Kerrville. I need you to drive the stage outta here tonight and park it a couple miles south of Kerrville, out in the brush. I'll meet you in the saloon on Main Street in Kerrville tomorrow night."

Simms stood and moved toward his whiskey bottle again. Blue watched him go, not sure if the meeting was over. Finally, he stood and went outside to get the horses and hitch up the stage. From what he had read on the telegram, it sounded like an army payroll was coming through next week. He wondered if Simms believed the part about him not being able to read.

———

I met Norah at the café for dinner and told her right away about the visit from Rangers McNelly and Ware. It did not surprise her that they had identified the guy who had attacked her as Frank Jackson. We'd been pretty sure that's who it was.

When I got to the part about King Simms, she put her fork down. I could see the worry on her face. "Has anybody seen him in this county?" was her first question.

I shook my head. "I'm not sure there's anybody in this county who would know what he looks like," I said. "I never got a look at him. He didn't come to the horse ranch when you were living there with Maribel, did he?"

She shook her head. I reached across the table to take her hand. "There's no reason to think he would be in Gillespie County," I said. "He wasn't tied in with Frank Jackson or the Sam Bass Gang. He was down near Laredo that whole time, smuggling cows out of Mexico. They would have never crossed paths."

She relaxed a little, gave my hand a squeeze, and went back to eating. "When does Lat Smith get back in town?" she asked.

"Tomorrow," I told her. "Should be in about midday. I don't expect he's had any trouble up there. I'll tell him about Frank Jackson and see if he's ever heard anything about King Simms."

She nodded and leaned in a little. "Promise me if you're doing anything you think is dangerous, you'll take Lat Smith," she said. "And if Lat isn't around, see if Boone will go with you. I don't have a good feeling about this. King Simms, whatever is left of the Sam Bass Gang, all of it sounds like trouble. Promise me."

I started to protest about how she shouldn't worry, but those beautiful eyes had me pinned to the wall. I promised. After that, we just talked about the new ranch, the house we were building, and the future we had ahead of us. I thought about showing her the King Simms poster, but I didn't wanna spoil the mood we had going.

I felt downright peaceful when I kissed her goodnight and strolled back to the office. Sometimes, my gut tells me when trouble is coming. Sometimes it doesn't. This turned out to be one of those times when it didn't.

Chapter 16

Trial Run

King Simms sat astride his horse in the sparse cover of a small stand of cedar elm trees. He glanced upward—the trees were about fifty feet high, the trunks were big enough to cover their presence if nobody was looking too hard. He glanced over at Blue, who was swatting at a mosquito, sweating in the heat, and swearing under his breath at all of it.

Simms was worried about having only the two of them on this job. The boy at the San Antonio stage stop had told him they usually had a shotgun rider on each stage. The driver might have a gun, but he was busying driving the stage. He and Blue should be enough, unless one or two of the passengers had a gun and knew how to use it. That's the part that had him worried.

These passengers were a family from back east, according to the kid in San Antonio. Simms forced himself to calm down. This one would go down like he'd planned it. He just had to replace Frank Jackson before he went after the next stage—the one with the payroll. That one might have a soldier riding in the coach or even on horseback beside the stage with all that money in the strongbox.

Simms glanced to his west. They had hidden his stage back in the trees in that direction. The horses were already hitched, and he had already tied two big branches to the back of the stage to drag behind and cover the trail. When they reached the first stream, moving east and south, he would cut the branches off. Then he would take the stage down a flat, shallow section of water for a few hundred feet, climb, and go east until they hit the stage road from Boerne to Stonewall.

Blue would leave separately and lead Simms's horse a few hours later to join him at the stage stop in Stonewall. Simms had decided he didn't trust Blue to drive the stage with the loot in it.

Simms's horse shifted his feet impatiently and Simms pulled the watch from his pocket while he patted the animal's neck. The stage was about ten minutes late by his figuring. "Not that unusual," he muttered to himself.

Blue glanced over. "D'ya think it's still comin'?"

Simms leaned over to spit in the dirt. "It's comin'," he growled. "Just be ready. Don't shoot nobody if you don't have to. We're just practicin' the route and such with this robbery."

Blue stared moodily down at the trail. He didn't like the way Simms talked to him. He thought again about the payroll robbery he'd read about in that telegram. A lot depended on the third guy Simms planned to hire for that one. It sounded like a lot of money, and he didn't plan to share it any more than he had to.

Dust rose from the trail below them, and both men leaned forward, staring to the south, straining to see the coach. The dust thickened, and the cloud grew, but it was another five minutes before the stage came into view—first the horses, then the coach.

"Don't shoot nobody 'less you have to," Simms hissed. "An' pull that bandana up over your nose. Pull yer hat down. We can't let 'em see our faces."

The coach slowed as it climbed the rise. Simms waited until it was near the top, then put his spurs to his horse. The startled animal jumped out from the trees onto the road. Blue followed. The shotgun rider saw them and reached for the double-barreled shotgun resting on the seat beside him.

"Don't," Simms barked. When the rider laid his hand on the shotgun, Simms put his fingers to his lips and cut loose a deafening whistle. The shotgun rider froze where he was. The stage horses reared, and the driver fought to get them under control.

Blue's horse pranced in a circle and he fought to bring the animal around. He glanced first at the shotgun rider, he'd seen the driver had his hands full with the horses. When he looked back at the driver, the man had a rifle halfway up from the floorboards beneath his legs. Blue's reaction was automatic. He pulled his Colt .45 and shot twice. He only needed the first one. It hit the driver full in the chest and he slumped back against his seat. The second shot exactly followed the path of the first. The driver laid pinned back against the back of the seat for a moment, then toppled sideways into the dust at the side of the road.

Screams sounded from inside the coach. Simms glared at Blue, then pointed at the shotgun rider with the barrel of his Winchester rifle. "Watch him!" he hissed, then rode around to the side of the coach. A family of four was crouched on the floor inside. Simms saw no weapons.

He forced calm into his voice. "Okay, folks," he said. "The driver was stupid enough to draw on us. Don't nobody else need to get hurt. Just come outta there real slow. I need to see your hands at all times." He waited while they came down from the coach—first the father, followed by the mother and children.

The shotgun rider was down on the ground at the side of the coach now. Blue held his pistol on the rider and had his other hand on the reins of the stage horses. Simms pulled two lengths of rope from his saddle. He pointed his pistol at the family. "Line up beside the coach and look the other way. Don't nobody look over here."

They did as they were told. Simms motioned at the shotgun rider to lie face-down on the ground. Simms knelt and tied his hands and feet. That done, he moved to the passengers and held a pistol on them as they gave him their money and jewels. They faced the other way and handed things back to him over their shoulders.

Simms climbed up to the driver's seat on the coach and looked around—there was a strongbox, but it was unlocked and proved empty when he opened it. He kicked the passenger luggage down to the ground and went through it quickly—there were a few more jewels, but no money.

Blue stayed beside the stage horses and watched as Simms threw the loot into a knapsack and tied it around the saddle horn on his horse. Simms rode back around and addressed the passengers.

"Nobody move for five minutes," he snarled in a low tone. "Then you can untie the shotgun rider and go on to Kerrville. One of us'll be watching you," he lied. "Anybody moves before five minutes is up, you get shot. Got it?" He saw all the heads nod up and down.

Simms rode around Blue and motioned at him. They galloped away, threading their way through the cedar elms until they reached the hidden stage. Simms vaulted off the horses, taking the knapsack with him and tossing his reins to Blue.

"He hauled out that rifle," Blue mumbled. "Didn't have no choice. He woulda plugged me in another two seconds."

"Shut up," Simms growled. "No time. Change of plans. Take my horse and ride south on the stage road back to Boerne. Put my hoss in the livery when you git there. Then take the stage road up to Stonewall and meet me there. Won't nobody think anything about your tracks on the stage road, but I don't want two sets of 'em. Leave my horse in Boerne. I'll git it later."

Simms watched him ride away, shaking his head and mumbling under his breath. The last thing they needed was a dead driver. Now, he'd have to think twice about robbing the payroll stage next week.

He tossed the knapsack into the box he'd built under the seat inside the stage, then climbed up on top and pulled out, following the route he'd taken over here. He held a course to the south and east, pulling up twice to see if the branches he'd tied to the back of the stage were doing enough to cover the tracks. He decided they were.

After an hour, he reached the stream he was looking for. It flowed south from the Pedernales River and would help him further cover his tracks. Simms cut the branches from the back of the stage. He'd planned to toss them aside here, but on impulse, he tossed them up on top of the stage and led the horses down into the water.

He followed the stream for two hundred yards and climbed out on the opposite bank.

When the rear wheels were out of the water, he tied the branches to the stage again and drove up and out of the stream. He held a course east and south again until he reached the stage road to Stonewall. Simms climbed down again, cut the branches loose, and took the stage road toward Stonewall. He relaxed a little for the first time that day.

Along the way, he stopped, climbed down, and went to count the money in the knapsack. One hundred fifty dollars, plus some jewelry that might be worth almost that much. Simms's lips curled into a smile for the first time that day. He'd tell Blue it was worth only two hundred altogether, then split that much with him. Not a bad day, he decided.

———

Blue rode south to Boerne like he'd been told. He saw only two lone riders on the way. He'd lowered his bandana, but kept his hat low and nodded to each of them on the way by. Blue got a nod and a wave in return. His stomach unknotted itself by the time he reached Boerne. Just a guy riding to town and leading a horse. Nobody would think twice about that, would they?

He left Simms's horse at the livery, then broke with Simms's orders for the first time. He stopped at the saloon, stayed an hour, and tossed down five whiskey shots before he took the stage road to Stonewall. Blue held the reins with one hand and the saddle horn with the other on the way out of Boerne. He had his wits about him enough to know he had to stay in the saddle.

It had kinda become routine—the best kind of routine —to meet Norah in the café for dinner several times a week. We had finished our meal and were holding hands across the table. I told her I'd had a quiet day. That was my favorite kind, after the Frank Jackson deal. Norah had spent the day working her horses, but told me that Zeb and Caleb had been around the whole time.

I was putting off going back to the office one last time, but when the door opened and Lat Smith came in, I had a feeling I would have to go back right away.

Lat took off his hat and nodded at Norah. "Ma'am," he said. He glanced at me. "The sheriff from Kerr County, a man named Marcus Bergen, is at the office, and he's plumb insisting he's got to talk to you."

I tried to remember what Jake McCabe had told me about the sheriff in the next county over. He'd said the sheriff there had been wanting to retire for a few years, but never quite got around to it. Probably needed the cash from working, he'd said.

I got up, leaned over the table, and gave Norah a kiss. I put a dollar on the table to pay for the meal. "See you later," I said.

Norah looked at Lat. "Watch after him," she said.

Lat grinned and put his hat back on his head. "I surely will," he told her.

Norah looked at me and pointed at Lat. "I've got to find a girl for him," she said.

I chuckled and led Lat over to the door. "Did she mean that?" he asked.

"Probably did," I told him. "She's a downright determined woman, too. This could be a good thing. Maybe she'll find you a keeper."

We reached the street and Lat told me more about Marcus Bergen's visit. "There was a stage robbed on the road from Boerne to Kerrville," he said. "Happened a little way east and south of Kerrville. Driver got kilt. Bergen wants you to help him find the robbers."

I stared at Lat. "Boerne and Kerrville aren't in my county," I told him. "Why's he want me to help?"

Lat shrugged. "He says the stage road crosses into Gillespie County for just about a ten-mile stretch, and that's where the holdup happened." He frowned and fell into step beside me as we reached the office. "If'n you ask me," he said, "I think he just don't want to get hisself shot at by stage robbers."

I chuckled one more time and opened the door to the jail and the office. "I expect you might just be right," I told him.

Bergen looked up when we came into the office, then got up to shake my hand. He looked like a man hoping for help. A man, like Jake had said, who wanted to retire and couldn't quite do it yet. He wanted no part of this robbery. You could see it in his face.

Bergen sat down and glanced at Lat, then at me. "Your deppity tell you what happened out there?" he asked.

I shook my head. "I just know a stage got robbed, just a few miles inside my county, from what Lat said. It was the stage from Boerne to Kerrville? And the driver got killed?"

Bergen nodded, his lips set in a thin line. "Shot through the heart twice. They got the drop on the shotgun rider and he couldn't give 'em no help. Driver shouldn't have gone for his Winchester a'tall, that's what the shotgun rider says. One family ridin' in the coach got all their money and jewelry stole. Didn't hurt the passengers none."

"Passengers and shotgun rider made it to Kerrville?" I asked.

Bergen nodded. "That's how I found out about it."

"Any idea where the robbers went?" I asked.

Bergen snorted. "One of 'em rode down to Boerne, we think. Somebody rode in leadin' another horse, and got drunker than Cooter Brown at a saloon in Boerne, from what I could find out. Barely settin' his horse on the way out of town, they said. Trail was too old to follow by the time I got down there."

"The other robber?" I asked. "The loot?"

Bergen shook his head. "Wasn't much of a trail there," he said. "There was some brushed-up ground going off east from there. Coulda been somebody covering tracks. Don't really know for sure. Loot was probly with the second guy. The one in Boerne left both hosses at the livery stable whilst he got stewed over at the saloon. Probly wouldn't have the hosses there if the saddlebags was full of money."

I thought on that for a minute. He was probably right. And if the second robber had come east, he was moving farther into my county.

I stood up. "My deputy and I will look into it," I offered. "We'll try to track that second varmint if he came east. I'll send a telegram if we come up with anything."

Bergen stood up, looking pretty relieved. "'Preciate it," was all he said. Lat saw him out, then came back inside. We made plans to ride out the next day to the robbery site.

King Simms laid out the cash from the stagecoach robbery and counted it again. One hundred fifty dollars. He took thirty dollars and stuffed it into his pocket. Next, he looked at the jewelry. He wasn't much of a jewelry expert, but he knew a guy in San Antonio who could sell it for him. Simms took about one-third of the jewelry pieces and put them in his saddlebags. He put the rest with the one hundred twenty dollars he would share with Blue. No way, he reasoned, that Blue knew for sure how much they had taken.

Blue had made a bad mistake back there. He hadn't been paying attention, and the driver had almost gotten off a shot. Now the driver was dead and there would be more guards riding with the coaches. Especially with the coach carrying the army payroll next week.

Simms heard a knock at the door. He figured it was likely Blue, coming back to meet up like he'd been told. Simms moved to the door. Blue was done after this next robbery, he was sure of that. Simms liked his helpers greedy, but not too greedy. And smart, but not too smart. Blue was a little too greedy and a little too smart. Careless, too. Simms could take care of that problem. Robbers got shot during holdups, didn't they?

Simms fixed Blue with a hard stare when he came into the stage stop. "Dead drivers weren't in the plans," he said in a low, threatening tone.

Blue shrugged and avoided Simms's glare. "Driver was haulin' out a Winchester," he pointed out. "It was him or me." He dragged his eyes up to meet Simms's stare.

Simms left off staring and moved across to the pile of

money and jewelry. He counted out half the money and gave it to Blue, who stuffed it into his pocket. Simms pointed at the jewelry. "You wanna take half, or you want me to sell it all and give you half the cash?"

Simms could see the distrust in Blue's eyes, plain as day. "I'll take half the stones," he said.

Simms turned and divided the pile in half. Blue took his half and jammed that in the pocket on top of the money.

"When we goin' next?" Blue asked.

"Next week," Simms answered. "I gotta get another gunman. They'll have more guards for the next one. I'll get a guy in San Antonio and be back."

"What day next week?" Blue asked. He had to remember that Simms didn't know he'd read the telegram —army payroll next Tuesday, it had said. Blue had to pretend he didn't know.

"Don't know," Simms lied. "Come back in three days and I'll tell you then."

Blue crossed to the door. "I left yer hoss at the livery in Boerne, like you told me," he said. Then he was gone.

Simms stared at the door after Blue left. Too smart and too greedy, just like he'd been thinking. He was pretty sure Blue knew about the army payroll shipment. Blue needed to have some bad luck during the robbery. Simms knew how to arrange for that.

CHAPTER 17

POSTER BOY

Finding the holdup scene wasn't hard. First, I rode over to Kerrville with Lat Smith and found the shotgun rider, still hanging around town. He's the one who'd had sense enough not to haul iron on the robbers. The family of passengers had already left on the stage for Fort Concho. It turns out the man on the stage had sent his money ahead of him to a bank in El Paso, using a service called Western Union. Don't ask me how that works. I just walk down the street to put my money in the bank and take it back out. Anyhow, this guy is a lot smarter than I because his money beat him there.

The passengers weren't there to help us, and the shotgun rider didn't seem to remember much. He was still in Kerrville, but somebody had conked him on the head with a pistol when the robbers left, and he was a little fuzzy. He didn't remember anything after getting hit on the noggin. He said both guys were wearing a bandana over their faces and had their hats down low when they rode up. He didn't recognize either of them and couldn't do much to describe 'em either. He thought they'd ridden away to the north, but he just got that from looking at the tracks after he came to.

That was pretty much the end of the trail for us in Kerrville, so we rode south on the stage road a few miles and found the stagecoach. It was still sitting there at the side of the road. The next stage through had picked up the passengers and the shotgun rider. They had the horses tied behind them when they rolled on to Kerrville. The coach was still there on the trail, where the high-waymen had left it, but we could find no clues in it.

Lat and I both dismounted and moved around the coach, studying the signs we could find on the trail. There wasn't much left to see. There were at least six sets of footprints in the dust, but the robbers had walked around and stepped on things enough to cover what they'd been doing. Blood on the trail told us we had found the spot where the driver had fallen. He had been taken away for burial now, but we could tell the robbers had left him where he fell.

We mounted and followed two sets of hoofprints to the north and west, away from the holdup spot. We found where the two robbers had stopped, then had gone in two different directions after the robbery. The set of hoof-prints leading away to the south rejoined the stage trail after just a couple of miles. There were two sets of hoof-prints, so we knew that the set going south would be the robber who led a horse back down to Boerne. Bergen had already told us about this guy. No point in following him.

Lat and I returned to the robber's meeting point and got down to study the tracks we had in front of us. Like Sheriff Bergen had said, they had covered the tracks over. Covered like somebody was hiding his trail on purpose.

I glanced at Lat. "Whaddya think?" I asked.

Lat stared at the ground. "Well, he covered his trail a-purpose, like we thought," Lat drawled. He moved away several feet and leaned down, studying the ground. "I think mebbe he tied off a couple branches and dragged them behind a wagon. Take a look at this."

I rose and went to kneel beside the tracks he was pointing at. It was a wagon wheel. I could only see one. The brush or branches he'd used had covered the other, but it looked like the second robber had ridden away in a wagon. Well, I thought, that was something we didn't know before.

We followed the brushed-over tracks for a while, but when the ground rose and came to some bare, dusty plateaus, the wind had done its work. We couldn't track any further. I pulled up, lifted my hat, and scratched my head. "He's gone west into our county, probly took the loot in that wagon," I said. "But I can't see how we can track him from here. He could have gone most any direction, I expect."

Lat stared moodily at the ground in front of us. "Nope," he agreed. "This here is a washed-out trail."

I shook my head, staring north and rethinking things. "I think maybe he went to a stream coming off the Pedernales, followed that up to the river and lost his tracks up there," I said. "Could be halfway to Austin or San Antonio by now. Didn't have that much loot accordin' to the shotgun rider. Mebbe ditched the wagon, put the loot in his saddlebag, and went on." I shook my head. "I guess they thought they'd have more loot than they got. One family's stuff wasn't that much to rob."

I reined my horse around and waved at Lat. "Let's get on back to town," I told him. "I'll send a telegram to the Rangers to see if they can help."

It was dark and shadowy in the saloon where King Simms went to meet one of his old gun hands from the cattle rustling days. Simms preferred it that way, dark and shadowy. There were newer, nicer saloons in San Antonio, but too many people in this town might know him. It had taken half the day to get a message to Zeke Rustin, known only as Rusty in the old days, but that was to be expected. Rusty was particular about who he hired out to.

Simms ordered a pitcher of beer and settled down to wait for his gun hand. He smoothed out the message the kid at the stage stop had slipped to him when Simms had slid into the café across the street. The kid was too nervous to come and talk to him, but he'd managed to drop a note on Simms's table when he walked through the café. Simms stared at the note. It looked like a telegram the kid had been getting ready to send.

Extry security on Tues stage. Stop

Guard inside plus guard ridin beside coach.

Watch yerself theyre ready. Stop

Simms growled to himself and shoved the note into his pocket. At least he knew how to get Blue off his payroll now. There would be a couple extra sets of guns for him to ride into. Simms was a lot more comfortable with Zeke Rustin. The man knew how to do his job, take his money, and disappear.

Rusty announced his arrival with the scrape of a chair being pulled back. He emptied the whiskey glass he was carrying, poured himself a beer, and chased the whiskey. The beer glass landed on the table with a thump. Rusty reached for the beer pitcher again. "Whaddya got?" he asked.

Simms snorted. "Good to see you too," he growled. "I got some good money if'n yore interested in workin'."

The second glass of beer vanished. "How much? When?" He stared at Simms over the top of the beer pitcher. Simms waved for another pitcher. Might as well keep the gunhand happy.

"Army payroll for four hunnerd sojers," Simms announced. "They don't get paid but once ever' two months. Next Tuesday is the day."

Rusty frowned as he did the arithmetic in his head. After a minute, he nodded. "How many of us?"

"Three," Simms told him. "After we're done, there won't be but two of us. We split fifty-fifty."

Rusty stared across the table. "We gonna kill one of our own boys?" he asked.

Simms shrugged. "He's greedy, and he's plannin' to play his own hand on this one," he explained. "Can't be trusted. We don't have to kill him. The sojers can take care of that. I got it all planned out."

The new pitcher arrived, and Rusty reached for it. He frowned again. "Brought me in kinda late, didn't you? Next Tuesday?"

Simms shrugged again. "I had me another partner to start with, but he got hisself shot and kilt. I brought in somebody I could find quick, but he ain't workin' out. I thought of you, thought you might like the money."

"How many sojers on that stagecoach?" Rusty asked.

"Two, one inside an' one ridin' alongside. Plus, the driver and I'm sure they'll have themselves a shotgun rider."

Rusty nodded and lit a foul-smelling cigar. He

squinted at Simms through the smoke. "There's four of them, an' only three of us," he pointed out. "An' one of us is fixing to get kilt during the robbery, only he don't know it yet. How's that gonna work? Sounds like they've got us outgunned."

Rusty wanted to ask how Simms knew about the army payroll and the guards, but he decided to trust his old boss on that one. Simms had paid somebody off, Rusty was sure of that. He waited for an answer to his question, still squinting through the smoke.

Simms leaned back. "I got the perfect spot," he said. "Sharp drop in the trail, driver'll have to slow the hosses almost to a stop. The sojer ridin' outside the coach will be on the driver's side, across from the shotgun rider. They always spread the guns that way. I'll have our other guy take out the rider. He won't know about the sojer inside. That's when he'll get himself shot. You an' me, on the other side, take out the shotgun rider and driver. If the hosses try to bolt, they'll turn over the coach on that turn at the bottom. The sojer inside will be a sittin' duck. We can smoke him out of there."

Rusty went to the bar for another whiskey, drained it, came back, and chased it with another beer. "How we gonna carry all the money?" he asked. "And get away with it? It'll be heavy. We'll need time to git out, probly out of Texas, what with the army chasing us."

Simms let a grin spread slowly across his mouth. "That's the best part," he said, leaning forward. "You won't believe how I set that up. Idea come from Sam Bass hisself. Too bad ole Sam didn't get to try it out." They leaned forward and talked for another twenty minutes. Then they drifted over to join a poker game.

Two hours later, they left the saloon. Simms had

planned on riding back tonight, but it was too late. He would have to look for a flophouse. He'd wanted to buy some ammo here too, but it was too late for that as well. He would have to leave early in the morning and get the ammo at the general store in Stonewall. The one with the nosy shopkeeper. Simms swore under his breath and went looking for the nearest flophouse. He was still itching from several bug bites he'd gotten the last time he'd stayed in one.

———

Norah pushed into the general store in Stonewall. The shopkeeper had said there would be a few packs of flower seeds coming in. She wanted to have them planted and blooming by the time she moved into the new ranch house. Norah hoped Pike would move in at the same time. They needed to get that wedding date set, she reminded herself. Today, she saw she would have to wait for the shopkeeper to help her—he was serving a customer at the counter.

"That's a lot of ammo," the shopkeeper observed, stacking several boxes on top of the counter.

Norah could only see the customer's back, but the shopkeeper looked at the customer's face, stiffened, and said nothing else. He glanced up only when he took the money and made change. The customer turned, and Norah saw his face clearly for just a moment. He was tall and dark with a big hook nose and deep-set eyes. When he saw Norah looking at him, he jammed his hat down hard on his head and pushed past her. He walked past without acknowledging her. The door slammed behind him.

Norah turned to look at the shopkeeper, who seemed a little shaken. Norah had always known the shopkeeper, Elmer, to be a friendly, breezy man. Not so today. Elmer forced a smile on his face.

"Miss Norah," he said. "I got yer flower seeds right here under the counter. How's that ranch house comin'?"

"Good," Norah said absently, staring back over her shoulder. "Who was that guy that just left?" she asked. "The one buying a lot of ammo?" Her instincts were telling her Pike might need to know about this guy.

Elmer's smile slipped several notches. "Oh," he said. "That there's the new stage owner. Bought the place from Werner a few weeks ago, I guess. Been in here, mebbe twice. Don't like to chit-chat much. Says his name is Jed Perkins. Likes to be left alone, from what I kin tell."

"Hmmm." Norah picked up the seed packets and put them in her purse. She took out some money to pay for them, staring curiously across the street. "Maybe I'll go over and say hello to him," she said.

Elmer shook his head, then shrugged. "Mebbe he'll be friendlier to you, ma'am," he said. Norah noticed he didn't sound like he believed it. When she left the general store, she noticed Elmer had moved to the store window. She had a feeling he was watching out for her.

Norah approached the front door of the stage stop and knocked, then pulled at the door. It was locked. She knocked again, then stepped to the side to look through the window. She could see no one. How could he not be there? He had come back from the general store just a few minutes ago. She stepped back to the door and knocked again. She got no answer.

A noise from the back of the shop got her attention. Norah turned just in time to see the stage pull out from behind the shop and take the road out of town, moving awfully fast. A shopper about to step out onto the street jumped back as the coach rolled past. Norah hadn't gotten a good look at the driver, but she was pretty sure it was the same man she'd seen in the general store.

———

Simms whipped the horses when he reached the edge of town, glad to leave the place behind him. He'd heard a knock at the front door of the stage stop just as he ducked out the back. Luckily, the horses were hitched, and he'd been ready to go, except for buying the ammo. Now he couldn't get out of this town fast enough.

He'd seen the woman at the front door when he pulled out, but of course, he had no intention of stopping. He didn't plan to sell any tickets for the stage, anyway. And, if it was just another nosy neighbor, he didn't need that.

Simms checked the overhead sun and eased the pace a little. Stages didn't generally move this fast. This needed to look like a normal stage run. He would meet Blue and his new man, Rusty, a little later. They would be ready for the stage carrying the army payroll by morning.

———

The stage from Austin had come in yesterday with a package for me from Ranger Ware. He'd sent a few posters of some folks wanted for robberies and cattle rustling and such. I shuffled through them until I found the one for King Simms. I took it over to the window and studied it in the light—I'd never laid eyes on this guy. That was good, I suppose, because he'd probably never laid eyes on me, either. That made us even if it came to a fight. I studied the poster for a couple seconds. Dark hair, big nose, scary eyes. I would know him now if I saw him.

Ranger Ware had been smart enough to send two posters. I let Lat Smith have a look at one, and he shook his head. "Never seen him," he told me. I let him take one, and I took the other. Between us, we had checked with most of the store owners in town, at the bank, and a few other places. Nobody had ever seen this guy.

By the time the shops were closing and folks were heading home, I met up with Lat at the sheriff's office. Lat's luck wasn't any better than mine. I shrugged, dropped both posters on my desk, and headed home. King Simms must have never worked this town. That was good, I figured. One less thing to worry about.

This morning, it had dawned on me I hadn't been by the livery stable, but when I did, it was more of the same. Old Wilson, the guy that owned the placed, took the poster and stared at it so long I thought he'd gone to sleep. Finally, he handed it back. "Never seen 'im before," he announced, then went back to shoveling stalls.

I took the poster with me and went straight to the café on Main Street, where Norah and I were meeting for breakfast. I tossed the poster on the table, gave her a kiss, and settled down for my first cup of coffee. That's when I noticed Norah staring at the poster. She reached down and swung it around to get a better look.

"That's King Simms?" She was still staring at the poster.

I sat up straight in my seat. The coffee cup had

stopped about halfway to my mouth. "That's him," I said. "You've seen him somewhere?"

She tore her eyes off the poster and looked up at me. "I think I saw him yesterday," she said, now staring back down at the poster. "It's hard to be sure, I only saw him for just a moment."

My coffee cup came clattering back down to the table. "Where?" I demanded. "Where did you see him?"

"In Stonewall!" she murmured. "There was a guy in the general store, bought a lot of ammo. He went past me on the way out. I just got a quick look, but maybe..." Her voice trailed off. Her head came up. "The guy I saw had bought the stage stop from Werner, the old owner, just a couple weeks ago. Elmer at the general store is a little scared of him, I think. I went over to the stage stop to meet him, but he was already leaving town, driving the stage. Going really fast, I thought."

My hat was already on my head, and I'd jumped up from my chair. "I'm going to Stonewall now," I told her. I stopped. "You think it's him, but you're not sure, right?" I asked. I snatched up the poster.

"Not sure," she agreed, then grabbed my arm as I was about to take off. "Elmer, that's who you need to talk to!" she said. "Elmer over at the general store has sold him things a couple of times. Show Elmer the poster! He'll know for sure."

I dashed out the door and ran down to the sheriff's office. "Lat!" I hollered on the way through the door. I found him in the back, letting out a couple boys who'd had too much firewater last night.

"We got to ride," I told him. "King Simms might be over in Stonewall. At least, he was maybe there yesterday."

Five minutes later, we were in the saddle and riding hard for Stonewall. If Simms had left town on the stage, we wouldn't find him there today, but we could talk to Elmer and maybe follow his tracks out of town.

CHAPTER 18

STAGE TO FORT CONCHO

King Simms crawled out from under the stagecoach, stretched, and stared around him, able to see little in the moonlight. He had parked the stage in a stand of burr oaks about one hundred yards from where he planned to hold up the stage from Boerne to Fort Concho. According to his stooge in San Antonio, the stage was scheduled to roll through later on this morning.

He cast a critical eye around. His getaway stage was hidden well enough, he felt sure of that. He had walked the area where the payroll stage would have to come down the incline from top to bottom—at no point could he see his getaway stage, hidden in the burr oaks.

Another glance around told him he had about an hour until the first daylight filtered through the trees. Time enough for coffee, he decided. First, he went to check the horses. He had the two he had used to pull the stage out here from Stonewall. One was his horse, the other was a nag with enough life left in him to make the round trip from Stonewall to here and back. After that, it didn't matter. Maybe he would decide on another robbery, but the smart thing now would be to move on.

Satisfied that both horses were still where he had hobbled them, he dug around in his saddlebags and came out with a battered coffeepot and some coffee. Simms squatted on his heels while he waited for the pot to boil. He planned to meet Rusty and Blue at the north edge of the town of Boerne this morning. At first light—he'd been clear about that.

A faint whistle from the coffeepot interrupted his thoughts. Simms poured a cup from the battered pot, spilling some on his hand in the process. He let loose some heartfelt oaths and sucked at his hand. When the burning eased, he dug around in the saddlebags again and swallowed a little jerky while he walked over to his horse and mounted up.

The moonlight was enough to guide him on the stage road south to Boerne. He was alone on the trail this morning, and he counted that as good luck. If his luck held, he would make it to town and back with his men without crossing paths with anybody. There was no telling what a total stranger might remember from crossing paths.

Simms's luck held when he reached the edge of town. Rusty and Blue were both there. Simms didn't know if they knew each other, but they were waiting together, so they must have figured things out. A few suspicious looks went back and forth, but that was fine with Simms. They didn't need to trust each other. Simms reined his horse around in the trail and waited for them to come to him. They fell in behind him without a word and the trio soon left Boerne behind.

One hour later, he pulled them off the trail a couple

hundred yards short of the sharp drop in the trail where he planned to make his move. He didn't want fresh droppings or hoofprints on the trail to tip anybody off. Those boys with the stage might be a little jumpy today, what with the big payload they were carrying. Simms led them parallel to the stage road until they reached a sharp descent through underbrush. He pulled them up at the bottom and motioned for both men to rein in their horses and listen.

"We take 'em out right here at the bottom," he told them. "Blue, you post up about fifty yards back up the trail, back in the brush. There's gonna be a sojer ridin' beside the coach. He'll be on the driver's side, this side of the trail. You take him down, then ride around behind the coach an' come up on the other side. That's where Rusty and me will be. We'll take care of the driver and shotgun rider. Shouldn't be nuthin' else you need to do by the time you git to us. Got it?"

Blue nodded. He was staring up the hill, off into the brush.

"What?" Simms barked.

Blue snapped his gaze back down to focus on Simms. "Nuthin', I, uh, was wonderin' where you got our getaway stage hid, is all."

Simms fought down the rage he felt flooding up inside him. Blue wanted to know about the getaway stage so he could take the money after he'd gotten rid of Simms and Rusty. Simms had caught Blue glancing sideways at Rusty once in a while. He was trying to figure out if he could take Rusty straight up, Simms thought. That's probably after Blue dry-gulched Simms, Simms decided.

"Up the hill a ways, in a stand of burr oaks," Simms

snapped, nodding his head vaguely to his right and off behind.

Blue nodded and looked down. He hadn't asked once what to do if there wasn't a rider or the rider was on the other side, Simms noticed. Simms now realized he'd left that out of his plan.

Rusty asked instead. "Whaddya want us to do if the rider is over on this side?"

Simms chewed on that one for a minute. "If'n they go by and there ain't no rider on yore side, you come around the stage an' take him down from behind," he told Blue. "Rusty and me will still shoot the driver and shotgun rider."

Blue nodded and rode back up the trail. Rusty followed Simms across the road and down to the bottom of the hill.

"What do I do if the sojer don't get Blue?" Rusty asked.

They pulled off into the brush at the bottom and Simms found the hiding spot he'd picked out yesterday.

"Shoot Blue first," he said. "I'll take down the driver. The shotgun rider'll be worried about the shooting goin' on behind him and he'll be looking that way. After you get Blue, get the shotgun guy if I haven't already dropped him."

Rusty moved off to pick his position, kneeling behind a small boulder that gave him cover up to his chest. Simms pulled out his pocket watch and checked it. According to the schedule he had for the stage and the distance from Boerne, he thought they had about an hour to wait.

———

Lat and I burned down the trail to Stonewall in record time. We made a beeline for the general store and busted in on Elmer. He was up on a ladder, stocking a top shelf and I thought he was gonna fall off with all the noise we made.

I waved the King Simms poster around in the air. "Have you seen this guy?" I hollered.

Elmer hustled down the ladder and grabbed the poster. He adjusted his specs on the top of his nose and rolled his eyeballs over it.

"Jed Perkins," he announced. "Bought the stage stop from Werner a couple weeks ago. I've filled a couple of orders for him. Kinda grouchy, he is." He stopped and adjusted the specs again. "King Simms," he mumbled. "Who's King Simms? Is that Jed's real name?"

I grabbed the poster back. Lat was already headed out the door. "Yup," I called over my shoulder. "King Simms is his real name. He's pretty salty. Don't mess with him."

"Didn't plan on it," I heard Elmer yell as the door shut behind me.

Lat was already knocking on the door of the stage stop as I reached the street. He'd shucked out his Colt and had it real handy. I did the same.

Knocking on the door did no good. We circled around to the back, and our pistols were still out. There was nothing in back of the place except a pile of half-rotted wood. The back door slid right open when we pushed at it. Lat and I spread out and charged right through the door.

Nothing. That's what we found. Absolutely nothing. We checked all the corners and poked around a little, but there wasn't much but some tools and papers. Finally, I spotted a little box under a bench. I pulled it out and slid the top open. There was some jewelry, but not much. I took it with me.

"Probly stole it," I said to Lat. We moved back outside and I knelt to study the tracks of the stage where it had rounded the building and hit the street. This had to be the spot where Norah saw him yesterday. I was staring at the tracks when it hit me.

"Wagon. We thought it was a wagon, over there where the stage got held up a couple days ago. Maybe it was a stage makin' them tracks."

Lat stared at me. "How could a stage rob another stage?"

I pictured the tracks back at the stage robbery. We didn't see these tracks at the robbery site," I reminded him. "We found the wheel tracks a little ways off, after they'd ridden their horses away from the robbery."

I was still staring at the stage tracks. "You make a getaway with the stage," I mumbled. "Who would ever stop a stagecoach if you're looking for stagecoach robbers?"

Lat trotted off to get his horse and I stood up. Then it hit me. He'd ridden away from here on the stage yesterday. If King Simms was our stage robber, he might've already left to rob another stage. I sprinted to my horse and jumped on.

"We got to get to Kerrville," I shouted. "There's a stage leaves Boerne at 10:00 on Tuesdays. Goes north to Fort Concho, then west to El Paso. We've got to get to that stage before he does!"

Simms wanted to pace back and forth. He always liked to pace, he could think better that way. He forced himself to stay down, hidden by the fallen log he'd picked out to give him cover. He glanced sideways. Rusty looked like he was setting in church, Simms thought, he was so quiet. Simms mumbled to himself and eased his watch out of a side pocket. The stage should be here anytime.

Simms hadn't heard a sound from Blue since he'd ridden up the trail to pick an ambush spot. That didn't mean anything bad, Blue needed to stay quiet. Simms mopped at the sweat trickling down his forehead with his bandana. He didn't bother to pull it up over his mouth—no need to cover his face. He didn't plan to leave anybody alive here except for Rusty. He might need Rusty again sometime.

Now he could hear something. Simms crouched down and concentrated. There was a low rumbling noise, he was sure of it now. The stagecoach was coming. To his right, Rusty lifted his Winchester and laid it across the boulder in front of him. It was time.

———

Blue could see dust before he heard anything. He had a good spot—there was a cedar elm with a good thick trunk between himself and the stage road. He took a knee behind waist-high brush and some scrubby mesquite trees in front of him, glancing over to check his horse. The horse was tied to the trunk of a live oak tree, a little farther back from the road.

The dust column grew and Blue strained to see. He remembered an old spyglass he'd taken from a dead guy one time, it was stuffed into his saddlebag. Blue trotted over to his horse and retrieved the spyglass. He came back, held it up and studied the stage as it came on. He grinned. Sure enough, there was a rider on his side of the stage. The driver and shotgun rider were up top. This was gonna be easy, he told himself.

Blue dropped the spyglass to the ground and grabbed his Winchester, bracing against the cedar elm. He frowned for a moment, they were moving awfully fast. He reminded himself they had to slow down when they got to the drop-off in the road—that's when he would take out the rider.

The driver must be a veteran of this run, Blue thought to himself. The driver pulled in on the reins and called to the horses just before the stage drew even with Blue. The soldier riding beside did the same. Blue laid his sights on the rider, let out his breath and squeezed the trigger just as the soldier's horse sidestepped a rock at the side of the trail.

The Winchester boomed in Blue's ears and the soldier lurched in the saddle when the shot hit him. Blue grabbed his Winchester and rushed over to his horse. The soldier was still in his saddle, leaning over and dropping back to move around the stage, looking for cover.

Blue fumbled to untie his horse, cursing at himself for the delay. Finally, the reins were freed and he jumped into the saddle. The soldier was on the other side of the stagecoach now. Blue glanced to his left as his horse galloped across the road. The driver and shotgun rider were firing to the front. No doubt Simms and Rusty had opened up on them.

Blue rounded the stage, pulled his Colt, and fired at the soldier riding escort. The soldier slid from the saddle and hit the road hard. Blue swung down, holding on to the reins and taking a step toward the fallen soldier. He had to finish the job. A single shot took care of it.

Blue checked the soldier. Then his eyes widened as he felt a blow in the middle of his chest. He tried to take a step, but his legs didn't seem to work. He fell and landed on the stage road just two feet away from the dead soldier.

———————

Simms took careful aim, Winchester resting on the fallen log, and dropped the shotgun rider, who had stood and started turning toward the back to get a shot at Blue. He slumped across the driver, who shoved him away and fought to keep the horses under control. The shotgun rider fell from the coach and landed on the road.

A boom from his right told him Rusty had fired his first shot. Simms risked a glance behind the coach. Blue, clutching his chest, stumbled backward, then fell to his knees and landed face first. He lay still as the stage reached the bottom of the incline.

Rusty's rifle boomed again and the driver slumped back in his seat. The horses were running free now. A shot cracked from inside the coach and Simms felt wood splinters from the fallen log flying into his cheek. He dropped his rifle and pawed at his face. He groped for the rifle on the ground, cursing and trying to focus on the stage.

The rider inside the coach was trying to crawl out of the window on the far side of the coach. He steadied himself on the top of the stage and fired again. Rusty yelled, grabbed at his shoulder, and returned fire.

The horses picked up speed and galloped around the

bend at the bottom of the road, gaining speed. The coach was already up on two wheels, then tipped when the horses, running free, rounded the curve and started up a small rise. Rusty, shaking his head to clear his vision, saw the soldier jump from the coach, then crawl to take cover behind it when the stage, lying on its side now, came to a stop. The horses dragged it for a few more feet, then stopped and stood trembling when the stage got stuck behind some rocks and fallen branches at the side of the road.

Simms took a chance and half-rose from his position. A shot tore through the leaves just above him. Simms dove to take cover behind the log. He stayed down to think about their position. They had the guard pinned behind the coach, but he had a field of fire and had them locked in place under cover behind their barricades. Simms looked to his left. Rusty seemed to be favoring his right shoulder, but he was sighting through his rifle, looking for a clear shot at the guard.

Simms swore under his breath, holstered his Colt, and laid the Winchester across the log again. This was a delay he hadn't counted on. First, they had to take out the remaining soldier. Then they could take the strongbox.

————

We thundered into Kerrville, horses lathered and tiring out. We reined up in front of the sheriff's office and burst in. Bergen, feet on the desk, stared at us, mouth open.

"Stage from Boerne," I shouted. "Is it here yet?"

Bergen swung his feet down from the desk and stood, looking from one of us to the other. As best I could tell, it was taking him about a year to answer me. "Uh, no, not here," he said.

"Could be a robbery on the trail coming here from Boerne," I shouted, only at a little less deafening level than before. "We got to meet that stage comin' in."

Bergen was still staring at me. I slapped my hand on his desk so hard he jumped and took a step back. "Horses," I said, leaning over the desk. "Our horses are tuckered out. We need fresh horses."

Bergen finally seemed to pull it together. Well, a little bit, anyway. "Livery stable," he said, pointing. "Tell Bert at the livery I told him to give you fresh horses."

We clattered out the door. "Come on!" I yelled at Bergen.

"Posse," I heard him say as we ran out the door. "I'll get together a posse for us."

"It'll be too late," I mumbled to myself. We mounted and rode three blocks to a livery stable. I gave the owner Bergen's message. He blinked a few times, then brought out two horses for us without saying a word. He was a little slow saddling them up, so Lat and I took over and did it ourselves.

"Think Bergen's gonna get there to help?" Lat yelled as we galloped south out of town.

I looked back over my shoulder. No sign of him. "If he does," I hollered, "it's gonna be way too late. Just you an' me, Lat."

Half an hour later, galloping at full speed south on the stage road, we heard gunfire.

CHAPTER 19

STAGECOACH SHOOTOUT

Hunched down behind the fallen log, King Simms tried to make sense out of what was happening. He and Rusty were under fire, that part was for sure. The second soldier, the one who'd been inside the coach, was the only guy left who could shoot at them. Everybody else was dead and lying on the road. The hard part was trying to figure out where he was shooting from.

Simms studied the stagecoach, overturned at the side of the road. The top-side wheels had finally quit spinning. The coach was turned over on its side, so the guy couldn't be shooting through the doors. There wasn't any room underneath to get a weapon through and squeeze off a shot, either.

That just left the front of the coach and the back. The soldier had to be lying down, probably shooting just over the traces where they were chained to the coach. Raising his head to spot the guy could be deadly, though. He seemed to have their positions zeroed in.

Motion from Rusty, behind a boulder to his right,

caught Simms's attention. Rusty, lying on his back behind the boulder, had his pistol in his hand. He made motions to let Simms know he planned to lift the pistol over the boulder and fire blindly toward the coach.

Simms got it. It was a good plan. While Rusty pinned him down with some blind shots, Simms could move out to his left and circle the coach. He could use the coach to shield himself until he came around the back and got a shot. Simms nodded and came up to his hands and knees, ready to move out.

Rusty lifted his pistol and fired four shots blindly at the coach. Simms came off the ground, staying low, and sprinted to the back end of the coach. He moved to the far side, waiting to jump out and fire. He would have only seconds to spot the shooter and take him out. He leaned against the back of the wagon and waited for another burst of fire from Rusty.

When it came, Simms darted from behind the stagecoach, crouched low, Colt extended in his hand. He searched the underbrush behind the front of the coach. There! The soldier was on his belly, firing the Winchester at Rusty's position.

Simms fired twice, aiming for the center of the soldier's chest. He heard a sigh and saw the Winchester slip from the soldier's hands. "Got 'im," he hollered at Rusty.

The strongbox had fallen from the top of the coach. Simms could see it lying at the side of the road, ten feet behind the overturned coach. He trotted over to the box and hauled it out, dragging it toward Rusty as he emerged from behind the boulder where he'd taken cover. The strongbox was heavy. Simms knew that was a good sign.

There was a lock on the hasp securing the strongbox. Simms trotted over to the dead driver and went through his pockets, finding the key. He hurried back, fit the key in the lock, and heaved the lid open. Simms and Rusty weren't disappointed. Hundreds of gold coins reflected the sunlight. Simms slammed the lid shut again, and both men ran for the thicket where the stage was ready to move. Simms climbed up on his getaway stage while Rusty mounted his horse.

Simms wheeled the getaway stagecoach around and pulled up next to the strongbox. Rusty followed and dismounted, waiting for him.

Simms pointed at the gold. "Load some into your saddlebags," Simms told him. "I'm gonna put the rest in the spot I made to hold 'em under the seat inside the coach." A few minutes later, they had moved the payroll coins. Simms noted with approval that Rusty had put only a few dozen coins in his saddlebags. He might need all the speed he could get from his horse before this was done.

Simms walked over and began unhooking his horse from the getaway stagecoach traces. He pointed at the escort soldier's horse, nibbling grass at the side of the road. "Shake out a loop, will ya?" he asked Rusty. "I'm gonna tie my horse off behind the stage in case we git chased and I need to ride him. I'll put that one in to pull the stage."

Ten minutes later, the switch had been made. Simms stepped back to check the reins and traces on his stage. Both he and Rusty jumped straight into the air and whirled when a shot sounded right behind them.

Both men drew as they turned. The soldier Simms had shot just a few minutes before had crawled up to the side of the road, pistol in hand. He'd gotten off one shot. Simms and Rusty fired two shots apiece. The soldier slumped back to the ground.

"Thought I got 'im before," Simms growled. He walked over to make sure the man was dead this time.

"Let's mount up," he told Rusty. "If we run into the law, we split up and meet at the stage stop in Stonewall, soon as we both can git there."

Simms pulled out and led the way north on the stage road. He planned to pull off the road after a few miles and take the same route he'd taken during the practice robbery last week. Ten minutes later, they saw two men coming toward them, riding hard.

————

They came into view shortly after we saw the dust rising. I could see the stagecoach plus a rider escorting the coach. The knot I'd had in my throat since this morning eased up. It looked like we were here in time to stop a robbery. I was wondering now if I'd made a big fuss over nothing.

After a minute, Lat Smith leaned over and hollered to make himself heard. "Hey Pike," he said, "how come that stage ain't got a shotgun rider?"

I stared. It was true. No chance, I figured, that a big army payroll didn't have a shotgun rider, even if they had themselves an escort alongside. I kept a hand on the reins and reached back to lift my Winchester from the scabbard. Lat Smith did the same.

What I saw next made that lump pop right back up in my throat. Plus, my stomach commenced to turning over and jumping around. The escort rider peeled off and took across country, going to the west. Crazier than that, the stagecoach left the trail and went more to the east and away from me. Even from this distance, I could see how rough a ride that was. The coach was bouncing so hard I knew he couldn't keep it up.

I figured King Simms would be on that stage. Whoever was on horseback was likely to be a bad hombre in his own right, but he couldn't be worse than King Simms.

"Go after the guy on horseback," I shouted at Lat. Then I pulled my horse off the trail. I was going after King Simms.

———

King Simms reacted immediately when he saw the riders ahead of them pull their rifles. No chance he was fooling anybody with the stagecoach now. He looked around at Rusty and pointed west. Rusty peeled off immediately and went west. Simms guided the stagecoach off the road, going east. He knew he couldn't keep up this speed. The coach couldn't take a ride this rough and he couldn't stay in the driver's seat.

His mind raced. Slowing down meant the law would catch him in no time. He reined in the stagecoach horses, fighting them until they stopped. He climbed down, leaped on his horse, and pulled the reins free. Simms dug in his spurs and the horse leaped forward. He would have to come back for the payroll later.

———

They'd given Lat Smith a mouse-colored mustang, but he wasn't complaining. He knew he wouldn't win any races with this horse at that illegal track operation they'd shut down, but this horse could go all day. He steered his horse a little left to catch up to the robber on horseback. With this angle, he could cut the distance between them in half.

The guy fired a wild shot or two over his shoulder, but Lat wasn't worried about that. It would have to be the luckiest shot ever to hit him from there. He hunched down and urged the mustang on. They reached a thin stand of burr oaks, but he knew the robber didn't have time to pull up his horse and take cover. Lat was too close now.

They burst out of the stand of burr oaks and hit a grassy meadow. The ground rose slightly, and the mustang made up ground. As Lat closed, he could see the robber glance behind him from time to time. Finally, the guy turned in his saddle and tried to line up a shot with his pistol.

Lat pulled his Colt with practiced ease, sighted, and squeezed the trigger. With the movement of both horses, it wasn't exactly where he'd aimed, but it was enough. The guy tumbled out of the saddle and landed hard.

As Lat rode up, the robber pushed himself to his knees and lifted his gun. Lat fired one more time, driving the outlaw back, then down on his knees. He collapsed in the grass. The pistol fell to the ground beside him.

Lat dismounted and checked to be sure the man was dead, then remounted and rode back toward the stage road. Pike might need help.

———

When King Simms stopped the stagecoach and jumped on his horse, I made up some ground. He was too smart to do what his fellow outlaw did, though. Instead of riding due east, he rode directly away from me, pointing south and east. Now it was just a straight-up horse race, and I didn't really know how good this livery stable horse was. At least, I thought, he was fresh.

After fifteen minutes, I knew the fresh horse I'd been given had some staying power. I slowly made up ground. I could see Simms looking over his shoulder now and then. I had him worried.

The flat meadow and thin stands of trees gave way to some rolling hills, and the distance between us closed. The hills were tuckering out his horse faster than they were tuckering out mine. I reached back to assure myself the Winchester was still in the scabbard.

As he galloped up a low, slow rise in front of me, I saw something that changed everything. I saw him pull his rifle from the scabbard, and as he went over the rise, he kicked his feet loose from the stirrups. I knew he'd bailed off the horse. He was on the ground over there. If I took my horse over that rise, he would blow me out of the saddle!

I reined in my horse sharply as we climbed the rise, then kicked out of the stirrups myself and dropped off the horse. I had to move fast—if he popped up over the rise with that Winchester, it was all over.

I took only my Colt as I dropped off the horse. This was going to be some in-close shooting, which meant only one of us was walking out of here. I slapped my horse on the rump to send him over the rise, then dove to the ground at the top of the rise on my side.

Hoping he would be foolish enough to shoot at the riderless horse did me no good. Simms was too smart to fall for that. Now he would know I was flat on the ground somewhere on the other side of the rise from him. Nothing stirred for several seconds. I saw a rock lying off to my right. My hand closed on it and I threw it to my left, letting it land on the ground, right about where I thought he must be.

He came up about ten yards down from me, Colt in hand. He was focused straight in front of him, which gave me a second or two. I came to my knees and fired. He tumbled backward, but I was pretty sure I'd only notched his shoulder. There was no time. It was now or never for me.

I hunched and ran those few steps to where I'd last seen him and came charging over the rise. I fired and missed, then launched myself at him feet-first. He fired as I came and I felt a heavy blow low down on my left side. I kept coming and kicked him in the chest with both feet.

He fell to his back but came up still holding his Colt. I landed, rolled, and came up firing. The first shot took him in the chest. He braced on his knees and the gun kept coming up. My second shot took him straight through the heart. He slumped over, rolled on his back, and stared up at the sky.

I staggered to my feet and went to check him. He was dead. I slumped to the ground and put my hand to my side. It came away bloody. His Winchester lay a few feet away. I used it to lever myself to my feet and hobbled over to my livery stable horse. He held still while I pulled myself into the saddle and tied my wrists to the saddle horn. I turned the horse toward the place where Simms had left the stagecoach during the chase. That stagecoach sounded like the easiest ride for help.

I think I passed out a time or two along the way. I would come to and look around once in a while. Every time, the horse had stopped and gone to grazing. I started him out again each time and wondered how far I had to go.

———

There was a voice coming from somewhere. I thought I knew that voice. I lifted my head up and saw I was still tied to the saddle. Looking around, I saw Lat Smith driving up to me in the getaway stagecoach. I gotta say, that was a pretty sight for some sore eyes. Mine, I mean.

Lat helped me down from the horse and into the stage. I slumped on the seat and hoped I wouldn't roll off.

"Don't know where the payroll is," Lat was saying. "Haven't seen it."

I can't say I was too worried about the stolen payroll just then. My head slumped to the side, and I was looking at some hinges. I reached out to touch one of them. The hinges were holding the seat on.

I pushed myself off the seat and knelt in front of it. I lifted the seat and looked inside. "Found the payroll," I told Lat.

He stuck his head in the coach and whistled. "You shore did," he said. He closed up the seat and helped me to lie back down on it. "I think I'm gonna take you to the doc in Kerrville," he said. "He's closer than your doc in Fredericksburg."

"Good," I told him. "I don't think the doc in Fredericksburg likes me very much."

Somewhere on the road to Kerrville, I guess I passed out again.

CHAPTER 20

NORAH

The light was hard on my eyes. I put my hand up and squinted, trying to work out where exactly I was. The stagecoach ride was the last thing I remembered. Most of it, anyway. I think Lat must have hit every bump in the road. The door opened and closed, then Norah came in and sat on the edge of my bed.

Things swam around in my brain. Norah leaned over and kissed me. That's when I worked out that I was in my own bed, back in Fredericksburg. Norah pushed my pillow under my head a little more and patted my cheek.

"Welcome back," she said. "Doc Freeman told us you'd wake up pretty soon."

I squinted at the light pouring through my window. "How long have I been gone?" I asked.

Norah got up to close the curtains, then came back to sit on the bed. "Two days," she said. "The doc in Kerrville patched you up. Lat sent a telegram to me. I got Doc Freeman to come with me from Fredericksburg and bring you back in a wagon."

My brain was still a little fuzzy, so I just laid there and

chewed on things for a while. "It was King Simms doing the robberies, like we thought," I said after a while. "I, well he's…"

"Yes, he's dead," Norah said. "After he got you to Kerrville, Lat went back to kind of clean things up. There were three outlaws. King Simms and a guy named Zeke Rustin, goes by the name of Rusty. There was a poster out for him. Lat killed him before he came back to help you. There was another outlaw at the site of the holdup. We don't know who he was. There were also two soldiers, the stage driver and a shotgun rider. All killed during the holdup."

"Wow," was all I could think of to say. I stared at the wall. "That's a lot of folks got killed for just doing their jobs."

"It is." She took my hand. "But you made sure these outlaws won't do this to anybody else."

I squeezed her hand and let my brain go back to sorting through everything she'd said.

After a while, Norah decided to talk about something else. She probably decided my brain was about to run up the white flag on all this news. Maybe my eyes rolled up in my head, I don't know.

"Would you like some good news now?" she asked.

I nodded and shifted a little on the bed. The pain in my side told me not to do that again.

"The gold we found was from the train robbery in Nebraska, like we thought. Probably Sam Bass's share of the money. It came to about ten thousand dollars, just about what we counted."

I blinked a couple times at that. I remembered the sight of all that gold when we hauled it out of the cave. That, plus the stagecoach money—I never thought I would be around that much money in my life. Didn't really care to do it again, either. Folks get downright rowdy when there's that much money up for grabs.

I focused on Norah. "What's the good news you was talkin' about?" I asked.

She grinned from ear to ear. "Union Pacific Railroad had a reward out for anybody who turned in those coins," she said. "Ten percent."

My brain was still way too fuzzy to be doing that arithmetic, but my old schoolmarm would have wanted me to try. "Uh, one thousand dollars!" I said, staring at Norah.

"Yep," she said. "They brought us one thousand dollars. I put it in the bank already. We can't have that much sitting around." She leaned in again. "There's more," she told me. "Bain and Company, the folks that own the stagecoach route, are giving you two hundred dollars. They had promised that much to whoever arrested the people behind last week's robbery. They're convinced it was King Simms and his boys who did the first job. Mr. Bain himself is bringing you the money."

My mouth opened and closed a couple times, like a guppy going for a worm on the hook. "Twelve hundred dollars," I breathed. Then I frowned a little. "I wouldn't be around for any of that money if it wasn't for Lat Smith," I said. "He saved my hide back there."

Norah nodded and waited.

"I'm thinkin' we need to split it three ways," I said. "You and me and Lat."

She thought it over and agreed. "Like you said, you wouldn't even be here now if it weren't for Lat."

My eyelids got heavy, and I dozed off for a while. I came to when there was a knock at the door. Norah got up to see who it was, then came back in with Lat Smith.

"You're just in time," I told him. "We've got some news." He took a chair and waited. I told him about the reward money I'd just found out about. "The thing is," I told him. "You saved my hide out there and covered my back several times. Norah and I want to split the money with you. Four hundred dollars for each of us."

Lat looked back and forth at us, then shook his head. Norah stopped him. "We both want you to have it, Lat," she said. "This job was a lot more dangerous than any of us knew."

Lat stared at the floor. "Okay," he agreed. "Thank you both. The thing is...it makes me feel kinda bad about what I come here to say." He looked up at me. I just waited. "I've been thinkin' I want to go back where I come from," he said. "Back to Colorado."

I was disappointed, I got to admit, but I didn't want to try to stop him. "That's okay," I told him. "You were here when I really needed you. Take the money and go on home."

"It's a girl, isn't it?" Norah teased. "I'll bet there's a girl back there in Colorado."

Lat's face got a little red then. "There was," he admitted. "I lost track of her along the way. Don't know if she's still there or not."

Norah walked him to the door. "Doc says Pike will be up and around in a few days," she said. "Can you stay until then?"

Lat agreed. The doc came to check me over and Norah said she'd be back in a few hours. I settled in for some poking and prodding from old Doc Freeman.

It must have been early evening when I came to again. There was another knock on the door, and Norah came in with Boone and his wife Alice, along with Jake and Julia McCabe. They gave me a hard time for a while about stepping in front of too many bullets, but I know they were as glad to see me as I was to see them. Good friends don't come along all that often.

They wanted to know about the robbery, and I told them everything I could remember. When it got quiet, I told them Lat was moving on and I'd be looking for a new deputy. I asked them if they knew of anybody.

Boone harrumphed a few times and looked over at his wife. "Well," he said, "the thing is, I think Alice is tired of havin' me hangin' around the cabin. Can't imagine why, me being a nice guy and all." He looked at me after everybody finished chuckling. "I'll be your deppity, Pike, if you'll have me," he said. "I figger you've kilt all the outlaws in Texas already, I mean all the ones that Jake, here, didn't finish off afore you come along. So, the way I figger it, this'll be the safest job in the county now."

"Downright glad to have you, Boone," I said, holding out my hand. I've got to admit, there was a little lump in my throat. Boone shook my hand, and they filed out the door. Boone stopped on the way out and looked back at me.

"I'll be available right away," he said. Then he looked over at Norah. "'Specially if you wanna get married and have a honeymoon or somethin'."

Norah pushed him out the door and came back to sit on the bed. "I didn't put him up to that," she said. Her cheeks were a little red, I think.

I took her hand. "I know," I assured her. "Thing is, Boone's right, for once or mebbe twice in his life. I been draggin' my feet too long. Next month, how 'bout that? Soon as I'm back on my feet and got the bounce back in my step. How about that?"

The look in her eyes told me I had the answer I wanted.

A Look At: Nash Walker: Feud on the Frontier

Nash Walker Book One

He came to Texas to outrun his past. What he found was a war he couldn't walk away from.

In the rugged aftermath of heartbreak, Nash Walker, a hardened moonshiner from the hills of Tennessee, rides west with nothing left to lose. Texas offers a chance at redemption— or ruin. From bounty hunter to reluctant Texas Ranger, Nash is soon swept into the bloody Sutton-Taylor feud, one of the deadliest range wars in frontier history.

When an enchanting singer named Victoria pleads for help protecting her family's land from a ruthless neighbor and his gang of hired guns, Nash can't turn his back. With bullets flying and loyalties tested, he'll need the grit of a frontiersman, the law of a Ranger, and the backing of cattle baron Charles Goodnight to survive.

Will Nash find peace on the Texas frontier, or will this new fight cost him everything he has left?

AVAILABLE NOVEMBER 2025

ABOUT THE AUTHOR

Patrick Lindsay came to Texas by way of Missouri, Canada, and California and has been proud to call the Lone Star State his home for more than forty years now. He retired in 2017 from "another life" as a CPA, whereafter he turned his hand to writing.

He has read just about everything by Louis L'Amour and first decided to give Western writing a try on his initial day of retirement. He has been writing ever since and loves the idea that so many people get enjoyment from his work.

Patrick and his wife Michelle live on a cattle ranch near Fort Worth along with cows, horses, chickens, and a very spoiled Great Pyrenees dog. He is an avid fan of the St. Louis Cardinals in baseball and the Kansas City Chiefs in football.

www.ingramcontent.com/pod-product-compliance
Lightning Source LLC
Chambersburg PA
CBHW011638010726
47495CB00011B/2814